AS MIRACULOUS AND ORDINARY AS ACORNS

The Story of a Friendship

Ellen Belitsky

As Miraculous and Ordinary As Acorns
by Ellen Belitsky

All author profits will go to charity.

Author contact: ellenbelitsky6@yahoo.com Please put Acorns in the subject line.

ISBN: 978-0-578-29559-6

Epigraphs

Remembering speechlessly we seek the great forgotten language,
the lost lane-end into heaven, a stone, a leaf, an unfound door.
Where? When
Look Homeward, Angel, by Thomas Wolfe

Now if a man tried to take his life on Earth
And prove before he died what one man's life could be worth
Well, I wonder what would happen to this world?
I Wonder What Would Happen To This World, from Cotton Patch
Gospel,
lyrics by Harry Chapin

All the world's a stage,
And all the men and women merely players;
They have their exits and their entrances;
And one man in his time plays many parts,
As You Like It, by William Shakespeare

Ripple in still water
When there is no pebble tossed
Nor wind to blow
Ripple, by Jerry Garcia and Robert Hunter

The Universe in a Nutshell, by Stephen Hawking

"*My religion is kindness*" The Dalai Lama

Dedications

With love and gratitude, I dedicate this book to the past, the present, and the future.

The Past: To the loving memory of my husband, Irwin, who always gave me the time to write, and the love that sustained me.

The Past into the Present: To my sons, Jason and Darren, who nurtured me and supported me through good times and bad. To their wives, Libby and Heather, who have enriched my life.

To friends too numerous to name, but not too numerous to love and be grateful for: Those I've had since early teens, those I've had since our children were infants, those I met in groups: social, book, volunteer, support and writers'. To family who are super-friends—my brother, Laurence, my sister-in-law, Helen, and their family; my cousins and Irwin's. All of you taught me what friendship is—or this book could never have come to be.

The Present: To the new friends I've made since moving to my current home in the midst of the pandemic—you've been the key to sane survival in the COVID years.

The future: Above all, to my granddaughter, Maeve, for the joy and love you bring me, and the hope for the future that you represent. May you someday live in a peaceful, disease-free world, in a nation truly united.

And Always: The Past, Present, and Future embodied in my currently ninety-nine year old aunt, Blossom Noll "Etc.", who is as vibrant and with-it as any twenty year old, and is my model and inspiration for aging without growing old. May she go on living "her way" for many more
years.

Notes From A Quirky Writer

1. Instead of chapters, the book is divided into Parts, Sections, Acts and Scenes. Read them as chapters filled with narrative and action—or imagine the words on the page as monologues and scenes. Maybe this is a novel. Maybe it's a play. Maybe it's a mashup of the two—a plovel? It's up to you.

2. The titles of the sections are all names of songs from Broadway shows. Most of the lyrics can be found by Googling the titles. Most are available on YouTube with the original cast—and/or covers. They can compliment your reading, or be listened to when you're in the mood for some top-notch entertainment—or ignored. Names of shows, composers and lyricists for each song are in an appendix at the end of the book.

3. It's not your eyes, and it's not a misprint. One of the characters speaks in a very soft voice. Rather than bore you with "said in a soft voice" whenever she speaks, her spoken words will appear lighter than the rest of the print.

4. As I complete this book in February, 2022, the events taking place up to the present day are grounded in real time. The main characters are now seventy-nine years old, and COVID is impacting every aspect of life. My apologies–I had to interject some scenes addressing this. Everything that comes afterward is grounded in an imagination—a wish for a future world in which disruptive disease is no longer a factor.

Contents

As Miraculous And Ordinary As Acorns

The Story Of A Friendship

PART ONE: <u>ONCE UPON A TIME AND LONG AGO</u>

Shanna, age 29

Hush. Listen. On an ordinary night, at the very same time, four girls heard the same story and wondered what would happen to the characters next. That night, they all dreamed the same dream. In time, they found each other and began a friendship forged in their shared dream. Bound together for the rest of their lives, they never had a fight, never uttered an unkind word amongst themselves, never failed to be the nets catching each other should one fall.

With the death of the last of the four at the age of one hundred one, I am now free to tell the story of a friendship that was anything but ordinary. And so, let it begin as it did for them, with the Teacher, and a dream.

ACT I: <u>A DREAM IS A WISH YOUR HEART MAKES</u>

The Teacher

Hush, listen, as I send a dream to four old souls embodied in seven year old girls, and introduce them to you one by one:

Scene 1: <u>Somewhere</u>

Wren Abramowitz, age 7

Fidelity. Fellowship. I used two of Father's vocabulary words today. I pull the covers over my head to block the moonlight filtering past the sides of the shade. Filtering. I'll have to check it off in my notebook tomorrow.

My mind drifts to the story I heard on the radio. It was fascinating, but frustrating. Where did the Piper take the children? It's as if the story stopped before the real end.

"Hush. Listen." I hear the words, yet there is no one nearby. I'm not thinking them, and yet, I hear them. A voice in my mind but not of my mind. A sense of rightness and happiness, as if the air around me is wrapping me in a blanket of safety and nothing-can-harm-you-ness.

And now, music. Not instruments, not voices, not birds. As if the air itself is singing.

Oh, no! The peace, the music—they're moving away. I sit up in bed, reach out my hand to grasp the Wonder that is retreating from my world. I have to stop it, have to catch up with it, go with it, wherever it leads.

"Follow!" I hear the soundless voice. No time for robe or slippers. I drop my feet to the floor and race-walk to keep up with the music, the peace. Out the door of my apartment. No time to

wait for the elevator. I run down the five flights of stairs. On the third floor, my friend, Shoshanna, joins me. As we leave our apartment building and pass neighboring ones, other children spill out and out, race to join us.

Leading us is a woman who seems to be—"dressed in light," Shoshanna says. Shoshanna is the best artist in second grade. She sees things other children can't. I strain to hear her funny almost-a-whisper voice, a voice that has sadness in it. But now, the unvoiced roar of excitement I sense coming from Shoshanna and the other children almost drowns out her so-soft voice.

"Dressed in light," I repeat and Shoshanna nods. The woman is glowing, brilliant, like a star. She's wearing clothes that float around her, clothes made up of more colors than there are in my large Crayola box.

Shoshanna and I clasp each other's hands so we won't lose each other in the crowd. Walk fast. Almost run. Keep up, I must keep up with the woman and the Wonder. Music and peace seem to come from the flute she's playing. Dancing now. All of us, following her dance, faster and faster, dancing forward. Such a merry dance!

Leaving the city, leaving Oceanport behind. Suddenly, the country! But there is no country like this near Oceanport! Only towns. "The suburbs" Mother calls them. Where are we? A shudder of fear slices through my peace and happiness, like a knife through a fresh loaf of bread. Quickly washed away by a warmth, a soothing melody, a renewed sense of peace. I feel it coming from the woman, from the air, from every child in the growing river of children who are following her.

We dance along a paved road that becomes a dirt path. Sunlight dims, blocked by a canopy of treetops above us. Wait! Wasn't it night when I left my bed? And—we're all barefoot, there are stones on the ground, and no one is complaining. Not a drop of pain or even annoyance.

And now! The path is blocked. We can go no further. I want to cry. I feel flooded by the disappointment I sense coming from every one of the children. What are we to do, with a large mountain up ahead stretching from woodland to woodland on either side? Surely the woman can't expect us to climb a whole mountain! Yet she plays her pipe. Yet music and peace drift over us. Yet we dance on.

And now the tune changes. The melody becomes the music on my favorite radio program, the music leading the listeners into Storyland. A memory of the radio voice softly guiding the audience through the woods, across a stile over a brook, into the land where stories are born.

The other children are scared. I can feel it. Remembering: yesterday, the tale on Children's Story Hour. It's tomorrow now, the new day the Pied Piper warned of in yesterday's story. If the mayor wouldn't pay him for ridding the town of rats, he would take the children of the town as his payment. He drove the rats out by making them follow his music. And now, that's what we're doing!

I tremble.

I'm overwhelmed by my sense of the other children's fear. "The Piper!" they're all mouthing to each other until it's a silent scream in my ears. "The Piper is stealing us away!" and then the feelings and voices fade as child after child disappears.

I stay, and so does Shoshanna. Faster and faster we dance to keep up with the Piper. So do two others: A girl with wild red curls, another with black hair and long-lashed deep blue eyes. We could be in danger and Father always sneers at me and calls me "timid" because I don't like to take risks, but I have to know. I must know. Shoshanna and I talked about it for hours after the program ended yesterday.

"Where did the Pied Piper take the children?" "What if the story is true?"

We reach the mountain.

The music stops.

The Piper reaches out with her flute and taps the mountain. Trees move to the sides, and the mountainside itself slides open. The Piper slips inside. I don't have to look at Shoshanna or the other girls. I know what they're feeling. What I'm feeling. It's something I'm sure of. Whatever is within the mountain is safe. A place of peace and wonder. We scramble in after the Piper, certain the mountain is going to swallow us up, and content with it.

The moment we are inside, the gateway starts to close like a sliding door.

I breathe, and it's as if I've never really breathed before. As if the air itself is made of magic molecules. Air, so fresh, so pure, so scented with serenity. I have never seen, smelled, heard or felt anything as lovely as where we are. Colors so vivid, like Dorothy coming to Oz and the black and white world bursting into color. Rainbows of birds fly overhead, add their voices to the song the air is singing. A welcome song, I think, just as the Piper says, "Welcome to—"

To where? I'm in my bed, waking from a dream. Welcome to where? How can I get back there? Tears wet my pillow, drip down my face. I have never felt so sad. Despair. I must get back there—to whatever the name of the place is. To wherever the Piper is. It's as if I'm homesick for a place I've never been.

And more. It's as if being inside the mountain with the Piper I found something I never knew I'd lost, something I've been looking for my whole life. Please, let me come back, I pray silently.

And then, a miracle. In the silent voice of the Piper, I hear *"Whenever you need me, I will be there."*

Isn't the way the Piper came to me last night, on one of the worst days of my life, proof that she will be? I think about yesterday, relive the day as if it's happening now:

Scene 2: <u>Don't Rain on My Parade</u>

Wren, age 7

Sunday is always the best day of the week. It starts with having bagels and cream cheese and lox for breakfast, and then playing quietly in my room while Mother and Father have their "peaceful breakfast." Then Father goes to visit his grandmother who is in something called an old age home and who forgot how to speak English, so I don't have to visit her anymore.

The really good part of the day starts when Shoshanna and I go to Mme. Simone's Dance Studio. Shoshana is going to be an artist when she grows up and I'm going to be an actress, like in <u>Kiss Me Kate</u> which was the first play I saw on Theater Row in Oceanport for my sixth birthday. Something happened when the curtain rose—as if a door was opening and letting me in to a land of magic. The whole audience felt it, expected it. The silence of all talk—of breathing itself suspended, broken by applause like a burst of thunder. I knew right then being an actress was the best, best job in the world. And knew, I'm going to be an actress when I grow up.

Actresses have to sing. Actress have to know how to dance. I begged and begged and—my dreams came true! Dance lessons!

But now, at the Dance Studio. Somersaults. Everyone turning with their heads below their feet and I try, but dizzy, so dizzy. I pick my head up, fall to my side. Over and over I spoil my somersault. It's better when we do regular dance things. I do some pretty good first positions and fifth positions and pliés, so I'm pretty happy with the lesson.

It's Mother's turn to pick us up. Mme. Simone wants to talk to her.

"Wait on the sidewalk," Mother tells Shoshanna and me.

We watch while she stands with Mme. Simone outside the doorway. I can't hear them, but I feel anger, like punches in the air between them. Mother looks like she wants to slap Mme. Simone. Is Mme. Simone talking about my somersault?

Mother stomps down the walk toward us, shouting, "I want a full refund."

"With pleasure, Mrs. Abramowitz," Mme. Simone calls to Mother's back.

Mother strides toward us—her feet hitting the pavement like hammers. When she's angry like this, I don't say a word. I move as far from her as I can, grab Shoshanna's hand, try to pull ahead of mother, but I'm stuck.

Shoshanna has turned into a statue rooted to the ground. I can feel how interested—fascinated—she is by something. A squirrel eating an acorn. I know exactly what Shoshanna is doing. Turning her eyes and her mind into a camera, taking a picture so she can draw it when she gets home. I wait for her, let Mother stamp on ahead.

"Stop dawdling, girls," she growls, and stops moving until we reach her. She grabs each of us by the hand and jerks us along. Neither of us says a word the whole way.

At home, I want to ask, but I don't dare, why Mother is so angry. What did Mme. Simone say? I know if I ask she'll grunt "children should be seen and not heard," and order me to go to my room.

At five o'clock, she barges into my room, turns on the radio, which is another good part of Sundays. She tunes it to the right station and storms out without saying a word to me. I can feel anger spilling off of her, but the radio—the sound of the music, the invitation to a story makes me forget about her, about somersaults, about everything else that was ever bad. It's the story of the Pied Piper. It ends too soon. I hope there's a book that tells the rest of the story—what happened to the children after he took them inside the mountain. I'm going to look for it the next time Mother takes me to the library. Is it magical inside the mountain? Marvelous or dreadful? I need to know.

She's still angry at dinner time. She slams my plate in front of me on the table in the dinette and goes back into the kitchen where she's preparing dinner for Father and herself.

Her meatballs are delicious. Everyone talks about what a

good cook Mother is. Except my aunt Mildred, her twin sister. Deborah's despicable mother. Father makes me learn new vocabulary words every day. The first thing I thought of when he told me about *despicable* was Aunt Mildred. The second thing was my cousin Deborah who thinks she's royalty because she's a year older than I am, and expects all the younger kids to bow down to her.

I eat fast because Mother is furiously stirring something on the stove and telling me to hurry up because Father will be home soon and will want his dinner on the table and will *not* want to be bothered by a silly child. I gulp down my Jell-O and scoot to my room. I try to be very quiet while Mother and Father are eating their dinner "in peace."

But I'm curious. I know Mother will tell Father whatever Mme. Simone said to make her so angry. When I hear their silverware clinking and their voices talking, I creep back, quiet as a mouse, and stand outside the dinette and listen.

"Kicked out of dancing school?" Father is laughing.

"Can you imagine?" Mother is indignant. "That woman won't even take our money!"

"Why did you even think of sending her for dancing lessons?" That's what Father always says to Mother. "Why did you even think of—" whatever it is she says or does.

"You think I don't know she's clumsy as an ox?" Mother asks. "I thought maybe dancing lessons would help. Mildred insists they've helped Deborah."

"With that personality, nothing will help your niece," Father laughs and Mother laughs along.

Oh, I didn't know grownups don't like Deborah. None of the kids do.

"It won't hurt Wren not to be a dancer," Father says. "It wasn't your dancing that made me fall for you. The way to a man's heart is his stomach. Let me have some more of that chicken."

Two thoughts clash, like Mother and Aunt Mildred. Chicken? I didn't get chicken. I got last night's leftovers. It's a quiet thought, drowned out by "It won't hurt Wren not to dance." An actress has to be able to dance!

There's a moment of silence, broken by sounds of food dished out, followed by Father's loud chewing.

I think about what I heard. I'm kicked out? Can't go back to dancing school? Mme. Simone doesn't think I'm a good enough dancer? I know I'm not the best, like I'm not the best reader. Josie is, and it makes Father furious with his face all red whenever he asks me if I'm first in my class and I say "sometimes second or third but Josie is always first," which is the truth. And I know a few of the girls are better at dancing than me, but I try so hard, and I love dancing school. Except for the somersault. Is that why Mme. Simone doesn't want me?

I hear Mother laugh. Did I miss something? "I suppose you're right," Mother is saying. "She's not going to dance her way into a man's heart. Not with that face!"

I run into Mother's and Father's bedroom where there's a big mirror. What's the matter with my face? I stand and stare at it. It's a perfectly good face. Is there something wrong with it that I don't know? Is that why Mother wouldn't sign the paper to have my picture taken in school?

"Your father has an expensive camera and we have a whole boxful of pictures of you. We don't have to pay someone else to take one," Mother says. But it felt so funny to have to sit in the auditorium by myself while the rest of the class lined up to go on stage and have their pictures taken. And the way the children looked at me, as if they were wondering what was wrong with me. "Is it because of your hair?" some of them asked.

I look at my hair in the mirror. "Frizzy," Mother says, and brushes and brushes it but it still sticks out all over the place.

I hear Mother and Father getting up. I run back to my room, grab my list of vocabulary words and pretend I'm studying them. "Furious," I say loudly, so he'll hear me.

Bath time is silent.

I fall asleep, thinking about never being able to go to dancing school again. And wondering—What if the story is real? What was in that mountain? Where was it? How can I get back there? What if? I wonder as musing turns into a dream.

Scene 3: <u>Mr. Cellophane</u>

Wren, age 7

I'm getting ready for school, washing, getting dressed, sitting alone at the dinette table eating my Farina with raisins and lots of cream so that I'll gain weight. Mother says I'm too thin. I'm still feeling sad, empty, wishing I could slip back into my dream. Wishing I could get to—where? It's a question wrapped in despair. Will I ever find out? Ever get back there?

I let my mind drift for a while. Something else is itching it. Was there a time when I saw the Piper's face before? Only the face wasn't the Piper's. The face was on a little girl, and it glowed exactly the way the Piper glowed. It was the day I found out that what would make Mother really happy would be for me to be invisible. Not here. I was two, and—

Wren, age 2

A new cousin! I never had a boy cousin before, or a cousin littler than me. I have my cousin Deborah, who is two years older than me and goes to nursery school, but now I have a boy cousin named Leonard. I hope I like Leonard better than I like Deborah. Leonard's mother is Aunt Dot, who's in the hospital now because that's where you go to get a baby born.

I get excited when Mother says we're going with Aunt Mildred to visit Aunt Dot in the hospital. I can't wait to meet my new cousin, Leonard.

Aunt Mildred says we have to go when Deborah is in nursery school.

"We'll have to take Wren," Mother says in this unhappy

voice. "I can't find a sitter."

Mother tells me about the rules—"You won't be allowed to see Leonard until he comes home next week," and then I feel the icy cold coming out of her that I feel whenever she looks at me, and she says "You have to pretend you're not there because it's against the rules for children to visit. You have to be so quiet no one will notice you." Which sounds really strange. I can be quiet, but I can't disappear.

We walk around the outside of the hospital looking for a door, but all the doors are the wrong ones until Mother says —"Deliveries—over there," and points.

"Pretend you're not here," she reminds me. She swings her coat open, pushes me against her legs and wraps the coat around me. "Be so quiet no one will guess you're hiding under my coat."

I tiptoe through the silly room. It has pipes in the ceiling and it's very dark. Mother's hand is so tight around mine that it hurts. Mother and Aunt Mildred are laughing about breaking rules and I don't understand because Mother and Father get very mad if I break a rule. Breaking a rule is almost as bad as doing a sin.

Mother and Aunt Mildred are looking for stairs because that's part of hiding, because someone might see me in an elevator or "Heaven forbid! What if someone walks into the elevator wearing perfume and she sneezes!"

Mother is walking fast now, with her fingers digging into my arm, dragging me like I drag my Betsy Wetsy doll. It hurts and I can't see where I'm going and I'm scared but I don't dare cry or even tell Mother she's holding me too tight or pulling me too fast because then the bad people who can't know I'm here will hear me and Mother will have to tell Father what a bad girl I was.

Aunt Mildred says, "He's gone now."

Who is gone? I can't ask.

Mother pulls a little bit of the coat off me so I can see the ground. We walk up a lot of stairs. I wish Mother would carry me. Stairs scare me and Mother knows, but "Just walk. Don't be a baby," she whispers.

We get to the room they're looking for, which is 203. Mother loosens her coat so I can see Aunt Dot in bed, but it's like a chair because Aunt Dot is sitting, but where did Aunt Dot's legs go?

Mother pushes me under the bed and whispers for me to sit still and not move, so I pretend I'm playing Statue. I look and look for Aunt Dot's legs but they're gone, and that's scary. I get all stiff playing Statue, wish we could go home now, but Aunt Dot and Aunt Mildred and Mother are laughing about making me disappear.

"She'll stay like that forever," Mother says in her icicle voice. "You don't have to worry about her. She does what she's told."

So I keep doing what I was told, but my legs hurt. My loneliness hurts. Pretending I'm not here hurts because I AM here, and I want to see my new cousin and I want to hug Aunt Dot who is my nice aunt, and above all, I want to know where Aunt Dot's legs are.

I feel something. Nice. Like waves of pink and softness and love. I turn my head. Someone is with me under the bed! Her finger is on her lips. *"Don't talk,"* she mouths, and it's as if I can hear her, even though she doesn't use her voice. She's a little girl, around my size. She's wearing a white party dress and she's all shiny and bright. How did she get here? I should be scared, but I'm not. She makes me feel safe, loved. She makes me feel HERE. With just my mother and my aunts, it as if I'm not here, not real, but now I am even though Mother and my aunts are still laughing and talking as if I'm not.

"I'll be with you whenever you feel lost," the girl tells me without using her voice. I hear her without using my ears, and know in a way that makes me feel certain and safe, that this girl will always be with me when I need her.

Wren, age 7

I think about the girl in the hospital, think about the bad day I had yesterday, think about the dream, and my sadness melts away. I feel loved, and safe, and will always know, no matter what, that the girl from the hospital, or the Piper in my dream, or whoever she is, will always be watching, always be near me when I need her. But I still yearn to get back to my dream, back to that enchanted place.

And I wonder again if Shoshanna had the same dream, because she was in mine and—what if? I'll have to ask her on the way to school.

ACT II: <u>THE IMPOSSIBLE DREAM</u>

The Teacher

The sadness of the child called Shoshanna rips through me. All of the children have woes. Apparently that is an important part of this stage of human development. But this child, in particular, reaches out to me. This child needs me as a bird needs air to keep it aloft. Her need to know I exist, and will always protect her, is overwhelming. When I decide to send the dream, it is for this child, that I do.

Scene 4: <u>No One is Alone</u>

Shoshanna Friedman, age 7

I huddle under my covers, want to disappear from the world. I whisper to Marigold, my Toni Doll. "He is bad, and I can't honor him, so I'm a sinner, and that means I'm—"

And then I'm holding Wren's hand and we're running after the lady. I'm trying to keep up with her, trying to take pictures of her in my mind and remember, remember, remember because I have to draw this. How? How is it possible to draw light, because she's glowing from inside her skin as if she's made of light itself. Her clothes! The colors glow from within, glow as if the woman is clothed in nothing but light! I wish I had a sketchbook and colored pencils with me, but how could I draw the impossible beauty of the woman I'm following?

The music changes to The Children's Story Hour theme. Oh, of course, this is the Piper. I have to know, must know where she is taking us. For she is not just light itself. She is Safety. Absolute Safety. It's just something I sense. Wren whispers something about peace and I feel the peace fill the inside of me, a kind of serenity that makes my heart beat slower, my breath deepen, the thrum of everything inside me say, "It's OK, let down your guard. Nothing can harm you now."

Haven't I learned, even today, especially today, that I can never let down my guard?

Except now, following the Piper, I am doing what my mind tells me not to do.

Impossibly, I follow the Piper through an opening, into a mountain. I look around, try to turn my mind into a camera so I won't forget an inch of this beauty. A grassy knoll in the center, ringed by flowers. Flowers, in colors richer and purer and just— how can there be such colors? A lake or pond off in the corner, its mirror surface reflecting a sky dotted by cotton-ball clouds. All surrounded by a forest of trees covered in spring-soft greenery.

With sunlight impossibly full on her face, the Piper welcomes us to a place where all is Love, where no harm can come.

I awaken, for a moment feeling snug and safe and loved. And then I remember. Be on guard. Always be on guard. Like yesterday. Finding out I'm doing one of the worst sins in the world. Finding out that even God is angry with me, because I'm breaking one of his biggest commandments. The lady said "No harm can come," which is all incredible and miraculous and perfect—if I'm in her world, but I'm not. I'm in my parents' world of rules and the Ten Commandments, so—

My thoughts are interrupted by a voice. The Piper's voice. "*I am always with you. You are loved, and you are safe.*"

Does she know my secrets? I think about yesterday, and it's as if it's happening now:

Scene 5: <u>What Have I Done?</u>

Shoshanna, age 7

My mother, Ima, surprises me. "How would you like to try Sunday School? It's on Sunday morning, early—You'll have plenty of time to come home and have lunch before dancing school."
I remind my mother I'm not in third grade. She leans forward to hear what I'm saying. I try to talk louder, but—that's what the problem is. I can't. Can't talk louder and can't go to Sunday school.

"I can't," I tell her. "If Deborah or any of the other third graders from our building see me walk into their third grade Sunday School class, they'll probably call me a second grade baby right in front of everyone."

Ima says that's nonsense. She tells me I'm smart and I'm reading on fourth grade level, so the people at the temple said I could try it. I know why Ima is doing this. "Trying something new," I overheard her tell Abba, my father. "Maybe something new will help." They were talking about my voice. The way my voice got whisper soft, so I won't be able to blurt out some secret. But how can I blurt it out when I don't remember what the secret is? All I remember is that Abba said I mustn't tell anyone. Ever. So I couldn't even tell Ima that's why my voice disappeared and "trying something new" isn't going to help.

But it's exciting to be doing something third graders do, and I like my <u>Children's Bible</u> and my prayers, so I'm looking forward to it. Even more exciting is that I get to wear my favorite yellow dress with white daisies all over it, which I usually only get to wear to temple, or to parties.

The teacher, Mrs. Braunstein, greets me with a big "Shalom, shalom!" which I know means hello, goodbye, and peace. It's so funny for a word to mean three things.

Mrs. Braunstein tells me to sit in the back of the room where there's an empty seat, which is good because Deborah is way up in front. I almost laugh at the way Deborah scowls when she sees me walk in. Her whole face scrunches up. I'll have to draw it. My chair is wobbly but I don't care. I'm doing such a grown-up thing!

Sunday school is so interesting! I know I'm going to love it. We're going to see a filmstrip. I adore filmstrips! It's about a new country called Israel. I raise my hand when Mrs. Braunstein asks if anyone remembers when Israel became a country. Almost everyone does, and we each get to say something about how we came to temple and sang and danced and had a huge birthday cake and as much grape juice as we wanted.

In the filmstrip, the children in Israel are playing in the snow. They never saw snow before! How can that be? I can't wait to tell Wren and the other kids in second grade about this strange place.

Snacks! They even have snack time! Oranges! I love oranges. These come all the way from Israel. Mrs. Braunstein cuts them into quarters and gives us each two pieces. I never ate an orange with the rind still on it. I watch the other children to see how to do it. Oh, sweetness! What delicious juice! What a beautiful shade of orange. I can't wait to draw it.

Oh no! the beautiful orange juice is dripping onto my starched party dress, getting orange all over the white daisies, turning the yellow dress orange. Ima will be so mad! I try to wipe it away with my napkin, but that just makes the wetness bigger. Is it a sin to spoil my best dress?

I'm wondering about this, getting more and more uncomfortable because if there's one thing that gets Ima mad it's dirtying my good clothes. My ears are half closed but they're open enough to know Mrs. Braunstein is talking about the Ten Commandments. I keep patting my dress with the napkin, barely listening to what she's saying. I know all about the Ten Commandments—how God gave them to Moses and let everyone know there's just one special God and how everyone should worship him. How could anyone not know that?

My mind is sloshing around God and sin and dripped juice when words blast through as if someone turned the radio way up.

"Thou shalt honor thy father and thy mother." The room spins while Mrs. Braunstein talks on and on about what that means. It makes me all dizzy. I have to hold onto my seat to keep from falling off into space. I take deep breaths and concentrate hard on not crying.

Because.

I can't honor Ima and Abba. I love them, but I can't honor them. Sometimes they do bad things. How can I honor Ima when she sends me to public school "to meet all kinds of children because you're going to live in a world where there are all sorts and you need to get used to them," and then doesn't let me play outside of school with Josie who lives down the block and is the smartest girl in our class? Just because she's a Negro. Wren's mother won't let her play with Josie either, so I guess Wren can't honor her mother.

And Abba. Thinking about Abba makes me feel like throwing up. I swallow hard and take deep breaths so I won't. I don't know why, but I know Abba did something very, very bad. Something so bad he said I had to keep it a secret but how can I tell when I don't remember what he did? I just know I can't, can't honor him.

When Ima comes to pick me up I say I was bored, that Sunday School is "monotonous" which is one of Wren's vocabulary words that we decided to learn together.

"OK, Ima says. "I guess we should have waited until you're in third grade. We'll try again next year. Maybe there'll be a different teacher." It makes me feel bad because I liked Mrs. Braunstein. I hope she doesn't get into trouble because I said she was boring.

At five o'clock, after dancing school, Ima turns on the radio and I listen to Story Hour. It's the story of the Pied Piper, which brings me into it while I'm listening. Afterward, I wonder where the Piper took the children, and wish he could take me away somewhere. But where?

I go upstairs to Wren's and we talk for a little while about where the children could be, but I have to go back down so that Wren can eat her dinner before her father gets home and has his with her mother. I'm glad I have a reason to leave. Wren's mother is in a nasty mood.

Later when I'm in bed, I whisper to Marigold, because she's a doll, so it's safe to tell her secrets. "I'll never be able to say, even in my softest voice 'I cannot be a Jew.' I can't be—I lied to Ima, which doesn't matter because I'm such a bad sinner that a little lie won't make a difference. I won't obey the Ten Commandments. I won't honor parents who do bad things.

"Nothing is more important to Ima and Abba than obeying the Jewish laws," I explain to Marigold. "Nothing is more important to me than knowing I can't, and I won't."

And then I dream.

My alarm clock wakes me up. I can still see the beautiful lady piper, still see the light and the colors and the flowers and— something else. Someone else shining with the same light as the lady, with the same face.

I brush my teeth and wash and put on the clothes Ima laid out last night but all the while I'm somewhere else—back when I was six, back when—

Scene 6: <u>Who Can I Turn To?</u>

Shoshanna, age 6

Ima is baking. Just the smell makes me hungry.

"I'm making cookies to take to the hospital for Esti. I'm leaving as soon as these finish baking. I made a double batch. I'll leave half for you. Wait until they cool before you touch them," she says.

I plead with Ima not to go out and leave me alone with Abba.

He scares me. I don't tell her he scares me. If she asked, I couldn't say why. He just does. He never takes me outside to play with the other kids from the apartment building. Even playing with the little ones is better than staying inside with Abba. I have to watch the clock and watch what he's doing and what mood he's in. Like, if he's got his boxes of prayers strapped to his forehead and his hands and is talking to God in Hebrew, I absolutely cannot go into the room he shares with Ima. And if I hear the radio on, that means he's listening to a ball game and "God forbid" I make him miss hearing the score or interrupt him when he's yelling at a player who's a numbskull and did something stupid. I can't tell Ima all that I'm thinking because—doesn't she know it already? She's not blind and deaf! I want to shout at her and say "I'm afraid of him! How can you leave me with him?" But she must know this, and still—

"Please call Wren's mother and ask if I can play at her apartment," I beg.

"I tried," she says. "Wren and her family are going to visit her grandmother."

"What about Deborah?" I ask and Ima looks at me kind of funny because she knows that Deborah is older than us and we don't like her because she bosses us around and calls us names.

"Wren's mother mentioned that Deborah is also going to visit their grandma."

Ima takes the cookies out of the oven, puts them on the counter, puts half in a cookie box, and takes the box with her.

"They're too hot to eat now. Wait a while till they cool and then take a few," she says and slams the door behind her.

I go to my room and read my Bobbsey Twins book until I get to the end, which is much too soon. I think I'll draw the story like a comic strip, but decide to have some cookies first. They're probably cool by now. Just the smell of them makes me feel melting chocolate on my tongue before I even get to the kitchen.

Oh no! Ima forgot to put the tray of cookies on the table I can reach. Ima likes to stand when she cooks, so the counter they're on is too high for me. I pull a chair up to the counter, climb onto it very carefully. I reach up, take a cookie. I'm just starting to bite into it, and oh my, the chips are still warm and soft and—

I sense someone behind me. A hand clamps down on my shoulder. A hurting hand. The pain goes down my arm and into my back. Abba.

"Stealing a cookie?" Abba asks.

"Ima said I could take some when they cool," I say. "Want to have some with me?"

"Lying too? Stealing and lying? One sin isn't bad enough? You have to make it worse with lying?" Abba's voice is soft, the kind of soft that's like angry yelling. His face is all red and his eyes look funny, kind of glittery. I never heard him talk like this before. "Two sins. Come with me."

He pulls my arm, his hand squeezing, hurting. Now is the time. I've never been spanked, but he's threatened it. Will he use his belt, like Robert's father does, or will he just hit me? My tummy hurts. I drop the uneaten half of the cookie onto the table as he pulls me away.

"Sit on my bed," he orders, and what can I do but sit there, shivering inside.

And then a miracle happens. A true miracle with an angel and everything. She's beautiful, in a white gown with big white wings like the angels in my <u>Children's Bible</u>. One minute I'm sitting on Abba's bed and the next I'm in the angel's arms. She carries me to a place of flowers, and the smell! Like the rose garden at the Botanic Gardens. The colors! Colors I've never seen before. More colors than there are in the world! And birdsong. I look at the angel and realize she's not an angel, she's Mother goose, with wings. She puts me down gently on the grass near the flowers. "Hide under my skirt," she says, in a voice I can hear even though it makes no sound. "Whenever you're frightened, just think of me and hide under my skirt."

I stay there for a long time, but then Mother Goose and the garden fade and I'm back in my parents' room. Back on Abba's bed. Back, trying to catch my breath. But why am I out of breath? All I was doing was sitting quietly under Mother Goose's skirt. Is it because I had to fly back here from so far away? Is that why I'm so tired, so out of breath?

And cold. Where are my clothes? Why are my clothes off? I don't remember taking them off. I was wearing clothes when I was with the Mother Goose angel.

"Here," Abba grunts and thrusts my clothes at me. "Put them on." His voice is that quiet screaming again. "I won't tell Ima about your sins and you can never tell anyone about this. Never, ever speak of it. To anyone. This will be our secret. Right, Shoshanna?"

"Yes, Abba," I say. Or try to say. Something has happened to my voice. As if my voice flew away. As if Abba crushed it in his bed, or I left it in the garden with the Mother Goose angel.

I still don't have much of a voice when Ima comes home.

I don't have a voice when I play with my friends, or at school.

I get dragged to doctors and they all agree. I'm doing it on purpose, and I can't tell anyone that Abba put me in his bed and stole it because I sinned.

Shoshanna, age 7

Two pictures float into my mind, like two people walking together, somehow wrapping me up in a bubble of safety. One is the lady in the dream, the Piper. The other has exactly the same face, but she is Mother Goose. I get ready for school, while my mind flies free, breathing in the memory that no matter what my life will bring, the Lady-Piper/Mother Goose person will keep me safe.

Scene 7: <u>**Happy Talk**</u>

Wren, age 7

I couldn't talk to Shoshanna on the way to school. Mother was walking us, and privacy was impossible. But Eugene's mother is walking us home now. Robert and Eugene are with her, ahead of Shoshanna and me.

I start cautiously. It's not that I think Shoshanna will laugh at me for dreaming about a story. No. I'm afraid to hear her answer. What if she dreamed of the same place I did? That's so totally weird. But if she didn't—.

Please, I think, please don't say you didn't dream it. She was there in the dream, and if she didn't dream it, it can't be real. But if she did dream it—what does that mean? What if the dream place is real? What if the Piper is real?

I'm afraid to ask, but I make myself. "Remember the story on <u>Story Hour</u> yesterday? My voice is almost as soft as Shoshanna's. Her words come out in a rush, with an undertone of excitement.

"Of course. I even had a dream about it. A beautiful dream. I drew a whole bunch of pictures about it when I got up this morning. There are still a few more I want to draw when I get home. Come down to play with me in about an hour. I have to do these drawings first. It's really important," Shoshanna says.

She had a dream? I can feel my heart bang around in my chest.

"Can I see them?" I ask.

She starts to say something about coming over after I have my milk and cookies. I interrupt her. The words start spilling out.

I tell her about how I left the building, and she was there, and how we were all running after this lady. "She—the Piper—was a lady, not a man like in the story. She was wearing this flowy kind of gown that came down to the floor and was more colors than Crayola has. Like the Pied Piper, she led all the children, lots and lots of children, out of the city, down a country road to a mountain. We were terrified that we wouldn't get to wherever she was taking us, but she touched the mountain and it opened up with a hole in its side like a sliding door. Most of the children started screaming about the Pied Piper and ran away, but a few of us followed her into the mountain. And—"

By now Shoshanna is kind of jumping around while we're walking and her whole body is bouncing, "And there was a garden inside," she says. "The most beautiful flowers I've ever seen, and it smelled so sweet and the music was so beautiful—"

"Not like anything I ever heard before," I say. "And there were woods, gorgeous, beautiful woods around the flowers, ex —"

"Except," Shoshanna interjects, "for the lake in the upper left if it was a picture and the sky was—"

By now we've stopped walking, are standing staring at each other, and Eugene's mother is yelling "Will you two stop dawdling and get over here before the light changes and we have to wait for it to change again."

"How," we ask each other when I'm in Shoshanna's room an hour later, looking at the pictures she drew of the dream. How is it possible we had the same dream?" Neither of us can answer it.

We both know. "We can't tell anyone about this. This is our secret." We link pinkies and promise to be friends forever.

I sense a soft sun-storm of happiness wrapping itself around Shoshanna. She smiles a smile from inside of her, the kind of smile she hasn't had for so, so long. Her happiness makes me happy.

Shoshanna, age 7

It's a puzzle, I think, after Wren goes home for dinner. I'm drawing more pictures. This time, with a face on one of the girls that's clearly Wren's. Two other faces I never saw before. But they were there in the dream. Maybe the drawings will help me understand.

Another thing to understand. How can this secret seem so

right, so full of happiness, while other secrets are so bad, so hurtful?

I hear a voice—the same soundless voice of the piper-lady, which is the same voice as the Mother Goose angel—the voice that's in my head, not my ears. *"Call me whatever you want,"* it says. *"You have many dresses in your closet. I have many costumes I can wear. Think of me whenever you need to call on me, as the Piper, or Mother Goose, or the Angel, or anything else. I will always hear your need, and be there to protect you. As I will always be there with your friend, Wren."*

It's like a big happiness ballooning inside of me. My voice may be gone, but my happiness is back.

ACT III: <u>BALI HAI</u>

The Teacher

I picture two streams, flowing gently. And then suddenly, their course turns. They surge toward one another until their waters splash over their banks, and the two streams merge in bubbles of jubilation. A confluence of two streams, each bearing a boat carrying a passenger: One, Wren, the other, Shoshanna.

Now, miles away, two more streams flow toward one another, each bearing another of my chosen children, neither suspecting that on a soon-coming night, a dream will change her life.

Scene 8: <u>Getting to Know You</u>

Gracie-Faye Callahan, age 7

"You'll forget it in no time, once y' see the grand house we'll be livin' in," Da says.

Da must have left his brains in Ireland. He wasn't on that boat. He wasn't there with Mam and all the family pukin' for nine days and the wee ones cryin' and the rain and waves and nothin' green and the sureness shamrocks and pots of gold weren't comin' with us on that boat. And Da surely wasn't with us when the rainbow burst out and filled the sky and turned the sea into a mirror so there was a rainbow above the ship and a rainbow below. "No, Da, I'm sure I won't forget that," I tell him, and it makes him laugh.

The taxi with Da, Patrick, Brigid and me—the older ones—threads through more cars than I thought there'd be in the entire world. It's a race. Will we get from the city called Oceanport to a suburb called Silver Birches first, or will the taxi with Mam and the three wee ones get there before us?

"'Tis the perfect place for our family," Da is tellin' us. "When Imported from Ireland transferred me across the sea to head the growin' company, I asked the folks already here where the best place would be, for it was clear Oceanport was no place for children. Children need green around them, don't y' know? And where would fairies be hidin' in a big city with no green? I looked at a map and saw a lovely county west of the city, with a brook runnin' through it, and a big Catholic church in the center of town. Investigated, I did," he turns and looks straight at each one of us, as if he's about to make a big announcement. "I discovered one train line better than the others. And then I investigated train stops, and there, only a half hour on a fast train, only forty minutes from my office, was a village called Silver Birches. The very one with the big Catholic church." He turns and grins at us again. "So I found us a grand house, with a patio that we'll put an awnin' over so we can sit outside in the rain and watch for rainbows." He glances at the thing that tells how many miles we've gone. "You'll be seein' it in less than ten minutes."

"What's a birch?" I ask, for the thought of a town made of silver doesn't sound soft or green, but Da explains that birches are trees, and these are called silver because their bark is white. A lovely picture fills m' mind and warms the cockles of m' heart. To live among trees so magic their bark is white!

"Is there a school?" Patrick asks. He would. Just two years older than me and already with his head livin' in books, even when there are butterflies overhead and fireflies, which are fairies in disguise, waitin' to be caught, and looked at, and then set free, their minds filled with our wishes.

"I told you about the beautiful church, and would you believe, right down the block, there's a lower school for the likes of you. When you get a little older, there's a girls' school on one side of the church, and one for the boys on the other side. Looked at the school registry, I did, and there are lots of children from other places in the world—names on the list from the likes of Italy and Poland and all other grand and glorious nations, but most of the names are familiar, which should make y' feel at home."

"Are there boys my age on the block our house is on?" Patrick asks the moment Da stops talkin'.

"Oh my heavens, yes." Da ruffles Patrick's hair. I'm sittin' on the other side of Da and I move a little away. Mam captured my curls into pigtails with new green ribbons and I don't want Da to touch it and mess it up before I meet the children who live near us, for Mam told us we'd be movin' to a street crowded with friends for all. Patrick mustn't have been listenin.'

"Lots of children fillin' the street where they all play together, all ages, for the street—Acorn Oval—is a safe one, with only cars that belong there—no cars passin' through on their way somewhere else. Now, mind you, not all the children are Catholic. Some are what's called Jewish and they go to the town schools, but I've met them and lovely folk they are, and I hope you'll all be good friends. Patrick, there's a family named Lieberman, and I believe they have a fellow your age, and Brigid, I think they also have a girl for you. For you, my little Gracie-Faye, there's a darlin' girl named Maura Reilly who was hoppin' up and down with excitement when she heard a girl her age was movin' in. Said she'd show you around and stay beside you in school.

The warm happiness inside me is more than I can take. I picture a girl—will she have red hair like mine? It's hard to sit still. I need to get up right now in the cab and hop up and down too. Or jig.

Dancin' a jig is the first thing I ask about, when I meet Maura the next day.

"Y' don't know how to jig?" I ask Maura. It's a bit of a shock when she says she doesn't. She talks funny and very fast and it's hard for me to follow what she's sayin' but I get that she's tryin' to tell me that if I show her how, she'll be jiggin' along with me. Learn it she does within the first hour I meet her. She's not at all what I imagined, but sometimes what's real is even nicer than pretend.

I was thinkin' wild curly red hair like m' own, but Maura is beautiful. Starin' is rude but I can't stop lookin' at Maura, with her black hair and eyelashes like black frames around her eyes. Those eyes! So big, so bright, bright blue. "Y' have the most beautiful eyes I've ever seen," I tell her. "Y' look like a princess or someone in a movie magazine!"

A whole string of words comes out of her mouth and I think m' ears hear less than half of them. "Thanks," I say a few times, and I think she's sayin' she likes the looks of me, with my green eyes and red curls but I can't be sure. Maybe something else is green or red. Or has freckles.

Brigid bubbles over talkin' about her new friend, Susie, so I tell her about Maura but I'm not bubblin'. I feel a tug like an undertow pullin' beneath the happy feelin' of havin' a new friend. "Maura's a nice girl and all, but she doesn't believe in fairies. She said she'll go fairy huntin' if that's what I want to do but I get the feelin' she's just bein' polite because I'm new, and I wonder if she still will when the newness gets old. Maura doesn't like poems or books, and it's a sadness we can't swap books or spend hours talkin' about the stories we read.

"That's too bad," Brigid says, "but a friend is a friend and never should y' turn one down." Which sounds like somethin' Mam would say. Brigid likes to repeat whatever Mam says even if it's a bigger idea than Brigid's brain can sort out, Brigid bein' only six.

I tell Da, "There's a problem with Maura but maybe it's just a gettin' used to problem. She talks so fast there's no understandin' her, and her thoughts get so jumbled that one sentence can go on for a half hour and mix up seven or a million different ideas, which Sister Mary Clare would never have allowed."

"Y'll get used to it in time, Da says. "Just try to catch every few words, and y'll get what she's tryin' to say."

Mam tells me to go knock on Maura's door and ask her to play, the way Patrick calls on David, and Brigid rings Susie's bell. I try to explain that Maura doesn't play what I like. All she wants to do is play kick ball or bouncin' ball or jump rope or a game the kids on the block call SPUD or the most horrible of all, dodge ball where everyone throws balls at you. Mam insists, so I do, but it's not fair, because Maura hardly ever comes over for a fairy or elf hunt.

So I call on her to get Mam off m' back, and sometimes magic surprises y' and comes along. I get to Maura's house, and she's playin' the piano! So I come in when her mam invites me, and Maura looks at me and turns the tune she's playin' into a jig. I start dancin' and we're laughin' because now there's somethin' we can do that we both like. When we finally get tired and stop she says "Y' taught me to jig. But do y' know how to step dance? I really want to learn."

Waves of happy wash away the undertow. "I'll teach y'" I say, and then she says the most excitin' thing. "With your dancin' and my music, maybe we can put on a show for the other children on the block. Or get all the children to be in our show and do it for the parents and—" She goes on and on and I just listen and maybe I understand and maybe I don't but I'm happy because maybe now I have a friend, a beautiful girl named Maura.

Scene 9: <u>I Won't Grow Up</u>

Maura Reilly, age 7

"I'm never, ever going back to school 'cause it's a terrible place and no one likes me and I have no friends and I'll sit in my room all day and you can teach me or I'll go to public school where no one knows me and I'll make new friends and maybe I'll learn to read and maybe I won't but I don't care what you say, I'm never ever going back to St. Ursula." I slam my book bag onto the kitchen table with the loudest bang I can and grab a cookie and stuff it in my mouth before Momma tells me I can't talk with my mouth full of food.

"Slow down, Maura," Momma says, but Momma has no idea how bad things are and how can I possibly explain that if she's a good mother she will never ever make me walk into that building again.

"Chew slowly, Maura," she says as if she hasn't been listening to a word I've said. "Just tell me what happened and we'll figure out what to do."

"There's no what happened to figure out, there were three things, one after the other and they kept getting worse and worse and first it was embarrassing and then it got so I couldn't look at anyone and then it got so no one would look at me or talk to me and I'm uninvited from Mary Alice's party and I'll be the only girl in the class who isn't invited and that's all anyone will talk about for weeks and years to come and I'll never have friends again so there's no what to do that will fix things and you're" I look around the kitchen, "You're a Brussel sprout if you think you can fix anything."

"Take a deep breath, Maura, and tell me the first thing. Just the first thing," Momma says in that extra calm voice that makes me angry because she should be getting upset now if she was paying any attention to me. I start to tell her the first thing. Maybe that will get her a little excited.

"The first thing that happened is that we were practicing for the spelling test, going around the room and Sister said a word and if it was your turn you had to spell the word and when it was my turn Sister said 'and' which she knows I know because it's the word I got right on the spelling test last week, but I spelled a-n-t and Declan started to laugh and Christine told him to stop and then I said, 'There's an ant crawling up my desk so if I made a mistake, it's the ant's fault,' and everyone laughed, even Sister kind of smiled like she was trying not to laugh and it's NOT FUNNY!"

I can see Momma holding in a smile and that makes me so angry I hit the table with my fist and she says in that calm voice I want to punch "Just go on, Maura," like she wants to get the story over with, so I go on because there's no point in getting Momma mad at me too because then there'd be four bad things happening today, so I say, "And then we had the spelling test and there were a lot of words I didn't know so I skipped them or guessed them but then there was the word 'was' and I know how to spell it, I know there's an 's' and a 'w' and an 'a' so it's a word I know but I couldn't remember what order to put them in but I knew I just needed a little hint, so I leaned over and looked at Peggy's paper to see what letter came first and Sister boomed out 'Maura keep your eyes on your own paper,' and everyone stopped writing and stared at me until Sister said the next word was rain which I guessed at and followed all the rules and wrote r-a-n-e and when I got my paper back I got 0% on the whole test and Christine saw it and told everyone so now everyone knows I'm dumb in spelling and—"

Momma comes around and hugs me but I shrug her off so I can tell her the third thing, but she's babbling on about how she'll talk to Sister tomorrow. "Maybe you can have your spelling tests privately, or your own list of words," she says. "We'll work something out. Maybe get you a tutor. And maybe she can talk to the class about how people can be very good at something and not so good at something else. I'm sure no one in your class can play the piano or sing as well as you. And Sister has told me you're the most popular girl in the class. That's not going to change. They're still your friends. They still li—"

"NO THEY'RE NOT!" I scream. "I told you there were three things but you don't remember or you weren't paying attention to me but the ant and the spelling test are only two and they were littler than the third thing which was the worst that ever happened to anyone anywhere and I lost all the friends I ever had and—"

"OK, Maura. I'm listening. What happened?" Momma interrupts but she really doesn't want to listen, which I can see from the way she's sighing and leaning her head on her hand as if she's the one who has a problem.

"The third is I asked Christine if she's coming to Mary-Jo's party on Saturday and Christine got all upset because Mary-Jo is one of her best friends and she didn't invite her so I said maybe the invitation got lost in the mail because remember when you got the letter that said you didn't pay the gas bill but you did pay it, and you had t—"

"Get back to Christine and Mary-Jo, Maura." Momma leans forward with her elbows on the table where she always tells us not to put them and puts her hands up to her forehead like she's trying to keep her head from falling off.

"I'm getting to that which is that I told Christine about the bill getting lost in the mail so she went to Mary-Jo and Mary-Jo asked how she knows about the party and Christine had to tell her I asked her if she was going and Mary-Jo got all upset because she had to let Christine know that the party is supposed to be a surprise for her because everyone knows Christine's mother is sick and can't make her parties and her birthday is coming up so now Christine knows the party is for her and she's all happy but everyone else was all excited about it being a surprise so I was uninvited and now they're having a party and everyone in my class is going and I'm the only girl in the whole class who isn't going and even Gracie-Faye who almost no one really knows was invited—so I have no friends left and—"

Momma puts her hand on my arm to stop me. "The party isn't for another week. Lots can happen in a week. I'll bet by then you'll be back with your friends and re-invited to the party. I'll bet a new record that you'll be at that party. Any record you want if Mary-Jo doesn't ask you to come. Now, why don't you go out and play."

"There's no one to play with, just boys and good heavens, how am I supposed to live on a street with only boys my age?" Sometimes Momma has turnips for brains.

"What about Gracie-Faye?" Momma asks.

"I told you, she's weird and it's not because she talks funny and is from far away and it's a different kind of weird because all she likes to do is read books and talk about God and Jesus and church or elves and fairies and leppersomethings and STOP!" Momma throws my jacket to me and the sleeve swings into my mouth so I toss it onto a chair and go into the living room and start to play the piano, which at least is something I can do without getting in trouble.

On Saturday we go on a family picnic so I don't have to think about school or friends but on Sunday Momma starts in with "It's almost time for your radio show," which is a good thing, but she spoils it with "Why don't you call for Gracie-Faye and Brigid and ask if they want to hear it with you?"

Momma's brains are as scrambled as eggs. "How can I ask them to listen to the show when Brigid is a baby and I told you, Gracie-Faye is in my class and I told you that no one in my class will play with me." I drop the carrot I'm supposed to be peeling onto the counter and start to leave the kitchen, but Momma's blabbing away.

"Gracie-Faye is new. She hasn't had a chance to make friends, and from what you've said about her, I'm sure she'd love Children's Story Hour," Momma says in that you-must-obey voice of hers. I can't argue and explain about Gracie-Faye's weird accent and how she'll never be my friend because she's in the top reading group and even sits on the steps with Patsy and reads books during recess when any normal girl would be jumping rope or playing potsie or A-My-Name-Is-Anna, but if I keep arguing I'll miss Story Hour so I put on my jacket and head down the street as slowly as I can and still get back in time for the story.

Scene 10: Finding Neverland

Gracie-Faye, age 7

I love this book! It's the story of Queen Maeve, tellin' how she saved the whole kingdom. I'm almost up to the best part when someone pounds on the door and Mam yells for me, sayin' Maura is here callin' for me to come out and play.

It isn't for play, I hear Maura tellin' her while I'm puttin' on m' shoes and headin' downstairs. It's to listen to a radio show called <u>Story Hour</u> and she goes on and on about how she knows I love stories. She sees me comin' down the stairs and starts with her runaway talkin'.

"You have to come right now, right this minute or we'll miss the walk into Storyland and the music is so great so come on." She practically pulls me out of the house, down the block. We sit in her kitchen, eatin' these happy-mouth chocolate brownies, and her mam turns on the radio and gets the right station.

It's the story of <u>The Pied Piper</u>, and isn't it lovely how he led the children away from their dishonest, greedy folk. For sure, he must be takin' them to Ireland where everything's green and I have dozens of friends who will help the children find Fairyland in the meadows.

Maura, age 7

When the story ends, we sit on my stoop and talk about it and I'm thinking, maybe Gracie-Faye can be my friend because we're sitting here talking for a long time and with no one else being willing to be my friend having Gracie-Faye might not be so bad.

"So where do you think he took the children?" she asks, and then she goes on with her idea the Piper took the children to Ireland, "where there are meadows with tall grasses and wildflowers where fairies, elves and leprechauns live."

Which I think is a little dumb but if Gracie-Faye is going to be my friend I have to be polite, so I don't say how dumb it is for the Piper to lead the children somewhere ordinary, that a story has to be exciting so if he did take the children, he certainly wouldn't take them to Ireland so I think about being polite and I just say, "Maybe he took them somewhere adventurous or dangerous like Never Never Land where there are pirates and crocodiles."

I hope I'm not hurting her feelings and I guess I'm not because she says "That's a good idea, Maura. Stories do have adventure and danger in them," and then she starts to go on about this Queen Maeve story she's in the middle of reading "for maybe the dozenth time," which is the dumbest thing I ever heard but I just let her talk without interrupting which I know I do a lot but I can't help it because I never know when people are finished and it's my turn to talk.

In the middle of her telling the story of Queen Maeve which it turns out is pretty interesting, her brother Patrick comes along and oh, my! he's so cute! maybe I'll marry him someday so I move over for him to sit next to me but he doesn't sit, he says he's there to get Gracie-Faye to come home to set the table.

"What?" I almost say because shouldn't her mom be setting the table but I catch myself before it comes out of my mouth because maybe that would be rude, and Momma always reminds me if I'm not sure if something is rude it's best not to say anything.

Gracie-Faye looks at me and says "We all have jobs. We take turns. It's m' turn to be settin' the table today."

I think for a minute and am about to ask if her mother can't do all the jobs because she's almost ready to have the next baby but Gracie-Faye is getting up and walking down the three steps to the front path where Patrick is waiting for her, so I just say "Nice to meet you Patrick, see you tomorrow, Gracie-Faye, we can talk more about the story on the bus." And then she's gone, and I sit for a while on the stoop watching the clouds because if I go into the house Momma will tell me to get my school bag ready for tomorrow or worse, come to my room and check to see if all my homework is done and it isn't because I couldn't read all the directions for the workbook page and she's going to sit with me and make me do it.

I'm lying in bed, thinking about the whole conversation with Gracie-Faye and wondering what kind of adventurous, dangerous place the Piper could be leading the children to—and then I'm walking down the road to Storyland, and I hear the narrator's voice but it's not his voice, it's a lady's voice—

"Hush. Listen." I hear the most beautiful music I ever heard, and the voice says "follow" and how can I not follow when the music is so beautiful and it sounds like a whole orchestra—I can hear every instrument but it's better than any instruments I ever heard or could imagine, so I follow the music down the street and Gracie-Faye is running with me and then lots of other children are coming from all sides and then we're out in the country and the music plays the tune of the <u>Story Hour</u> but it's different because it's so beautiful but the other children start screaming "the Piper!" and maybe it's the Piper who's playing the music and maybe she's stealing us and taking us somewhere but that's OK because if she does I won't have to go to school again and I keep following the lady and the music and so does Gracie-Faye and a very small girl who isn't pretty at all and has glasses and frizzy sticking-out hair and a girl holding her hand who has brown hair with some blond in it and big gray eyes and is very pretty but the other children are screaming "The Piper" and disappear and then we get to this mountain and my goodness, the whole mountain splits open and we run inside and the music gets even better and how is that possible? And there are flowers everywhere and the Piper stands on top of this hill to welcome the children to—

But I wake up and don't hear where and I'm filled with sadness because I know that's where I belong, in a place like Never-Never Land.

I think some more and didn't the lady in the dream look like the lady who came out of nowhere and took my hand and led me back to Momma when I walked away from her in Great Expectations when I was four because she was shopping for nightgowns to wear to the hospital because Bobby was going to be born and I didn't want a new baby, it was bad enough having Kevin who's two years older than me and if it turned out that it was a girl it would live in my room and if it was a boy it would live in Kevin's but I didn't want a girl in my room and I didn't want another boy. So I walked away and got out of the store into the mall and a lady walked me back to Momma and whispered *"I'll always be here when you need me,"* in this voice only I could hear and then disappeared so I couldn't even point her out to Momma so she could thank her, and I'm sure it's the same person.

"I'll always be with you," I hear in my head now, and it makes me really happy and makes me think someday, maybe someday, I'll learn to read and spell and maybe I'll get re-invited to the party or at least, Gracie-Faye will be my friend.

Scene 11: <u>Oh What a Beautiful Mornin'</u>

Gracie-Faye, age 7

All through the table settin' and the dinner I'm thinkin' about the Pied Piper and how maybe he took the children back to Ireland or maybe Maura's right and he took them to a new adventure.

I'm still wonderin' about it when I fall asleep, and then I hear music, and—

I'm followin' the lovely lady and her magical music, the music of fairies. It bids me to listen and follow. Surely, the lady must be leadin' me back to the green of Ireland or a glorious adventure. Sure as there is God and magic, I will not miss an adventure or a chance to go back home.

The lady is movin' so fast I don't have time to grab m'robe and slippers. Down the stairs, out the front door. Barely time to close it behind me and no time at all to be sure it's locked, but this is a grand land, and surely lockin' doors can't be necessary.

Maura is runnin' down the street with me and now other children are joinin' us and they're dancin'! Such lovely steps! I want to pirouette and do soarin' leaps but the lady is leadin' us all so fast, so fast I can only do the forward-movin' steps or I would fall behind. Now the music changes to the music of The Story Hour *and "The Piper!" children are screamin' and runnin' away and disappearin', as if the Piper is someone bad. The children are all gone except for me and Maura who is still dancin' and so are the smallish girl with sitckin' out hair holdin' hands with the regular-size pretty girl.*

A mountain! A mountain in front of us! What to do? But the lady must say some magic words, call upon the dwarfs who can tunnel through hills, or maybe she herself is a fairy queen or an elf-maid. A door opens right in front o' her, a slidin' door, and the lady goes inside and I follow and so do Maura and the two other girls and yes! We're back in Ireland with green all around us. But where in Ireland is there such a beautiful garden?

The lady stands on top of a hill and says "Welcome to—"

But before she tells us where we are, everythin' disappears. Everythin'.

I'm sittin' in m' bed with a grin on m' face so big it hurts m' cheeks. I know why the lady looks so familiar. Her face is the same as the face of the leprechaun who talked to me before we set sail. He came up to me as I was waitin' to board the ship, feelin' sad sayin' goodbye to our land, and Mam sayin' "We'll come back and visit, often," which will never be enough. The leprechaun came right over to me, stood there beside me, with no one seein' him but me, and I bent down so he could whisper in m' ear, *"I'll always be there with you, with Ireland in m' pocket."*

Sure and there's no question about it—she may seem like a lady, but the lady is my leprechaun, come to me from Ireland, with a piece of m' homeland hidden in his trousers.

Scene 12: <u>Friendship</u>

Maura, age 7

"You have to be nice, Maura," Momma says and she always says that because I used to hate having to go to Gracie-Faye's house and walk with her to the bus stop and sit with her on the bus, and how is Momma to know that I can't wait to see Gracie-Faye today because for one thing, she's my only friend in the entire world which Sister says is the whole universe with all the stars and planets and everything and besides being my only friend she was there with me in the dream and I wonder if she'll like it when I tell her about it and "STOP!"

Momma is combing through my bookbag like going through my hair with a fine-tooth comb to get the sand out after we go to the beach but she's in my bookbag making sure I have my books and my homework and lunch and I understand she has to but I don't like it and I tell her so. I let her pin my hanky to my sleeve, put on the jacket she's holding out and take the bookbag she sticks into my hand and I almost forget to kiss her goodbye which I do even though she's a mushroom who can't understand why I shouldn't be going to school today or ever, and skip down the street to pick up Gracie-Faye because today I want to get there fast because something in me just says I should.

Gracie-Faye, age 7

I can't wait for slow-poke Maura to get to my house. I have to grab her and talk to her before we're at the bus stop with all those other children. We *must* talk alone. I walk as fast as I can toward her house, meet her in the middle of Acorn Oval and she starts talkin', babblin' with her words all pilin' up and makin' no sense, so I stop her with my hand on her arm.

As loud as I can, I say "Did y' dream last night?" Before Maura can begin an answer that will take longer than our walk, I add, "I dreamed where the Piper took the children, and it was beautiful, all green and lush like Ireland and would you believe it, right in the middle of a mountain! A green space with food-o'-the-fairies flowers dancin' around it and woods beyond for elves to play."

Maura stops walkin'. Just stands there starin' at me with those big eyes of hers like she's forgotten how to speak.

Finally she starts with her babblin', words comin' so fast they're tumblin' all over each other. "Was there a lady leading the children, a beautiful lady with a dress with every color ever invented and my goodness! the music! the most beautiful music I ever heard and instruments that haven't been invented and it was like the air was singing and the flowers were singing and"

"Yes! Yes!" I'm shoutin' and jumpin' up, clickin' my heels right there in the street. I can't help m'self, it's such a joy.

Maura grabs my hands and we face each other jumpin' and dancin' and "How is it possible?" I ask and it's hard to make out Maura's words because she's out of breath and we're still starin' at each other. People don't have the same dream. It's not possible.

But we did.

"For sure the fairies had something to do with it," I say. "For sure the fairies sent us the same dream to be sure we'd be friends."

OK. Maybe I shouldn't have said that because Maura is lookin' at me, and I don't have to make out her words to know she's thinkin' 'How can I be friends with the crazy girl with her eyes in a book and her head all filled with fairies?'

But I'm wrong, because she's sayin' "Like sisters, forever, sisters and best friends forever," and she hugs me and m' heart explodes with joy at bein' in this strange new country and havin' this strange girl who all the other girls say is the most popular in the school tellin' me she'll be my best friend.

It's almost more wonderful than knowin' the leprechaun-lady will always be with me.

ACT IV: <u>WE GO TOGETHER</u>

The Teacher

Two together in Oceanport now, two together in Silver Birches. Time goes by, streams flow on, pathways turn.

One stream splits off, turns toward two that are distant. With more Time, the lone stream turns to join the three that now flow together, the Gathering complete.

I see this, and, send a dream to the four who saw, the four who know, before two plus two become One. I stand before them atop the hill in the meadow of flowers. Trees greening with new spring leaves shine in sunlight brushing over the woods surrounding the meadow. In each of the four corners stands a girl. First, the dark haired one comes forward from the far left corner. From the far right, a freckled red-head dances toward her. They meet, join hands, and dance toward me. Hesitantly, a blond girl from the lower left devours the scene with her eyes and moves toward us. Coming closer, she breaks into a run, clasps hands with the other two girls and joins their dance. Time moves on, until the small girl from the bottom right peaks out from behind a tree, sees the dancers and seems to fly, bird-like, to join them in their circle of joy. Grasping their hands, she closes the ring, now complete.

Scene 13: <u>Something Sort of Grandish</u>

Shoshanna, age 10

"We don't have a choice, Shoshanna," Ima says. Ten minutes ago I walked into the kitchen, drawn by the scent of the chicken fat Ima is making. The kitchen still smells of simmering onions and blobs of chicken fat melting into liquid that will harden into the scrumptiousness we'll put on potatoes and bread when we have meat meals and can't use butter. I love to watch the onions turn translucent before they're swallowed up by the melting fat.

"Here, Shoshanna," Ima says and hands me a dish of the solid pieces left after she pours the liquefied fat into jars to put in the refrigerator.

I take a bite and the fat melts into my mouth, and I wonder if anything in the world could be more scrumptious. And then she starts to talk, and how can your whole life change in ten seconds? I'm eating food fit for kings and she's sitting here opposite me at the kitchen table telling me they've found a house in a place I've never heard of and "we're moving as soon as our mortgage is approved," which I gather has something to do with money.

"Look at your class," Ima says. "The 'One' class is supposed to be for the brightest children and now half of your class is Negro and half of them can't even read."

I try to tell Ima she's all wrong. "The only Negroes in my class are Josie, who's the best student in the whole world, and Malcolm, who's certainly at least as smart as Wren or me. And Roland and Trisha who have trouble reading but are smart in everything else. Yes, the three and four classes are mostly Negro, but that has nothing to do with my class, and besides, they're nice children and they probably are as smart as the one and two classes, maybe they just don't have books at home—most of them live in the projects—so I don't see what difference it makes."

Which doesn't stop Ima from ranting on. "The exception proves the rule. We have to get you out of that school."

I discuss it with Wren. Her parents are also looking for a house. "And it's so ridiculous," Wren says. "Josie is my next best friend after you and I can't even tell my mother about her because she'd never let me play with her."

"But you do on the street," I remind her.

"Only when my mother isn't around."

"Yeah. Well, you won't have that problem when you move.

For sure your parents will find a suburb where there are no Negroes. That's what my parents did. I don't get it," I say. Wren is inching closer—reading my lips? I try to speak more loudly.

Abba drives us to the new house, on a street called Acorn Oval in the village of Silver Birches. They say it only takes a half hour by commuter train from the city of Oceanport which has been my home since I was born, but it takes a whole hour in Abba's car. Finally we arrive at the house. It looks like the picture they showed me. Drab.

There are girls I see playing on the street. They're wearing uniforms, and Abba says that means they go to "parochial school" which is a school for children who are Catholic, and I'll be going to public school. I'm allowed to play with them, Ima says, but we won't be going to school together, so how am I going to meet children from my school? I hate it here already.

My biggest concern, which of course I can hardly mention to my parents or any other living being, is who I can talk to about the dreams Wren and I have. The ones about the lady Wren and I call the Piper. The place we call the Haven. My parents have made it very clear to me—phone calls to Oceanport are long-distance, which is expensive, which means I can only call Wren once a week, for three minutes. You can't have a conversation about a dream in three minutes—or wait seven days to talk about it.

My room has possibilities, though. Whether my parents like it or not, I'm going to make it really mine.

"Here are some wallpaper samples." Ima thrusts a large envelope toward me. I push it away.

"I don't want wallpaper. This is a must. I want white walls. Plain white walls. And I need you to drive me to The Artists' Attic for paints. I'm going to paint a mural." It's not a statement. It's a demand.

"Suit yourself," Ima says.

In the weeks it takes between the purchase of the house and

moving-in day, I give up my last precious days in Oceanport with my friends and go with my mother to Silver Birches, where I can close the door to my room and create a mural on the four walls. Twice, Ima lets Wren come with me, which is really nice, but really sad, because it reminds us of how far apart we're going to be. Almost a whole hour door to door! Or forever, unless we can get one of our parents to drive us.

The day after I move in, the two girls I saw on the street knock on our door. I feel a twinge in my stomach when I see them, as if it's tumbling around. Could it be? Are they really who they seem to be?

I focus on the girls. The beautiful dark haired one with the big blue eyes introduces herself to Ima and me in a rush of tangled up words.

"Hi, I'm Maura and this is Gracie-Faye and we don't go to public school but our parents said we can all play together when we're not in school and Gracie-Faye got here from Ireland three years ago and don't mind her if she talks funny, it's because she's from so far away."

The girl with the green eyes and mop of red curls holds out her hand and says "Hi."

Before I can say anything, Ima is saying, "My daughter is happy to have friends here. Why don't you girls go up to Shoshanna's room and get to know each other. I was just about to make a batch of oatmeal cookies. I'll call you down when they're done."

"Come on," I say. "My room is upstairs."

We traipse up the stairs. Will they think I'm weird with a mural going all around my four walls? Or will they…

We walk through the door. I look at their faces, try to capture their reaction, and my breath catches. I almost can't breathe. Gracie-Faye and Maura are standing there staring, gasping at the sight of the oasis of flowers in the middle of the forest. Frozen like statues staring at the woman dressed in panels of flowing multicolored fabric that dances in the wind. Gracie-Faye's face has turned so white it looks like her freckles are jumping out.

"Did y' dream it?" Gracie-Faye asks, her widened eyes glued to the mural.

"It's the dream place and how did you know and do you see the beautiful lady when you go there and my goodness, Shoshanna, do you dream it too?" Maura also has a just-seen-a ghost look. Just seen a ghost, or witnessed a miracle.

We sit on the floor so we can all face the mural and stare at it. Come to the wonder of realizing that the three of us all dream of the same place. "And my friend," I say. "My friend, Wren, dreams of it too. We call the lady the Piper, because that's how she first appeared to us."

"To us, too," Gracie-Faye says, "but we think of it as school, and call her the Teacher."

"A teacher, yes," I say. I can tell they have to strain to hear me. I try to speak as loudly as I can. "We should agree on her name, and the name of the place. I think of it as the safest place there is. Wren and I call it the Haven."

"Well, we can compromise and use Gracie-Faye's Teacher name for the lady who I agree is like a teacher but a nice one and Shoshanna's name for the place because my goodness, when I'm there I feel as if no one can tell me I'm talking too fast or not paying attention, or—"

'Tis all right with me," Gracie-Faye interrupts Maura.

"OK, it's the Haven and the lady is the Teacher but Wow! How did we all dream it?" I look at them as if one of them might have an answer. Maybe they learn something in their Catholic school that can explain it, but all I see on their faces is question marks.

"I dreamed of you coming here the night before you came and my goodness, yes! I dreamed the lady—the Teacher—said that a bird will be coming soon too, but of course, maybe it's not a bird maybe it's your friend with the bird name and my goodness, how can this be?" Maura's face is a mask of confusion, disbelief—and I think, awe.

"And how"—my voice gets even softer than usual. My new

friends move closer to hear me—"How is it possible that I dreamed the same thing and saw the two of you peeking out from behind the trees?"

Gracie-Faye crosses herself. "It's the doin' of God," she says, her voice filled with wonder. "Maybe magic, but I think this is bigger than magic. This is God's doin'."

I see a doorway to Hope crack open. God has been a question mark ever since I lost most of my voice. Could this be God's way of saying "I'm here?"

"Don't mind Gracie-Faye, everything she says is about God or Jesus or Mary or one of the saints, unless it's about fairies and elves and leprechauns and gremlins and who knows what other magical creatures come out of her mind and mouth," Maura says, but her voice is shaky.

No matter, I think. Whether God or coincidence or magic or that ESP thing Wren read about, there is something miraculous about it. Something greater and grander than real.

Scene 14: I'm All Alone

Wren, age 10

Three minutes on the phone with Shoshanna is the ultimate challenge. For one thing, by the time we say hello, it's time to say goodbye. And then there's the matter of hearing her. I can't. Not very well. So we decided that the best thing to do is write letters to each other. But what can I say? I tell her about the things going on in school. How Mrs. Rome, who I have for fifth grade this year, actually has a shoe monitor who goes back and forth between Mrs. Rome's feet and the closet exchanging her spikey heels and these ballet slippers she teaches in. I tell Shoshanna how Mr. Brand, whose room is fortunately on the first floor, sat on his window sill and fell out the window and landed in an evergreen bush and returned to the classroom covered in needles.

One week I tell her that Carol and Susan aren't talking to each other and are dividing the girls in the class into factions which I'm keeping out of it because neither Carol nor Susan is a friend of mine. The next week, I tell her that Carol and Susan are best friends but they're not talking to Diane. "I miss you," I say in every letter. "There's no one I can call my friend. Except Josie, and I can't invite her home after school. My mother would never allow it. The only Negro she lets into our house is Marfa, and she's our maid. My mother calls her "the girl" which is preposterous. I love Marfa. She's really nice. But she's no girl. She says she has a daughter my age. Sometimes I wish she was my mother."

Every letter ends with almost the same paragraph—how Mother and Aunt Mildred went house-hunting that weekend. Not together. They take turns. One week Mother goes on Saturday and Aunt Mildred goes on Sunday, and then they reverse the next weekend. They both want houses and they're afraid if they go together they'll both want the same house. This way, whoever finds one first is the one who gets it. The result is always the same—"this is wrong with this house," or "that was wrong with that house." So I'm stuck here, and the worst part is that I'm trapped here with Deborah, and we have to spend our weekends together so that the mother not house hunting can be stuck with us. "Can you imagine being stuck with Deborah every weekend?"

Sometimes my letter tells Shoshanna about Mother and Aunt Mildred:

> Dear Shoshanna—They want to move near each other. They shop together every day. You'd think they liked each other, but when they talk about each other, you'd never believe it.
>
> 'Mother: "Mildred thinks her blueberry muffins are so wonderful. They taste like straw."
>
> 'Aunt Mildred: "Wren, you have to taste my blueberry muffins—those things your mother feeds you are like rocks."

'Mother: "Can you believe that hat Mildred was wearing? She must have bought it in the five and ten."

'Aunt Mildred: "I can't believe your mother would go house-hunting wearing a rag like that.'

"And so on. I think Aunt Mildred's worse than Mother. She's so critical of Deborah. You know how Deborah is always making fun of everyone and acting like she's better than them and making them feel like they can't do anything right? And you know that's how Mother treats me some of the time, but that's the way Aunt Mildred treats Deborah ALL of the time. So sometimes I feel sorry for my cousin because maybe she's trying to please Aunt Mildred by acting like her. She's always looking up at Aunt Mildred after she says something mean to me, as if she expects Aunt Mildred to pat her on the head or give her a hug. Which she never does.

"I miss you," I say at the end of every letter.

I'm lonely. Most of the other kids I was sort of friendly with have found houses and moved away. I keep hoping Mother will find a house near Shoshanna's, where I can go to the same school she goes to. I'm not good at making new friends. It scares me. I never know what to say so I don't say anything. I just stand there being scared.

Wren, age 11

I finish eating my dinner of leftovers alone, go to my room while Mother and Father eat, finish my homework, and start to read my new <u>Nancy Drew.</u>

"Come into the living room, Wren," Mother calls. "Father and I have something to discuss with you." I try to think of what I did wrong. I go as slowly as I can.

"Sit down, Wren," Mother says. I don't sense anger. In fact, Father actually is almost smiling.

I sit.

"There's going to be a big change in our family." Mother has this look on her face, like she's trying to hide the greatest secret in the world. I figure, she found a house—maybe right next door to one Deborah's family found. It's the kind of thing Aunt Mildred and Mother would do—find a way to be neighbors.

Mother nods to Father and he puffs up to make the big announcement: "Your mother is pregnant. You're going to be a big sister."

Oh! "That's great, congratulations, Mother," I say and sense Father is annoyed that I don't thank him, too. But really—she's the one who's been throwing up so much. She thought it was nerves.

> Dear Shoshanna—It's like the best and worst thing is happening at once. Deborah is moving near you. I don't know how close—not to your street, but to Silver Birches. Her street is Poplar Place. So, good news, I'll be rid of her for a while.
>
> Because—bad news. You'd think that with Deborah's family in Silver Birches Mother would focus on house-hunting in your town, but now she's got some kind of problem and has to stay in bed except for going to the bathroom and taking a shower every other day until the baby is born, which is another three months. So there's no house hunting going on now. And the worst part of that is that when the baby is born, it's going to live in my room.
>
> As far as the rest of my life is concerned, it's awful. Almost everyone you know has moved away. My only friend at school is Josie, and I don't have to tell you about that. What's new, though, is that even in school, I can't sit and discuss the books Josie and I are both reading because she spends recess jumping Double Dutch. So I spend recess sitting by myself, watching the other kids. Or sometimes I play single rope jump rope. It's the one thing the girls in my class like about me. I'm so bad at jumping in, and jumping in the rhythm of the rope, that I'm a

steady-ender.

I miss you...

I am so tired. The baby cries all night. Geoffrey. A boy. I wanted a sister. It turns out that everyone else in the world thinks it's great that it's a boy. "Thank God it's a boy," my grandparents, and the cards from Shoshanna's parents and my parents' friends who are religious Jews all say.

"Now I have a child I can take to a ball game who won't make me leave in the second inning like this *girl* did," father tells everyone he passes, pointing at me and snarling at the word "girl."

It doesn't hurt me. Nothing can hurt me. I'm going to be an actress when I grow up. It doesn't matter that I'm not pretty. Not every person in a show is beautiful. I practice now, pretend I'm a soldier from back in the old days. I'm cloaked in armor—their words ping off it and don't touch me. Nothing they say or do can hurt me.

Scene 15: <u>Bosom Buddies</u>

Wren, age 12

"God must be looking out for us," Mother says into the phone, which is kind of weird because she never goes to temple or prays or talks God talk the way Shoshanna and her parents do.

Clearly something is up, so I pick up the extension very quietly, with my finger pressing the button down. When the phone is against my ear, I release the button very, very slowly. Barely breathe. I can't let Mother know I'm listening in. I recognize the voice on the other end. It's Shoshanna's Ima, who never calls Mother. Very few people do. I can see why. No one really likes Mother besides Aunt Mildred.

"It's right on our block," Mrs. Friedman is saying. "The Baxters are putting their house on the market. I told Rhoda

Baxter, 'Don't dare put it on the market until I call Gertrude Abramowitz,' so Gertrude, her asking price is $17,000. Three bedrooms, three bathrooms, screened in porch, a backyard you can fence in for Geoffrey, and—"

"Tell her I'll be there on whatever train leaves around nine, as soon as Wren's off to school and Marfa comes to clean. She can watch Geoffrey—I'll give her a few extra dollars."

"You leave your children with Marfa? She's your girl!"

I almost choke, manage to hold it back. Mother would be furious if she knew I was listening in.

"Of course I do," Mother says. "Marfa is perfectly trustworthy. And she's a mother herself."

I have to sneeze! Fast, press the button, return the receiver to its cradle a tenth of a second before the sneeze bursts out. Whew! Hooray! I whip to my room, shut the door, turn on my Victrola, blast <u>Rock Around the Clock</u> as loud as it goes, drop a pile of books on the floor to mask the sound of my jubilant scream. "YAHOO!" I know my mother. Keeping up with the Joneses or whoever else. If the neighborhood and house are good enough for the Friedmans, it will be good enough for Gertrude Abramowitz. And it's Mother's precious sister's town! No way is Mother going to turn this house down! And no way will Father say "no." YAHOO! Before I know it, I'll have my own room again, and it will be within spitting distance of Shoshanna's.

Moving day. The first day of summer vacation. We've barely gotten to the house. The moving men are still standing in the living room waiting for Father to finish writing a check. I'm in my new room, moving my things from where Mother told the moving men to put them to where I want them. I turn around and there's Shoshanna, running up the stairs, two steps at a time. She grabs me with "You can fix up your room later. My friends are waiting to meet you."

Does Shoshanna remember who I am? How scared I get of meeting new people? *Her* friends. Have they replaced me? But she wants me to meet them, so—

I don't really have a choice. She grabs my hand and—if I didn't grab the bannister I'd fall head over heels down the stairs to keep up with her. She drags me across the street and down the block, knocks on a door, makes an introduction to a girl who—I can't complete the thought. *I know her!* My stomach is somersaulting and Shoshanna is dragging me back to my end of the block to a house right across the street from mine, as if it's a race, where the goal is for all of us to keep up with each other. Knock on another door. Sit on a stoop. Oh, my God!

"So I dreamed about y' last night," the red haired girl, Gracie-Faye, says in this strange musical way she has of speaking. Which is shocking, because I also dreamed of her, and of the other new girl, Maura, on whose stoop we're sitting. And the dream took place—

I can feel the blood draining from my face. "Do they know about—" I turn to Shoshanna and start to ask.

"I told them about—"

And now everyone is laughing and jumping all over the place in front of Maura's steps and we're all talking at once and—

"I've known you forever!" I explode, "since the first dream!"

We hug and dance and shout and go to Shoshanna's room for me to see her finished mural and then down to her kitchen because her mother just took a batch of cream-cheese brownies out of the oven.

"It was so hard. I wanted to tell you," Shoshanna says, "but I was afraid you'd feel left out—and that you needed to keep it special between you and me."

Talk goes on from what Gracie-Faye, Shoshanna and Maura consider vital information about the other families on the block, and life on Acorn Oval, to a lament that we won't all be going to the same school.

But it doesn't matter a bit, I think, because we're all going to be friends forever. "The fabric of a friendship woven in a dream," I write in my diary and lock it closed with the key I hide inside a sanitary napkin at the bottom of the box so Mother will never be able to read my private thoughts.

PART TWO: <u>AS WE STUMBLE ALONG</u>

ACT V: <u>FALLING SLOWLY</u>

The Teacher

Danger waters! One stream flows serenely, joyfully along, never noticing the sudden falls ahead.

Scene 16: <u>If This Isn't Love</u>

Gracie, age 13

I'm getting used to being just Gracie. I announced to the world that junior high is too old to be Gracie-Faye. I'm also getting used to walkin' down the block after school to Elm Street to cram onto the bus that's already picked up kids from Silver Birches High. Getting used to standin' and waitin' for a bus to have room for us, and so are guys from St. Francis, waitin' right on the same corner.

The gaggle of kids waitin' today is huger than usual, I guess because of the rain. Maybe some kids walk on nice days. Umbrellas are bangin' into other umbrellas and lots of kids are getting pushy and rude. It's cold and wet and it's "outa my way, I'm getting on the next one."

I'm hummin', trying to think happy thoughts that will raise me above the crowd and let me soar home.

"Hey, Red, can I share your umbrella?" I hear a guy's voice and assume he's talking to me. No one else has an out of control mop of bright orange hair. I peer out from under Mam's big umbrella which I had to take because Brigid took mine when she couldn't find hers. I don't know the guy—guys from several elementaries pour into St. Francis. Whoever he is, he's really, seriously cute. The kind of cute that goes with girls like Maura and her friends and has nothin' to do with me and mine. Even if he's really talking to me, there's no way I could possibly reach high enough to get the umbrella over his head. So I say, and I don't know where I get the audacity to say it, "You can if y' hold it, Blondie."

He takes the umbrella, is careful to position it to be sure I stay dry. Somethin' likeable about him.

"Irish." It's a statement, not a question. I'm working on my accent, but apparently it's still here.

"New here myself," he says. "To Silver Birches. I'm from upstate. Ian Quinn."

"Gracie F—" I stop myself. "Gracie Callahan."

We stand for a few minutes without talking. A bus comes and kids from all around us push, but this Ian Quinn is the gentlemanly sort, and we wait patiently. I'm in no rush, willing to stand here a while gettin' to know him. Another bus passes us, so full it doesn't even stop.

He turns toward me. "Where do you live?"

I tell him Acorn Oval. He tells me he lives on Maple Lane, just two short blocks apart.

"Would be faster if we walked," he says.

We start walkin' and before I can understand what's happening we're practically skipping down Elm, singin' <u>Singing in the Rain.</u>

We get to a puddle and he starts singin' louder and dancing and I sing and dance along with him not even caring if I'm on key. Gene Kelly would be proud, I'm thinkin' but Ian's loudly proclaiming "Puddle wonderful," and what is there for me to do but laugh back, "mud luscious!"

We continue on, sharin' favorite lines from e.e. cummings' poems and say together "Children guessed, but only a few, and down they forgot as up they grew," which makes us promise each other we'll never grow up so much that we forget, which makes both of us burst into Peter Pan's <u>I Won't Grow Up</u> manifesto.

We approach the corner where we should go our separate ways and I can't believe myself, I'm always so shy, but I say "I'll walk y' to your door so y' won't get wet."

"See you tomorrow, Gracie Callahan. Same corner," he says

when we turn into his street. "Look for the rainbow when this rain stops, and maybe you'll find a pot of gold."

We're at his door, no time left to tell him about my family's hunts for pots of gold at rainbows' ends, or our shamrock hunts. Maybe tomorrow I'll tell him. Or the tomorrow after.

I sit in my room after the warming cocoa Mam made, and tell the picture of Mary hanging over Brigid's bed and the one of Jesus hangin' over mine, "I've met a fellow with golden hair covering his head, wanderin' around Fairyland. Bless Ian Quinn, for the lad is my pot o' gold."

"Did y' ever see <u>Finian's Rainbow?</u>" I ask Ian.

"How could I be Irish and not go, when it was playing in Oceanport?"

"So what character did y' like the best?" I don't know why I'm asking, but it seems important.

"Well now, that's an easy one. See, you've probably noticed I'm not a go-out-for-football kind of guy if you know what I mean. I'd rather sit and read poetry. And write a little, here and there. So the character that touched my heart and sang my soul was Og, the leprechaun." He looks at me and grins. "And when he sang about loving the girl he's near, well, that's me, all the way. So what about you, Gracie?"

Do I dare say what I'm thinkin'? Because if he loves the girl he's near, the way he's looking at me—but what if some other girl is near? Does he look at her the same way?

I dither. "Sharon, for a while. I mean a girl comin' over here from Ireland, missin' the homeland, and a part of me is her Da, believing in finding pots of gold at the end of rainbows just over the next hill, but finally," I stop. Take a deep breath, a swallow of hope, and make myself say it. "The one I really feel the most is Susan, because she's a dancer, sort of like me, but mainly because she ended up with Og."

I bite my tongue and don't say it aloud, but I'm thinkin' as loud as I can, Someday I'm goin' to marry a leprechaun named Ian.

Scene 17: Hurry Back

Gracie, age 15

We're meeting and meeting after school every day. Eighth grade, ninth grade, now tenth! Used to be, he walked me home, but now, I'm a trainee for Toe to Tap, a group good enough, diverse enough—everything from step dancin' to classic ballet— why, we're known so well it's not outlandish to think about getting on Ed Sullivan! It means as soon as school is over I have to get to the train station to catch the 3:47 to Oceanport. Which gives me a half hour to be with Ian, who hasn't missed a day walkin' me there and standing chatting until the train swallows me up.

We've a problem, though. I'd make a bet—the hours and minutes and sweet seconds with Ian add up to more than a year. All the talk of magic and poetry and theater and rainbows, fairy-folk, wishes and dreams and singing as we walk. Ian reciting poetry he made up by himself, and some of them even about me! Which is all well and good and lovely, but NO DATES! Not that Ian hasn't come right out and asked. No. It's my da and my mam. The Callahans have a rule. "No datin' until you're sixteen," Mam says, and "If the law says you're not old enough to drive until sixteen then you're not old enough to date, either," Da insists.

I should be in heaven now, but instead I'm lost in a sadness. Ian has invited me to a dance at St. Francis, and I know Da and Mam's answer will be "sixteen."

"It's not fair, Da! Everyone is going to the dance! Even the nuns are going. They're going to be chaperones. And you let me go to dancin' school, where there are boys." Whinin' I am. I can hear m'self whining. I'll do whatever it takes. Maura suggested tears but I'm not that good an actress. Whining is as close as I can get.

"Ah, dance class. Well, y' know that Irish dancin' with y're arms down at y're sides and all the dancin' done by y're feet isn't the same as American dancin' with boys' arms tight around y'. Sixteen, Gracie-Faye. Not a minute sooner."

Oh, Da, if you only knew, I think. The leaps into men's arms, all the different kinds of holds. I thank God and all the angels for Da's ignorance, but gratitude does nothing to lessen my distress.

"I'm Gracie. Not Gracie-Faye. I'm not a child," I snipe and turn from the room, but not fast enough to miss hearin' Da laugh. "Not a child," he mutters to himself and laughs some more.

Goin' up the stairs, my eyes gulp back tears that threaten to fall.

By the time I reach my room, I'm plottin' for the fairy queen to use her wits and her magic to break out of her dungeon and imprison Da in her place.

The minute Brigid walks toward the house, dirty from playing SPUD with the kids in the street, I accost her on the front stoop. "I need a favor, please say yes."

"Depends. What do you want and what will I get?"

My sister is the bane of my existence. Better to have asked one of my brothers, but Brigid is the one I need. "What you'll get is the favor I need," I say. "Please let me do your job tonight, which, in case you forgot, is peelin' potatoes."

"And I suppose you expect me to clear the table tonight, when we're having chicken with all the bones and mess, which, may I remind you, is your job today." Brigid turns to go inside.

"No wait," I say. "I'll do your job and mine. And I'll let you borrow my red sweater when you go to Katie's party on Saturday."

The red sweater does it.

Tonight is my only chance. The only time Mam is alone, without a toddler tugging at her or the older ones askin' homework questions is when Mam is cooking dinner. While I'm peelin' potatoes and she's chopping onions and readying the chicken, I'll have my chance.

I plead. "Mam, I'm fifteen and a half. More. Just five more months and I'll be sixteen. Please, please, can I go to the dance at

St. Francis? Just the dance. Not out afterward like Maura and the other girls. Just the dance, Mam, where there'll be nuns all over the place, and Maura says they have rulers that they poke between the boys and the girls remindin' them to 'leave room for the Holy Ghost' so for sure the boys aren't going to be doing any of the things that get Da so wild."

Mam puts down her stirrin' spoon. "Is it that important, Gracie? Is there a special lad or somethin'? I've seen that look in y're eye, and it's not history or math or even dancin' y're thinkin' of."

What to say? I've never lied to my parents—or to anyone that I can think of, and right now, I'm not thinkin' anything, but—I take a deep breath, gamble on the truth, as Da always says.

"Yes, Mam. I walk most of the way home or to the train station almost every day with a lovely Irish Catholic boy, and he's asked me to the dance."

I hold my breath, can see in my mother's face that she's looking back in time to her own first dance.

"His name is Ian Quinn, and his da is from County Kerry and his mam was born in Dublin.

"Well now, I'll talk to your da. I can't promise any more. Now get those potatoes done. It's gettin' time to be putting them in the pot."

"Thank you Mam," I say and silently thank God, Mary, Jesus and all the saints there be.

When Mam tells Da somethin' must be, he lets it be. "Peace in the house," he always says.

And peace there shall be. It worked! "Yes," Da says. "I'll drive y' there. Pick up the young lad on the way. I'll make it my business, I will, to find out the exact time the dance is over, and I expect you and the lad to be waitin' in the parkin' lot within five minutes of the end."

Ian agrees. He wanted to take me to Cohen's Cones or The Chocolate Tree afterward, but he understands. At least we'll have the dance.

I'm getting more excited by the day. By the minute. I keep looking at the calendar and the clock as if by looking I'll make the dance come sooner.

A week before the dance, I'm standing here, waitin' at the corner, and where is Ian? He's never late! Must have gotten caught up in a discussion with one of his classmates. He comes to me, with a look on his face of sadness, and starts talkin' about his English test. He's avoiding something I think and in the pit of my stomach I'm hopin' he's not backin' out of the dance and maybe he just wants to be friends and never thought of me as a girlfriend kind of friend. Something in me tells me to run away and hide, disappear into the dungeon of the troll forever. Something is wrong. Not just his strange talk about his English test. The slump of his shoulders, the sadness of his face. The pain of waiting for the fire breathin' dragon to burn away all hope forces me to say somethin', to ask if I've done somethin' to upset him, and I hear an answer even my wild imagination couldn't ever have conjured.

"We're moving. I'm moving. I just found out. The business trip my Da is on is in Texas. He's been transferred there and they didn't tell us! Mam and Da kept it a big secret that Da has already started working down there and he's bought a house and now it's ready and we're moving in three days. Just two days to say goodbye and pack up and leave my whole life and—"

The street has sprung a sink hole and we've both fallen through. We're drowning in a grave of dreams in a place beyond the reach of tears.

We grasp for footholds. "Phone calls," Ian says.

"But long distance is so expensive. Three minute rule in our house and no more than once a month for calls to Ireland. Probably the same for Texas," I say.

So, letters. "I'll write every day," we both promise. "And we still have today and tomorrow at least," Ian says.

I don't go to dance class. He walks me home and we sit on the stoop and talk and talk and then all of a sudden he gets a gleam in his eye, drops to one knee and says, "Gracie-Faye

Callahan, would you be my guest tomorrow evening for dinner at the Arbor Inn?"

He would choose Arbor Inn, the finest restaurant in town, with its gardens and wishing well and "Of course, Ian Declan Quinn," I say and stand and curtsy.

My first date! There is no way Mam and Da won't allow it. I try to brush away the thought that it might well be my last. We promise each other to enjoy every minute we have left together. To make memories last until—

"When I graduate from high school I'll come back up here for college. Maybe we can both go to the same one," Ian says.

But what is a promise for a fifteen year old boy whose life has gone out of control? The next day, he is even more morose. "My last day of school. Gracie, our last day together. We're flying down tomorrow."

"We have tonight," I tell him, but "No," he says, his voice so low I can barely hear it. "I called for a reservation. Arbor Inn is closed tonight. They're having some kind of private event."

We spend the rest of the day together. Da drives us to Silver Diner for dinner. Neither of us feels like eatin'. We sit on our front stoop after Da drives us home, and even Da doesn't stop us from sittin' close together, Ian's arms around my shoulders. Even Da understands my first kiss will be a kiss goodbye.

We don't say goodbye. We can't say goodbye. We make promises.

"College wherever you are," Ian says. "Phone calls.

"I'll write every day," we both promise, as we've already promised a hundred times or more.

Days become weeks. Weeks become months. Months become years. Every day becomes every other day, and then gaps of three or four days, gaps of a week, gaps, I think. The distance over the phone of awkward three minute calls grows and grows until it dies.

ACT VI: <u>I GOT LOST IN HIS ARMS</u>

The Teacher

I watch, as three streams struggle on, tight together. Watch, as gravity sucks another stream downhill. Watch, in horror, as it separates from the others, and catapults one of the girls, from youth to adulthood.

Scene 18: <u>No Other Love</u>

Shoshanna, age 15

Next to Wren, I think Tommy is the best friend I have. He sits at my table in our sculpture elective, and we talk for the entire period. We're so alike—sometimes it's as if we're thinking the same thoughts. I'm thinking about this while I'm walking down the hall with him toward his calculus room. We get there, and I'm about to turn off and continue on to trigonometry when he motions me over to the side of the hall so others can pass us, and says, "We could use some cheerleaders. No one comes out to cheer for the track team. Gets lonely out there. So how about it, Shoshanna? Want to be a cheerleader?"

"*But,*" I say. Is he making fun of my voice? Of me?

"Hey, I get it, Miss Soft Voice," he says in a way that erases any possibility that he's mocking me. "But you have friends. All those girls at your lunch table. You might be the last ones picked to *run* track," he says, alluding to our announcement of the formation of the Last Ones Picked Club after an unfortunate gym incident, "but I'm asking you to become the first ones picked to *cheer* track."

"I'd have to ask them," I say. What is he really asking? Does he really want the group, or is he asking because he knows I won't come without them, or is it someone else in the group he wants?

"Seriously, Shoshanna, the whole team would love to have them, but as for me, it's you I want there," he says, as if he's reading my mind. "Come to the game and we'll all go over to The Chocolate Tree afterward. Sodas, hot chocolate, sundaes—whatever you girls want."

I guess he sees the look on my face. "You do like chocolate, don't you?"

"I don't like it, I love it, but—" I'm about to explain about the Chocolate Tree not being kosher, but he turns to go into his calculus class with, "No buts. Be at the track at one-thirty this Saturday," as the door closes behind him.

I ring Wren's doorbell, start talking the moment she opens the door. "What am I going to do? Saturday!"

"Slow down. You sound like Maura. Do about what, and what does Saturday have to do with it?"

I try to explain the situation to her. I love how cool she is, but sometimes—I wish she'd join me in getting a bit hysterical.

"First of all," she says, "you can stop whining. Second of all, you can come inside and sit down or we can stay out here and sit down on the stoop. We'll figure this out. I figure better sitting down."

"There's nothing to figure. It's impossible. And wrong. If he was Jewish I'd be doing cartwheels down the street," I say.

"You? You had to go to gymnastics help-class. The chance of you cartwheeling down the street is as likely as—"

"As me going out for chocolate whatever on a Saturday. And with a guy who's not Jewish." I try to stop the tears threatening to fill my eyes, just barely manage to keep them from spilling over.

"Who are you talking about? What chocolate? What non-Jew?" Wren asks, her eyes widening as if they want to swallow me.

I sigh, "Tommy Greene. He's in my sculpture class and we've become friends and now he wants me to get a group of girls to cheer for the track team and then go out to the Chocolate Tree afterward—on Saturday." My tears start to fall.

Wren puts her arm around me, pulls me up from the stoop and guides me to a chair on the screened in porch. "Do you really like him, like, boyfriend like?" she asks.

"How do I know? I've never had a boyfriend. I mean, I'm not supposed to—orthodox men and women aren't supposed to touch each other unless they're married, so I don't exactly encourage dates. I would, but—my parents."

"I know," Wren says, with a look that screams she may know but she certainly doesn't understand or accept it. "So why now?" She looks down. "Maybe I shouldn't say this, but I was walking behind a group of guys in the hall last week—guys from the track team—the ones who couldn't make it to the football team—the smaller guys. Anyway, they were laughing about dates and betting each other that the first one to get a date with a pretty girl would get a dollar from each of the others to take the girl out for a Big Bathtub Sundae at the Chocolate Tree. I'm sorry. I just don't want you to get hurt."

"Tommy's not like that," I say. "Maybe the others are, and if he was with them he sort of had to go along with them, but that's definitely not what he's like. Hey, he's short, so I'll wear flats if we ever go somewhere anyone would notice. We talk every day. He walks with me from sculpture to our math classes. He's a genius—taking calculus. No other boy ever walked me to my class, or talked about real things. Interesting things. Like books. We've read some of the same ones and we talk about them while we're sculpting or walking to our next classes. He's just so easy to talk to. So comfortable. It makes me feel good. Special. I don't know if that's boyfriend-liking, but I know it's liking. What else do I need?" By now my tears are flowing.

Wren hands me a tissue from her pocket. "Wow. OK. So we have to make this cheerleading, Chocolate Tree thing happen. Yes, I'll go with you and I'm sure most of the other girls from our lunch table will. We'll make it happen."

My lunch table is fabulous, and full of ideas. It turns out Jean Black's father's name was Schwartz before he changed it to Black to get into med. school. Not only is Jean Jewish, her mother's kitchen is kosher. I'm going to get out of the family lunch on Saturday by claiming that my social studies class was divided into project teams and mine meets on Saturdays—at Jean's kosher house. Just reading and discussing. I won't have to do any of the writing or hands-on work. Problem one solved. Problem two: Clothing. I'll be going directly from temple. Wren will bring clothes appropriate for cheerleading and I'll change in the high school girls' room—and change back before I go home.

Problem three—where to meet. It turns out that Jean's house is in the opposite direction from the school, with the temple in the middle.

"The library," Caroline says. "It's between the temple and the school. Tell your parents that's where you're going—not Jean's house. That your project group is doing research at the library and Jean will bring a sandwich for you. You can change your clothes in the bathroom there and show up at the track meet in casual clothes, or change in the girls' locker room at school. They'll both work for changing back after the meet."

Problem four—The Chocolate Tree. "What about suggesting Cohen's Cones—they have a kosher sign in the window," Caroline says, and is surprised when I tell her it's closed on Saturday.

"It has to be The Chocolate Tree," I lament, "and the problem isn't just the not kosher. To be honest, the kosher thing is my parents. What my parents don't know won't kill them. I don't think God cares what I eat. The whole Orthodox thing—it's too much for me. Works for some people, and sometimes I wish it would work for me, but it doesn't. Like seeing a nice pair of shoes and trying them on and—even if they say they're your size —they're just not a perfect fit. No matter what you do, they're not comfortable. So kosher doesn't matter to me, but it's everything to my parents. I won't be hurtful to them, so—"

Wren raises her hand in a stop-sign. "But chocolate is

chocolate and your parents are never going to know. They go to temple and then go home. They're nowhere near The Chocolate Tree."

"But what if one of their friends or someone sees Shoshanna there and says something?" Jean asks. The location issue. The glass storefront issue. A guillotine crashing down, beheading a possibility.

There's no way to politely tell Tommy I can't ever sit with him and have a soda because he's not Jewish and someone might tell my parents. But I can play the Sabbath card.

When I see Tommy in sculpture class, it's the card I play. I explain I have to go to temple in the morning, explain the whole plan for getting to the track meet. "But the Chocolate Tree? I can't go anywhere in this gossipy town without someone seeing me and telling my parents I was spending money on Satur—"

Tommy starts to say that he expects to treat me, but I insist that I can't be seen sitting in a restaurant on the Sabbath.

"Hey, no problem," he says. "Joey has a cooler. Sam does, too. We use them for water during the meet, but we can fill them with sodas and bring bags of snacks and hang out on the field after the match."

"Hallelujah!" I laugh. Between Tommy and my friends, life couldn't be more perfect. A sense of peace, a sense of well-being, a sense of friendship as a force stronger than the force of religious mandates. A stomach-churning sense of anticipation, of danger to come. Because this will not just be one afternoon of cheering and snacks. Problem solved for today. A door opening just a crack. Unlocking of the possibility of the door swinging wide. A tiny solution opening the way for a gargantuan problem.

Which will be solved by my friends.

Shoshanna, age 16

I've rushed to grab the mail before my parents can get it every day for the last two weeks. Now it's here. Now, on an eighty-seven degree day, a chill runs through me. I shudder.

"Apply for it," Tommy said. "It will be perfect. It's only half a day, and then we can go to museums and parks and stores—whatever you want—for a few hours and take the train home in time for dinner."

I applied and the response is here and now I'm afraid to open it. My hands tremble. I'm afraid I'll accidentally tear a piece off an edge or corner of something I need to fill out and mail back. I inch out the one-page letter and peek at the first paragraph. At the first word.

"Congratulations."

I wait until dinner is over. Wait until Abba is in the living room, ensconced in his over-stuffed chair with a book in his hands. Ima starts to clear the table.

"Sit a minute, Ima," I say. "There's something I need to discuss."

"I knew," Ima says. "An actress you're not. Fidgeting like a jumping bean all through dinner. So tell me, is it science you're failing? Math?"

"No, Ima. Just the opposite," I say. "Something wonderful. I was accepted into a program for talented high school students. At Oceanport Visual Arts, Ima—the most prestigious art school in the country. And Ima, if I do well at their program, I might even be able to go there for college. I might even be able to get a scholarship!"

"Not so fast about college, young lady. For college you'll go to a Jewish school. Mid-Atlantic Hebrew, or if you want to go away and God willing get a scholarship, Yeshiva of New England. But this program for the super-smart artists, wait until we tell Abba! A real blessing it is. But can we afford it? The train fare alone—"

"I'll pay the train fare with my baby-sitting money. I'll get a job after school if I need to. And it's subsidized by Oceanport Arts. It's only five dollars a week," I say.

I see my mother's face. Under the table, I cross my fingers for luck even though it's not a Jewish thing—it's something Gracie and Maura do. It can't hurt and it might help.

"Five dollars is a lot of money, Shoshanna. But such an honor it is, too good to pass by. We'll manage. So tell me, how many days a week is this, so we know what train fare we're talking about." I can see Ima adding figures in her mind, but it's not that. Not the money at all that's dropping molten lead into my stomach.

"One day. Just once a week, Ima," I manage to squeak out.

"After school, or Sunday?"

The question that could ruin everything, and no way to avoid it. I can lie about the time, turn a two hour course into a six hour one, but the day? I'm trapped with a rifle to my head and a bayonet to my heart.

"Saturday, Ima. It's Saturday, from ten to four."

"Oy! Saturday! How could you think such a thing?"

"I thought, Ima. I searched my soul. I prayed to God. And God sent me dreams, and my dreams said I have a God-given talent and that it would be a sin not to nurture it."

"So nurture it six days a week, but on the seventh day, God said 'rest.'"

"But that's just it, Ima. To me, art isn't work. Painting pictures is like saying prayers. And riding in a train? Walking is work. Sitting in a train is restful. And I can use every minute on the train to pray. I'll take my prayer book and go through the whole service. And I'll bring my lunch like I bring my lunch to school, so there'll be no temptation to eat non-kosher food. I won't be spending money. I'll buy my train tickets during the week. Please, Ima."

Unbidden, unwanted, tears start to fall.

"Shush, Shoshanna," Ima says. "Your father and I will talk."

"Over my dead and buried body," Abba is saying. "Sinful. School on the Sabbath."

"Remember Miriam Katz?" Ima asks.

Listening at the top of the stairs, I want to yell, "No, stay with the school. Tell Abba what I told you about my dream about God and my talent. What does Miriam Katz, that girl who disappeared five years ago, have to do with this?"

"Who?" Abba is asking.

"Miriam. Chaya and Yossi Katz's fourth daughter. Same situation. They didn't let her do what she wanted to do—something about not letting her do it because it was on a Saturday. So she packed her bags and disappeared. Not kidnapped. The police said she's accounted for and fine and since she was eighteen, she's an adult and free to live where she likes. They never heard from her again. No. We have one child. I'm not losing her. We have to let her go. She'll grow up and come to her senses. And if she doesn't, at least we'll have a daughter. There are worse things for an Orthodox family than having a daughter turn Conservative. Or God forbid, Reform even. Worse things, like running away."

Shoshanna, age 17

On Chanukah, I give my mother a painting copied from a photograph of the grandmother I never knew. Ima is moved to tears.

"See what the course is doing for me?" I tell her. "I wanted to use my time there to thank you for letting me be in the program."

I thank God and my mother for every Saturday I have with the course—and with Tommy. The program is truly wonderful. I'm in awe of what I'm learning, stunned by the level of artistry the course is bringing me to. But when the course ends at noon—that's when my day, my joy, really begins.

We start with lunch. Not the crappy sandwich I always show my mother I'm making. We have a routine. "No meat," I told Tommy, so we go to Chock Full o' Nuts. Tommy insists on paying. "What kind of guy would let a girl pay for a date?"

I get the same thing every week. A rich layer of cream cheese on thick slices of date-nut bread. Heaven on a plate. How can something so good not be kosher? Because no one paid a rabbi to bless the food and get a piece of paper certifying that it's kosher? More to the point—how can it matter to God?

Adventures every week. Museums. The zoo. A costume museum. A sculpture garden. A movie—<u>The Apartment</u>. Casual kisses, which never feel right.

"Hey, girl, you can't always worry about someone you know seeing you. Relax," Tommy says, whenever I stiffen.

He gets it, I tell myself.

Scene 19: <u>Soon It's Gonna Rain</u>

Shoshanna, age 17

"Surprise today," Tommy says.

I thought we were going to the natural history museum, but if Tommy has something else planned—why not? We take a bus to a part of Oceanport I've never been in before. Apartment houses? No museums? Tommy is happy, excited. But—I don't know why—something makes my stomach feel tight, as if it's caught in a vise. Something in me wants to insist on going back to Museum Mile. Something is—

"My brother, Ralph, got a Saturday job. His apartment is free for the whole afternoon," Tommy says. "Every Saturday." His grin. His sparkling eyes.

I make myself say "great," as if I'm so overcome with delight that words won't work. I squeeze his hand. I can't let him know. I'm scared, but it's not just that. I feel—I don't understand what I feel. It's like, I should be over the moon. We'll finally be able to make-out in private the way normal couples do. Kiss. Pet. It's what girls my age do, I tell myself. Nice girls. The ones at my lunch table who swear they won't give their virginity away to anyone but a husband.

We lie on Ralph's bed. Tommy holds me, kisses me gently. I'm sure he senses my hesitation. He makes no move to get beneath my clothes. He is so warm, so loving. It's nice to have a man hold me like this. And yet, when his hands brush lightly over my breasts, I can't stop myself from twitching, as if my body wants to pull away.

"That really excites you," he says when I shudder. But it's not excitement. It's the opposite. It's nice when he strokes my arm or my back, but when he touches my front—it's as if his fingers are fire and I jerk to get away.

Why did I feel warm and loved earlier today, when he kissed my cheek on a street corner while we were waiting for the bus, and I feel nothing when he kisses me now, the way I've always wanted to be kissed? Nothing, with a faint touch of nausea in the background.

I'm sure I'm in love. We've been using Ralph's apartment for months, and we've talked about it. Tommy's gotten the protection he promised. Every moment I'm with him, I feel wanted and cared for. And if the moments I like least, the ones where my body feels nothing as his hands sweep over it like a shower of down that feels like thorns on my skin are the moments that bring him delight? Maybe that's the difference between men and women. Even if it's not, when my body goes numb and my skin stings at his touch, I feel his delight. I feel loved, cared for. How can I not give him what he's waited for so patiently? And maybe —maybe this is what I need to do to bring me to ecstasy. My friends talk about waiting for marriage, but isn't that where our relationship is headed?

He's inside me and it feels—It doesn't feel. It feels as if I'm dead. I go through the motions, do what he tells me to do, move when he tells me to move, and I love him and I'm happy to be with him, but my body is dead. I find myself thinking about the Haven, picturing the pinks and pale yellows of spring, seeing the Teacher, hearing her say, "I'm here."

When it's over, I pretend. I tell him I liked it. I tell him I love him, which is true. I love him. I just don't love sex. It's O.K., I think. He loves football and it bores me to death, but I sit with him when he watches, and enjoy his enjoyment. How is this different?

He laughs and jokes and holds my hands under the jacket on his lap on the train ride home, where we have to look like two strangers or school friends who just happened to run into each other in case people we know see us. He's relaxed and happier than I've ever seen him. I'm happy, too. What we did was distasteful to me, but if it makes him happy—giving a gift is a great happiness, and I'll give it whenever I can.

I lie in bed, reliving the afternoon. As sleep shuts out thought, I see Abba's face.

For months, I've gifted Tommy every Saturday afternoon, delighted with the way an act as exciting for me as washing the dishes brings him such joy. But now! Now! Oh merciful God, Now!

"Meet me after school. Usual place," I tell Tommy on our way out of animation class.

"Can't. Practice," he says.

"Please. It's crucial." I'm sure he can see that I'm close to tears.

"Hey, if it's that important. But just two minutes," Tommy says and rockets off to his Spanish class. I saunter toward French.

I stand under a tree—our tree—where we often meet. Right where the path splits into a fork, leading to a street on one side where I would normally head home, and to the stadium on the other, where Tommy would normally head for practice. He comes along, just another student stopping for a friendly chat.

"What?" he asks. "Practice is starting. Big meet this Sunday."

"I went to the doctor." I take a long breath. "I had this test."

"Are you sick?" His voice is gentle now, concerned.

My whisper is softer than usual. It's the most I can get out. Tommy leans in to hear. "Not that kind of test. The kind. Oh, Tommy, the rabbit died. I'm pregnant."

Tommy laughs. Laughs? A sword made of ice stabs me, shatters within me, spewing frigid shards throughout my being. I can barely hear the words riding on his laughter.

"Oh, is that all. Hey, calm down. We'll take care of it. Johnny's girl got pregnant last year. Stu's also. There's this terrific doctor—just two hundred dollars. You don't even have to go to Oceanport. He's right here in Twin Oaks. Fifteen minutes away. I can drive you there after school and get you home by dinner time. I'll get the number from Johnny or one of the other guys and make the arrangements. Don't worry about the money. I'll come up with it. You know, you had me worried. I thought you were sick or something."

No! No! No! I breathe deeply to keep from fainting. Or vomiting. Or both. The world is spinning and everything is upside down. I start to shake. "It's not." I can't find air to get words out. "It's part of you and me." Deep, deep breath. "It's our child." I grasp his shirt in my fist. "We can go to a state where we're old enough and get married."

Tommy glares at me as if I've morphed into a monster. I can't look at him. I turn my head away. It's just a flash, but the image of his horror is seared into my mind. His anger! I'm so cold, shaking so hard, I'm going to—I take a step back and lean against the tree to keep me upright.

His face, his voice soften as if he's fighting for control. "Oh Shoshanna, where did you ever get such an idea? Don't you realize I was accepted to Ivy on a scholarship? I thought we had an understanding. We never discussed anything permanent. Hey, I'll do right by you. I'll pay for the whole thing, drive you there, drive you home, stick by you until we graduate, but—that's all this ever was. I never lied to you. I never said a word about marriage or anything after Silver Birches High. I always told you I was headed for Ivy or one of the other top schools. We never talked about going to colleges near each other, so I just assumed, and thought you did, too, that this was strictly a high school thing. Hey, we could visit each other in college, and maybe it could lead somewhere, but marriage? I'm going to be a doctor. I'm not going to think about marriage until I'm out of med school. So—you want this baby—Shoshanna, it's yours. If you don't—I'll do everything needed to get rid of it. Your choice.

Make the right one," he says while he's turning away from me, stomping angrily toward the practice field. As if he wants to kick something.

The next day he nods toward the empty seat next to him when I start to walk into art class, just as he always does. As if nothing has changed.

Doesn't he understand that everything has?

Scene 20: <u>On My Own</u>

Shoshanna, age 17

I've only shelled half of the top layer of the bowl of pea pods beside me when—I can't help it. Tears start to drip into the bowl of shelled peas.

"Shoshanna, what's the matter?" Ima asks, in a voice of such softness, such concern that I feel a lifeline pulling me toward the cradle of her arms.

With three words, I ruin everything. "Ima, I'm pregnant."

Ima jumps back. "Oy, Shoshanna, that such a thing should happen!" Ima turns aside. I can hear her sharp intake of breath. She turns to me, tears in her eyes, stiffens and hugs me in a way that feels as if she's pushing me from her even as she draws me close. She makes a cup of tea, as if that will help, and says, "We have to plan, then I'll tell your father and we'll talk."

Which certainly won't help.

She sits down at the table with a look—so tired, so beaten down. Could she have aged in the last five minutes? "So who's the boy? We'll call his parents, arrange a wedding." She struggles to talk, choking on unshed tears. "Not what we planned for you, but people get married young, have babies and work out schedules so they can go to college. We'll help and God willing maybe the boy's parents will help. We won't be the first to help raise a grandchild. Your grandmother was seventeen when she had me. Not such a terrible thing. So tell me, the boy?

I shiver. Ima doesn't understand at all. This isn't the turn of the century, and Tommy isn't—

There's no way not to say it. I wait until the tremor shaking my core subsides and say, "Ima, he's not Jewish."

"Not Jewish!" Ima shrieks. My eyes dart to the window to see if it's open, to know if the whole neighborhood heard. No. Thankfully, it's closed and only I see her, hear her charging across the room back and forth like a madwoman. "Oy, such a sin!" She stops, thinks for a minute.

"Maybe he'll convert. Such things happen," she says in a voice as cold and hard as a stone shrouded in ice.

"No, Ima, he won't, and he won't get married."

"Go to your room!" It's a shriek from the depth of her soul.

Ima's words slice through me, turn my legs to jelly. Half crawling with hands and feet, I make it up the stairs and collapse onto my bed.

Downstairs, she rages, "I'll talk to your father. We'll talk to the rabbi."

The rabbi. I know the rules. I should start packing, stay dressed because I know, the minute my father comes home—or if he waits that long—from the minute he gets off the phone with the rabbi—I know. I should be packing but I'm frozen on my bed, shivering, trembling, waiting. Waiting. Remembering—it's Tuesday. Abba will have a sandwich while he's on the commuter train, go directly to the temple for the board meeting. Nine-thirty. The earliest he'll be home.

I'm so cold. So cold. I get into my nightgown and slip under the covers but the blankets don't warm me enough, not even the extra blanket on top of the winter quilt, so I lie there and shiver and cry and time. Time. Time. Every second taking an hour.

Time. The door opening. Abba calling out his "Hello," his "where is everyone?"

Ima's footsteps. Ima raging.

Abba, the scream of a wounded animal, "Shoshanna, get down here."

I cling to the banister, drag myself down the stairs. When I'm halfway down, I hear Abba's voice, like a voice from another planet, like sound under water, "Get out. Now. You're dead to us. Go to your goy, you little whore. OUT! OUT! NOW!" A throat-searing screech.

Abba moves toward the door, opens it. What choice do I have? I drag myself to the door, hold the wall for support. Start through it before the foot he's raising can kick me.

"Moishe, her coat." Ima is pleading. "Shoes!"

But Abba is thundering "NOW!" with his raised foot moving toward me.

Somehow, I make it to Wren's, the closest house to mine.

Wren, age 17

My heart is racing. My parents are off at a meeting at Geoff's school and he's sleeping at his friend's house. I'm here alone and I should definitely not be reading The Telltale Heart. Poe never intended for this to be read when you're home alone. After dark. My heart is beating in a rhythm with the buried heart in the story, and what will my parents do if they come home and find me dead of a heart attack?

Banging. Is that my heart? No. The doorbell! Someone is ringing the doorbell and banging on the door. I pull the afghan on my lap over my head. If he breaks in, I'll play dead. Or deep sleep, or something.

The banging and ringing won't stop.

The rule is that if Geoff or I are home alone, the door is NOT to be answered. But the banging and ringing persist. I have to find out what I'm up against. Call the police if necessary. I slither into Geoff's room, grab his baseball bat. I don't turn on any lights, walk close to the wall so I won't be seen through the window. I slip down the stairs as quietly as I can, wall-hug my way to the kitchen and take a carving knife. Crawl beneath a window to get to the door. Stand on my toes, stretch to my tallest and peek through the little hole.

Shoshanna???

I drop the bat and the knife, unlock the two locks and the chain and Shoshanna is standing there sobbing, shaking like a seedling in a hurricane, wearing nothing but her nightgown. Barefoot. I'm overwhelmed by the tsunami of fear and anguish gushing out of her.

I pull her into the house. Can she walk? She seems frozen, as if her feet have forgotten how to move. She's so much taller and stronger than I am but I manage to drag and maneuver her onto the couch in the living room. I wrap the afghan over her, around her. The way you'd swaddle a baby. I'm almost knocked down by the depth of despair filling the space surrounding her.

Shock. The word pops into my mind, a heading on a page. "Tea," I say. "I'll put up tea and get some more blankets."

"No," Shoshanna manages to gasp between sobs. "Just sit here with me. Don't leave me alone."

"Just to the kitchen. You need something warm." The page of my first aid book is still there, in front of me. But now, Shoshanna insists, grasps my arm, begs for me to just sit beside her. I put my arms around her, try to warm her hands with mine.

Finally, between sobs words pour out and out and out. "Pregnant." I tighten my arms around her, try to keep myself from reacting. Shock, terror, grief, anger all tightly entwined— Shoshana's feelings and my feelings all blurred together and I can't, can't react.

In phrases whispered between sobs I get that she told Tommy about the pregnancy, that he thought two hundred dollars would fix everything, that he threw her out of his life. "It's his baby and mine. I'm not getting rid of it."

If there were something I could say—but there is nothing. All I can do is listen. Listen in horror, without reacting to Tommy's tantrum when she suggested marriage. Listen in horror to how the man she thought loved her stormed out of her life. Listen in disbelief as she relates how her parents threw her out of the house. Just sit there helplessly listening, feeling the impact of her emotions assaulting me, but not reacting. Yet. Not when I'm with her.

When she finally lets me leave her for "just a few minutes, to put up some tea, I promise," I call Gracie. Apologize to her mother for calling so late and blurt out the situation. Then I talk to Gracie and ask her to call Maura.

By the time I get off the phone the kettle is whistling. Moments later I put a cup of tea on the coffee table beside Shoshanna.

The doorbell rings. Gracie and Maura scramble in, seat themselves beside Shoshanna, hear her say in this ghostly monotone, "I'm dead. My parents declared me dead. I told them I'm pregnant and about Tommy and they threw me out and said I'm dead. They're going to sit Shiva for me."

Gracie and Maura question me with their eyes. "Her parents are going to have everyone come over to offer condolences—and say prayers and other ritual stuff."

"Mam said we should deal with tonight," Gracie says. "You can sleep at my house. 'There's always room for one more,' Da always says. My parents would do anything to avoid an abortion. They'll treat you like a heroine for wanting to keep the baby."

"So would mine," Maura says, "and I have that chair that opens into a bed and—"

"You can stay here—we have the guest room," I say. It's clearly the best option. No one will say it, but this could be for a lot longer than one night. I'll deal with Mother. I know she won't be as welcoming as Gracie's or Maura's mothers, but this is really the best option with school in the picture. "Shoshanna is here already."

"Mam says you should go to school tomorrow. She said you may be dead to your parents and as good as dead to Tommy, but you need to go on with your life," Gracie says.

"You know, you could give it up for adoption and they have these homes, I saw a program on TV where pregnant girls all live together and if they're your age they have teachers who come and they do schoolwork with you and it's like a vacation or sleep-away camp and then it's sad that you say good-bye to your baby and all the friends you made in the house, but you know the baby will have—"

Shoshanna's eyes come alive for the first time tonight. She glares at Maura. "It's my baby and I'm keeping it."

She turns to Gracie. "I'll stay here. I can't say at your house, Gracie—it's crowded enough as it is—but thank your parents for the offer."

Her eyes start to fill again but now she breathes, deeply. Once. Twice. "I'm two months pregnant. I'll start to show soon. They won't let me stay in school."

"Huh?" Gracie grunts.

"She's right," I say. "They made our gym teacher, Mrs. King, go on leave the minute she started to show. Even married teachers can't be pregnant in public school. Let's deal with today. My clothes won't fit you."

"Shoshanna's one size smaller than me," Gracie says. "You may need things a little loose." Her hands twist around each other. "I'll go get some stuff for tomorrow. Be back in a jiff."

Mother takes over the minute she gets home and assesses the situation. Her favorite occupation—taking charge of other people's lives. This time, I appreciate it.

"I always thought that woman was a dishrag," Mother says. "I always tell Wren, and I'm telling the rest of you. You have to be strong and stand up for yourself. Never let your husband get the upper hand."

She makes phone calls. When we're in school tomorrow, our mothers and some of the other women on the block will go over to the Friedmans and try to talk some sense into them. The other women on the block are aghast. How can a mother declare her daughter dead?

The doorbell rings. The first few of a troop of neighbors coming over to strategize.

"Come on," I say. With some help from Maura, I manage to get Shoshanna up the stairs and into the bed in the guest room.

When we get home from school the next day, Mother sends

us upstairs to do our homework. I'm figuring out the math problem when she calls me down to the kitchen. She has the good sense not to tell me what happened at Shoshanna's house in front of her.

"It's hard for us to understand," Mother says. "I'm a Jew, and I don't get it. As far as I'm concerned they're a bunch of table scraps and I hope they rot, but they insist they're just obeying a religious mandate. They have the backing of their rabbi. A full Shiva. Their mirrors are covered, they have prayer times set, the two of them are sitting on low stools so they're beneath everyone. Their clothes are torn. I mean, everything."

"It's hard to believe," I say.

"They're so dense," she says. "When the eight of us came marching in, they thought we were there to commiserate with them. I had a few choice things to say. Everyone else did, but mine, of course, were the most honest. I mean, being Jewish, I could say how un-Jewish throwing your child out is."

"But you don't practice the religion—Are you sure?" I ask.

"I don't know about practices but I know about Jewish values and children are valuable! When it was clear there was nothing we could say or do, we went home, got suitcases and boxes, came back and marched upstairs, figured out which room was Shoshanna's and took everything that wasn't nailed down. Her parents couldn't get up off their stools to stop us!"

I go upstairs schlepping a suitcase that Mother packed, filled with Shoshanna's stuff. Shoshanna comes down with me to retrieve boxes filled with art supplies, books, and stuffed animals.

"At least we don't have to call social services," Father says at dinner. "We—and the neighbors—will take care of you. You're almost eighteen. You can go anywhere you want, but you're welcome to stay here. It would be a different story if you were a little child."

But she is, I think when we go back upstairs. I feel her shaking inside, so cold it makes me shiver. See her staring into space, hugging her stuffed panda. That's just what she is. A lost, lonely, terrified little girl.

Little girls get taken care of. On one shopping trip after another, with every neighbor chipping in, Shoshanna acquires a full wardrobe. Thank goodness overblouses are in style.

Shoshanna, age 17

School is unbearable, especially sculpture class, where I always sit at the same table as Tommy. I straggle into the room, and he's sitting in the same seat, at the same table we always sit at together. He's motioning to me to come sit with him, as if he hasn't a clue that my whole world has collapsed, that I can't take a step back to yesterday, that there's no ground to step on.

Room spinning. Feeling faint. Turn around. Must turn around. Must leave. Hobble to the door but Mr. Tobias is there in his clay-smeared apron welcoming me in. I brush past him, drop down into the closest empty seat. Bethany Roberts' seat. She starts toward it, takes one look at me, makes eye contact, glances up at Tommy sitting alone at our table and breathes "Oh." She looks at me again, whispers, "Hey, it's OK. I'll go sit somewhere else."

I think about my parents. If they've declared me dead, then they are dead to me. I cannot mourn. When it comes to my parents, they're just dead.

And God, I think. I haven't considered myself a Jew since I was seven. Now I can't grasp the concept of how any valid religion could make parents disown a child because she violated some religious law. One idea, one thought leads to another to the ultimate conclusion that religion is an artifact invented by people, with all the faults people have. Religion works for people like Gracie who believe that religion comes from God. For Gracie, there's no way to separate God and Religion. It's a matter of faith. For me—God is a matter of faith, but I look at the multiplicity of religions around the world, all believed by their followers to be the word of God, the one true religion, and see— not their culture growing out of their religion, but their religion growing out of their culture, which grew out of their environment and their history. It must be nice to have Faith that religion is the word of God, but it will never work that way for me. Nothing proves that more than where I am today.

Questioning—If God is one thing and religion something else, how can God allow parents to declare a child dead?

I've lost too much. I'm going to have a baby and I need God to make my baby healthy and help me find a way to care for it. I can lose my parents but I can't lose God. I must separate God from religion. Something in me whispers that God has a plan for me. Faith. It's the choice I need to make. Like the choice to lose everything to keep my baby.

Scene 21: <u>Movin' Out</u>

Shoshanna, age 17

It's the day that had to come. A messenger knocks on the door of my English class, hands Mrs. Hewitt a note, right in the middle of her school-famous rendition of Marc Anthony's speech, seconds away from spewing forth her proclamation that "Brutus is an honorable man." Everyone is prepared, with hands over our mouths, teeth clenched together to keep from laughing.

She scowls, pierces the messenger with her eyes, reads the note, snarls, "Shoshanna, please report to the main office. Take your things." Everyone stares at me as I gather my books. My pen drops. My heart drops with it. No one moves to help me retrieve it.

I walk out of the room with "They are all honorable men" booming in the background.

The principal is waiting in her office. So is the nurse. So is the guidance counselor. The secretary ushers me in and closes the door behind me.

"Lift your shirt," the nurse says.

The principal turns to the nurse. "Better call her parents to come get her," she says, with a sarcastic emphasis on the word parents.

I'm told to empty my locker, take all my belongings and go to the nurse's office.

"Disgusting!" I hear the guidance counselor say as I stumble out the door. It's only partially closed. I was meant to hear her.

"Don't bother to call my parents," I tell the nurse, but she keeps on dialing.

It's almost enjoyable—the shocked look on the nurse's face when she reaches Ima, tells her to pick up her pregnant daughter and is told the person named Shoshanna is dead to her.

There are limits to how much I can burden Wren's family. I can see that the only reason her mother is putting up with me is that she's looked at as the neighborhood heroine. Gertrude Abramowitz, savior of young pregnant girls!

I lie in bed listening to Sidney Abramowitz leaving for his office, to Wren leaving for school, to Gertrude Abramowitz pushing Geoffrey out the door in time for his bus, to Gertrude leaving for her "hair appointment."

The dream I had last night is the strangest I've ever had. I look at the scrap of paper I wrote everything on as soon as I awoke. "The train to Oceanport. Bus number seven to the 8th Street stop. Bus number nine to Avenue C. Walk two blocks east, one block south." I fold the paper and secure it in a pocket of my purse.

I'm awake but the dream overpowers all thought. I see the Teacher, leading me. See the house. The man. The people reaching out to welcome me.

It makes no sense to trust, but trust is all I have.

There are suitcases in the basement. I fill one with the new clothes the neighbors have bought for me. I take the "stash of cash" Wren keeps in her desk for things like gifts and cigarettes. I take the cash from the jar in the kitchen where everyone drops their change for some charity. I'm not a thief. I know they'll understand. "Don't worry about me," I write. "I'm going to stay with friends in the city. I'll pay you back, I promise. I'll be OK. I'll call when I get settled." I leave the note on the kitchen counter.

It's only half a lie. I don't exactly know people in the city, but I trust the Teacher. I trust God, though I'm certain I shouldn't. What other choices do I have?

I stand beside the railroad track, a ticket to Oceanport in my hand, my suitcase beside me. It would be so easy, so very easy to jump as the train approaches the station. I would, but—

But there's a child within me, a hope for the future, and I will love it, and nurture it, and never, ever turn my back on it no matter what it does. So I fidget, pace, step onto the train.

Breathe. Scared. Where? I let the crowd swallow me and move me to the Oceanport station. Follow the directions on my scrap of paper. What else can I do?

Take a bus. Then another. Which way do I turn? Where do I go now? I look down at the address. Avenue A. Which way is Avenue A? Did I mix up the directions? Reverse east and west, or north and south?

"Can I help you?" a man asks.

"Trust," I hear the Teacher's voice. "Trust."

There is no way in the world an intelligent woman should trust a strange man coming over to someone who's obviously young and lost, especially in a big city, and yet, it's as if there's an aura of calm, peace, and caring about him. Almost as if he's wearing a sign proclaiming himself safe. And he looks like the man in my dream, doesn't he? I trust. It's all I can do.

"Are you looking for 938 Avenue A?" he asks, in the softest, friendliest voice I've ever heard. I feel calmer, more taken care of, than I have since I found out I'm pregnant. How could he know what I'm looking for?

"The Caring House," he says. "I was waiting for you to come this way." Either he's a master con artist or—I can't even let myself think *or*. Probably just a very nice man, maybe someone who works at the Caring House, maybe I have the look of the people who come there.

He introduces himself as Leaf, takes my suitcase, walks me to the corner. We turn, and there it is. A brownstone house, with a whole bunch of kids sitting on the steps, smoking and laughing. The air is weed-scented. How can I expose my baby to that? But what choice do I have? My arms twitch with exhaustion—I can't take my suitcase back—and my legs—.

Someone sees me approaching, comes down the stairs and holds out her hand. "Liberty," she says, and puts her hand on mine. Another comes down. "Redwood," he says and points to his red hair. I meet Harmony and Summer and a few others and —. Redwood asks my name. I hesitate. "Little Momma?" Harmony suggests. I hear affirmative mumbles that feel like a welcome to their clan. I smile. My whole self smiles. I have a name, and somehow, that name makes me real.

Dear Wren, Gracie and Maura,

I'm here in Oceanport living in a commune called The Caring House with the most loving, caring people I've ever met—with the exception of the three of you. I don't know how to thank all of you for what you've done for me. And Wren, please thank your parents for me. A bank check for the money I borrowed is enclosed.

I earned every penny of it. This is a real tourist area. They come to see the hippies. Hey! I'm an attraction. Not sure I'm a hippie, but they think I am. Anyway, there are all these stores selling all kinds of crafts that the tourists eat up. The easiest, fastest way to make money is to make love beads. I've been here almost two weeks and already I've earned enough to pay your family back. Everyone—tell me what color you want and I'll make you each a strand.

Love—Shoshanna—"Little Momma"

Dear Wren, Gracie and Maura,

The people here are amazing. One, Leaf, is like the leader. Not in telling us what to do—we have meetings to make group decisions. He's older—I think maybe twenty-five—so we look up to him. I've never met anyone so caring, so compassionate. He's a carpenter and would you believe? He's making a cradle for the baby. In between stringing love beads I'm knitting a blanket for it. I'm also learning to weave.

I have to go now. It's my turn to make the salad.

Oh, if you write back, be sure to address it to Little Momma Free. They call me Little Momma. We've all let go of the names our parents gave us. I went to court, kept my first name, Shoshanna, but—you can't imagine how thrilling it was to change Friedman to Free. It's the name I'll have to give my baby.

Love,
Shoshanna Free, "Little Momma"

Dear Wren, Maura and Gracie,

Here it is! A picture of Dandi-Lion Free. Three weeks old and smiling already.

Sorry it took me so long to draw it, but—you wouldn't believe how little sleep I get. But she's a darling. It was worth everything I went through to have her.

Love to all you "aunts"
Little Momma

PART THREE: <u>MOVE ON</u>

The Teacher

The flow of time is relentless. Change lurks around every bend.

Shoshanna, eventually relocates with some of her housemates to a cabin far north, near the Canadian border, on the shore of a mountain lake filled with calming waters. There, she raises her daughter, Dandi Lion. There, on the banks of peace, she names her newborn son Pax.

I watch, as streams twist and cross as the others grow past youth, and leave Silver Birches one by one. Watch through time as streams recross and twist, again, and yet again. Watch as streams bubble over rocks, plummet down valleys, glide through time. Watch as streams merge with new streams, as mergers spew forth young streams, as families grow. Watch, as three of the four find themselves on the shores of Lake Kinde. Apart, not yet together as they were as children, yet closer, ever closer. And the fourth—distance could never keep one of the four apart.

ACT VII: <u>WHAT I DID FOR LOVE</u>

The Teacher

Shoshanna was the first. Gracie follows soon afterward, borne through time by a smooth surfaced stream, headed toward lands long dreamed of. But wait—there's always a bend with the unforeseeable ahead.

Scene 22: <u>A New Life</u>

Gracie, age 18

Rusty O'Rourke. My senior prom date. I almost said "no" when he asked me, but he looked so hopeful, and really, we're friends. So I can't say I'm not having a good time, now that I'm here. And I can't feel guilty about the price of a gown. For one thing, I got it at Dexter's Discounts. For another—Brigid is my size, and never needing for a date. So she came with me to shop, and we bought a dress we both like, and she's already picturing herself wearing it to her prom, next year.

That's the problem. I'm dancing with Rusty, and thinking about my dress. The music is kind of loud, so it's hard to talk. My thoughts are pirouetting around in circles from my first, and maybe-ever gown, to the sadness of packing up and leaving Acorn Oval to go touring with Toe to Tap, not just for a summer, but maybe forever—or until I'm too old to dance. Bad enough not having Shoshanna a few houses away, but the sadness of not having Wren and Maura within almost shouting distance is a sadness I shouldn't be dwelling on at a dance. I focus on Rusty's face, on how happy he looks, try to make my face as happy as his, and focus on the joy of spending my life doing what I love. The thrill of a leap across the stage, as if I have wings, soaring into the arms of a partner I know will be there to catch me while my wings are still outspread. And then my mind soars as if it's dancing, and the joy of it brings me to the feel of a man's arms holding me, but it's not Rusty. I have leaped across the stage, into Ian's arms. I just catch myself before I whisper his name.

Two weeks later, I board a bus filled with my fellow Toe to Tappers. It's not good-bye, I tell myself. For sure, I'll be back home to visit my family every time there are a few days between shows. Wren and Maura swear we'll get together whenever I'm near their college towns. We book a lot of colleges. Maybe I'll even get to stay in their dorms when we're at theirs.

The bus starts to move. I wave to my family, and am swept into the joyous cheer of my fellow dancers, as we move toward day-one of our summer tour. Saints be praised, it's really happening! I'm a professional dancer, on the first leg of a career!

Gracie, age 20

It's an excitement every time we set up in a new town. It's been two years, and a thrill still runs through me every time I see a poster or an ad proclaiming "Toe to Tap. Tour the world through dance. From Formal ballet to polkas and jigs to Rock 'n' Roll. Our dancers do it all." And here I am, decked out for Irish step dancing, between Bessie in a tutu, en pointe, and Anna, in her Russian folk Barynya costume.

We're hanging out in the dressing room, waiting for the crew to finish setting up so we can rehearse. Not for the dances—we have the program encoded in our muscles and minds. But each stage is different, and adjustments have to be made. In small groups, we walk across the stage, taking note of any differences we're going to have to accommodate.

Everything goes well. It's a sell-out audience, an enthusiastic crowd. As the music begins, I move with the chorus, dancing across the stage, our arms at our sides, our feet moving fast as hummingbird wings. As the music builds to a crescendo, I leap from the center of the chorus to begin my solo.

Catch my foot in a cable that's come loose and fall flat on the floor.

The doctor is cheerful. "You've broken three bones in your foot, and two of your toes. A few weeks of being off your feet, and you'll be good as new. Walking as well as you ever did." Does the man see beyond my foot? Has he looked up a few inches to see how I'm dressed?

"I'm a dancer," I say.

"What difference does that make?" the doctor asks.

I demand to see an orthopedist. "A foot specialist."

The foot specialist confirms what every dancer knows. Bones heal, but not for the way a dancer abuses her feet.

I go home. Time to make other plans. And didn't I always know there would be a life after dancing? God has other plans for me. Didn't I always have plans? I laugh at the thought I once had of becoming a nun. No. I want a man. I'll find my leprechaun someday, marry him and have a houseful of children. And a job —a job where I can be useful, serve people. Once I got over the nun idea, didn't I always think, when I got too old to dance, that I'd love to be a nurse? So I didn't get too old. I broke my foot.

I tell my parents, and my mother reminds me, "Didn't I always say if this dancin' thing doesn't pan out, we're keepin' the money we set aside for y' to go to college. Y' can have it whenever you want." I tell them they're getting their dream. Dancing will always be in my heart, but I'm going to be dancing away to the Oceanport University School of Nursing. Earning my B.S. and R.N.

Scene 23: I'll Know

Gracie, age 26

I'm living in Oceanport, where I have a wonderful job as a pediatric nurse at the hospital, making children laugh and curing their ills with promises of elves and fairies dancing through their IVs to slay the trolls causing their cancers. Every once in a while there's a date—a doctor or a patient's uncle or a man met at a church social or a blind date—but they're not finding-a-husband dates. I've learned by now and accepted by now that no man will ever live up to my memory of Ian. Maybe not even Ian. For people change. People grow up.

I grab the ringing phone. My friend Felice. Another blind date. "I gave him your name and number."

"Without asking me?" The hand not holding the phone fists. My stomach clenches.

Felice ignores the anger in my voice she can't help but hear. She knows my blind-date history! She blathers on. "He's perfect. He's Joe's best friend. We can double or you can go out with him alone but you can't turn this guy down. You'd be a fool and a half if you did. He's a professor at Oceanport U. A poetry professor, Gracie. I mean, English, but he likes teaching poetry best. He's even written a book of poetry that's going to be published. And he's Irish. And a practicing Catholic. What more could you want?"

A poet who won't grow up. A poet who didn't forget the boy as he became a man, I think.

"Does he have ears, eyes, nose and mouth?" I ask.

"Just answer the phone when it rings," Felice says.

"What's his name?

"Didn't catch his last name. Something Irish. First name, too. Sean or Ian or Declan. One of those."

"Thanks. I could end up talking to the wrong guy."

"Maybe it was Liam, or Ian. Something like ia-ish. "

The voice on the other end does indeed belong to a man named Ian. Yes, he says, he knows she works at the hospital. Does she know Bailey's Pub on Twentieth Street? How could she not—it's only three blocks from the hospital. He'll meet her there after work.

"How will I know you?" he asks.

"Wild red hair and I'll wear something green. I can get there around 5:15ish," she says.

"Perfect. Looking forward to meeting you," he says, and I swear I can hear a grin on the other side of the phone line.

I'm sitting in a booth on the left side, facing the door, wearing one of those new polyester pants suits. My deep forest green one. I check my watch. I got here early, so he's not really late. Just about four or five minutes—and maybe my watch is running fast.

I look up and—How is it possible? No. I'm sitting too far from the door. I can't possibly make out the man's features from here. And this man—If my date is coming from work, he would be carrying a briefcase, or a book bag, or books, but this fellow's arms are wrapped around a big brown bag. Did he bring his groceries here?

He nods toward the bar-tender. Someone turns on the juke box. Or is it a tape recorder because it seems as if—It can't really be playing Look to the Rainbow.

But it is, and he's coming closer and closer and I'm not dreaming. He's real and he's—

I jump up and I'm sliding out of the booth and he's running up the aisle and he's here already. Ian, my Ian Quinn, dumping the bag on the table and throwing his arms around me and I'm crying and he's crying, our arms and hearts wrapped around each other. And then he's ripping the brown paper off a pot covered with gold foil, filled with golden marigolds and gold-foil-wrapped chocolate coins. "I thought you'd be needing a pot of gold," he says when he can speak. "The rain has gone on long enough. Time for our lives to be filled with rainbows."

A week later he moves into my apartment.

Three months later, we wed in church, me in a white gown, Ian in a midnight blue suit. Afterward, we stand together in my parents' backyard, under a rainbow made of flowers. He, in a leprechaun suit, me, in a fairy dress.

"I promise you rainbows for the rest of your life," he vows.

"And pots of gold at their ends," I promise.

Gracie, age 27

If there are to be rainbows, there must be rain, and if there be rain, sometimes there are storms so torrential as to wipe away hope and throw us to our knees in despair. A rainbow first—I'm pregnant, and not just with one, but the double blessing of twins. And then the storm.

Not every wish comes true. Not every pregnancy ends in a child. Weeks before breath is possible, the two babies die. Two daughters. I think of them as Hope and Joy. I never have the chance to see them, never have a chance to hold them. But I know them, have felt their heart beats, felt their tiny fists and feet moving within me, and their loss is devastating.

Until—three months later, another baby starts to grow within, and nine months beyond that, another girl, named Arwen, an elvish name, is born. Arwen, for the magic of hope and joy returned.

Gracie, age 28

Ian bursts through the door to our Oceanport apartment. "Gracie, a pot of gold just fell from the sky and landed on my desk!"

"Mine just spit up on me," I laugh, wiping off three month old Arwen's mess. Ian takes his daughter and dances her around the room, while I finish cleaning myself.

"A phone call from Schrodinger U. They want me to head up their poetry department! And there's a raise! And we can get out of this apartment and buy a house!" Joy is spewing from Ian's mouth.

"Where is this Schrodinger?" I ask. I vaguely remember Wren talking about it when we were kids, wishing she could afford to go there. Buying a house or moving to a larger apartment is a necessity. Arwen can't stay in a crib in our bedroom much longer, and for sure there'll be brothers and/or sisters as time goes by.

"About an hour and a half north of here, on Lake Kinde," Ian says.

I love the name of it, but names can be deceiving.

"There's a hospital at the southern end of the lake where you could work."

He sees the look on my face, adds, "when the little ones are in school," he promises.

We make an appointment with a real estate agent, visit Lake Kinde, pass through Markettown, the small city on the south-western side of the lake, drive past working farms and small villages, see houses in a few.

The agent chatters brightly about life on the lake. "Lake Kinde was named for the first European settlers here. As time went by, the people—mostly farmers—who live on lakefront property formed an association, which grew to include the entire county. Everyone belongs. Mainly, they arrange social activities, but they also meet regularly to address any problems that occur lakeside. They stand together against outside developers taking over land. In one instance, lakeside residents bought a farm whose owners were selling and relocating to live near children. A developer had a vision of putting up a large mall that would 'bring tourists and shoppers from all over the state.' Just what the residents didn't want."

She goes on—The residents decided that on a lake named Kinde, kindness should inform everything done here. There's one overriding rule—the rule of kindness. Any time anyone does anything unkind, they put some money into a jar—they determine the amount based on what they did and what they can afford. Every spring, the jars are all collected. The residents gather for a major social event, using some of the funds, and give the majority to local charities."

Ian and I look at each other. What could be more perfect? We put a deposit on a four bedroom house in Harvey's Harbor, on the western shore, midway between Schrodinger, on the east coast, and Markettown, where the only public schools at present are located.

"For now," the real estate agent assures us. "With farmers selling out to real estate developers, and zoning codes insuring that all property will remain farmland or become residential properties, there's already talk of opening elementary schools midway down both the east and west shores of the lake. Probably be up and running well before your little one is ready."

It's something to hope for. "And I could get a job as a school nurse," I whisper to Ian, because the thought of being apart from Arwen, even for a few hours a day, is a hard one.

ACT VIII: <u>A WONDERFUL GUY</u>

The Teacher

As streams separate and go their own ways, one stream turns from an expected path. Sailing upon it, one woman looks back and laughs at the shades of gray world she expected to find in adulthood, looks to the future and sees nothing but love and joy. What she doesn't see, what she couldn't imagine in an eternity of time, is what lies ahead, with the next turning.

Scene 24: <u>The Best Night Of My Life</u>

Maura, age 17-21

Dates and dates and dates and dates. I hate the school work, but I love high school. My goodness, I'm majoring in dates, with a different one every week! For sure I'll get married almost right after high school so what difference do grades make anyway? What else can I do with my life because I'll never get into college and it makes me really mad, the way my brother, Kevin, is home from Ivy U. on vacation and my goodness, he's yapping on about college and how he found this great one for me.

It's not my fault. It's his. He's making me scream—really scream—"You know damn well I don't want to go to college and even if I did I wouldn't get in so stop sounding like your parents telling me I'm going to go when I'm planning on auditioning for walking across a stage and smiling if it pays enough to move into the city or maybe I can get a job singing back-up or playing a musical instrument on a local radio commercial. I mean I know I'm not going to be a pop-star—that's been made clear—or maybe I will be but it will take a lot of years of work and that's what I plan to do—work doing something with music and not going to college."

Kevin doesn't even blink, let alone apologize for his insensitivity. He just says, "Maura if you stop talking for a minute I'll explain."

I glare at him and shriek. "EXPLAIN, nothing you say will change my mind and"

Again he interrupts me with "just sit and listen." He flops down onto the couch in the den and I keep standing. He goes on blabbering about how his friend's sister got into some Sommerville College which I never heard of in some small town I never heard of and who would want to go there? But he goes on and on about how his friend's sister's grades were like mine and how she was like me, hated academics but the way I like music she liked drama so she goes to this school where they have a drama department and now "they're opening a separate music school, The Leonard Bernstein Conservatory" and musical theater and dance are going to be part of it which starts to sound a little better than college, I mean the conservatory part, and he's going on and on about how I could become a real professional and then he says these golden words: "admission is based on audition."

I'll never forget those words, I mean with an audition I have a fair chance of getting in.

I audition and my goodness and as Gracie would say, "thank you all the saints that be," I get in. I love it. I take drama and dance classes because my major is musical theater and I'll need all those skills, but it's the music classes I love and not just singing because for electives I'm taking the basics of other instruments because just in case the musical theater doesn't pan out, I'm taking music education courses, I mean teaching music could be fun, I like working with children and all, and actually the thought of running a children's musical theater is something I'd consider but mainly I'm involved in what's most important. I mean, my goodness, finding a husband has to take precedence over a career! I have dates and dates and dates, but none of them ever work out for very long but there's always another guy to take his place, and if I don't find someone here, I figure when I graduate I'll find someone.

Maura, age 22

I graduated and I got an apartment in Oceanport where you'd think I'd meet someone, I mean my goodness, a whole year has gone by and I'm still single and don't even have a steady at the moment, I mean I do have dates and dates and dates, but every relationship ends, which is usually by being asked out by another boy and liking him better but sometimes the guy found another girl. It never mattered much, I knew the right one would come along, and now!

I can't stop grinning, can't stop the music playing I my mind, "No more a smart little girl with no heart," I sing along with the music, raise my voice and blast "I'M IN LOVE WITH A WONDERFUL GUY!" I jump in the air, spin around, land with a thud and pirouette across the room and bang, bang, bang from that sourpuss downstairs banging on his ceiling with his broomstick or something else long enough because he's tall but even standing on his bed or a chair he's not that tall. I stick out my tongue pointed toward the floor and start in on the next verse a little softer, but I have to tell someone and obviously blasting it through the apartment walls and ceiling and floor to all my neighbors isn't the way to do it, which it should be but I look at my watch and my goodness, how did it get this late? I can't call Gracie or Shoshanna but Wren is a night owl and maybe she's reading a good book, when she does, she forgets to go to sleep so I dance to the phone and dial Wren's number.

"Who is this?"

Whoops! bad mistake. "It's Maura and once you hear my news you're going to be so excited you won't even care that I woke you up and"—

She's not listening to me, she's practically screaming "What's wrong?"

"You're not listening to me, why should anything be wrong? I'm in love with the most wonderful guy in the whole entire world and I'm going to marry him and we're going to have six kids or maybe more and"

"Maura, it's four A.M. I'm going back to sleep. I'll call you tomorrow when I wake up." Wren slams down the receiver.

OK, maybe I shouldn't have called, but there's this excited energy bubbling around inside me and I should go to bed for a while but how can I when I have all this energy but maybe I'll fall asleep and dream about Chris with brown hair and eyes that look right into mine and a dark blue Nehru jacket and light blue turtle neck and a string of love beads and he loves the music I love and he plays the guitar and he loves the Broadway shows that come to Oceanport and "Would you like to see <u>Hello Dolly?</u> I can try to get tickets for next week—and if not, we'll do something else and I'll get the tickets for whenever they're available," and when was the last time anyone went to a singles' night at a singles' bar and went in single and came out with the man of her dreams?"

In the morning, I tell Wren and then Gracie and then Shoshanna, "His name is Chris Rossi, his father owns a furniture business and he's being trained to be an executive but he's in graduate school now to keep from getting drafted and to learn more about business."

We go out to dinner at The Castle and it's romantic and the food oh, my goodness, the food is incredible and something isn't right because maybe Chris didn't know how expensive this place was going to be because he's really quiet and something seems to be bothering him, he keeps looking around and poking around his pocket and he starts to get up and mumbles to himself, "no, not here," and sits down but then we pay the bill and we start to drive home but we're going in the wrong direction, he pulls into some garden and it's night time, who goes to a garden at night, but there are lights so we go in and we're the only ones there and all of a sudden he drops down onto one knee and oh my god! oh my god! he says he loves me and wants to spend his life with me and before he can ask, I blurt out "Yes! Yes! and he pulls this ring out of the box that was in his pocket and it's gorgeous and how did he know my size because it fits, and I'm engaged!

"You've got to come with me to order the invitations," I tell Wren. "We're getting married in September because he's graduating in two weeks, and he'll lose his education draft deferment so we need to get a marriage deferment as fast as we can."

"So why are you waiting for September?" she asks, like she's living on another planet and doesn't realize we're waiting that long because of all the time it takes to get everything done, with the designing and calligraphy and addressing and printing—and that's just the invitations. I remind her there's the dress, and dresses for the bridesmaids, and fittings, flowers, table cloths, place cards. "There's so much to do and so little time so I made a list and invitations are at the top of the list and you have to come with me and so does Shoshanna because she's the artist and of course I need you and Gracie there because the three of you are like sisters, and"

"Do you even have a place and a date?" Wren asks.

"Of course, how could I possibly have a wedding without a date and a place and my goodness, it's at St. Joseph's in Oceanport and then the Grand Hotel and we have the big ballroom and the All Stars, which is the best band in the whole world and oh—I want you to be one of my bridesmaids and it will be beautiful and—oh yes, the first date we could get where the hotel and the band are both free is September 30."

Scene 25: <u>Something Bad</u>

Chanel 1, Your place for local news, broadcasting from Oceanport

"To repeat the national news reported in our lead feature: Due to the urgent need for an increased military presence, there will be no new draft deferments for reason of marriage, effective today, August 25, 1965. The entire announcement and follow-up will be rebroadcast on the 11 P.M. news."

Maura, age 22

Shoshanna is dense. I told her, "You can't just go to a Justice of the Peace or a priest or anyone else and get married, I mean, you need a license and a blood test and my goodness, those things take time and we did them, we got the license and the blood test and the church was booked solid so we stood on line for hours at Town Hall with my bladder bursting until finally pee was dripping down and thank goodness I was wearing a dress with a long, very full skirt and we finally got married, but it was a full week after the announcement and even if it was just one minute after it would be too late because the justice wouldn't listen to reason and put last week's date on the marriage certificate and here we are married, which is wonderful and we'll have our big church wedding and party at the Grand Hotel in a month, and I expect you to still come down and be one of my bridesmaids, but…"

Wren, age 23

Chris's draft notice arrives on September first.

I wait for the Teacher to speak. Wait to hear words of comfort, explanation, and hear silence. No dream foretelling, no dream to soothe.

Just events, and Maura's raw anxiety turning to terror, ending in grief so intense that it takes all my strength to be near her, to support her: Getting married after the deadline doesn't keep Chris out of the army, but it does let him leave for Vietnam a married man. It does make Maura a veteran's wife, entitled to benefits.

It does make Maura a widow.

Obituary in the Oceanport Gazette, January 15, 1966

"Private Christopher Rossi will be buried with full military honors at the Veteran's Cemetery in Oakwood on January 16, 1966, at one o'clock in the afternoon…He is survived by Maura Reilly Rossi, his wife of five months, and by…

ACT IX: I'M NOT AT ALL IN LOVE

The Teacher

One stream flows into a placid creek in the distant north. One stream melds with a loving stream crossed in human teen years. One stream is crammed with heinous debris and must find a way around it. And one stream flows on through time and space seemingly unchanging. Until clouds overhead clear, and sun shines through.

Scene 26: It's Too Damn Hot

Wren, age 24

"If the next apartment isn't suitable, I'll just live home and commute." I turn toward the waitress. "Iced tea. Large. Emphasis on the ice."

The waitress laughs.

"Vanilla ice cream," Gracie says. "With two spoons. And iced tea."

We're at a coffee shop half a block from Gracie's apartment in Oceanport. She hasn't been walking in the record-breaking weather for the last three hours, going into one inappropriate apartment after another. Her feet don't hurt from traipsing from one end of the city to the other. She isn't stopping every few blocks to get something to drink, and sweating it out before she gets to the next chance to go inside, buy a drink, and breathe conditioned air for three minutes.

"You're really going to commute from Silver Birches to O'port every day?" Gracie asks.

I remind her that our fathers have been doing it for years. "I gave my notice in Silver Birches, and accepted the position in

O'port—it's a great opportunity, reading specialist—so yes, I'll commute. For a few months. Until the fall. Until it's cool and comfortable and I'm not going to roast to death walking the streets of the city. I'll get an apartment eventually, but there's just one in this neighborhood left to look at, and if I get there and find out its been taken, or it turns out to be a fourth floor walk-up, I'll commute. I can't walk to the one after that—it's ten blocks away. Not in this heat."

The first thing I do when I get home is turn my air-conditioner up to the highest setting. The second thing I do is grab the phone. "I took the apartment, Gracie. Two blocks from yours. And six from Maura's. I can't believe we'll all be so near each other again!

"It's a lovely building. The apartment's a studio, with space for a couch that opens into a bed at one end and a dinette set at the other end, a kitchen small enough to stand outside, poke in a mop, and wash the floor, and a bathroom with a shower-tub combo."

Gracie answers with a list of questions. I answer every one: "Yes, it's air conditioned." "No, not central. Individual units." "Of course there's an elevator." "Second floor." "Yes, there's security. There's a doorman." "A hundred thirty a month."

I throw in a question of my own. "Can you meet me at The Furniture Farm on Saturday? It's supposed to cool down by then. I'll ask Maura to join us."

"Eleven? Then we can go to lunch afterward. I'm so excited that you're going to be my neighbor," Gracie says.

I tell her I am, too, but honestly, all I really feel is exhaustion —and relief.

Scene 27: <u>No More</u>

Wren, age 28

Dear Shoshanna,

...If I met a man worth talking about, you'd know it. If I had to send smoke signals up to the north woods to get to you, I would. Skywriting and blimps trailing strings of advertising-style banners. So, NO MAN. Yes, I've tried mixers, blind dates, bars—I even tried this new computer thing. I filled out this questionnaire and they sent me the names of three men they gave my number to. Man One is a lovely guy who took me to the penthouse restaurant at the Grand Hotel. Dining, dancing, ambiance galore, money-no-object. Only problem, here I am at twenty-eight and there he is at forty something with a teen-age daughter, the focus of his conversation.

Number two is all for the war. Thinks Nixon is the greatest person on the planet—He took one look at the peace posters decorating my apartment when he came to pick me up, grumbled something about "this" being a mistake, and how ashamed I should be about not supporting Nixon and the war, and left. Good riddance.

Man number three? He was apologetic, he really was. A genuinely nice guy. I felt sorry for him. He lives with his parents—his mother filled out the application and sent it in, and then she usurped the reply with my number on it before he got home and insisted that he call me and ask me out. The problem is that he's "not into girls." He had to kill time before he went home, so I went to a movie with him, then for a late night snack. We laughed a lot, conjured up terrible things about me to tell his mother who's convinced that if he meets the right girl she'll "turn him around." I told him to hang onto my number—to get together as friends, or to use me if he ever needs a woman to take somewhere, like a family Bar Mitzvah or something. What's wrong with having him as a friend, the way I have girl friends? Does sex have to be a part of everything? So thank you, computer. I found a new friend.

But not a boy-friend.

So that's it. Nothing new here. Please organize your community to demand that they get your phone service working. I'd much rather talk than write a letter.
Love, Wren

Wren, age 29

Dear Family and Friends,

I'm mimeographing this and handing it or mailing it to everyone dedicated to finding me a husband. I DON'T WANT YOUR HELP!

No, I haven't found a husband on my own. Yes, I have been trying. You have all been trying.

I'm getting sick of it. Do I need a husband? NO! The only thing I need one for is to have children and you know what? One of the teachers at my school, a single woman, just adopted a lovely two year old. So I can have children without a husband.

The bottom line is that I'm happy living alone. No need to have another human being in my apartment. If I find the right man, fine, but if I don't, that's fine, too.

I won't turn away Mr. Right if I happen to bump into him, but I'm fine if I don't, and I refuse to go out of my way to be in a place where I might have that bump. It will happen naturally, or it won't, and I'm happy either way.

Thank you for backing off and respecting my needs.
Love, Wren

Scene 28: <u>Maybe This Time</u>

Wren, age 31

On sunny days with low humidity and a soft breeze, I enjoy sitting in the park, accompanied only by a good book. If the park is crowded, a passerby sometimes asks if "that seat is taken," when it clearly isn't, and ends up sitting down. Or, it's happened that a clod plops him/herself down, but that's rare. Usually there's a "nice day today" comment and my seat-mate and I retreat into our own heads—or books.

Sometimes, though—it's happened a few times—someone will sit next to me and ask what I'm reading. Usually the person will be a man—young, single, and looking for a Saturday night date. It turns out that the odds of finding someone I'd like to spend time with are better here than they are at mixers and singles nights at bars. I've had some pleasant dates as a result—and have met some interesting women. Many interesting conversations. Usually, it's the book I'm holding they're attracted to, not me, and most of the time I meet no one, which is OK. Books make fascinating companions.

I'm sitting here now on a sunlit afternoon wondering who, if anyone, will be drawn to <u>Siddhartha</u> by Herman Hesse. About a quarter of the way through, a man slides onto the other end of the bench. I can always sense whether anyone that close to me is just interested in a seat or if he's looking for conversation. Now, I feel loneliness sitting there. Loneliness, and hope. I turn toward him, am amazed by how cute he is. A man looking like him wouldn't be interested in me, so I start to turn back to my book, but "You like Herman Hesse?" he asks.

I blurt out "I'm reading everything he's written. This is my second time reading this." I hear my father's "You're nuts!" in my head and hope I'm not making a fool of myself for coming across as so intellectual I'd turn off Einstein if he perched next to me. But—is it possible? The guy is practically bouncing with excitement.

"I've read it several times. I always find something I missed the last few times I read it. I'm also working my way through Hesse. Did you know he was analyzed by Carl Jung? Have you ever read anything by him?" He asks.

By now I'm sailing straight toward Venus. "Yes, I know about Hesse and yes, I've read Jung. There's something about him. As if I get him on a level that's more than just cognitive. I feel him and his ideas." I'm babbling but I can't stop myself. "I read Freud and got A's on college tests but he made no sense to me. As if I was reading a list of facts, which are really theories, not facts, but appealing to that part of my brain. Jung was grabbing my feelings. Like reading poetry. Even things I couldn't totally understand felt true. As if I grasped them with some part of my brain that isn't all words and intellect."

I laugh, embarrassed, am about to say "Don't say I'm nuts," but he's running with my comment, expanding on it.

I want to jump out of my seat, stand and scream and dance and sing. I'm exploding with joy and excitement and hope because if this man isn't married or engaged or not interested in women—but even if he's all of the above, wouldn't it be wonderful just to have him as a friend? As someone to meet with every week or so to bounce books and ideas back and forth? It's the best feeling there is. The strongest feeling I've ever had. It's just joy and what could be more perfect and wonderful and—

"Are you free for dinner tonight?" he asks.

—and life just got more wonderful, more perfect.

It's almost torture to separate, to go to my apartment on one side of the park and his on the other because "I can't exactly walk into a nice restaurant on Saturday night in shorts," he says, and I look down at my sundress and say "I need to change, too."

He picks me up at my apartment. We walk to a neighborhood eatery and talk and talk and he walks me home and comes in for coffee. By the time he leaves somewhere around two A.M.—and only because I have a friend's baby shower tomorrow and need to get some sleep—he asks if I'll be back from the shower by dinner time because—

I call Gracie, Maura and Shoshanna. "His name is Tim Rose. Timothy—and I'm going to marry him."

Tim arrives the next evening weighted down by an overloaded shopping bag.

"What?" I ask. I was ready for a hello kiss when I opened the door. I stand there like a lox, dumbfounded as he walks past me and drops the bag onto the kitchen counter.

"Surprise!" he says, and finally kisses me.

"What?" I ask, as if it's the only word in my vocabulary. My heart is beating so forcefully I can barely hear my own thoughts. Breathe, I tell myself, as if I'm talking to Maura.

"I'm making dinner. Sit down. Where do you keep your glasses?"

I follow Tim into the kitchen, show him where everything he needs is. He leads me back to the living room, brings me a glass of wine. "I've got it all prepared. I just have to mix it together while the oven is preheating. Then I'll join you for appetizers."

Ten eternally long minutes later, Tim places a platter of French bread rounds smothered in black olive tapenade on the coffee table and slips onto the couch beside me. He explains that he's a trained chef, working at his uncle's restaurant, Maison Française.

"I'm trying to save for my own place," he says. We talk about his job, how he's learning every aspect of the business. I tell him about my job as a teacher, my dream of opening a bookstore with enough space to serve coffee and tea, with chairs arranged in a circle so the patrons can discuss books and ideas and—"

"Someday," Tim mumbles and darts into the kitchen to check on the main course.

Someday? Is that a promise? I can't ask—he's back in the kitchen, and anyway, how could I ask something like that? But I can hope.

Only after he leaves, as I'm taking plates and glasses out of the dishwasher, do I realize I was the only one drinking the wine.

Four months later, we're on a city bus, headed toward a seafood restaurant. "I got a call from my friend, Al. He wants to know when we're going to have some news."

When. Not *if.* "So am I," I say, praying we're both thinking the same thing.

"I was thinking of June," Tim says. "It seems to be the traditional time for weddings."

"Is that a proposal?" I ask.

"I guess so," Tim says. "I mean, I just sort of assumed."

I grab my seat to keep from flying out of it. Wren Abramowitz, the girl who made it through high school without a single date, is getting married!

"Order lobster," Tim says.

"But it's so—" I start to say.

"It's the specialty here. In the ocean this morning, on your table tonight," he insists. "How often do we get engaged?"

We can't decide on an appetizer or a salad, so we order one of each and share them. While we're picking at the salad, a flower salesman walks in. Tim buys me a long stemmed rose. The proprietor charges out of the kitchen and orders the salesman out of his "establishment."

Tim looks like a little boy who's been scolded for doing something he thought was good. I can feel his bewildered sadness.

"We just got engaged! We're getting married," I cry out. The entire restaurant bursts into applause, the proprietor runs to the kitchen and the flower salesman ducks out before the proprietor can get the information he needs to report him. But he wouldn't anyway. He charges into the kitchen, runs back to our table with two glasses of champagne. Tim pushes his over to me after the proprietor leaves. How can he not like champagne? Or is he just giving his to me because he knows how much I love it?

I suggest elopement to Tim. "My mother. She'll over-manage the event to the point where it's her showcase rather than our wedding."

"So let her," Tim says. "Let her have her day. We'll have the rest of our lives." Tim's parents, it turns out, expect him to have a traditional, large wedding, which is exactly what Mother plans to make. Exactly, I find out later, it's what Tim wanted—to the extent that he planned it all out to the smallest detail, and then conferred with my mother and managed to convince her that all the ideas were hers. Only the entire guest list for my side of the affair is left up to my mother. She doesn't consult me.

I don't know half the people on my mother's guest list. More than half. Strangers to me. Rungs on my parents' business and social climbing ladders.

"Tim, do you know these people?" I hold up his mother's list. Strangers to him.

Getting married surrounded by strangers in the Grand Hotel ballroom was something I never wanted. Tim is thrilled by it. "No one organizes big parties as well as the Grand," he exults.

Bridesmaids! Whose wedding is this? I start to wonder, but Tim must have ushers for business reasons, so—bridesmaids. Thank heaven for Maura, Gracie and Shoshanna being at my side, but it's too formal, not at all what I dreamed of. I certainly never envisioned bridesmaids and absolutely not Deborah in my bridal party, but here she is. My mother insisted. "A cousin is a cousin."

Deborah turns the fun of fittings into torture sessions. "You expect me to wear this rag?" "Gracie, peach is not your color." "Maura, this style makes you look like a cow," and during the procession itself, "Shoshanna, you're clomping along like a hippopotamus on those heels."

Besides being able to hear Deborah's comments, my father is whispering in my ear, telling me that by cutting the veil off the floral headband my mother ordered after I told her I wouldn't wear a veil, makes me look like a slut. I may be the only bride in history walking down the aisle scowling. I try to smile when I get up front beside Tim, but he's frozen, his face blank. I sense terror, as if he's about to make the mistake of a lifetime.

"It'll be over in a few minutes," I whisper, as if his terror just relates to the ceremony, but *what if?* I think. I blot out the thought.

The standard, impersonal mumbo-jumbo of the service slides over me. I come alive at the end. "I now pronounce you man and wife," the judge says, and sexist though the wording and the ritual may be, it's ecstasy enough for Tim to wrap his arms around me and brush his lips over mine in response to "You may now kiss the bride."

I grip Tim's hand and practically skip back down the aisle with him as the ceremony ends. It's more joy than my body can hold, along with the thought singing through my mind, "I'm normal now." Married, like most women my age. A member of the human community. I am in love. I am married. I love being married.

At the reception, I search for my friends in the sea of strangers, find them perched on a sofa outside the ballroom, where the music is distant enough to allow conversation. Gracie and Ian, Maura, Shoshanna. I want Tim to join us, but he, too, has found his friends, congregated with them in a bar in another corridor to watch a ball game on TV. I shrink into my comfort-circle of friends, try to disappear into their midst.

Scene 29: <u>Life's a Funny Proposition After All</u>

Wren, Age 35, Journal Excerpts

I miss everything. My friends. Books. Ideas. MYSELF! I don't even feel like myself anymore. And above all, I miss sleep! I didn't get it when my friends with babies talked about exhaustion. Exhaustion—the word doesn't come close. There is no word for tiredness that's painful. Tiredness that seeps into every cell.

And tedium. I finish doing one wash in time to start the next one. Diapers. Will Janna ever learn to use the potty? She's almost three, and still not consistent. And Ethan! He's only eighteen months old! And in six months, one more!! I'll never be done with diapers!

Who am I kidding? It's not the kids. It's not the exhaustion. Or the tedium. It's the silence. Yes, Janna is becoming a regular chatterbox and Ethan has a few words.
No. The problem I have to face is that it's Tim. We haven't had one—not one real discussion like the ones we had before we were married. Not one word touching on an interesting idea or substantial thought for months and months. Maybe since our wedding. Oh, we talk, about money—as in how not to spend it so that he can save to open his own restaurant.
And Schedules. Tim's schedules. They're driving me crazy. Two children under three and one on the way and he expects his schedule to take priority over everything. His breakfast on the table at seven. The house clean, no toys on the floor, a newspaper on his chair, his perfectly heated tea on the table beside it when he walks in the door at eleven on working nights. Scheduled, pre-planned activities on Monday, when the restaurant's closed.

The house was in disarray last night when Tim got home. No tea or newspaper ready for him! Just a puking child and me washing sheets! Imagine that! And he was furious!!!!
Gracie suggested leaving him, but how? Two babies and another on the way! He's a good provider. And I keep telling myself, it will get better. There really are moments when I love him. If only we could talk…

Hallelujah! The Cranstons on the second floor are moving out and their three bedroom apartment will be available in a month. Sue let me know so I can grab it before anyone else. Can't wait to tell Tim tonight."

What is the matter with Tim? I told him about the Cranstons' apartment and he launched into this tirade to the tune of we can't afford it because he has to save our money for his dreamed of restaurant. "Three children in one room, including a baby who will wake the other two up?" I shot back. And he spat back, "So put the baby in our room next to your bed. You have to grab it so it doesn't wake me up, anyway. I can't nurse it! Be reasonable, Wren."

Wren, age 36

The mailman knocks with a registered letter addressed to me. Ethan is trying to reach the door handle to open it and Janna is trying to push her brother aside. Zachary is latched onto a breast as I stick one hand out to take the letter. Sign it? I get Janna to hold it while I jot some squiggles where my name belongs. I watch her carefully open the desk drawer I point to and put the letter in.

When Zachary finally nods off, I look at it. From Roger Cooper, a lawyer in Markettown. Up in the country somewhere. Whatever. Tim is better at legal stuff than I am. I put it back in the drawer, don't even think about it until after the children are bedded down and I'm attacking the dinner dishes.

"Tim," I call into the living room, "There's a registered letter that came today from some lawyer. It's in the desk drawer where we keep the extra pens." I go back to washing the dishes.

"Wren, come here!" Tim screams.

What awful thing has happened? Is someone suing us?

"Your Uncle Ned left you property upstate! You're a landowner. Look—twenty acres of property on Lake Kinde. At the north end of the lake."

"You're kidding! What are we going to do with land up there? Are there any buildings on it?" I ask.

"You bet. Listen to this: Farmland, a small apple orchard, virgin forest land, grass covered, treed land abutting the lake, a three bedroom farmhouse, a silo, a barn, six hens, three goats. The chickens and goats are cared for by members of the local 4-H club, who are paid for their efforts." He puts down the page he was reading, picks up another.

"There's another note—from your uncle—private to you." He hands it to me.

I read it aloud. Private does not exclude husbands. "My two stipulations are that you continue my relationship with the 4-H youngsters and that you retain the name of the property— Blossom Knolls. Blossom was my mother—a wonderful woman who ran a successful flower farm. I had no interest in farming or flowers, lived in the city and let the land go fallow until I retired there and found life on Lake Kinde most pleasant. Frankly, I obtained the goats to trim the grass.

"The property is ten miles from Schrodinger University— With your interests, I think you might enjoy taking courses should you decide to move here. I fear the house may need some work before you bring up your family, but I sincerely hope my favorite niece and her family will find happiness here. Your loving Uncle, Ned."

Tim mentions starting a restaurant there, which I'm sure he won't follow up on once we visit the area. In my quest for interesting day trips for the kids, I've never seen anything to indicate that the area appeals to tourists or has attractions of any kind. Farmland. Just farmland, small villages—really, housing developments—and Markettown—originally a farmers' market, now a small city. If there are any restaurants, that's where they'd be.

Thoughts of Schrodinger drown out all else. My whole body screams YES at the thought of taking courses there. It was the college I wanted to go to—if my parents had the money. The college there would have been money for, if I'd been a boy. The idea of taking even a single class there makes me drool. Schrodinger, I think, "where there are no right or wrong answers

—just the excitement of the pursuit, the journey of learning."
Yipes! I actually remember the blurb in the brochure!

Another joyous thought. Ian teaches poetry at Schrodinger. Gracie lives somewhere on Lake Kinde in the village of Harvey's Harbor. How far away can that be? It's too late to call her. And time to be with Tim now. Time for us to celebrate together.

Something for us to work on together. My soul smiles.

Monday, the first day Tim isn't working, we bundle the kids into the car and head upstate. Please, I pray. Please be perfect!

No, it's not, I think the moment I see it. This is not going to work. Not without a heap of money. The house doesn't need work. It needs to be torn down, a new house built. And what can we use for a restaurant? The silo looks kind of cute, so I open the door—

"Mommy, it stinks!" Janna screams. I shoo the kids away, almost puke from the smell. I push Zach's carriage as far from the silo as I can before going back to slam the door shut. I retch. Rotten apples and corn cobs—a playpen for whole tribes of mice.

Tim calls from the distance. "Come and see the barn! It's perfect!" I can feel great waves of ecstasy enveloping him.

My heart sinks. I've been picturing a little restaurant with a half dozen tables or so. Maybe a dozen. The barn can accommodate at least four times that. Preposterous! A restaurant miles from the highway, in farmland. How will it find customers seven nights a week? Maybe the college students, but most college students don't have cars. There apparently are buses looping the lake, but I just don't have a good feeling about it.

"Look at it! It's gorgeous!" Tim grabs my hand and pulls me into the barn. "We can put a wall up, separate the goats and chickens from the restaurant. A glass wall—so our patrons can watch them. Maybe have a kind of petting zoo," he says, with a glance toward Janna, chasing the chickens, and Ethan petting a sleeping goat.

Seeing my children, realizing what the open space will mean to them after living in a city apartment, glimmers of possibility start to form.

"Le Maison Française de Norde!" Tim shouts.

Are you for real? I think, but don't say. Who, up here, is going to eat fancy French food? Who will be able to afford it?

I can't burst his bubble. This is the happiest I've seen him in years. But there's no way we can do anything now. We just don't have the cash.

But we do. We go to the lawyer's office in Markettown to work out the particulars, children in tow. Tim insists, "I'm working. Keep it all in Wren's name. I can't get here every time something needs to be signed," he says.

"Mrs. Rose," the lawyer says, "Ned Abramowitz didn't just leave you the land." It turns out there's money for me. A lot of money. Enough money to pay for a new house for our family, a restaurant for Tim, and anything else we could possibly want. I look at my children, think of how happy they were running around the farm, think of how excited and happy Tim is at the prospect of starting his own restaurant, and optimism wins. Even though I know a fancy French restaurant is wrong, he's my husband, it's his dream, and manna has fallen from the sky.

We have the house built, the silo cleaned up. Workmen turn the barn into a fancy French restaurant. I love Tim's exuberance, his utter belief in his vision, but I swallow back tears every time I see him exulting. My heart is sinking and I am terrified. The higher you go the further you fall, the further you fall, the more damaged you are. He is flying as high as a human can.

I meet with the lawyer without him, set up bank accounts. "Don't you want to make the checking account joint?" he asks. I assure him my husband is a busy man who will appreciate my handling of it. I also—it's wrong, I think, but do I have a choice? I set up two savings accounts. One joint, with a nice sum. Enough to do all the work we need to do to renovate the barn and get the restaurant running. The other in my name. In case.

Tim ties a blindfold over my eyes, leads me into his "Maison de Francaise de Nord," tells me to open my eyes. From where he's positioned me, I can see the entire establishment at one glance.

No! One glance, and the room starts to spin. I drop down into the nearest seat, force myself to pretend to appreciate what I'm seeing. It's a clone of his uncle's upscale restaurant. The exact same dining area size. The same placement of tables. The same mural of the Eiffel Tower on the wall facing the entrance, the same maroon carpeting, the same white tablecloths, design of glasses, patterns of plates and silverware. The only difference is a glass wall separating the dining area from an animal enclosure that gives far too much space to the diners, not nearly enough to the poor animals.

I feel bile rising. I swallow hard. I will not vomit on his new carpet. My vertigo worsens. He hands me a menu, a huge smile beaming light in my direction. I force a smile back. "It's lovely," I say with as much enthusiasm as I can dredge up. My hand shakes as I open the menu. Why bother? I know what I'll see. It's identical to his uncle's, except for our name and address. His uncle's menu, down to the last sliver of brie, meant for people affluent enough not to care about the cost. The nail on the coffin.

I am overwhelmed by my own unease clashing against Tim's joy coursing through my mind. It will never work. And it will destroy Tim.

I push myself up and hug him, so he won't see my face. Kiss him, so I won't have to tell a lie.

The restaurant opens.

Almost no one comes.

No one ever returns.

Wren, age 37

Three children, one on the way, and a restaurant almost bankrupt—at least as far as Tim is aware. He doesn't know about the money I've hidden away. As far as the money he knows about goes, almost nothing is left. I need him to understand that, but "Give it time for word of mouth to build up a clientele," he keeps saying.

It's been over a year. He's had time. He has no interest in seeing the books. I'm walking a tightrope between forcing him to see the reality of the situation, and keeping enough available to him to keep the restaurant open. The thought of what would happen if he had to close is too devastating.

Incident after incident screams, "This is not working!" but he doesn't, won't hear it. But I do. Saturday night used to be date night. Now I get a baby sitter and sit alone in the restaurant. Sometimes, I'm the only customer.

I'm there when the Hensons, who sell us eggs and chickens, come. Doesn't he hear them? "What is this? Is this food?" Barbara asks. Patsy, our one waitress, helps them order. "Let's go out for burgers next time," I hear Joe say as they leave.

Last Saturday night there were only two couples, here on a camping trip, eating at the restaurant to get in from a heavy downpour.

The restaurant is losing money on a daily basis. I keep siphoning money from my secret savings account into the checking account.

I hear the comments, the things his friends try to tell him. "This BYOB thing is what's dragging you down. No one wants to go to a fancy French restaurant and have to schlep a bottle of wine," and "Tim, food doesn't make money in a restaurant. Alcohol does. For heaven's sake, get yourself a liquor license. Buy some good stuff and get a bartender. The college kids will come here to drink."

"It's something to think about," Tim says.

Wren, age 38

Tim's late again. The restaurant closes at ten—just in case someone stops by for a late meal. It's after midnight. Not that I don't know where he is, what he's doing, what he's going to be like when he gets home. Night after night, surly, angry, verbally abusive. Drunk. I can smell it but I don't have to.

He walks in, screaming, "You bitch, you got me into this." Pounding his fist on the walls, on the table. Lightning bolts of rage fly toward me. The baby, Kimberly, starts to wail. The older three stick their heads out of their rooms, huddle together outside the kitchen, where he's found me. They start to laugh—the kind of nervous, scared, someone-please-protect-me-or-tell-me-nothing's-wrong kind of laugh. Tim rages toward them, reaches for Janna. I throw myself between the children and him. His fist lands on my face.

Blood streams from my nose. "Leave! NOW!" I breathe through gritted teeth.

He storms out of the house.

To where? I have visions of him setting the restaurant on fire. Or going back and pouring the contents of his entire bar down his throat.

The children are terrified, screaming. I pick up the phone and call the Markettown Police. "Just get someone up here and let the children know you'll keep him away," and add, almost as an afterthought, "and lock him up until he's sober. Protect him from himself."

Someone is pounding on the door. I grab a butcher knife, tell the children to go hide, call them back when I hear the shout from outside, "Markettown Police." I open the door and there's Grant, our dairy supplier.

"Volunteer police up here. I'm on the force," he explains. They have Tim. "He's OK now. He took the car, managed to get into town without killing anyone. He went to Harry's Bar and Rocky refused to serve him, so Tim reached over the counter, was stopped by Hickey, who ended up being punched in the face. Tim proceeded to break everything he could reach. I was in the bar myself, so he wasn't able to do much damage, and Harry's insurance will cover it. We'll keep Tim in lock-up overnight. Look, everyone on the lake knows him, knows his restaurant is failing, knows he's a drunk. Harry has no desire to prosecute. What he wants, what we all want, is to get help for Tim. We came up with a plan, if you'll go along with it. We'll get him over to Oceanport Municipal Rehab. Not the best place in the world, and they'll only keep him a week. Healing House in O'port is top of the line. They keep patients for several months, and they have excellent results for all kinds of addictions, but with the restaurant, I'm sure—"

I interrupt him. "Grant, I have money. I have a solid bank account, and if need be, I could sell off a part of Blossom Knolls. Please give him a choice of jail or Healing House. And please mention that I won't hesitate to have him charged with assault and file for divorce if he doesn't make the right choice."

Wren, age 39

The right choice. It's my final visit to Harmony House. It's time to discuss what I know in my heart, and hope Tim knows in his.

He says it first. "I really care for you, Wren. I love your friendship, your mind, your ideas. But I can't live your free and easy life. I can't get up in the morning and think I'm going to have breakfast and then at ten o'clock, sit down to fill out my tax return, and then have a kid screaming she just puked and another one run in and fall and scrape his knee. I can't live with seeing your disappointment when you want to pick apples on a beautiful day and I say "but we scheduled a movie," and make you stick to it. We're meant to be friends, Wren. Not spouses. Not co-parents. I don't want to terminate my relationship with the kids—I just want to have short planned visits with them. Know beforehand what I'm going to be doing."

It's as if I'm in the Haven, living a dream. The relief, the peace. Tim said everything I would have said. He kisses me on the cheek, checks his watch.

Ten minutes later, on the dot, we walk into the social worker's office to make final arrangements for Tim's release. He'll remain in Oceanport where he can continue as an outpatient for as long as he needs it. He's already found an apartment, and his uncle has assured the social worker he'd be "delighted" to have Tim back as maitre d' of his restaurant, while gradually taking over the business, "for when I retire." Supervised visitation schedules with the children are planned. The legal divorce to follow will be just a formality.

"And Wren, can we meet once a week, or a month—whatever works for you? Go out for dinner, or tea—just the two of us? Just talk? About books and ideas—the way we started out?"

"I'd love that, Tim," I say. "I think that's what we were both in love with—the talk. It was a cerebral relationship. We should have kept it that way." Horrible thought. "But I'm glad we didn't. The children…"

We meet at his uncle's restaurant. "Go ahead and have a glass of champagne," Tim tells me. No way. Not in front of him. Not even for a celebration of our divorce. We discuss the book we've both read in preparation for our meeting. Formalize Thursdays at four as our getting together time in Markettown for "high tea." I should be flying, ecstatic. Or grieving. Isn't the death of a marriage supposed to be sad? But what I feel is relief, and gratitude that Tim is making this so easy, honoring our mutual need to be free of our marriage, while retaining what was best of our relationship.

"Friends. Thursdays at four," he says.

"And any time you need me, even if it's not scheduled." I assure him.

Wren, age 50
Lake Kinde Neighborly News

All Kinds Live on Lake Kinde

To those new to this feature, we are touring the lake, going from property to property, learning about our lakeside neighbors: fruit, vegetable, dairy, chicken 'n' eggs farms, a dairy farm, fishing sites, boat rentals and harbor, a university, suburban and rural villages, three sets of schools —all filled with people living together as good neighbors should. In peace, with a deep sense of community.

Take this week's visit to Blossom Knolls, on the north-east edge of the lake. We are warmly greeted by Wren Rose, owner of the property. Before Mrs. Rose —"Please, call me Wren,"—inherited the property, it was a flower farm owned by her great aunt, Blossom Abramowitz. Some residents may recall the French restaurant that filled the spacious barn when Wren and her former husband moved in, but, as Wren said "I knew from the start that the folks of Lake Kinde would prefer a cozy all-day brunch place. When I closed the French Restaurant, I kept the chef and waitress, and opened Chew and Chat—a restaurant where people come to feed their bodies and their minds, with friendship as the main course."

Blossom Knolls is divided into two distinct areas—a public area and a private one, with hedges and white picket fences dividing the two. Chew and Chat is located in the public space, in the original silo. Entering it is like entering a conversation-centered living room in a friendly home. The room is ringed by tables with washable tops covered by placemats—"Handwoven by Shoshanna Free," Wren asks me to be sure to mention. The seats all face the center of the circle. Few are empty. A lively discussion is taking place, including all the diners. I ask how discussion topics are chosen, and am told "It's organic. One idea grows out of another."

We continue our walk through the property with a visit to the barn, which has become Banquet at the Barn, with bookings going a year or more into the future.

"We used the barn as a day-care center, run by a licensed teacher—my friend, Maura Rossi. Youngsters snacked on healthy food and enjoyed structured activities and supervised play while their mothers enjoyed 'adult time' at Chew and Chat." When the clock turned and most moms became working mothers, we converted the barn to a banquet hall, Banquet at the Barn."

Wren tells me they thought of having an organic farm to grow their own produce, "but then the Robinsons opened their organic farm, and getting our produce from them just seemed like the thing to do. All our supplies come from lakeside farms."

"That's the Lake Kinde way," I agree with Wren. "Cooperating and supporting one another."

We enter the private area, walk through woods to a paved road and sidewalk. "Acorn Circle," is named for Acorn Oval in Silver Birches, where Wren and her friends grew up. The circular street in Blossom Knolls is lined by three-bedroom cabins, and the Rose family's large ranch home. The cabins were built as vacation homes for Wren's three friends and their family members. "New cabins are added whenever children become adults," Wren says, noting the construction of a second road around Acorn Circle, where the next set of cabins will be built.

Paths lead through wooded areas to a large grass-covered field. "On holidays, when all the families are here, the teens like to camp out on warm nights, and the youngsters turn the area into a playground." Indeed, off to the side, I see an area filled with climbing structures, swings, and slides.

At the far end of our walk, we come to the lake, where shade trees stand guard over the shore.

I thank Wren at the end of the tour, and recommend that you come to visit Blossom Knolls, and have a meal at

Chew and Chat yourself.

I put down the newsletter, satisfied that it included all the pertinent public information. But it says nothing about raising my four children. Nothing about the break-up of my marriage. Nothing about the way this has become a second home for my friends and all of their family members. We're a town unto itself here. Just as Lake Kinde is, for all who live around the lake.

My one regret about the article, though, is—why did I tell her about Tim and the restaurant? It will be so hurtful to Tim," I think, then realize he'll never read it. Even so, I put a double contribution into my Lake Kinde fines can.

PART FOUR: <u>THE WAY BACK</u>

ACT X: CHANGE, CHANGE, CHANGE

The Teacher

Time flows on, for earth years upon earth years. Today, I send a dream. Streams torn apart for years, with occasional crossings and recrossings, flow toward one another, merge onto a common course. One by one they come, until four streams bleed into each other, and become one inseparable river. A river mirroring a river of the past. A river bordered by oak trees, dropping piles of acorns on the shore.

This, the women see.

I float above the streams, say to the four who dream, "The time for the gathering has come, that you shall be as once you were." This, the women hear.

Scene 30: The Telephone Hour

Wren, age 71

"No," we tell each other. This time, the Teacher is wrong. We all have our lives, all are happy where we are, doing what we do. The dream? The Gathering? People have free will, we assure each other, even as questions lurk in the recesses of our minds. No one is moving anywhere, so, except for holiday get-togethers, no gathering of any sort is going to happen. Unless it's via technology.

I think of all we've gone through since we graduated from high school, moved on to college, to careers, to marriages, parenting, to where we are today. I think of Gracie's career as a nurse, Maura's years as a music teacher, Shoshanna's success as an artist, my life as proprietor of Chew and Chat.

Chew and Chat. Blossom Knolls. I sit on my front porch with

a cup of tea and some fruit compote and muse about the dream. No way could I ever leave Blossom Knolls, or Chew and Chat. The discussions we have there!

I think about the cabins! One of the best decisions I ever made. "Why not?" I asked anyone who cared to listen. I think of how I inherited the land, and enough cash to build three cabins. The look on Shoshanna's, Gracie's and Maura's faces when I casually said to each of them, "It's yours! To live in, vacation in, anything you want it for, any time you want to use it!" I relive the pleasure it gave me each time one of my children and then our grandchildren, reached responsible adulthood, and I gifted them with their own cabins.

I implore the Teacher, "We practically have a city! A city that fills up with everyone on holidays and vacations. "Is that what you meant by The Gathering?"

I get no answer. Thoughts come and go. Our friendship has helped us survive the hurdles we've jumped over, the laughs and tears we've shed as we've lived apart for the last fifty-or so years. What need have we to gather? And we do gather, I think again. Every holiday, we're together at Blossom Knolls. And while we don't live together, I live at the north end of Lake Kinde, Gracie lives minutes away on the west shore, and Maura an hour down-lake in Markettown, on the south-western tip. It's really only Shoshanna who lives afar. So what need do we have to "gather?" There is so much glue holding us together—our holidays at Blossom Knolls, our phone calls in between, letters when we were young, now e-mail. But more—so much more. Dreams. There is nothing in life as intimate as living within the same dream. But more still—there is nothing in life as intimate as a friendship so deep, we can sense each other around us always and ever.

I start the conference call. "Impossible," Gracie says.

"I'm aghast, how could she suggest that I'd move," Shoshanna says, and adds, "the part about as we once were. I assume she means when we all lived on the same street."

"If you want to live on the same street, move down to Markettown, because, my goodness, there are always empty apartments in my neighborhood and I'm not going anywhere," Maura says.

"This is my home, and my job," I say. "Janna's family lives here!"

None of us will consider moving. Gracie certainly can't. "Ian is far too sick to move him—and everything I need is in the house we raised our kids in. Including room for a full-time aide, but that's never going to happen. I really can't visualize being unable to care for him myself."

So—Shoshanna. "Leave my cabin in the woods?" she laughs. I think of her, half-isolated from anywhere large enough for a name. "It's a few miles from Canada", she says, whenever people ask for the name of a recognizable town. I turn my attention back to her. "The beauty! The mountains! The woods! The creek!" she proclaims when I suggest that she could come back to civilization. "I have the post office," she reminds us. We know. It allows her to get her packages of materials, and mail back the crafts that people pay megabucks for.

So, Gracie isn't moving, and neither is Shoshanna. And Maura?

"My goodness, no! Hey Teacher, listen to me, I'm not moving. I love my apartment in Markettown and my goodness, I'm in the high school this year and I'm teaching a jazz group and musical theater group and would you believe a classical group and the lower grade choirs and we're putting on Bye Bye Birdie and NO! I'm not going anywhere."

Surely, I try to make the Teacher understand, getting together for holidays at Blossom Knolls is the only way we're ever going to be gathered together in one place for longer than a few hours of shopping, restauranting, theatering, whatever.

We leave the Teacher to digest our refusal to listen to her dream, and go on to talking about other things, as closely linked as if we were in the same room.

Scene 31: <u>I Belong Here</u>

Wren, age 71

Crumbcakes! I don't answer the phone. Hope it stops ringing, or if it leaves a message, it's from a telemarketer. I just warmed up a piece of pumpkin bread and am taking the cream cheese out of the refrigerator. It's the middle of the afternoon, my personal, private relaxation time. I don't bother to check the caller ID. My friends know not to call me now.

Maura's voice blasts out at me from the answering machine. "Pick up your phone, it's an emergency and what am I going to do and I need to talk to you and I know you're there, so—"

I reach for the phone. "Calm down, what's the matter?" I take a bite of the bread, know whatever the matter is I'll have plenty of time to chew it before Maura comes up for air and I'll have to speak.

"Did you read the paper? I mean, the Righteous Flock took over the school board in last week's election and their first act has been to cancel all art, music and gym classes and fire all the teachers of any subjects that aren't state mandated and what am I going to do? I could continue to teach music as a volunteer, the paper said they'd allow teachers to continue to work as volunteers and anyone else who wants to volunteer but where am I going to live because on top of losing my job, on page six of the paper there was this little article that said the Righteous Flock has purchased three apartment buildings and mine is one of them and everyone has to move out within two months because they're turning them into six-bedroom condos exclusively for people belonging to their organization which everyone knows is a cult."

What am I going to do? Or tell her? I can feel her anguish, and it's overwhelming. I was tired before, planned on taking a walk, coming back and either finishing the book I'm reading or taking a nap. Now I'm on full alert.

"Calm down," I repeat, trying to model soft, slow speech. Telling Maura to calm down is as productive as telling an infant not to cry. "You know you'll always have a place to live. Sell or give away your furniture or just walk out and leave it there. Pack up your other stuff. Whenever you're ready I'll have someone come down with a truck and bring up everything you want to keep. Your new home is your vacation cabin up here. You know this is your home." I say it in as many different ways as I can. When Maura is in this kind of a state, that's what it takes. "And you can do things slowly. You just paid your rent for the month, so there's no rush. Move a few things at a time."

"But I want to volunteer in the schools, and—"

I cut her off. "And you will. You'll set your alarm, get yourself up, and drive down to Markettown. There's no law saying volunteers have to get there by the first period late bell."

Call it serendipity. Call it coincidence. Call it chance. Luck. Call it—

A flier in the window of a store the day after The Righteous Flock's takeover of the Markettown Schools and three apartment buildings catches Maura's eye. The following day, the same flier arrives in every mailbox in the villages surrounding Lake Kinde:

You are invited to attend the opening of The COVE: A Community of Vibrant Elders located on the south-east shore of Lake Kinde. Beautiful one and two bedroom apartment style condominiums are now available for occupancy...

Come one, come all—our friendly staff is ready to introduce you to your new home!

A flurry of phone calls. "It's less than a half hour from Markettown," Maura screams into my ears, Gracie's ears, Shoshanna's ears. "I'm going tomorrow and signing up and that's the answer to all my problems, it's an easy commute and I can retire and get my pension and social security and keep helping those kids as a volunteer and my goodness, I'd go now but they said the office closes at five and it's four fifty-five and I can't possibly get there in time but I'll be there at nine tomorrow when they open and I have to get off the phone so I can find a mover who will pack for me and get me in as soon as they say I can come but I have to get off because there are some things I want to pack and I have to start now."

The next phone call from Maura lets me know, "I saw it and it's beautiful and I can afford it and my goodness, you have to come next week and see it because I gave them a down payment and I called my brother, and Kevin said his law firm can handle it and my goodness, by tomorrow or the next day he's going to have all the legal and bank stuff done and I have a two bedroom apartment and as soon as I get off the phone with you and then Gracie and then Shoshanna I'm calling the mover with the move-in date because the lady at the COVE said I can move in any day this week, whenever I'm ready and the moving company will pack up everything I don't pack, I mean, how much do I have in my apartment here, and by next weekend I can entertain you all at my new home."

Apparently no one apprised Maura of the myriad details involved in a move. Shoshanna came down to Blossom Knolls the previous day. We arrive at Maura's as per her "next weekend to entertain you" invitation. As expected, we walk into a shambles, ready to turn chaos into livable.

"Where do you want this to go?" I hold up a framed picture.

"Wherever you want, as long as they all go up. My goodness, what difference does it make where the pictures go, I don't ca—"

"Give me the pictures. I'll figure out the best places," Shoshanna says, "but let's get your stuff unpacked first."

"Maura, why don't you go organize your clothes closet? Winter stuff on one side, summer stuff on the other." I head into the kitchen, look in dismay at the cabinets filled with pots on top of plates with cans of food beside them, start to take everything out before putting it back in organized spaces.

The intercom rings and we buzz Gracie into the building.

"I didn't think you could make it," Shoshanna says.

"Arwen came over and threw me out of the house. Says she's

perfectly capable of taking care of her father. She thinks she is, but she's not a nurse. I wasn't going to come, but she insisted," Gracie says, and picks up a dust-rag. "I'm just staying an hour. Ian's *my* husband, *my* responsibility."

"So how do you like it here?" I ask Maura. We're all in the living room, gobbling the pastries I brought down from Chew and Chat, with Maura pulling things out of cartons and the rest of us sorting them into piles destined for the master bedroom, the guest room, the living room, dining area, and kitchen.

"I think I fell out of my apartment and landed in Neverland! This place is phenomenal. I mean, they have no activities during the weekdays because we're expected to have lives outside the COVE and those lives are supposed to include volunteering. I mean I'm going to go to the Markettown schools five days a week and if no other music teacher goes I'll do one school a day which is convenient because there are three elementaries and the junior high and senior high and Sylvia who I taught with is going to volunteer to teach home and career skills and Florence and Sam who I met here are going to teach gym and Rayna and Jane who I also met here volunteer at Markettown Hospital. Everyone I've met here volunteers at something, and then at night they have all these clubs and you should see how many people signed up for my COVE Chorus. You should all move here—it's fabulous. Beverly—my new friend who volunteers here as the social director said we should all get our friends to move in and fill up the place because now we're only at thirty percent capacity and right here on my hall there are four apartments still available and the introductory price isn't going to last forever and—"

"You know, it's an idea," Gracie says. "I'm certainly not about to move now, but the time will come when I'll want to move. Look, when this drug stops working, Ian's going on hospice care. It's just a matter of time. I'm not moving from the house while he's alive. I'm going to be his caregiver, twenty-four/ seven, but—the time will come. I like it here. Your apartment is lovely, Maura, and the location is perfect. I love the idea of a community where everyone volunteers. It will attract the kind of people I want to live near. I can't volunteer for anything now but —the time will come when I'll have the hours free to volunteer as a nurse in the Markettown schools or hospital. So—it's something to think about."

"The time will come for me to move, too," Shoshanna surprises us by saying. "When I moved up to North Woods, every owner of a house on the lake was a year-rounder. Now there are just two of us left. All the other houses have become summer rentals. Or the year rounders still own the places, but they go south or travel during the winters. It's getting very isolated. If my neighbor Marti ever moves, or if her handyman ever quits, there'll be no one to shovel me out when it snows. Whenever that is—buying in now isn't a bad idea."

By the time they've gobbled up the last piece of pastry, Gracie and Shoshanna are ready to head down to the sales office. As Gracie says, "The prices are only going to go up. I have to get back to Ian. I'm just going to let them know my intent and take whatever paperwork there is home."

"Did Arwen give you a time she needed to leave?" I ask.

"She just showed up and threw me out. I'm her mother. I'll get home and throw her back to her own home where she belongs. I love her and appreciate it, and if she wants to stay to visit with her father, that's fine, but someone has to take care of him, and that's my job, not hers," Gracie says. There's no way we're going to be able to convince Gracie to stay for a while longer.

I think about the COVE. I live more than an hour north of here. I still help out at Chew and Chat even though Janna is running it now, and she and her husband and my grandchildren all live at Blossom Knolls. I don't see myself moving. But—"If the three of you are living here—maybe I should buy a condo to stay at so I can visit and be with you on weekends."

I join Gracie and Shoshanna when they go down to speak to the sales agent.

We walk out with paperwork to fill out, and promises made to arrange for down-payments.

"What if?" We ask each other the next time we meet at Maura's. The breakfast casserole I brought down from Chew and Chat has finished heating, and I'm doling it out. The fruit salad bowl is being passed around. "The gathering. The thing the Teacher said was going to happen, in that dream we had about two months ago. What if she knew?"

"What if it was God's will," Gracie says. This time, her son, Oberon, has taken over and mandated that she join us.

"What if it was fate, like—from the day we were born. That we were meant to live together on Acorn Oval and meant to come together again now—or whenever the rest of us move in," Shoshanna says.

"Chance? Coincidence? Karma? Fate?" I ask. "What if it's Consequence? We do X, and Y naturally follows. I think that could explain it," I say, and then counter myself. "But most of the time, most of our lives could be Reaction. We find ourselves in situations, and then free will takes over, and we choose to react in a certain way, and that sets up another X, and we have to choose another Y, and so on and so on. So—maybe luck or fate or something sets things up and then free will takes over. The COVE opened and then we all reacted. Freely. By our own choice," I say.

"But the Teacher did say it was time for the Gathering. And we all protested, and look at us now," Gracie says.

"I just had another idea," I say. "Sort of mashing up all of the ideas. What if everything is fated, preordained—as if life is a play. The script is written. But every actor that plays a part plays it differently. And that makes the other actors react differently. So —Life could be scripted, as it were, and yet, each actor could have free will in how the script is interpreted. Two people might read the same script and one could turn it into a comedy and another could turn it into tragedy. Just an idea—another what if."

"What if you pass the dressing and stop what-iffing," Maura says.

What if. "*The time for gathering has come.*"

Scene 32: <u>Good Friends</u>

Wren, age 71

Before we're actually gathered, Shoshanna and I are going to use our apartments—me, on occasional weekends, Shoshanna for the one or two weeks a year she comes down from the north woods and joins civilization. There's one thing we're going to need when we do—something to sleep on at the COVE. Gracie doesn't need anything—she lives in Harvey's Harbor, a short drive from here, and certainly isn't going to leave Ian for a night out with the girls.

But she joins us on a trip to the Markettown Mall to purchase futons, and of course Maura comes along.

Our orders placed, we stroll through the mall toward the parking lot, our eyes taking in store windows, alert for signs of interesting sales. Shoshanna suddenly grabs my arm. I look in the direction she's looking. Josie? Our childhood friend from Oceanport and Silver Birches?

I pull away from Shoshanna, bolt through a gaggle of window shoppers. "Josie!" I scream. In the middle of the outdoor mall, in front of Patsy's Pancake Palace, the three of us jump around, hugging and laughing. Gracie and Maura stand there bemused, confused, and—I can sense it—embarrassed. Shoshanna and I reintroduce them to the friend we knew in elementary school, who followed us to Silver Birches. We haven't really been with her since high school graduation, except for one day, when we ran into her unexpectedly.

It's not really a decision. The Pancake Palace is right here. We have to get out of everyone's way. And we need to talk for a while—Josie has about two hours before she has to meet her daughter. "She lives in Markettown, and just found a house in George's Gorge. She had to get her children out of the Markettown schools. I'm helping her move, but she had a meeting this afternoon, so I'm picking her children up at three fifteen. Just killing time here until I have to go for them."

Which gives us plenty of time for loaded dessert pancakes before Josie has to surprise her grandchildren, Gracie has to get back to Ian, Maura has to get back to the COVE to prepare for a chorus meeting this evening, and Shoshanna and I have to head up to Blossom Knolls where Shoshanna is spending the night before going back home.

We go around the table, catching each other up on our lives. Josie talks about being a doctor, living on the west coast. "Semi-retired now. I just go to the hospital two days a week. I like living on the West Coast. The weather, the light, the lifestyle. But I come east to visit my daughter and grandchildren pretty often. She's really busy, so I like to visit frequently to help out with the children," she says.

"What keeps her so busy?" Gracie asks.

"Her work. She's a family court judge here in the county," Josie says. "She never knows. She tries to keep her schedule manageable, but let's face it, when it comes to families, there are always emergencies. Keep her in mind. You never know when you'll need her help."

"My goodness, once upon a time I could have used her help, I mean, terrible things happen." Maura's face clouds over. Sudden quiet.

Gabrielle, I think. Her foster child. Something Josie knows nothing about, so I keep the thought to myself.

We fill Josie in on years that seemed to crawl by as they occurred, but swept by in a flash as we remember them now. There are a few surprises.

"I certainly would have connected with you if I was aware that you were at Chew and Chat. My daughter has taken me there," Josie assures me.

Maura mentions teaching music in Markettown.

"Are you Mrs. Rossi?" Josie asks.

"One and the same," Maura says.

"Oh wow! My grandchildren adore you! You're the only teacher they talk about—constantly. Harriet and Douglass

Spencer."

"My goodness, they're two of my best elementary students, such lovely voices and they're always so polite and attentive, I just wish every child was like them," Maura says.

"So what about you?" Josie turns to Gracie.

"I'm a nurse."

"But—the last time I saw you—we were in high school—you were dancing for Toe to Tap. You'd already started on a dance career," Josie says. Gracie fills her in on her change of career, her husband, children, grandchildren. "We're up to five, with another one on the way," she gloats.

Gracie's voice quiets. "My husband." She stops, takes a deep breath. "Ian has pancreatic cancer. It's just a matter of time. I—we—Maura moved into the COVE, the Community for Vibrant Elders, and the rest of us all bought apartments for—whenever. When the day comes that I'm alone in our big house—the COVE. That's where I'll be."

Maura smiles. "So I'm there already and I guess it's perfectly obvious—you can figure out that I lost my job so I'm volunteering but I also lost my apartment so I moved to the COVE, and my goodness, you should come visit there! It's wonderful, and everyone there volunteers somewhere and I'm teaching music in all the schools, one school each day and life is good and it's so great to run into you."

"Good for you!" Josie says when Maura stops for a breath. She turns toward Shoshanna. "What have you been up to? I expected to see your work in museums, but I haven't—"

I see the grin on Shoshanna's face and I know very well what she's going to say. "Your bag—look at your bag." Josie pulls a purse constructed of magnificently woven fabric up where the rest of us can see it.

"Look at the label," Shoshanna says.

"Shoshanna Free," Josie reads and her hand flies up to her mouth. "You're?"

"Yes, I changed my name from Friedman to Free as soon as I left high school," Shoshanna says.

"Oh wow! You're really famous! I've seen your crafts and art at shows all over the country. There's a store right in my town that has a whole section of Shoshanna Free crafts—jewelry, weavings, pottery. I have several of your things in my home. Who knew when I bought them that Shoshanna Friedman had become Shoshanna Free?"

We go on talking for a while longer, Shoshanna filling Josie in on her home up north, her two children, and her grandchildren.

Talk goes on to memories of our mothers. The utter shock of going to the funeral of the woman who'd cleaned our houses for years and learning that Marfa was Josie's mother.

"I loved her," I say. "I used to have fantasies that she'd take me home with her and adopt me."

"Honestly, she did come home and moan that she wished she could rescue Deborah from her mother—and she sometimes added you. I guess when you were having a particularly bad day," Josie says. "She said she tried to keep you and Deborah near her when she was cleaning your houses, just to keep you out of your mothers' way."

"Deborah's mother was worse than yours, but yours wasn't much better, Wren," Shoshanna says.

"What made your mother so cold and scary was the way she looked down at everyone," Gracie says. "As Maura used to say, but in a nicer way, is that she made everyone feel like shit. Smelly shit. Sorry, Wren, but—"

"No need for sorry," I say. "You're absolutely right."

A few minutes of reflective quiet. What is there to say?

Gracie breaks the silence. "What did you all think of my Mam?"

"I loved coming to your house. I mean I loved that there were always people tumbling all over the place and you had to be careful where you stepped because there were always toys on the floor and baskets of clean clothes waiting to be folded and my goodness, the things that your family was always doing together made me jealous even though I was always invited and I thought things like shamrock hunts were silly until I grew up and realized it was a great way for your Mam and Da to get the whole neighborhood to weed their lawn," Maura says.

"I loved your mother too, Gracie. And your mother made me feel like royalty when I came over," I say to Maura. I turn to Shoshanna and blurt out, "Your mother made the best cookies and always made me feel at home." Everyone agrees, but I realize—and everyone else does, that she may have made the best cookies and was a very good mom—but she turned out to be the very worst. I quickly ask Josie if her mother had anything to say about any of the other mothers.

Josie laughs. "Well, she didn't work for Gracie's family, or I'm sure she would have griped about having to make all those beds! But she did have some words to say about the disarray in Maura's house—especially in your room, Maura," and she did mention the state of your kitchen and the bowls and pans your mother left for her to wash, Shoshanna," Josie says. "But she enjoyed working for them. She was always happy when she headed out to work in your houses. Not so for Wren's day or Deborah's. Sorry."

"Never be sorry for honesty," I say. "My mother was very abusive to her—verbally. I don't know how she put up with it."

"Money," Josie says, and adds—"She knew when she was there that she could be a buffer between you and your mother. She wouldn't stop working for you. At least one day a week, she felt as if she was giving you a little respite."

Wrapped in the sweetness of an afternoon spent with an old friend, we don't notice how fast time is turning until Josie looks at her watch. "Oh! I have to pick up the kids," she says.

"Promise you'll let us know the next time you're here," I say. "For sure."

"And maybe you should think about taking an apartment at the COVE to use when you visit your daughter," I suggest.

"No chance," she laughs. "My daughter made sure the house she bought had a guest bedroom—with me as the intended guest. But I'll come over to the COVE to visit. Promise."

ACT XI: <u>CONSIDER YOURSELF</u> (AT HOME)

The Teacher

These humans! They can laugh at the promise of a gathering, laugh at the promise of all living together, but the streams carrying them through life go where they will, and laughter cannot make them alter their course. Maura has arrived, and now, one by one, other streams will join hers in a lake of kindness, where they have always belonged.

Scene 33: <u>Finishing the Hat</u>

Shoshanna, age 72

The light. The whiteness. The infinite quiet. I stare out the window until the scene is etched in my mind for all time. Time. What I don't have now. No time to even brush my teeth—I'll do that after. Shower after.

I set up my easel at the window, mix the paints, but how, how am I going to replicate that brilliant whiteness—whiteness that seems to be made of light itself? White light, the sum of all colors. The opposite of the blackness that would happen if I mixed the paints.

Close. I've got it close. Not perfect, but enough to paint the scene—the trees outside my bedroom window, boughs weighted down by whiteness. There should be shadow, but no, there is none. Just this perfect white.

Yesterday, there were no leaves left on the tree. Were there? Two leaves are falling now. Red leaves. How could I have missed them? One lands on the cushion of white snow. The other drifts down, and—how did that happen? It lands directly atop the first. I paint them mid-flight, one following the lead of the other.

I put my brushes down, step back. Far from perfect—no human could capture that whiteness painted by God—but maybe the best work I've ever done. What a way to end! The thought startles me.

Showering, I find myself singing—or as close to singing as I can come. <u>Finishing the Hat.</u> The song about Seurat finishing a part of a painting. It reminds me of how, from the first time—I think we were twelve—Maura, Wren, Gracie and I were allowed to take the train from Silver Birches to Oceanport to see the latest "Play for a Sunday Afternoon" put on by an amateur theater specializing in Broadway musicals. We could do that now, I think, which is a strange thought, because I live hours and hours away from Oceanport—and from my friends.

Maybe my mind is trying to tell me something. Oceanport is just about an hour from the COVE. I've said I would move into the COVE eventually. Maybe eventually is now. This snow is proof of it. It will be devastating to leave this beauty. Fifty-three years—from boisterous Hippy commune to home owning member of a year-round community to utter isolation.

Didn't I always tell myself I'd move if I got too isolated? I look out the window. How am I going to shovel all this by myself? It's one thing that the summer people have all packed up, stopped by to say "See you next year," and snow-birded to points south. But since last month when Marti, the only remaining year-long resident fell and broke her hip and her kids carted her off to wherever it is they live—This loneliness isn't good, I think, and hear Pax's voice in my head—"It's not safe, Mom." Dandi's voice joins her brother's, "Mom, come live with us."

No, Dandi, I'm not that old.

I glance out the window again. At least a foot or more of snow since I woke up. Beautiful—but the road to town hasn't been been plowed yet. With the silence of the snow, I would have heard it. And my driveway! What was shovel-able an hour ago—Who is going to shovel it? With Marti's aide gone, who can even get me out of here?"

For the first time, I realize how trapped, how alone I am. I sit at the table sipping coffee. Maybe it's time for the COVE.

<u>Finishing the Hat,</u> I hum. Not just finishing the painting. It's time to say, "Yes, this piece of my life, these glorious years of living in this wonderland, raising my children, supporting the family doing the artwork I love, is over. Time to put the final dot of paint on the picture, the final period at the end of the sentence. Time to leave the aloneness of the woods and the lake, and live among my forever friends at the COVE."

I look out the window again. White snow. A red leaf fallen atop another. The wind blows, a branch sways. Two more red leaves waiting to fall become visible.

And when they do, I think, there will be four at the COVE, and the picture will be finished. The gathering complete.

Scene 34: <u>Open a New Window</u>

Gracie, age 72

"Please God," I pray. "Please God, today, or tomorrow if it be thy will, let me get through this as his wife, not as a nurse. Let me do what he wants, what must be done, and not what I've been trained to do. Let love triumph over what's been drilled into me."

I think of my children, a six hour plane ride away. "Go," Ian told them when they realized how ill he was. "Go—it gives me great joy to know your two families will be vacationing together. I guess your mother and I did something right." He tried to laugh and almost ended everything on the spot with a coughing fit. "Don't worry about me," he continued, "the angels will guide me and your spirits will be with me, wherever you are."

But now—I don't want them to get on a plane—they might not make it back in time, but they can say good-bye from there. I call them on FaceTime. "You can't wait to get here," I tell them, when their immediate response is to yell to their spouses to start packing. "Please," My voice chokes. How can I say this to Ian's beloved children? "Say goodbye now," slips from my mouth.

I bring the tablet with images of his children and their families to the bedroom.

"Ian," I wake him, and blessed be, he is conscious and able to say goodbye to our children, their spouses and our grandchildren. Moments of deepest sorrow, deepest gratitude, deepest peace.

I sit beside him, listen to his labored breathing. I will not call 911. I adjust the painkillers in his IV. No machines. No extraordinary care. He's had a wonderful life. Every item on his bucket list has been crossed out, replaced by joyful memories. He's watched himself waste away, endured pain no person should have to endure, and now—it's time. I sit beside him, hold his hand, moisten his lips as he drifts in and out of consciousness.

I call our priest. He hurries over, administers last rites, sits with us for a while, until he has to leave to perform a baptism. "Life," we both say at the same moment. One life ends, another begins.

Memories. Ian wanted the music of memories. As the afternoon goes by, we listen to I Won't Grow Up, and retell the story of our first meeting. Over the Rainbow and Look to the Rainbow.

"Don't forget," he's instructed me, "The green leprechaun suit I wore to the wedding is what I want to wear to the funeral." How could I forget?

The room darkens. The photo sensor turns on the nightlight in the hall outside the room. Just that. I play I'm Not Down Yet and remind him of all the hardships he's overcome.

He's quiet, his breath thready.

"Open the window," he manages to say. "I love you, Gracie-Faye Callahan Quinn."

And then the only sound is his labored breathing. I open the window.

The end is near. I switch the CD. Hymns now, to guide him home.

I sit with him and talk softly as his mind fades and returns, fades and returns, until he is silent, the only sound in the room the music and his ragged breath. I hold his hand, whisper my love.

"Call 911!" the nurse in my head screams, but that is exactly what neither of us wants.

"You are the love of my life," I say, to drown out the thought of making him stay with me for even a moment more than he and God want. I remind him, and myself, that he will soon be with Jesus and Mary and all the Blessed Saints. "And I'll be with you, Ian. When my time comes, I'll be with you for all eternity, and until it does, I know you will never leave my side."

The room gets night-dark, but there is no reason to turn on any more lights. The pale beams of the nightlight through the open door are all I need. Through the window, a full moon rises, tears falling from its eyes. Without thought, I reach for the afghan on the back of my chair and wrap it around myself.

Ragged breath. Rattling. I hold Ian's hand, whisper love and wish him a peaceful journey.

Breaths further apart.

Time.

Breath.

Time.

Breath.

Time.

Time.

Time.

"Oh Ian, my love!" I close his eyes, kiss him gently.

When I'm ready, I call the children, reach them just as they're about to board a plane home. I call the hospice volunteer, Julie, who is befuddled. "I would have been with you! Why didn't you call me?"

"It was a private moment," I try to explain and thank her for her help.

"I'll call a doctor and the funeral home and be right over," Julie says. I start to tell her I can handle it myself, realize she needs to do this, and thank her for handling the logistics.

"Time of death was 12:27," I say.

"That was an hour ago!"

"Private time," I remind her and can hear her wordless lack of understanding.

Even my friends don't understand when I call them. "I'll be right there," Wren says. "I'm on my way," Shoshanna says, and offers to call Maura." I thank her.

At the Wake, a multitude of visitors—it seems every student Ian ever taught, every person I ever worked with, every friend we, and our children ever had—comes to say their good-byes. People who only knew Ian and me professionally or casually roll their eyes and are aghast at the sight of the open woven-reed casket, the sight of Ian bedecked in his leprechaun suit. People who knew us well smile and congratulate me on honoring who Ian was. Surely, this is what Ian wanted.

There is a lovely funeral mass in the Church of Saint Therese. The casket is closed, blanketed by wildflowers that Shoshanna wove. Father Joseph leads a beautiful service. Wearing the fairy dress I was wed in, I speak lovingly of my life with Ian. Maura sings a solo as the choir sings Ian's favorite hymn, <u>Be Not Afraid.</u>

The casket is carried to the cemetery adjacent to the church. "A green burial," Ian insisted, "but in a Catholic cemetery." The priest conducts the burial service.

The casket is covered by rich soil, with apple seeds sown below the surface, for Ian loved apples and trees.

"The worms crawl in, the worms crawl out" sings through my mind and I almost laugh, because the voice singing it is Ian's. No one notices. I'm sure no one notices, but just as I'm hearing the song, a worm slithers through the soil. Maybe it was the sight of the worm that brought on the song. Or maybe—? I choose *maybe,* and silently thank Ian.

After the service my family and our close friends gather at Banquet at the Barn at Blossom Knolls. Memories are shared, toasts are made, and in Ian's honor, I lead an Irish jig in a chorus line that snakes around the tables.

"Oh, how he would have loved to be here," I hear someone say, and I have all I can do to keep myself from turning around and saying, "But he is here!"

A week later, I get into my luggage-filled car and drive to my new home at the COVE.

"The welcome committee wants to know if we should have the Welcome Ceremony," Shoshanna asks.

"Of course! Why not?" I think they're a little shocked, but I'm here, I'm alive, and don't I deserve to be welcomed? More to the point, if I refuse the welcome, they'll give me all kinds of special treatment, as if I'm in need of their support. I'm not. I appreciate their condolences, but I'm moving here on my own steam, just like everyone else.

I can't tell them how deep the emptiness, the sadness, the grieving goes. I can't speak of being hollowed out, the magnitude of the loss unimaginable. But each moment is a choice. I can wallow in my grief or choose to make each moment the best it can be. It's what Ian, in his infinite generosity would want for me. A door is closing on years of bliss. But a new door is opening and I will walk through it smiling. Who is to say that the next doorway won't lead to a life as grand as the life I'm leaving behind?

Scene 35: <u>Who Am I?</u>

Wren, age 72

The Teacher was right, as always. "I'll-never-move-Wren," is completing what the Teacher called The Gathering, moving downlake from Blossom Knolls to the COVE. Bringing the four of us together the way we were when we all lived on Acorn Oval. It's nice to fantasize going back to that time, but we've changed. We've all changed in so many ways. The first time around we were children, then teens, filled with hope and open to all the possibilities life holds. Look at us now, every one of us wearing scars as badges of survival.

There are a thousand reasons not to move. I said I never would. But here I am, realizing that retirement is boring—that I could be living with my friends with activities and volunteer opportunities. Ian dying and Gracie moving in kind of cements it. If ever she needed the four of us to be together, that time is now.

There are a thousand reasons not to get out of bed today, to pull the covers over my head and go back to sleep. One reason to throw the covers off and start the day. It's moving day and if I don't get going, I won't get to the COVE in time to settle in before my friends get back from volunteering. I know myself. I'll need time to relax before they bombard me with welcomes, which are ridiculous, given that I've been staying down at the COVE at least once a month, visiting them.

The snooze alarm is screaming "Stop hiding. Get on with it." I swing my legs over the side of my bed. My knees protest. I drop my feet to the floor as gently as I can but the moment I put my weight on them, my back screams. Pop-up-too-fast-dizziness sings a wake-up song. I gingerly take my first few steps toward the rest of my life.

I brush my teeth and wonder if I really chose to move or if I'm just pleasing others again, moving because I retired and Janna is doing a fine job of running the restaurant and overseeing the catering hall, as I've trained her to do since she was a young teen and expressed interest in taking over the business. Or am I just skimming along on the current of "Come on, we need you here," and "It's the right thing to do—there's nothing for you anymore at Blossom Knolls," and "You'll love the evening clubs and the volunteer opportunities and how close we are to Markettown and the train down to Oceanport," and above all, "The three of us are here. You're not moving away from something—You're moving toward your friends."

I find myself belting Who Am I? from Les Miserables in the

shower and instead of answering with a bunch of numbers or a name, I lustily sing in my repertoire of three or fewer notes, "I'm Wren Zelda Abramowitz Rose. Former wife of Timothy. Daughter of Gertrude and Abraham Abramowitz. Sister of Geoffrey Abramowitz. Mother of Janna, Ethan, Zachary and Kimberly. Grandmother of Kayla, Jake, Samantha, Alexander, Olivia and Emma. Owner of Blossom Knolls. Owner of Chew and Chat and Banquet at the Barn. Forever friend of Shoshanna Free, Gracie Callahan Quinn and Maura Reilly Rossi. Friend of"—too many to list. But who am I, apart from other people's names and expectations?

Who am I? I ask myself as I drive downlake in my loaded car, a question and an acknowledgement of the way my past has imprisoned me, turned me into a false *Who*. I knew who I was at Blossom Knolls. Mrs. Chew and Chat. Who will I be at the COVE? The soundtrack of my mind flips to <u>Another Opening Another Show</u> and yes, this is the fount of the joy I've been feeling on and off at surprise moments. I've been playing roles all my life—the roles other people expected of me. Well then, I tell myself, it's time to try out a new role—the role of an old woman adventuring to find herself. Project New Life. The thought is warming, joyful.

I think about the Welcome Ceremony which against all reason and my impassioned "I don't want it!" I know will happen tonight. A memory from the past brings me back to the last time I was welcomed in a formal ceremony:

Wren, age 19

I've just transferred from New England State, after an abysmal year. Now, I was doing what I was determined never to do—living back in my parents' home, commuting to Forest College of Liberal Arts in Pinegrove. A big three mile commute. "We can afford Forest, New England, or a state teachers' college." I was told. With mandates: I still have to take education courses, but at least here I can major in something else. Maybe philosophy. Or biology. I have room to take electives in both and then make up my mind.

Which I shouldn't be thinking about now. I'm sitting in this auditorium, wondering why transfers need to be at an orientation, and I should at least try to listen to the shrill, gesticulating woman at the podium. The Dean of Women. "The most important thing," she preaches, "is to join a sorority."

What sorority is going to want a girl like me? I had a small group of friends in high school. Clearly not the popular girls. I've already spent a horrible year at New England University where I was definitively not sorority material. But the Dean stresses, emphasizes, accentuates that in a commuter college, the one thing that matters is to belong to a sorority—any sorority. It's the only way to have a social life. There's a women's dorm for the few students who live on campus. The sororities—all of them—share the entire first floor. Each sorority has a section with couches in the main room, and a table in the dining room, she explains, implying that anyone not lunching in that room is an absolute campus-nonentity.

"But you must realize," she admonishes, with her finger shaking and pointing around the crowded auditorium, "that all the Greeks are together. All campus activities revolve around the Greeks, and if you want to have any experience of college at all beyond your classes, you must, MUST," she shouts, her finger wagging more wildly, "join a sorority."

But what if no sorority will take me?

I certainly wasn't wanted by any of the ones at New England last year. Not that there was one with women I'd want to spend time with. So why bother here?

"You have to try," Shoshanna says.

"You can't just go to classes," Gracie says.

"My goodness, if you want to meet a husband you have to go to those fraternity parties and from what I hear the only way to get invited to them is to belong to a sorority so…" Maura concurs.

I force myself to "rush," to try out, to walk through that door into Sorority Row. I make it through the entrance and plop down onto the first couch I come to. I'm actually welcomed! I come again, and sit on the same couch. It takes me two or three times to realize I'm sitting with women like myself. Women who wouldn't be accepted into the sorority where all the girls are pretty, or the one where all the girls ooze money. This is the one where the women actually study and are in college to learn, not here to get husbands. Rich ones. In my English class, I hear a woman in the "best" sorority stick her nose up in the air and announce to her friend and everyone she hopes is eavesdropping, "I wouldn't consider marrying anyone who doesn't give me at least a four carat diamond."

It takes me just one visit to realize that all the women in the sorority I'm sitting with are Jewish, that three of the other sororities—the one for pretty girls who aren't rich, the one for pretty girls who are very rich, the one for rich girls who aren't pretty—are also exclusively Jewish, with the exception of one very wealthy Negro girl. The other sororities are clearly Christian. And white. No exceptions. What if one of them had been the couch I'd fallen—tripped—onto? I can't believe how lucky I was to literally fall into this sorority's section. The one for women who aren't particularly pretty and who aren't advertising wealth.

I can't believe how wrong the system is—why are we divided by religion? The thought that Gracie and Maura wouldn't be welcome in any sorority that would consider me rankles. Yet I don't walk out. I stay, and know I'll come back.

To my amazement, I actually enjoy coming here. It's only for a while, though. I'm certain that as soon as they have to vote on who gets in and who doesn't, I won't be able to come here anymore. It makes me kind of sad, because I'd like to be friends with these women.

It's probably a waste of time, but I fill out and submit the form that indicates my sorority of choice. No second or third choice. Those rushees who are accepted will receive invitations to join by special delivery tonight.

I lie in bed awake, listening, my stomach churning, part of me wishing, part of me certain I might as well try to sleep because nothing is going to happen.

Nothing does. Hours go by. No doorbell rings. No knock on the door. I'm not surprised. I tell myself, there's no reason to be surprised. What did I expect? But still, as the night goes on, unreasonable hope slides down to sadness. Sadness to grief.

I have to go to school. I can't miss my classes. I want to wear a mask, to make myself unrecognizable to the sorority sisters who are in my classes, those I might pass on campus. The embarrassment of showing up every day on their couches, the arrogance of indicating I wanted to join and thought they might accept me!

I make myself get out of bed, go downstairs for breakfast. Not dressed in the blue and gold outfit I'd selected—the sorority colors. Dressed in a drab brown skirt and beige shirt.

I walk down the stairs. One at a time, slow motion.

I'm halfway down—and I see it! A big blue and gold envelope on the dining room table, near the front door. My invitation!

"Oh," Mother says. "It came when your father was just getting home, so he left it on the table for you. He said he didn't want to wake you up, and he never mentioned it to me when he came upstairs. I know what a slow-poke you are in the morning so when I came down and saw it I didn't want to delay you. I decided to let you find it for yourself when you came down.

I grab the invitation, run back upstairs, elated, overwhelmed. Change into the blue skirt and gold sweater I'd put out last night in hope. Gulp down breakfast.

"I don't understand why you're so excited," Mother says. "It certainly isn't the sorority I would have chosen." Waves of disappointment drift from her.

I will not let her ruin this day. I jump from the breakfast table, grab my jacket and wait on the front stoop for the carpool to pick me up. I fly into sorority row as soon as I get to school. All the rushees from all the sororities are there in the hallway, forming lines. It's easy to see what line I belong in from the colors the women are wearing.

The groups of new pledges form lines. That's what I am now —a sorority pledge—Hooray!!! One by one the lines are all brought down to the basement cafeteria. My line is one of the last. From above, I hear the anthems of each sorority being sung as their new pledges come down. Then my sorority is called, but instead of its anthem, I hear "Consider yourself at home. Consider yourself part of the family. We've taken to you so strong…" Taken to me? <u>Consider Yourself?</u> Consider *me*? Part of the family? My eyes fill with tears—I'm sure they glisten. I will myself not to cry as I'm enfolded in hugs by several of the sisters. For the first time in my life, I feel as if I've been freely chosen just for being me.

I promise myself that whatever it takes, I won't make them regret accepting me. I will fit in.

Wren, age 72

Worsening road conditions draw me back to the present. Plump lace-flakes are starting to sink to the ground, and stick. This road has one blind curve after another. Which was always OK, when the only people using it were the residents, but since the ski center opened in the mountains a few miles north of Blossom Knolls, there are always tourists unfamiliar with the terrain zipping around twenty mph curves at sixty.

I pass Schrodinger University, pass George's Gorge and the snow lightens to a small-flake flurry right at the point where the road straightens. I breathe a sigh of relief, allow myself to take one hand off the wheel to reach for my water bottle and take a sip.

Shit! I jam my foot on the brake, swerve to avoid hitting a teen with skis flopping on a rack atop his car.

No more thinking, Wren. Just drive.

At this moment, the most appreciated sign in the world is

"Welcome to the COVE. A Community of Vibrant Elders."

"Wait until they meet you," I tell my back and knees as I park. "They'll find out you're not so vibrant." I get out of the car carefully. "So we just won't tell them, will we?"

PART FIVE: <u>SEASONS OF LOVE</u>

The Teacher

Spirit, the maker of water, the holder of water, the oneness encompassing and breathing and being the All, of which water is but a part: Spirit watches and knows. I watch and know. The year of final lessons is about to begin.

SECTION A: <u>THE LITTLE THINGS YOU DO TOGETHER</u>

Waters flow to pasts, presents, futures. Water knows—All time is Now. Streams merge together in a river carrying memories of rocks, falls, and detritus of times past. Yet the river of time flows on, carrying four souls, now gathering once again. I watch them as they enter a new year, floating on the current of years past as three streams together, are joined by a fourth in a bath of bubbling joy and the sweet serenity of home-now. Streams and rivers, family and friends unite in one soft-flowing river, emptying into a lake of love.

ACT XII: <u>HERE WE ARE AGAIN</u>

The Teacher

Sometimes water is deceptive. Sometimes, water that seems clear and tranquil lets boats glide easily over the surface. Sometimes there is an unseen undertow, or a sharp rock jutting up from the sediment at the bottom. Sometimes a time-worn fossil surfaces. Sometimes...

Scene 36: <u>Willkommen</u>

Wren, age 72

Garbed in resolve to be my own person, to honor my inner Me and throw off all remnants of the Wren-who-fits-in, it takes me about five minutes of being at the COVE to discard my resolve. For tonight only, I tell myself. Walking past the dining hall, peering through the open door, I see the big Welcome Wren sign hanging on the wall, and know I cannot disappoint the friends I'm moving to be near, the acquaintances I've made and the friends waiting to meet Mrs. Chew and Chat. I steel myself for the unwanted attention about to swoop in on me like a storm of a foul scent.

Tomorrow, I promise myself. Tomorrow Project New Life will start, and I'll find the Real Wren.

Together, Shoshanna, Gracie, Maura and I take the elevator down to the first floor, walk toward the dining hall. Maura scoots ahead and enters before the rest of us. Gracie and Shoshanna stand on either side of me, lead me through the door. I can feel their excitement—but I feel the blood drain out of my face, hope Shoshanna and Gracie will catch me if I start to faint. The residents are lined up on both sides of the aisle they've created for my friends to lead me down. Led by Maura, they welcome me, lustily singing <u>Willkommen</u> with "Wren" and "COVE" booming out in almost every line of their adulterated lyrics.

My knees start wobbling and threatening to quit completely, and just when I'm sure I'm going to fall flat on my face if I take another step, Gracie starts doing a jig, pulling me down the aisle. Somehow my feet join the line now forming behind us, snaking around tables, dropping residents off at their seats.

The room quiets and Beverly, the big, trumpet-voiced president of the Residents' Council, welcomes me. The whole ceremony is exactly what I expected, but I'm surprised, amazed, at how warm and welcomed it makes me feel. My whole body relaxes and hey! Maybe this is OK! <u>I Think I'm Gonna Like It Here</u> starts to sing in my mind, filling me with a comforting warmth.

I'm seated with my friends and some of the friends they've made here. Normally, I just listen when I'm in the company of people with whom I'm unfamiliar, but I surprise myself by joining in the conversation.

Back in my apartment, my friends tell me they've been having dinner in the dining hall. Tables seat six or eight, so they always have friends join them.

Maura takes ten minutes to explain that they're all volunteering at the Markettown schools, where they bring sandwiches and eat them wherever, whenever they have a few minutes free. I keep trying to interrupt, to tell her I know this, but she surges on.

They don't have to tell me about weekends. We've been spending weekends together, either at the COVE or up at Blossom Knolls. What they do have to tell me about is breakfast.

"We take turns making it for each other. Eight A.M. weekdays, ten on the weekend," Shoshanna says.

"We go first-name-alphabetically," Gracie says. "I made it this morning. Maura's tomorrow, then Shoshanna, and then you.

Are you OK with that?

The new Me, the Me who can be eccentric or fit in—whatever is authentic—wants to shout, No, I'm not! I haven't cooked for myself for—I can't remember how long. I've been eating at Chew and Chat. But—"It sounds like fun," I say.

They go on talking about clubs and weekend trips and—

Enough, I think. They're my friends and I love them but I need some alone-time. There are only so many seconds I can spend with other people. New Wren or old, that's who I am, something I'm sure will never change.

Thankfully, my friends know me well enough to sense my flagging energy. Shoshanna stands up, "It's been a long day for Wren," she says and they all head toward the door.

Scene 37: <u>Doin' What Comes Natur'lly</u>

Wren, age 72

I awake with the strange thought—Did my friends and I choose each other, or—are we just meeting The Teacher's expectations? We're very different people, with different interests, different lives. When we were in high school, I had my friends and Shoshanna had hers. Maura had her friends and Gracie had hers. It was only on Acorn Oval—and even there, Gracie's sister Brigid and her friends, Susan and Bailey, were close to us in age, and we socialized with them sometimes, but— It wasn't the same. The Teacher chose the four of us, brought us together, made us a private club. Will being part of that club be who I am here at the COVE?

I dress for the day, psych myself up for breakfast at Maura's. I'm directed to her apartment by the sound of a fire alarm and the scent of burning toast wafting from her doorway into the hall. I enter to see Shoshanna teetering on a step ladder reaching for the smoke alarm, and Gracie throwing the glowing toast into the sink.

We open the windows and head for Shoshanna's apartment.

When we're all seated at her glass table eating the scrambled eggs she whipped up, and toast cooked to perfection, I ask the question that's a bee buzzing in my mind. "If we'd never dreamed of the Haven, would we still be friends?" Eyes turn toward the wall where Shoshanna has recreated the lake and woods.

"We've discussed this, Wren. We know we would never have gotten together. Maybe we'd have been friends on the street, but that kind of thing doesn't last when everyone gets into their own crowds in high school, and then drifts away for college and men and children and—no, we wouldn't have gotten together the way we did," Gracie says.

"I don't mean at the beginning. We know, we didn't choose each other. The Teacher put us together. But would we have stayed if we didn't keep having the dreams? What is it that keeps our friendship going?" I ask.

"Maybe it's the cabins you had built for us at Blossom Knolls, how we've all come together with our families and everybody for vacations," Shoshanna says.

"One thing for sure—you've all always been there for us whenever Ian and I needed help. So many of our friends drifted away as he had one illness after another, but you never abandoned us," Gracie says.

"My goodness," Maura says. "Yes, we're all different and have different quirks and stuff and that makes you all interesting. I mean, no one else on earth believes in fairies the way Gracie does and frankly I find that very entertaining and Shoshanna makes me see things I wouldn't notice and good heavens, I wouldn't have gotten through high school without Wren helping me out and then the way you were all with me at the times my life was falling apart, and we like to do a lot of the same things like going to theater and eating good food and just being together is fun and kind of like we're a family."

"Maybe that's it. We *are* a kind of family. We know each

other's histories, know each others' parents, know all the things that made us who we are. We've shared those histories. We've shared each others' joyful moments, but we've also grieved with each other—shared experiences almost as intensely as we would if they were our own. It's something new friends will never have," Shoshanna says.

I sense sadness, and realize how important we are to Shoshanna. Aside from her children, who didn't share her past, we're her only family.

"I think there's more," I say. "It's that thing lucky families have—I guess, and I apologize for being corny—we love each other. Deeply. Like sisters."

"Sisters of the soul," Gracie says.

Breakfast finished, I set out on today's mission: signing up for volunteer work. I drive down to Markettown, to the school Maura and Shoshanna will be at today. "I'll take my own car," I tell them. "You're committed for the day. They'll probably sign me up and tell me to come back tomorrow."

But they don't. I walk into the principal's office. Mrs. Dugan welcomes me warmly. "We love our volunteers, Mrs. Rose. I assume you want to help out with our lunch program. You could bring so much to it."

I look at her more closely. Yes, she has been a customer at Chew and Chat. I sink down in my seat. If she thinks I'm here because I'm in a position to provide lunches for the entire school, she's going to be sadly disappointed.

I come right out and say it. "I'm not here because of Chew and Chat. I'm living at the COVE now."

Her jaw quivers a little.

"I'm here because before I began moderating the discussions at Chew and Chat, I was a teacher, specializing in reading. What I was thinking I can offer is if any of the teachers would like me to assist them in working with children having reading difficulties, or would want me to work with individuals on a one to one or small group basis, I'd be happy to do so."

As I speak, I can feel Mrs. Dugan's waves of relief. "We've lost our reading specialist—one of the teachers we had to let go. It would be such a help to have you. But—I hope you have your own materials. Somehow, the workbooks we had have all been used up over the past few years as funding dwindled, and our specialist seems to have taken our phonetic readers, so—"

The poor woman looks close to tears.

"I'm pretty good at creating my own materials," I say, "and I'll talk to some people at the COVE and find out if it's possible for us to hold a fund-raiser to subsidize whatever materials the teachers and I need."

I thought I'd be able to go home and finish my apartment set-up, but Mrs. Dugan has other ideas. I leave at the school day's end, starved because I didn't bring a sandwich. But my hunger for fulfillment has been assuaged, knowing that four children are going home proud of having learned something no one else ever taught them. Feeling good about doing something to please myself.

I go directly to the COVE office, ask about speaking to the program director.

"I guess you mean Beverly, the president of the Residents' Council." I'm directed to her apartment.

Approaching anyone I'm not well acquainted with is out of my comfort zone. Approaching Beverly takes my discomfort from standing on the third step of a kitchen step stool up to standing at the top of a ten foot ladder. She's overpowering. I shrink down into myself, lose precious inches, cringe in preparation for the onslaught of her trumpeting voice. Even when she's practically whispering, I want to turn the volume down.

I hesitate, timidly tap her door, and walk out with a banquet of fruit and cheese in my stomach, a plan for an emergency fundraising boutique on Martin Luther King Day, a promise from Beverly to organize the entire event, and a new friend.

Moving to the COVE might be one of the best things I've done in a long time.

I'm feeling good about myself, good about the COVE. I made a new friend, helped the children. Doubts I had about moving here fade, as if I'm wrapped in a quiet shawl of satisfaction.

And then. I'm waiting at the elevator for Shoshanna, Gracie and Maura, for us to go down to dinner, and I hear IT. That all-too-recognizable voice—footsteps on dry, crisp leaves. "Wren! Wren!" I want to run back into my apartment, pack my bags and disappear. If there's one person on the entire planet I do not want to live near, it's my cousin, Deborah. And what door is she coming out of? The empty apartment, directly across the hall from mine.

I wince. "Deborah, I didn't know you were living here."

"I just moved in today," she chirps. "I called our cousin Leonard to congratulate him on his promotion, which I wonder if you had the courtesy to do—and he told me that you were moving here. I'd been considering it, so when I heard there was someone here I know, I immediately called and made arrangements for myself and requested the nearest apartment to yours I could get. And they had one right across from yours! Isn't that wonderful?"

No. No. It's awful. Dreadful. Then I have a thought that almost makes me laugh. The Kinde Association Rules. Every farm, every business, every group residence, Blossom Knolls and yes, the COVE—everyone who lives or works on the shores of Lake Kinde has voluntarily signed a pact to live up to the name of our lake. To be kind. Every one of us has pledged to pay a fine for every unkind word we utter, every unkind action we take. Everyone at the COVE has signed it, knowing the money from fines will go to a lake-wide celebratory gathering at year's end, and most if it to charities.

I almost laugh aloud. I can just see Deborah being fined more and more each time she opens her mouth. She'll be paying more in fines than she does in rent.

Maura and Gracie open their doors and spare me the necessity of lying and welcoming Deborah. I reintroduce them to her, since they haven't seen her since we all lived in Silver Birches. No introduction is apparently necessary. They both look as if they want to spit. Shoshanna comes out a minute or so later and looks as if she wants to turn around and go back to her apartment, but she walks toward us. There are so many bad vibes, the air itself seems clouded and cold, but there's no way around it—we have to tell Deborah we're on our way down to dinner.

"Of course, I'll join you," she says, as if there's no possibility of there not being room at our table.

There's nothing any of us can say without being fined for unkindness.

"Where did you get that rag you're wearing, Shoshanna?" Deborah asks in the elevator.

Shoshanna doesn't answer.

"Wren, in this light your lipstick is far too dark," Deborah says.

"These are my lips, Deborah. I haven't put on lipstick since this morning. It's completely rubbed off," I say.

At dinner—"I wouldn't take that roll if I were you," Deborah warns Maura who has lost five pounds and reached her goal weight.

After dinner, I put a folding step-stool next to my apartment door. I'm too short to see out of the peephole. In the future, I'll check before I open my door. I do *not* want to run into Deborah again.

But I know I will.

I'm the breakfast host. The way Gracie, Shoshanna and Maura slip into my apartment—one by one, tiptoeing, in utter silence—is almost comical. No one says a word until my door is closed.

"I love this quiche." Shoshanna reaches for another piece.

"Courtesy of Chew and Chat and my freezer," I say, lest anyone get the remote notion that I've taken up cooking in my new life.

There are footsteps in the hall. We all look up. I can feel the collective anxiety, the collective "whew" as the footsteps continue down the hall. No question. Deborah is on everyone's mind.

"She's your cousin," Maura says. "It's uncharitable and unkind and never mind the Kinde fines—my goodness, I'll have to go to confession for saying this, but you have to do something about her. I'm not eating another meal with Deborah and if she invites herself to our breakfast—"

"Which she might," I say. "But it won't work. Whoever's door she knocks on can just politely tell her she only had enough eggs or bread or whatever for the four of us."

"And dinner?" Gracie asks.

"I don't know about you, but there are eight seats at the table and if each of you doesn't find someone else to join us, I'll find four more myself. Those seats will be full," Shoshanna says.

"Every night," Gracie adds.

I'm in total agreement, and I say as much, but "You have to understand where she's coming from. She's had a horrible life. Anyone who went through what she went through would be bitter. I mean, you all remember my mother—and you met my Aunt Mildred, who was ten times worse. That's what Deborah learned. She thinks her sarcastic remarks are clever."

"Your mother was the same way," Gracie says. "And look at you—it's as if you look at your mother and see her as a model of lessons in how NOT to relate to people. Deborah had the same model and took it as Gospel."

"But I had the three of you. I had your mothers. I had the Teacher. Deborah didn't have anyone. And her adult life was one misery after another."

"I know she majored in accounting and then couldn't get a job doing anything but book-keeping because she's a woman, even though she was first in her class," Shoshanna says.

"And making coffee—a bookkeeper's responsibility. That was just the start," I say. "She had this boss, Herman Gross, who knew a good thing when he saw it. Hired her as a bookkeeper and let her do everyone's accounting work—not meeting with clients —just doing all the hours and hours of math. I mean, this was before computers. And she did have to make the coffee—and serve it to the clients as if she was the maid. But that was just the start.

"He saw her getting dissatisfied, so he started dating her. But she wanted more. In order to keep her, he married her. Which worked, sort of. Who knows what kind of relationship they had. He never came to family gatherings with her. Obviously, it was bad enough that when she got pregnant and insisted that she was going to stay home and raise Rue, her daughter, he told her if she didn't work he would divorce her. Which is what happened."

I help myself to another slice of quiche.

"Sad," Shoshanna says. "But I'm still inviting a friend to dinner."

We all agree that would be the best idea, and that it would also be appropriate for each of us to drop a fiver into our Kinde jars.

Scene 38: <u>Love Makes the World Go Round</u>

Wren, age 72

I take one look at the flyer and a soft gust of sadness wafts over me. Visions of high school, not just for myself, but for all of us except Maura float on the feeling. Only Maura will be thrilled with the idea of a sock hop. Valentine's Day won't be easy for anyone at the COVE, except for the four couples. And maybe the six single men. It'll be interesting to see if they try to couple-up with any of the women. They haven't so far. Probably mired in the same searing sense of loss of the recently widowed or the softened sense of loss the divorced and long-term widowed women feel.

I don't know. Maybe we need to acknowledge Valentine's Day. Everyone's story is different.

Maura waves the flyer in front of me when she storms into my apartment for breakfast.

"What on earth is a sock-hop?" Maura starts in.

"Dances!" Shoshanna and I say in unison. We explain why they were called sock hops.

"My goodness, we didn't wear socks and saddle shoes. We wore stockings and heels and party dresses and—"

"Pass the butter, please," I say. I don't really want it, but someone had to say something to cut off the list of dates to dances Maura is beginning spew forth. It doesn't stop her, but it does get her to change the topic.

"My goodness," she bubbles, "There are so many great songs from the fifties. I have to set up meetings for the COVE Chorus right away to start rehearsing."

The rest of us look at each other. Yes, our schools had dances, but Ian moved away before Gracie got to one, and afterward came home in tears after every event, because all she thought of as she danced with another partner was Ian. Shoshanna had Tommy—She certainly couldn't go to a dance with him. Dancing with a boy was absolutely forbidden in their religion as Shoshanna's parents adhered to it. And I—I simply didn't go to a dance because no one ever asked me.

We look at one another, and Shoshanna shrugs and says her art committee will do the decorations. Gracie's dancers will prepare to lead and teach the fifties' dances, and what can I say? Even if I don't volunteer it, Banquet at the Barn will be catering the event, so I might as well form a committee to make up the menu.

So we plan, and prepare, and reminisce.

Shoshanna, age 72

I'm making soup, chopping vegetables, but my thoughts are on the sock hop. Guys invited me, but always "I'm so sorry. It would have been fun, but Orthodox girls aren't allowed to dance with boys," I said. The word got around.

I have to wonder. What if I could have gone to a dance with Tommy? What if my parents were like Wren's, or my other Jewish friends' parents? They'd want me to marry a Jew, but a high school dance? If we'd been able to make out in cars or the movies or the park—if we didn't have to hide out in Ralph's apartment where there was nothing to do but sex…Who knows?

I have to tell myself, one of the answers to all the *what ifs* is that if life hadn't happened as it did, I wouldn't have my Dandi, and maybe not my Pax, who came from another feel-nothing affair. Nor would I have my grandchildren. Or my new great-grandson. I wouldn't have found my home in the woods or met the people at the commune. Like Leaf. I wonder what became of him, what became of the rest of them.

I lower the flame under the boiling soup, sit down with a sketch pad and start to design decorations for the sock hop. And costumes for Gracie, Wren, Maura and myself. If we're going to go to a fifties'-style dance, we're going to go as fifties' teens. Hey world! I'm going to my first sock hop!

Gracie, 72

Oh, Ian. We had it all planned, all worked out. Our first dance. Oh, we did dance years later starting with down the street after you walked into the coffee shop carrying that pot of gold. But a high school dance? Well, Ian, we're about to dance our first dance together—bobby sox and all.

Wren, age 72

My first, I think. Finally, I can go to a sock hop I was invited to. I think about high school, the few dates I had in college that never turned into relationships. The effort to meet men for all the years I worked as a teacher, living in an apartment in Oceanport. I think about mixers and singles' nights at bars. Looking back, I have to wonder if all that effort was driven by a desire for Romance, or by my need to fit in, my need to fulfill everyone else's expectations for the direction my life should take. I lived alone, and except for the voices telling me I needed a partner, I was happy alone. I wanted to have children, but children can be adopted, and there's always artificial insemination.

Then I think about love. Maybe for me, love isn't about Romance. There are all kinds of love. I think of Tim—marriage didn't work, but I love him with all my heart. It's a different kind of love, a family kind of love, like the love I have for my forever friends. A kind of love mixed with the kind of love I feel for our four children, and our grandchildren. The kind of love that screams "They are the center of my world, and nothing, including my own needs, comes before them"—It's a kind of love that doesn't need dates, or proms, or sock-hops. It's the air I breathe —at least when it comes to my children. But sadly, I think, when it comes to Tim, it's as if a glass of wine was diluted with water. Love remains, but passion—Was there ever passion? For talk and ideas, but for Tim? There are so many questions I have that I can't answer.

I dream. The dream is still with me when I awake. I wrench myself out of bed—it's going to be a busy day. Valentine's Day. Tonight—the Sock Hop. I'm still in my dream, still reliving my wedding. Tim standing at the alter, frozen. I can feel his terror, his sense that he's about to make the mistake of a lifetime. We were so in love. In that moment, how did he know? Maybe I should have invited him tonight. I picture Tim at the Hop. Better that I didn't. It's not Thursday afternoon. Not the time locked in, on his schedule. Maybe it hit him, up there on the alter—we were meant to be friends. Maybe he understood, moments before saying "I do," that we're like two magnets—my charge needing to live a disorganized, spontaneous life, his charge needing a hyper-organized, rigidly scheduled life. Attracting each other now, as we stood with magnets aligned to attract. But turn them in time, so that negative faces negative, and positive faces positive? Maybe he sensed in that moment how our lifestyles would repel each other. We are both poles of magnets, both made of iron, and we understand each other as no one else can.

I bring my thoughts back to now. Breakfast. It's my turn. I know what we're having tonight, so—something light and simple. Toast and tea, coffee. Maybe poached eggs. But I'm still foggy, still back in a dream I had last night. So, frozen waffles. No work at all.

The dream presses in on me, insists on intruding into the present. A wedding memory—I'm sure it was mine alone, also sure the rest of the dream was one we all had. I defrost a package of frozen strawberries and am putting a can of Creamy-Whip onto the table just as the door opens and Maura pops in.

"I had a dream and did you and it was so beautiful and sad and sweet and—" Gracie and Shoshanna join us. The food is on the table, so they sit there and poke at it, with Maura exulting, "It was as if I was dancing at the wedding Chris and I planned to have and it was so real and the music! and to be there with Chris and—" Maura stops talking. I can feel a wave of sadness, as that part of the dream ended. Chris, and—Is she also thinking of lost hope—of Gabrielle?

I can feel emotion, like a cloud of joy floating around Gracie. I see her beatific look and know she's still there, in the dream. "Gracie," I say. "What do you remember?"

"It started the way it always does," Gracie begins, "but this time, we were teens—kind of high school age, I guess. The four of us were walking down the path through the woods and came to the foot of the mountain. A door swung open and we walked through and found ourselves in the Haven. Everything was as usual—the incredible flowers, the waterfall in the distance, the forest surrounding us. It looked very spring-like.

"The Teacher was standing there, dressed in her usual multi-colored flowing gown. Her hair was long, floating on the breeze, and colored—How can I describe it?" Gracie turns toward Shoshanna.

"The color of the sun. Like pure light."

"And then she spoke, and said one word. The only word the Teacher said."

A chorus of voices—"Dance!"

Gracie starts to resume the story but Maura overpowers her. "Oh, my goodness, she said 'dance' and there was this music, like nothing I've ever heard, like listening to heaven sing and maybe there are choirs of angels but anyway, we were all with the guys we were with in high school, except Wren, you were off somewhere out of the dream for this part, but Shoshanna was off in the forest kind of hidden by the trees dancing with Tommy, and Gracie, you were off on the side, kind of not on the dance floor but you were there with Ian—like dancing in a puddle on a street and I was there on the dance floor with Michael O'Donahue who I dated in I think eleventh grade."

Maura stops to take a sip of coffee and I grab the story. "And then everything changed. The three of us who got married were wearing our wedding gowns, dancing with our husbands.

Shoshanna, you were dancing with a man—who?"

"Strange," she says. "His name is Leaf. From when I lived in the commune after I left Silver Birches. I don't think I ever knew his real name. He was older than the rest of us. I don't know why he came into the dream. I never danced with him or anything. He was just a lovely man who made me feel safe and protected. Who made me believe everything would be O.K. Anyway, as we danced in the dream, Leaf drifted away, and then we all started aging, and one by one your spouses drifted away, but Wren, this is weird—at the very end, at least of my dream, you and Tim were dancing toward each other, and weirder still, it could have been shadows or the pattern of the leaves—the way they were dancing in the wind—but for a second, I glimpsed Leaf's face, peering out from behind a tree."

"Really, I didn't see anyone at the end like that," I say. "Or dancing toward Tim. The last thing I remember is him drifting away, but then when I woke up, I remember dreaming about being at my wedding."

"Maybe the Teacher sent the dream to tell us to dance with our memories tonight," Shoshanna says.

Scene 39: <u>My Funny Valentine</u>

Gracie, age 72

"Bet we do better in the laugh department than you," I say. I stuff another bite of waffle into my mouth. "The minute I swallow it, I have to get my dancers together. If they perform the way they did at yesterday's rehearsal, we'll be the comedy act of the century instead of a dance act." Eating should be slow but—I shovel a final forkful of waffle into my mouth.

My friends look at me. "You don't have to dance, Gracie," Shoshanna says.

"Everyone will understand if you let those dancers go on without you," Wren adds.

No one understands. Yes, it's Valentine's Day and yes, I just buried Ian. What my friends don't understand is that mentoring the dance club, doing the choreography, teaching the dances, and leading them tonight gives me a reason for getting out of bed, a sense of being needed, a reason for being joyful.

Shoshanna, age 72

With the last decoration in place, the stereo playing <u>At the Hop,</u> I stand near the door and watch vibrant elders decked out in felt skirts, pleated skirts, jeans with rolled cuffs, Keds and saddle shoes with bobby-sox, pony tails or short hair with head bands spill into the dining hall. They stare at the photographs of their high school selves scattered around the walls of the dining hall and squeal "I think this is you, Florence," and "I can't believe that's you, Donna, are you sure?"

When everyone settles down, we have to get up again, one table at a time, for the costume parade. No surprise, but it pleases me when the skirts over starched crinolines—felt skirts adorned by poodles, their leashes reaching up to our waists—pin-up girl sweaters, choker scarfs, bobby-sox and Keds, cats' eye glasses and pony-tails that I engineered and gleaned from the internet for the four of us wins first prize.

Wren, age 72

We're joined at our dinner table by four of our friends—Jane, who used to be our family dentist, Rayna and Nancy, new friends we've made, and Claire, who was once a high finance specialist who gave it all up to clean our apartments because it's what she loves to do. And Deborah. We managed to exclude her from our costume group, but— It was so pathetic to see her come in late every night, and scan the room for an empty chair, that we've been inviting her to join us. One night out of every seven. Yes, it's difficult at times. Most of the time. Tonight, we reserve the one table that seats ten. When Deborah walks in and scans the room, I wave her over. Her joy is palpable.

Waitresses, clad in jeans with rolled up cuffs and large, untucked men's shirts, bring steaming chafing dishes of fondue, and platters of bread cubes to the tables.

Between dipping the bread into the melted cheese, we talk of love.

"I love the fifties sock hop theme," Maura says. "I mean the costumes and my goodness, this fondue is fabulous, but the idea of this being a Valentine's celebration is creepy. I mean, *love,* why have this party honoring Romantic love when we're almost all widows? As far as I'm concerned, love is a demon stealing your soul away, making you love and love and love and then your husband is killed while you're still newlyweds and you try to adopt a child and—" And she doesn't say it, but I know. Her next word could be "Gabrielle."

Jane cuts her off. "Yes, Maura, losing love hurts. My Jacob died two years ago. One day we were hiking and he was fine and the next day he was sitting in a chair waiting for me to finish making dinner, and—." She takes a breath. "His heart just stopped. So I miss him, every single day. It's painful. If I'd never loved, I wouldn't have this pain. But if I'd never loved, my God!

the joy I would have missed. The memories of that joy far outweigh the pain. I try to use them as a balm for my pain. Try it, Maura." She spears a bread cube and dips it into the fondue.

"You said it all, Jane," Gracie says. "Ian was sick. Death was no surprise. But you're never really prepared. Joy. Memories. Absolutely, Jane. And something else. I feel Ian beside me. I feel him sharing the memories, and at my side always. Does anyone else? Please pass the bread bowl."

"I do," Nancy says. "I feel Greg's touch. I hear his words, talk to him and have a deep sense he's hearing me. More than he did in the last years of his life, when his mind was so gone he didn't even know who I was. But he knew I was someone who loved him. In the end, we didn't need words. We just knew. And I still know."

"I have to say it," Rayna says. "I share the pain of loss, but I also feel the pain of regret. Our marriage—there were some shaky times, and the last year of his life was one of those times. He was Mr. Grumpy and I was Mrs. Leave-Me-Alone. And then he suddenly died, and—I have so much regret. Underneath it all, I loved him desperately. How many chances did I miss to tell him I loved him no matter how curmudgeonly he'd become? I mourn for him and for those opportunities."

"He knew," Claire says softly, then perks up. "I never married. I was married to my career. But there are other kinds of love. I've loved and lost a sister, loved and lost good friends. And I'm sure they knew I loved them, and I'm sure they're with me still, as Gracie said." Claire picks up the forkful of cheese-infused bread cooling on her plate and pops it into her mouth. "Shoshanna, you haven't said anything."

"Parenting. Love is when you care so much for another person that you'd give up everything you are to keep her—or him —safe and well and happy. The kind of love for your baby even before it's born. The kind of explosion of joy you feel when you're with them, and all is well for them." Shoshanna reaches toward the steaming pot and puts down her fork. "Don't forget all the food coming," she says.

Rayna laughs and dunks another bite, waves the drenched bread in the air to cool and says, "In the same vein you're happier when the person you love is around than when he's not. When you just feel good and warm and care about doing things to make that person feel as good as you feel. You care and feel cared for. It could be your parents, grandparents, family, friends. People whose lives you want to share."

"Maybe it boils down to love being the feeling of God," Gracie says. "Like," she stops and struggles for a way to explain. "As if love is the thing that ties the world together. As if the object of your love is infused with God and that part is reaching out to the part of you that's filled with God and those parts are touching."

The waitress comes to clear the table, prepare it for the main course.

Have I ever loved, I wonder? Love the way Rayna described it, love for my children, of course. But for Tim? Did I ever let myself love the way those others who had husbands did? I listen to their talk of passion. For a moment, I feel a twinge of the regret for the opportunities missed for showing Tim my love that Rayna described feeling for her husband. But Tim is still alive, I think, and—Shoshanna said she saw Tim dancing toward me in the dream. Maybe it's I who should dance toward him.

Usually, when she dines with us, Deborah's lips are in constant motion, crafting snide comments. Few of them are voiced, though. She's learning. On her weekly dinners with us, we've stared her down and ignored her when she starts in. Clearly, she's still having the thoughts, but not saying them aloud? That's huge! Still I can't help noticing that tonight, her lips are unusually still, her sadness and loneliness more potent than usual.

All conversation ends when the food arrives on the tables. For the rest of the time devoted to enjoying the dinner, our table is besieged by visitors from other tables wandering over to comment on the food. I did nothing more than plan the menu with my committee. My chefs from Banquet at the Barn took over and instructed the chefs here on how to heat and present it. Still, I'm warmed by the steady stream of people I hardly know coming over to tell me how delicious the food is, how the Jell-O mold brought back memories, the pigs in blankets and stuffed derma reminded them of this or that affair, how the green-bean casserole was better than any they'd ever had, and the mashed potatoes, the fried chicken and Salisbury steak—

After the dessert parfaits and finger cakes, the entertainment begins. I'm delighted that Maura's COVE Chorus is wildly applauded in spite of her apprehension. Everyone joins in for the choruses of <u>Bye Bye Love</u>, <u>Peggy Sue</u>, <u>Lollipop</u>, <u>In the Still of the Night</u>, <u>At the Hop</u>…Maura looks so happy when an encore is demanded.

When the audience quiets down, Gracie leads her six dancers onto the stage. They perform flawlessly—the Mambo, the fox trot, the Lindy, with some Cha Cha thrown in. An encore is demanded, and "Everybody join in," Gracie shouts. No one misses out as those seated and those able to dance rock the room to <u>Rock Around the Clock.</u>

Gracie, age 72

The way the residents react to my Steppers is heartwarming, but for me, nothing matters as much as the final dance I've been told about. It's the start of a COVE tradition—to end the evening with <u>My Funny Valentine.</u> Sure, the four married couples at the COVE are on the dance floor and the single men have all found partners. Mostly, women are dancing with women, or dancing together in circles.

But some, like me, dance alone, our arms wrapped around the living past. "One soul for all eternity," I tell Ian, who holds me in his arms.

ACT XIII: <u>THIS TIME OF THE YEAR</u>

The Teacher

As if it senses the holiness in the air, the river flows smoothly, through sun and through shadow, as if Time has slowed down, and kindness is in the air.

To Gracie, I send a private dream: Two elves, hoppity, skippity hide-and-seeking within the flowers on the Haven floor. Happy and laughing and life-is-magic-ing in the forever-always of flowers foresting. But forever is never. One elf flits away, one elf left alone. Colors turn black and colors turn white, magic is nowhere and day's turned to night. I stand on the hilltop and say, "and day will follow night, as rain will yield to bow's light."

Scene 40: <u>Jubilation</u>

Advertisement in The Lake Kinde Newsletter

Chew and Chat and Banquet at the Barn will be closed to customers as "the family who are friends and the friends who are like family" of the Rose clan take over Blossom knolls and all that's on it from Thursday, April 2 to Tuesday, April 7 as we celebrate Passover and Easter.

We are grateful to you, our customers, and hope you understand that holidays are family times, and it is truly a blessing that we can provide a suitable venue for our family, our friends, and their growing families. We'll still be here to provide the feast you wish to serve your holiday guests. Directions for ordering and pick up can be accessed on our webpage—or just give us a call.

Have a wonderful holiday.

The Rose Family

Wren, age 72

I look at the crowd gathered for the first Seder. On this night, families sit together, many branches of which haven't seen each other in the flesh for several months. Clouds of happiness and warmth so thick it's hard to tell where one person's happiness begins and the next ends. Except Deborah, who sits scowling at my table. Where else could I put her?

And Gracie. I sense something dark and sad. Loneliness, in the midst of the tight togetherness of her family surrounding her. This isn't the moment to take Gracie aside to talk. She'll be the one to find the moment, if talk is what she wants.

I shake my head, let the joy in the room overtake any sorrow. Look at this room! It seems as if the barn is filled with every race and religion in the world! Passover is a celebration of freeing an enslaved people—something everyone can celebrate—at least when the children are around.

I know from the past what will follow around a campfire, and in the dormitory. The teens, who didn't learn the bitter lesson those of us who were young in the sixties have had to swallow: You can dream and march, give money, preach, sit-in, protest and above all believe that what you're doing will change the world. Maybe it will, a little, but not the way you believed, not the way you hoped.

Words will be thrown around. Names of countries, names of dictators, incidents in our own country, income disparity figures, terms like "human trafficking," "racism," "income disparity."

But for now, for the Seder, Shoshanna's granddaughter, Sunny, leads the pre-dinner service, and the freeing of one People is celebrated.

Our truncated service is over within a half hour or so. How long can children sit waiting for dinner?

Finally, hard boiled eggs in dishes of salt water are served. New life, arising from tears. A nice sentiment, maybe thought of by whoever made up the service centuries ago. It makes me laugh, though, because from the eggs on Passover to Easter eggs, it seems to me as if we're celebrating the start of spring as the pagan people celebrated from the beginning of time.

Hard boiled eggs—proclaimed by one of the toddlers as the best part of the meal—followed by a feast as only the Banquet at the Barn chefs can create.

The Seder ends with the words "Next year in Jerusalem," which to those gathered at our service means "Next year in Peace." Together, we sing Let There be Peace on Earth.

I sit back and survey the crowd. This room: This place of magic, this space where all can come together. This event. Our Jerusalem.

I think of how the childhood friendship I've had with Shoshanna, Gracie and Maura has lasted, without ever an angry word. The way our friendship has extended into a friendship of families that has gown and grown and grown as families expanded and generations grew. I sense the entire assemblage as being one living, breathing organism at peace with itself.

As if an oak rained down four acorns, and four acorns grew into oaks that produced a forest, with all the roots intertwined. Our Jerusalem, our world of peace. As ordinary and miraculous as any acorn. As ordinary and miraculous as people understanding the intertwining of roots and living in peace.

But one acorn is in distress, and I can't quite wipe out my awareness.

Scene 41: Nobody Told Me

Gracie, age 72

I sit, surrounded by family, and friends who are as close as family. Surrounded by love. The Seder goes on around me but I sit, overwhelmed by loneliness. The prayer over wine is chanted by those who know it, and all partake of wine or grape juice. I sip the wine and swallow back a sob that threatens to escape. There should be an empty chair beside me. Ian's chair. To remind everyone. How can everyone sit here and not be overwhelmed by his absence?

Arwen is beside me. How can I reach out to hold my daughter's hand? Ian's hand should be here touching mine, wordlessly communicating love, laughs and "did you notice what he did?" and "I love you's," but Ian isn't here, and that's an emptiness that will never be filled, a wound that will never heal.

Nobody told me this would happen. The service goes on, but my mind drifts into a litany of life for the last four months.

Nobody told me that the first week after Ian died I would float on a raft of relief that his suffering had ended.

Nobody told me that during that week, and a few that followed, I would feel nothing but the love and support of those around me.

Nobody told me that the first month or so would be spent in a bubble, participating in life enveloped in numbness.

Nobody told me about the surges of energy, the frenetic doing and doing and doing and moving to the COVE and engaging in activities and waking in the middle of the night to measure for new furniture, and making new friends, always with people and doing, doing, doing, busy, busy, busy.

Nobody told me about waking hours early with lists and lists and have to and should do spinning in circles on and on with no beginning, no end.

Nobody told me of a cold deep within me, a cold hot drinks and blankets and all the hugs in the world can't warm.

Nobody told me of fragility, of being so light and insubstantial that I'd need wrapping to hold me together.

Nobody told me about sudden sights, smells, songs, memories ripping through my soul in shuddering sobs that scream Ian's name and plummet me to my knees.

Nobody told me of happiness and playfulness and serenity returning. Of passing store windows and seeing my reflection smiling.

Nobody told me a supermarket background song I hardly

noticed would suddenly pierce my smile and make me fight back public tears.

Nobody told me that tears would always be ready, waiting in a box behind my eyelids, waiting for the word, the song, the scent that will lift the box-lid.

Nobody told me that in time, I'd warm from the cold inside, that I'd feel solid, and safe, and secure in myself.

Nobody told me, as I sit here at the Seder table, how fragile that feeling still is.

Nobody told me of the vast difference between loneliness and alone. A phone call can end loneliness. Alone, is alone, even in a crowd.

Nobody told me how easily a person alone could break, even here, even now, caressed by caring, surrounded by love.

Nobody told me, nothing can make a half feel like a whole.

I'm afraid to go to church on Easter. After the sorrow of the Seder, I'm afraid that church, the place I most associate with Ian, will force loud sobs to burst from the depths of my soul in a very public place. Sobs are private things, saved for moments alone. And mercifully rare now.

When was the last? I can't remember.

I put on my finery, get into the car with Oberon's family and am driven by my son from Blossom Knolls to Harvey's Harbor. Arwen and her family are waiting for us outside the church. Aren't Oberon's little ones cute in their dress-up attire? And Arwen's children are so grown-up looking! I latch onto the children, will myself to focus on them no matter what.

We go into the church, the organ playing, incense in the air. It's as it was last year.

Except.

Except that instead of sitting beside Ian, on the aisle, in a row with our children and grandchildren, I sit behind my family. "I need to keep my eyes on the children," I explain to Arwen and Oberon. If I get weepy, just seeing them will remind me of joy."

I wanted to keep the seat next to me empty, but Easter is a

crowded time, a time when every seat is needed. I hold Ian's warm winter scarf in my hands, hug it to my heart, and he is here with me. I feel his spirit cloaked around me like a prayer shawl.

I accept Communion, feel Christ's spirt reborn within me, feel Ian's spirit enmeshed with Christ's. And thank God for the serenity of Grace.

At the Blossom Knolls Easter egg hunt that afternoon, I crawl across the grass and help my youngest grandchildren win first prize.

"Can we tell Grand Da?" Mary Breena, who's only three, asks.

"Of course," I tell her. "Hold up your eggs, children." The youngest—Oberon's children—hold up their baskets. I look to the sky and call out, "Ian, we did it! Your grandchildren and I collected the most eggs!"

At dinner, I tell Shoshanna, Maura and Wren, "I told Ian that we'd won, and I swear, I heard him laugh and say, "Leprechaun luck.

PART FIVE: <u>SEASONS OF LOVE</u>

SECTION B: <u>BEING ALIVE</u>

The Teacher

Smooth current skims o'er the surface of Time, through dawns of tranquility, days of serenity, nights of peace. Four women trust in the water to drift them through hours, with time as a lullaby and space as a playground. I watch, as the current of Time carries the four women through memories of the past to now—the lessons of the present. They do not know, I cannot show the lessons ahead, the jagged thrusts of under-river rocks, the violent vortexes churning beneath falling waters, the broken boughs piling into barriers.

I wrap all I can reveal in a dream: The women stand in the Haven, swathed in tranquility. White on white. Downy feathers drifting earthward.

"Hush, listen," I say. "Time has turned and the time has come. Final Lessons must be learned." I whisper in each one's ear. To Gracie, "embrace vulnerability, accept assistance." To Shoshanna, "forgive, love without fear." To Maura, "trust, believe." To Wren, "Feel your own feelings, welcome them in."

I point to the woods edging the Haven, push my palms outward and a hedge in front of them opens wide, wide enough to see colors making those in the Haven pale in comparison, making the Haven seem but shades of gray. "Behold Om-eh, the world beyond," I say. Scents that set brains afire with joy, and music beyond the range of human hearing. Air soft as angel wings. I watch them reach out as if they could grab everything on the other side of the hedge. I wave my hand, and let the parting in the hedges gently glide closed.

They will yearn. For the rest of their lives, they will yearn. "When your tasks are done, the lessons learned, a key to open Om-eh must be turned, a word spoken," I say to all, then whisper a word in each one's ear, and kiss her awake.

ACT XIV: <u>MY CHILD WILL FORGIVE ME</u>

Scene 42: <u>All That Matters</u>

Wren, age 72

"M-A-R-T. Mart, like the Make-up Mart and my goodness, I got the greatest lotion there, and—"

"Maura, we know what a mart is. Twelve points. I spin the lazy Susan so that the Scrabble board faces Gracie.

"Axle. Nineteen points," Gracie says and spins the board toward Shoshanna, who stares at it for a moment, her eyes darting from mart to axle and back to the letters arranged in front of her. One at a time, she puts down l-i-v-e.

A feeling from nowhere, as if a cold wind is passing through my closed windows, makes me shudder.

"A problem?" Shoshanna asks.

I gather myself and add an s to axle. "Just this," I say. "All I can do. I have no vowels. Seventeen points."

"Just this!" Gracie laughs.

The game goes on. Maura, "kite." Gracie, "wing." Shoshanna, "wings." "Wren, "kite"

"You can't." Maura starts to say.

"I can, no rule against using the same word twice," I say. "Go on, Maura."

The game continues. Shoshanna is picking up a letter to put on the board when her cell phone rings. She looks at it. "My cousin Rachel. I'll call her back later." She puts down a c, is about to add another letter when her phone rings again. "That's the message ring. Hang on." She pulls her phone out of her pocket and looks at it. Her face blanches. I feel her terror. She reads the message aloud: "Rachel. Emergency. Call as soon as you get this." She leaves the table, walks into my bedroom.

Her mother died, I think.

I'm certain my fears are confirmed when Shoshanna stumbles

back to the table, her face ashen. Her mother isn't dead. "She's dying, and she's asking for me. She needs to apologize to me. She needs me to forgive her. I can't do it. How can a human being forgive someone who treats them as no animal should be treated?"

In the frozen bodies, the mask-still faces, I see no answers, nor can I think of one myself. I feel confusion from Gracie and Maura, helplessness from Shoshanna. "Will you deny her dying wish?" I ask.

"I might not—that's the problem. I still love her. She was my mother. Until that moment, she was a loving mother. She may have erased all feeling she ever had for me, but if she's asking for me now, maybe she didn't. Maybe she's loved me all these years."

"So why not go see her, talk to her, and then decide whether to tell her how she's hurt you, or forgive her," Gracie suggests.

"We could go with you," I say. "Drive down to Silver Birches together."

"She hasn't been there for years. She's been on the west coast near her sister, Rachel's mother, who passed away two or three years ago. She's near Rachel," Shoshanna says.

"Jesus—God—would say to go," Gracie says softly. "God forgives and we should, too."

"Maybe you're right. Maybe I need to see her to know. Rachel said it could happen at any time. I could start out and she could be dead by the time I get there. But Rachel said—and I think apparently the doctors think—if they tell her I'm on the way she could hold on until I get there. I think Gracie and Wren are right. I've got to get started."

I go online and work on booking a flight.

Gracie helps Shoshanna pack, while Maura looks up the weather on the west coast and flutters around Shoshanna's apartment.

Another phone call confirms that Shoshanna will sleep at Rachel's house, and that she'll pick Shoshanna up at the airport when her plane arrives.

We decide I'll drive her to the O'port airport, Gracie and Maura will come along.

Shoshanna, age 72

I have a few hours to sleep before I have to get up to make it to the airport. Like a filmstrip unspooling through the night, I relive a childhood of motherly warmth. My mother, my Ima. The sunlight of my life. The sun I revolved around. The sun that warmed me and nourished me, smiled at me and was always happy to see me no matter what I did. The best mother in the world, I thought, back when I was a child. Every time I saw Wren's or Deborah's horrible mothers, I thanked God for my own.

Images flash by of hugs and shopping and warm cookies and giggles over surprising things that set her off—and blind eyes turned toward Abba's abuse. Of Ima believing my lies—of library study sessions when I was going to Tommy's track meets, of day-long art classes in Oceanport when the classes lasted only two hours. Of Ima convincing Abba to allow me to take those classes on Saturday. That was huge, I now realize. Even without Abba's ire, just for Orthodox Ima to understand my need to go to school on the Sabbath. Until it all changed. Until the best mother in the world became the worst.

Scene 43: <u>Let the Sun Shine In</u>

Shoshanna, age 72

The purr of the engine sings me to sleep.

The Teacher

The Haven, its colors bleached to winter's white. I stand atop the snow-swathed hilltop. Around me, predator animals, from eagles to lions to sharks to people. From the distance, transported by song, prey animals come, from field mice and zebras to trout to ravens—and people. The prey animals stand before their predators and sing, "We forgive." The predators lower their heads in acceptance. All walk through the snow, swim in the snowmelt and fly through the snowfall together to the lake, and together, they drink.

Above the song, my voice, One word: Forgive.

Shoshanna, age 72

The seatbelt sign goes on. The captain's voice jerks me from the dream to the tasks of the present. "Fasten your seatbelts and return your seats to their upright position…" I go through the motions, flooded by dread at what lies ahead.

For the half hour it takes for the plane to land and get to a terminal, the time it takes to disembark, the dream weaves its way through my thoughts. A dream for me alone, I'm sure. The word *forgive* tumbles through memories. I remind myself that some of the best things in my life happened because of the worst Ima did to me. And she was a good mother. I run through a list of the times we laughed together, how we would talk in the evening while she washed the dishes and I dried them, how we would laugh our way through stores, how she paid for the "artsy" clothes that were my taste, not hers. I remind myself of how Wren's mother went to stores alone to buy Wren clothes that were never in style, never reflected Wren's casual taste. With each item on the list I see the joy that once was, yet feel no joy. As if the colors of the pre-pregnant past are painted over with a color-leaching veneer of what came next.

Robotic reunion with Rachel in the airport, dinner with Rachel and her husband, Mark, mindless talk. Sleep—with memories of my dream of the Teacher, and "forgive" resounding in my mind.

I try to meditate, but my mind flutters through fantasies of what the day will bring. I breakfast with Rachel and Mark, where we speak of everything except what I'm supposed to be here for.

I walk through hospital corridors, my heart pounding, and stand outside the door to room 115, with "Sarah Friedman" in the name slot on the door. There's still time. I could turn around, call a cab, pick up my bags from Rachel's and take the next flight home. I stand, staring at the door with "Sarah Friedman" on it and wonder what she has to do with the Ima I knew. Will I recognize anything about her? Will she know me? My stomach clenches. I feel my heart beat, my face pale.

I take a deep breath.

And open the door.

The woman in the bed is intubated, cannot speak, but is she even awake? Her eyes are open but she doesn't seem to be focusing on anything, doesn't seem to be aware of my presence.

Again, the thought, I could leave.

It's not the IVs and tubes that make the woman in bed a stranger, nor is it the wrinkled cheeks, the unkempt gray hair. It's the blankness, the emptiness I feel. I walked into the room with all my anger and yearning, all my love and resentment, and feel them whoosh out of me—air escaping from a balloon. I feel only emptiness. I grope for the chair beside me, my eyes pinned to Sarah Friedman. Wait. Hope. For a sign, any sign, that Ima is present.

Feelings bubble to the surface. I stare at the woman lying in the bed. I want to scream, but I swallow the words before letting them out: Look at me. I'm the child you didn't protect. I'm the woman you wouldn't let be your child. I'm the child you declared dead.

I sit for what seems like a long while, my thoughts overtaken by unbidden memories of Abba, and his death.

Shoshanna, age 60

I visualize Rachel fidgeting on her couch, still tied to the wall by the cord of her old phone. Still smoking, I think, as she exhales into the phone. Rachel and I rarely speak—she's five years older than I am. Five years is an eternity when you're a child, and then—

After I was dead to the rest of the family, Rachel made it her business to contact my friends and establish a tie to me. Maybe if we'd lived closer to each other, but—here she is, calling in the middle of the day from across the continent—morning where she is. There must be a reason, and that makes me feel my muscles tighten, and wish pregnancy hadn't stopped me from smoking just as I was starting.

"Your parents were in an accident. Your father died," Rachel says after the obligatory warning that she had bad news. Of course. Why else would she call? But bad? My father dead after declaring me dead?

Hallelujah! I don't need a cigarette. I need champagne! "Well, I can't do anything about that," I say, but I can. I have a cordless phone and I can dance and thank heaven phones don't have cameras because I'm chicken-dancing around the room like a chicken escaping a farmer with dinner on his mind.

"You could at least put on a show and come to the funeral and spend some time with the rest of the family," Rachel says, and goes on to reiterate that Ima was also badly injured in the accident and will definitely not be at the funeral—no possible chance of running into her. I'm grateful she doesn't suggest visiting Ima. She knows my answer.

The thought of throwing dirt on Abba's coffin is appealing. And it might bring some kind of closure, so I agree to come. It's in Silver Birches. Gracie's family still lives there. I can stay with them.

For some reason, I think of capital punishment. I'm totally opposed to it and yet—waiting for Abba's funeral, I understand the solace victims' families must get from watching executions.

I choose my clothes for the funeral carefully. Abba delighted in calling me a slut, so I dress as close to one as I dare without embarrassing myself. A black suit, with a camisole under it low enough for cleavage to show. Not at all my style. Something red.

I hear Abba yelling at me, see the fury on his contorted face whenever he saw me in something red. Shrieking for the world to hear that I'm a slut. Well, Abba, I guess you were right.

I rarely wear my hair in a pony tail, but I can't resist. I carefully gather my hair and secure it with my largest scrunchee, which happens to be flaming red. I don't speak at my father's funeral. I let my clothes speak for me. "Look at me. I was Abba's slut."

I lift a shovel heavy with earth and drop it on the lowered coffin. With the first shovelful, I delight in the thought of throwing dirt on him, as he tossed dirt on me for as long as I lived in his house. But as the grains of soil hit the coffin, the air changes, softens. The sounds of the cemetery silence. A cloud of loving pink surrounds me and the grave. Nothing else exists. I lift another shovelful and drop it slowly into the grave. "May you find peace, Abba," I silently say. "I forgive you."

Shoshanna, age 72

I look at the woman in the bed now. My mother. Feeling nothing, I whisper in the dying woman's ear, "Go in peace. I forgive you." Not the forgiveness of saying "Hey, it's OK that you didn't protect me from my father. No problem that you had me declared dead and thrust me out of your life." Not at all. Forgiveness saying, "You made some really bad decisions, but they came from who you were in this life, and I wish you peace and goodness in your next life, wherever your journey takes you." A forgiveness that cancels anger and replaces it with something soft and serene.

I rest my hand on my mother's. "I forgive you and wish you peace," I say again, in a voice the color of serenity.

I turn from the room, never to see Ima again, with a lightness I haven't felt since leaving her home fifty-six years ago. Forgiveness now filling the backpack where anger formerly festered.

The Teacher

I peer through a scrim to the souls traversing flowing streams, struggle to glean their feelings, to see as humans do.

I watch as Death touches a woman lying in a hospital bed. Watch as Death carries her to Awareness, where she will be washed clean, and readied for the life to come.

I watch Shoshanna, but I also watch her friends at the COVE. When they offered to come out to the funeral, Shoshanna was adamant.

"It's ridiculous. She's going to be buried out here. There's no reason for you to fly eleven hours round trip and be with me at a graveside funeral that's going to last around fifteen minutes. Rachel and her family will be with me. Pax and Dandi understand there's no reason for them to fly out. It's not as if they ever met their grandmother. I'll be fine. I lost my mother when I was seventeen. This is no loss now."

But Shoshanna's friends want to be with her, so I let them.

Shoshanna stands at the graveside, shovel in hand, and feels the loving-kindness of the Universe wrap itself around her like a cloud. A pink cloud, a vision of family and friends gathered around the edge of the cloud, supporting her, feeding her their energy and caring.

At the COVE, Wren puts down the book she's reading, moves to the chair she uses for meditation, and waits. Gracie puts down the pencil she was using to correct her granddaughter's essay, and waits. Maura signals the tenth grade chorus to keep singing and walks out into the hall to wait.

Each alone and yet together, I let them see Shoshanna, shovel in hand, gently sprinkling earth on the grave. I let them hear Shoshanna's voice, choking with forgiveness, yet strong, in a way it hasn't been since she was a child: "You did the best you could, given who you were in this lifetime. May you find peace in the next." She looks down, as if looking into the coffin, into her mother's lifeless eyes. "Till we meet again."

Shoshanna, age 72

I look up, and it's as if I'm seeing through The Teacher's eyes. I'm surrounded by love made manifest: My children, Pax and Dandi and their spouses and children, although they are all living across the land. Wren, Gracie and Maura, though they are all near Lake Kinde. All, all are here, as if standing around me, along with Rachel and her family, who are beside me at the gravesite. It's as if together, they are wrapping me in a cloak of love and warmth, as if the Universe is giving me all the hugs my mother denied me, all at once, for now, for forever.

ACT XV: <u>MIRACLE OF MIRACLES</u>

The Teacher

*I watch, as if I were human and the beat of breaths has stilled.
Watch, as a brook from afar struggles over rocks, watch as it
crashes over the rim of a waterfall, watch as it slides
groundward, watch as it bubbles forward toward four streams,
and merges into a river of love.*

Scene 44: <u>Where Do I Go?</u>

Gabrielle DeLucca, age 34

Lost. Lonely. Alone. Pregnant. That above all. This time, I'm
going to keep it. I remind myself—I've been clean ever since I
found out three months ago. I *will* keep it. But how?

How can I do it when I can't even pay next month's rent, now
that my hours have been cut back and I've lost my full-time
benefits? "It's the competition from the new supermarket," my
boss explained just before closing time. "No one's losing a job—
you're just all going from full time to part time." He smiled—
actually smiled—as if any of us can live on that.

I trudge on feet swollen from supporting my weight for the
past eight hours. Painful step after painful step from Franny's
Fine Foods to the apartment I've been avoiding since I found out
I was pregnant. The place I lived in. I shouldn't be coming here.
But it's where my friends are, and I have to be with them tonight
—and I know they'll take me back when my money runs out.

Arms wrap me in warmth and wipe away my aloneness. Food
—a table with bowls of hot food and "take all you want, it's so
good to see you!" But no! They're not just talking about the food,

they're referring to the buffet in the center of the table: Wine, pills—I can identify every one by its color and shape.

"No thank you," I say, over and over again.

Dessert. The joint being rolled, passed around.

"NO!" I scream, and run from the apartment. Before I can smell it and be tempted and the baby—God, no! Before the baby can breathe the fumes I'm down the two flights of stairs, running into the street, running to my fourth floor walk-up apartment that swallowed almost every penny I made as a full-time cashier. What will happen now? Part time? I can taste the bitterness of it.

The temptress, "abortion." The word floats through my mind. I've done it before. Why not now? "Because I'm going to keep this baby," my heart screams. I tell her "You're not an *it* any more. You're a *she,* and I love you, and I *will* find a way."

I'm Old Mother Hubbard, with a bare cupboard. She had broth and bread. "I have to give you more than that," I tell my baby. I have to eat vegetables, fruit, protein if she's going to be born healthy. But how? For the last two weeks, since going part-time, every penny has been put away for rent. There's nothing left for decent food. I can't do this alone. I try to think of people I know, all the people I've ever known who showed me a kindness or took me in. I cross out the last half of my life on the street. My friends would take me in, but. BUT! Look what happened when I tried—I had to run out of their apartment, out of their lives.

I am so hungry! I open the last can of soup I have. At least it has some vegetables floating in it. I heat half of it and put the other half in the refrigerator for tomorrow. I need protein. The baby needs protein. Eggs? I already had one for lunch. I have six left. Six days. I check the package of hot dogs in the freezer. Five left… I'm so hungry.

I'll eat the soup.

Thoughts of my grandma drift in on waves of sorrow. Grandma, who took me in when the social worker took me away from Mommy Toni's string of "your uncles" living in our apartment after Daddy Clyde disappeared. A different one every night. How dumb did Mommy Toni think I was? A fat lot of good Mommy Toni would do me now. If she's even alive. And who cares, anyway?

Grandma, you took me in and would take me in again. How did you get AIDs? How could you die? They have meds… "Grandma, I miss you." Unstoppable tears fall.

An image of a woman wiping my tears. Someone else I called Mommy. My foster mother. What was her name? The one who took care of me until I was three. I go to the dresser, pull out the envelope hidden beneath my underwear. Look at the picture I haven't looked at for years. The face in the picture I found stuffed into the pocket of my favorite dress when I was taken to live with Mommy Toni. A sudden memory of singing, and the sound of nonstop, fast, fast talk.

My eyes fill with tears. I stick the picture into my pocket.

I sip my soup slowly, so each spoonful lasts in my mouth. Like a blessing, a name comes to me. Like a whisper in my mind. Like a voice from a dream. *"Maura Rossi."* Maybe. I could have heard it, remembered it from anywhere. But it's a name, a hope.

I nuke a hot dog and race-walk two miles to the library. I have to get there before they close. Almost running, jogging. I'm not even sure what closing time is. It could be closed already. I just know, I have to get there. I grasp the hotdog in my hand, nibble a tiny bite every two blocks to make it last.

The library is open! I run to the computer room. Google. White pages. Maura Rossi. Damn! A whole list. I force myself to take deep breaths, gulp for air. One at a time, Gabrielle. One small manageable step at a time.

I try Facebook. No, not her—too young. No, she didn't look like that at all. No. No. No.

My heart stops. Thumps. I tremble. Chills. Mommy Maura's face. Like the face in the picture I found. The picture I hid so Mommy Toni couldn't take it away. Gray hair, rounder face, but yes! My heart races. YES! Seventy-two years old. Seems right. Mommy Maura who told me she wanted to be my always-mommy more than anything. Sorrow crashes down with the memory of how Mommy Maura promised to adopt me, how she let me pick out the prettiest pink dress in the store for my "'doption day."

I blink back tears. Coming home from nursery school. Momma Maura sobbing. Mean, ugly words about something called the Law saying she couldn't adopt me, that I had to go live with Mommy Toni and Daddy Clyde because they were my real parents. They didn't even need to adopt me!

How could anyone expect a three year old to understand? They took me away from my Mommy and made me live with my bad, bad pretend-mommy.

I clear the tears from my eyes and focus on the computer screen. Is she still alive? I read the last entry. Blessedly, it gives an address. "…So I finally made the move and here I am at the COVE on Lake Kinde and my address is… and my phone number is still…"

Lake Kinde! The COVE! A short bus ride away! I'll work tomorrow, maybe they'll break the rules and pay me for what I've earned this week so I can pay for the bus. It's a pipe dream. I know they won't.

I push the thought aside. Let hope take over. I can call now! The library has phones! I explain to the librarian that I have an emergency call to make and—She hands me the phone, sparing me from explaining that I can't afford a cell phone and I couldn't pay the landline bill.

I dial, one hopeful number at a time. Choke on tears when I hear Maura's silky voice, the swift surge of her words flowing into one another on the backs of memories. "Hi there, glad to hear from you unless you're a telemarketer but if you're anyone else leave a message and have a harmonious day."

I choke on a laugh tangled around a sob of pure joy and fear and words wanting to come out in paragraphs. I take a deep breath, and let out one word at a time: "I hope you remember me. My name is Gabrielle DeLucca. I'll try to reach you again tomorrow."

Scene 45: <u>Luck Be A Lady</u>

Wren, age 72

WHAT? I throw my book to the side, catapult out of bed, grab the robe at its foot with one hand, and the strap of my bag on my night table as I lurch toward the bedroom door. If the banging on the door to the apartment means the building is on fire, I'll need the cash, phone, and documents the bag holds. If it's a false alarm, I'm going to stuff someone's mouth with an onion and roast her head. Slippers, in the middle of the floor. Glad I didn't put them away. I slide into them. Make it to the door and peer out through the peep hole.

Maura? Maura with a wild look in her eyes, her pajama top half buttoned over the jeans she was wearing at dinner.

"What's going on?"

She stumbles, lets me guide her to a chair. At the best of times, her lips move faster than hummingbirds' wings and now —"Maura. I can't understand a word. Slow down!"

In a double-time rush, words tumble over each other: "It's Gabrielle. I knew you'd be in bed but I had to wake somebody up and you go to bed later than Shoshanna and Gracie and sometimes you read and forget the time, but I had to call someone because I was watching the news and just started getting undressed when I noticed the red light blinking and I mean who looks at the answering machine on their landline when everyone knows my cell but there it was blinking and heaven knows for how long so I listened to it and it was Gabrielle and no phone number or anything just she'll call back tomorrow and what if I'm not home, I have to—"

"STOP! BREATHE! Are you sure it's really Gabrielle? It's been over thirty years since you've seen her. She was only three when her birth parents refused to sign the papers. How could she have found you?" I feel the weight of the pain Maura endured when her foster child was ripped from her arms, from her life, feel the hope and fear radiating from Maura in tumultuous waves.

"I don't know how she found me and it has to be her, who else could it be and who would say it was her and—"

"Did she say anything about where she is and why she's calling?"

"No. And I—"

"No ands—please, Maura. Focus. Just answer my questions. No or yes and what she said. Did she leave a number or e-address?"

"No"

"All she said is she's going to call tomorrow?"

"Yes."

"Did she say what time?"

"No."

"And you want to be home when she calls but the Summer Teen Theater production is next week and you have to be at school for the rehearsal."

"Yes."

"And teachers can take personal days and my god, Maura volunteers can, too."

"There are no teachers. Everyone's a volunteer. I'm in charge and if I don't—"

More knocking on my door. Shoshanna and Gracie are standing there, both talking at once. "We heard banging on your door and then we heard you yell "Breathe," so we know something happened to Maura. Is she all right?" "What's going on? Maura are you—"

I explain the situation, as well as I understand it. We all remember Gabrielle, all remember the horror of helplessly watching her pulled from the arms of the only mother she'd ever known. All remember the horror of the social worker jamming the hysterical child into the car while we held, rocked, comforted Maura through the initial shock, through days of wailing and weeks of inconsolable sorrow, through years of quiet mourning.

Other memories flit through my mind, of the years before Gabrielle came into our lives, of Maura's brief marriage to Chris, of his death, of her many relationships that all ended when they started to become serious. "Because I can't go through it again. I can't let someone become the center of my life and then lose him again."

I look at Maura and am floored by the courage it took for her to bring in Gabrielle as a foster-with-intent-to-adopt when the child's parents were jailed on drug charges. The shock of the call telling her that Gabrielle's parents had gotten out of jail, and decided not to give up their child.

And. And here we are now, with Shoshanna asking, "Why did she call?"

"Damn it! I don't know! She could be hurt, starving, or maybe she's just in the area for one night and wanted to get together and now there's no chance and no call-back or at least the time she's going to call. I mean I'd give up anything for myself, but those kids have been working so hard, and Grease is —"

"Grease is almost as much dance as music," Gracie says. "If I didn't have to be at Obie's tomorrow—"

"They can manage without both of you," Shoshanna says. For a moment I'm distracted by her newly strong voice. I tune back in. "Mackenzie is a trained dancer—she's totally on top of her role, and she can handle the chorus. She can read dance-notation —all of Gracie's notes. And Allison B. is a piano whiz. She can't lead the band, but she can provide piano background for the singers and dancers. I can't be there. I promised one of my COVE art club members, Loretta, that I'd drive her to her chemo appointment in Oceanport and wait there to drive her home. I think she said three hours, plus all the driving time, so that takes care of the whole day."

Gracie picks up where she left off when Shoshanna started to speak. "I have to be at Obie's to take care of his children. Their nanny went to Michigan to visit her parents, and Obie and Dana both have meetings and appointments or whatever that they can't get out of. I'm the sitter for the week. The nanny's supposed to be back next week."

All eyes turn to me, "I have an appointment with my ophthalmologist. It took three months to get it," I say. "I can't give it up. My night vision is getting worse. Cataract surgery scheduled for next Monday and they have to do measurements or something. Twelve o'clock. In O'port. So I could listen for the phone until ten or so and I should be back by two."

"We'll ask around in the dining hall at breakfast tomorrow," Gracie says. "Someone will be willing to phone-sit for four hours. Or two shifts."

I guide everyone to the door, see Deborah standing in the hall. "Well, you could have invited me in to the party," she sneers. "If you're going to wake up the whole hall you might as well have an open house."

"Not a party, Deborah. An emergency," I say. Deborah Gross, winner of the COVE Volunteer of the Month Award every month since she moved in is about to get another opportunity to win again.

I explain to Deborah that Maura has to be in two places at once, and that one of those places is "right here, in the apartment almost across the hall from your own." I lay it on thick. "We know how overworked you are, what with working with the high school and junior high mathletes down in Markettown and helping half the population here deal with their finances and balancing their checkbooks, not to mention the clean-up committee at every COVE event, so we hesitated to ask you, but we're really desperate, could you possibly…" Maura may hate me for it, and I'm going put a fiver into my unkindness-fines can and feel guilty every time I see Deborah, but—

Maura has her phone sitter for the hours she's at her rehearsal.

I maneuver my arthritic knee joints back into bed, but sleep apparently isn't an option. From my spinning mind to my palpitating heart to my churning stomach to—Schrodinger's cat? Why am I thinking of Schrodinger's thought experiment? The cat is in the box with the poison and the radioactive source. If the radioactivity is detected the flask of poison will open and the cat will die. If not, it won't, and the cat will live. Since quantum theory says all things are possible until observed, until the box is opened, the cat is simultaneously alive and dead. Simultaneously, the caller is Gabrielle and an imposter. Simultaneously, Gabrielle will call tomorrow and she won't.

Simultaneously, I'm trying to fall asleep and I'm doing my damnedest to keep myself awake with thought experiments. My way of distracting myself from what's real. From letting myself feel.

I shift my thoughts to Maura, what she must be going through, and distract myself with memories. Think about the way Maura organized shows on the block—talent shows and concerts, with every child on Acorn Oval included, and at least one adult from each family in the audience. The show she put on to welcome me when I moved to the block. All those children! That's her talent, where she's a superstar. Working with children. Her life now, volunteering in the Markettown schools.

I'm jolted out of my reverie, back to the present, by the screech of a wounded lion.

Leave her alone, I tell myself. Let her get it all out.

Maura, age 72

I pace. Stop. Take off my shoes so I won't bother the woman downstairs. Pace. Back and forth, back and forth, to every tune I sang with Gabrielle, to the vision of every toy we played with together and her smile and her laugh and her tears when she fell and every outfit she ever wore and every word she ever said and I pace and pace and review how careful I was not to get hurt again the way I was when Chris was killed and how careful I was with getting not just a foster child but one I could adopt the minute her parents got out of jail and signed the papers and I had to do it because I wanted children and how could I wait, they said it was dangerous to have a child after you're thirty five because of that stuff with chromosomes being damaged so of course I put in for adoption because my goodness, I wasn't going to get trapped into marrying someone else who could get himself killed or walk out on me and then I couldn't adopt because they said I was too old but then they said there was a baby who'd been abused and maybe there could be permanent brain damage but I said I didn't care so they gave me Gabrielle and—

"NO!" I scream. "NO! NO! NO!" over and over and what if it isn't Gabrielle? What if it's someone who just wants money from me and is pretending to be Gabrielle—maybe she heard her story somewhere or maybe it could be Gabrielle and she could just want my money and "NO!"

"You have to trust," the Teacher said as if it was something I'm supposed to learn. But hasn't life taught me over and over that only a fool would trust? Didn't I trust when I let myself fall in love with Chris, and didn't I trust when I agreed to take Gabrielle with all the possibilities of problems down the pike? And didn't I trust God and lose everything? Chris, Gabrielle, God! All gone. And now they're saying get through tonight and however much time it will take for Gabrielle to contact me and trust she will and what if she doesn't?

The hands on the clock turn slowly so I pace faster. Pace and pace and pace and tell myself what I wished for harder than anything in my life is happening. Tell myself it could happen— Gabrielle could be my daughter again, I could love her again, which is terrifying. I am terrified. What if I do love her again, what if I fall in love with her again, what if I lose her to some man, and she loves him more than me or what if she is already married and is dragging some man here to do heaven knows what?

And what about promises? I promised to take Gabrielle ice skating but that was before—so I promised her and of course that never happened so I broke my last promise to her and maybe she hasn't forgiven me and maybe all she wants is to tell me over the phone how I ruined her life by making her trust, promising to adopt her and take her ice skating and…

I'm so tired, so dizzy. I fall onto the couch.

I see the Teacher atop her little hill in the midst of the

meadow.

"Trust," she says. *"Trust and Patience."*

How can I trust? My goodness, I haven't trusted anyone or anything including God for over thirty years.

Gabrielle, age 34

Impossible for the alarm to be going off. I haven't fallen asleep! The whole night has been spent tossing and turning and remembering and scared and hopeful and praying and—I must have slept, because here I am, with the alarm going off, and no phone. No food. No money. Just an address. An address worth more than all the money in the world.

Miraculously, an address just a short bus ride from George's Gorge. Just downlake. In my mind, I map the landmarks between here and the COVE, think of my trips to Markettown, on the lakeside shuttle, passing it by.

Everything in me wants to get on the first shuttle that comes by this morning, but buses cost money, and I have none. Seventy cents will not buy a bus ticket, even for that short distance. How far? Ten miles? I'm going to have to walk. Even if I go to work first, Donald is a stickler—payday is Friday, and not a cent before. He's not the type who will give in to pleading or tears.

My legs are strong. I can make it from here to my job as cashier at Franny's in fifteen minutes when I'm running late and have to high-tail it, but I'll never be able to do ten miles at that pace. But a half hour a mile? I can make it in five hours. Maybe six, if I have to stop to rest.

It's seven o'clock. I have to show up at work, can't just not be there. Maybe work a few hours before I take off. Maybe get Glen in the deli to give me a few scraps that he can't sell—he's done that before. Even slipped me broken pieces of bread. It will mean walking a mile out of the way, but—I can't just leave them. I'll work until noon, then—can I get there by dinnertime? If I'm lucky, I'll get to the COVE by dark.

And then? Oh, then. What? I can't let myself think of the

possibilities. Out on the street in the cold and the dark, or—No, don't think. Just do it.

Scene 46: <u>This Is The Moment</u>

Wren, age 72

I detour to my mailbox on my way up from dinner. All this junk mail. I must be on every mailing list there is. I stand over the garbage can. This can go. A bill—keep it. Charity—go—it's the tenth envelope I've gotten from this one. Political—toss.

A gust of warm air—the front door opening. Who's that? An old woman. Feeble. So thin. Wobbling. Looks close to fainting. No one else is around. I shove my mail into my tote and rush across the lobby floor as fast as my knees allow. But—it's not an old woman. Not a resident or anyone over fifty. Pregnant? Could it b—? I spring toward her.

Close enough now to see the woman's face. The scar on her chin. "Gabrielle!" I scream. "Oh, my god!" My God, help her! I wrap my arms around her. I'm inches shorter than she is, but she slumps onto me.

Someone calls out "Do you need help, Wren?"

The girl picks up her head and gapes. "Aunt Wren?" she asks. "Aunt Wren, are you here, too?" She would collapse into my arms, land both of us on the floor if the bridge players weren't sauntering toward the card room. I'm not even sure who's lifting her off me—a few people.

Gabrielle opens her eyes, assures everyone she's OK, and "I just need to see Maura Rossi," she says. She leans on me as we take the elevator up to the third floor.

I knock. The door opens. Maura stands there staring, white faced, arms reaching out. Gabrielle slips from my grasp, falls into Maura's hug, sobs, "Mommy, can I come home?"

"Yes, yes," Maura weeps. "Always, of course, what a question. Why my home will always be your home and my goodness, are you pregnant, can I be a grandma and oh, have you had dinner—Wren go get something out of your freezer and defrost it for her, she looks like she hasn't eaten in weeks."

I get back to Maura's apartment with a container of chicken stew. Gabrielle is lying on the couch, explaining that she didn't have money for the bus and that she walked all the way from George's Gorge without eating. I slam the stew into Maura's microwave and hear Gabrielle's whole story, as do Shoshanna and Grace whose doors I kicked on my way in with the food. We gather around Gabrielle, latch onto every word she says. Even Maura is silent. We're all her "aunts," we've all missed most of her life. We all want to know everything, but for Gabrielle, there's only one other person in the room.

"I always remembered you and wished you were my real mom." Gabrielle manages to say, choking on the unshed tears of the years apart.

"Real is what's in your heart, not on a piece of paper." Maura takes a breath, swallows back her own tears. "Welcome home. My goodness, I've been waiting a long time for you and I even have a spare room hoping against hope that somehow you'd find me and how did you do it? How did you find your way back to me? And—"

By the end of the evening, Gabrielle has been fed. Her new room has been set up. Gracie has volunteered to speak to the management of the COVE about hiring Gabrielle to replace the receptionist who is getting married next week and moving to another state. While Maura's busy rehearsing, I'm going to take her for the first obstetrician appointment I can get for her, and Shoshanna will take her shopping tomorrow for maternity clothes.

"And you can call Franny's first thing tomorrow and let them know you're not coming in—ever. Except as a customer," I say.

All Gabrielle can do is cry. "I came here hoping for some help, but what I really wanted, what I really need is a family, and I feel—I feel like—" sobs blot out her words.

No one has to say it—we all know. Maura puts it into words: "I think you're feeling what we all feel, especially me. I mean, I'd almost given up hope but you were in my heart every day and you're part of the family now and my goodness, welcome home! Wherever I live, whether you live with me or in your own place with your baby, my home will be your home, and you never have to worry about rent or food money or anything you want because my home will always be yours, and—"

Gracie cuts Maura off and says it all in one short sentence.

"You will always be cared for, by all of us."

Gabrielle, age 34

It doesn't seem possible. It's too much. This bed, this comforter! The softness! The feel of a full stomach. The food! Even if I could only nibble it. But the way they heated it for me, let me nibble some more an hour later. My stomach will stretch back to normal size. I'll get used to eating!

I try to close my eyes, try to sleep, but memories of how I got here, of everything that happened to me, cascade through my mind, toss my thoughts around in an unstoppable waterfall of time:

Falling off a sled, and Mommy lying in the snow with me, hugging me and rolling, rolling, rolling down the hill and laughing. I remember the laughing, hard to breathe laughing that wouldn't stop. Mommy's hug, I wanted to roll inside Mommy's hug forever.

But forever never came and the hug—I was torn from the hug. I won't go back there, won't remember or relive or think about Mommy crying that she's not my real mommy. Visits to my real mommy, Mommy Toni and Daddy Clyde, sleeping at their house and being bad, bad, bad so they wouldn't want me but they kept me and said "The Law says," and I didn't know who the Law was but I hated him. I still do. What a horrible law!

Because of the law, the day came when the visit never ended. NO. I won't think about that. It's ridiculous to spend the night—

this beautiful, wonderful night thinking of the past. I picture a trash can, throw all the bad things into it: how that terrible lady took me away from Mommy Maura and made me live with Toni and Clyde, how social services took me away and let me live with Grandma—and took me away again when when she got sick. The group home where I had to shop-lift, smoke and drink to get along with the other girls. Then "happy eighteenth birthday, Gabrielle." A hundred and thirteen dollars for a present, collected from the staff, a suitcase filled with my clothes, and a bus ticket to Oceanport. The man who helped me when I got off the bus and didn't know which way to turn in the crowds of people. Drake. Drake who brought me home, slept with me and then started inviting his "friends" over to sleep with me. Drake, my pimp. What could I have done? I had nowhere to go. Jail. That was a place to go for a while. Free food. Then another group home, this time with drugs, drink, and men. Staying with my friends, with drugs, drink. Getting pregnant. Getting out. The apartment. The cashier's job. The cut to half-time.

I take the trash can filled with my past, give it wings, and watch it fly away.

So here I am! Thank you, God! Here I am. I want to get down on my knees and thank the Lord for bringing me here, but I'm afraid Maura will hear me. I lie back against my pillows, tears streaming, and whisper my thanks.

The enormity of where I am—thank you, God. The way these women have welcomed me—thank you, God. I'm overwhelmed. Tears of thanks, a heart so full it might explode. The way they're all acting, as if I'm the most exciting thing to ever come into their lives. As if they're all about to become grandparents. As if I'm a princess about to produce an heir to the throne. As if—as if they really love me. Love ME!—Gabrielle! Love me the way they loved me when I was a child and Maura was my Mommy. I clench my jaw, my fists, double over to keep the scream of joy rising in my throat from escaping on a rushing waterfall of blissful tears.

I replay the evening, hear Maura say again, "You can still call me Mommy. It's OK." Then, softly, as if talking to herself in a voice of wonder, "My daughter, Gabrielle. My daughter, home at last."

Maura's daughter. How is it possible for one person to contain such happiness?

Maura, age 72

I drop to my knees and thank the God I haven't believed in since Gabrielle was torn from my arms.

"But you're there, God. My goodness, I thought you'd abandoned me but it was me who abandoned you and now I see that you were always there and this was the plan and thank you, thank you, thank you and I promise that I will trust you from now on and I'll be a good mother and a good grandmother and my God how is it possible for me to be so blessed? I feel like a balloon, soaring over the world, buoyed by the blessing you've bestowed upon me. The Teacher was right. Trust. If I'd only trusted that this day would come. But it did! And now, for the first time in thirty-one years, all is right in my world."

I'd say more, but I'm crying too loud. I hope Gabrielle can't hear me.

ACT XVI: <u>IF I ONLY HAD A HEART</u>

The Teacher

One stream flowing with the other gets caught in a logjam, is jettisoned back to the rocks and debris of the past. Freed at last, it slides down a slope to a loving lake below.

Scene 47: <u>It's a Hard Knock Life</u>

Wren, age 72

I cram the packages into the freezer. Impossible for me to visit Blossom Knolls without coming home with more food than it can hold. What a weekend! Three weeks to go before my granddaughter Kayla's wedding. Being with all those hyped up people was overwhelming. Being near Janna, alone, was like being in the midst of a tornado. Her combination of mother-of-the-bride joy and anxiety topped by the stress of planning for the most important banquet of her career was quite enough for me to process. But then throw in my friends' excitement and happiness seasoned by Maura's "Look at this list of songs. How am I ever going to get the kids to learn all these songs they're totally unfamiliar with…?" and Shoshanna's "Janna won't let me start decorating until that week—there are other affairs between now and then, and I can't possibly do what I planned to do in one week!" And helping Gabrielle move into her new two bedroom apartment a mile away from the COVE. I'm exhausted by all the happiness!

Everyone's but mine.

I maneuver the last package into the freezer.

Even the joy in the car coming home was a weight, crushing me. *Their* joy. As if Kayla were Shoshanna, Maura and Gracie's granddaughter and not mine. I felt their joy, and—shouldn't I have felt mine? Muted happiness, yes. But not the I-am-so-ecstatic-my-whole-body-wants-to-dance feeling I should be having. As if happiness is a thought, not an emotion.

Emotions. I turn on the stove under my teapot. Do I have real emotions? I'm sure there must have been a time when I could feel. How is it possible for emotions to up and wander away? How can feelings get lost?

Love. I married Tim because I thought I loved him.

I didn't. I liked him. I enjoyed his company. I still do, as I still love his ideas. I'm fond of him. Fond isn't romantic love. I love him as a friend loves a friend. I loved the idea of being in love, the idea of getting married. What I felt for Tim was what I felt this weekend. There were my friends, feeling everything from intense frustration and anxiety to child-like exuberance. I could feel their feelings. They felt, and felt deeply. Always, always, I can feel what others are feeling. Emotions like deeply saturated colors—emerald green, ruby red, sapphire blue. But my own feelings? Over-diluted water colors washed over a white page. Pallid hints of emotion but no—not the real thing. I can feel the symphony of joy exuding from everyone who mentions Kayla's upcoming wedding, and all I can feel is a happiness so distant that if it were music, it would be hard to tell the tune.

The kettle whistles. I pour it, sit in my rocker sipping Wild Orange tea.

Where did my feelings go? As I sit and rock, memories well up, each memory a brick in a wall separating me from my feelings.

Brick—Three years old: A memory of myself, walking with a friend and her mother. I'm crying. My friend has had the same disappointment, but she's shedding no tears.

Mother, "Big girls don't cry." "You should be ashamed of yourself, crying like a baby."

Brick—six years old, first grade rules: Sit quietly. Don't react.

Don't cause trouble. Obey the teacher. Clasp your hands on your desk when you're not writing.

Mrs. Grumbly, "Put down your hand, Wren."

"But I have to go to the Girls' Room really bad."

"Bathroom time is in fifteen minutes. Self control, children."

I have no self control. The pee pours out of me. No one can laugh, or they'll be punished. Mrs. Grumbly yells. I don't cry.

Maybe my tears were turning into pee, I think now, looking
back.

Brick—three, four, five… years old: Whenever I made too much noise. Whenever I disobeyed a rule I hardly knew. Whenever I got my clothes dirty, Mother—"If you don't behave, I'll put you up for adoption." I try to be good. I don't cry.

Brick—: Each time I offer an idea at the dinner table, or comment on something on TV, or in the news. Father—"What a stupid idea." "You're nuts." "Where did you get a crazy idea like that?" When did it start? It never ended until he died.

Brick—elementary school: "Are you first in your class?"

"No, Josie is. She always gets the most stars. I'm second, or sometimes third." Father. Tight-fisted, red-faced rage.

Brick—after the high school algebra state exam: "Why did you only get a ninety-seven?"

"I forgot the plus/minus sign," I say.

Father. Rage on his face. Fists lifted. Words shouted. Father trying to grab me. Running and locking the bathroom door. No tears. No feelings. Can't let it hurt.

Brick—junior high: Books piled on the seat I usually take at the lunch table. "Sorry, Wren, we're saving the seat for Marcia." The three Marcia's are already seated at other tables. The books remain on the seat. I sit at a table where there's an empty chair. The leftover girls' table. The table for the ones who aren't part of a social clique. That's what I am, a leftover girl. It doesn't hurt me. I can't let it hurt or they would see it, and no one can ever see that I hurt.

Brick—junior high: "I was invited to sixteen Bar Mitzvahs," Karen says. "I was invited to eighteen," Shelly says. "I was only invited to twelve," Sue says. "Oh, but you just moved here—not that many boys know you, Sue. How many were you invited to, Wren?"

"One." My mother's friend's son.

Brick—elementary through high school: Teams are picked. I'm left, the only one not on a team. A captain one player short scowls at me. "Wren," she concedes. "Go stand in the outfield," she says if the game is softball. "Stand near Josie or Alice and get out of the way if the ball/puck seems headed toward you," she says if the game is volleyball, soccer, field hockey or basketball.

Bricks—college: "Why are you wasting your time on those courses?" Father.

"You're nuts." Father.

"How is any boy going to ask you out with hair like that?" Mother.

"You're nuts." Father.

"You're eating too much of that college food, you look like a cow." Mother. "But why do you send all those packages of cookies and cakes?" I ask. "So you can share them. How else are you going to make friends?" she says.

"You're nuts," Father says again. And again.

Brick—college. A boyfriend. My freshman year at New England U. Half a dozen dates. He joins me in the dining hall where I'm sitting with a few of my dorm-mates.

Later that evening. Studying in a quiet room. Friends gathered in the adjoining lounge. A phone call for Susie Abel is announced. "Greg Winston just called and asked me out. Who is he? I never heard of him."

I try to close my ears.—"The guy Wren's been dating." Quiet whispers. I won't cry. I won't feel. I won't hurt. He's just a guy.

Bricks—adult years before Tim: I won't hurt. I won't feel. They're just guys. The ones in college. The ones for years afterward when I'm living and teaching in Oceanport. Blind dates. One look at me, and I see on their faces—it's only manners and decency that stops them from turning around and walking away. Others ask me out a few times. Disappear.

Bricks—adult years before Tim, continued: A constant barrage from my parents.

"You're nuts." Father.

"You're too fat…too thin….Your hair is too long…too short…" Mother.

"You're never going to attract a man like that…" both.

"How do you expect a man to be interested in someone who's always talking about books?" the daily chorus.

It's pretty obvious why I don't feel. I relegate the empty teacup to the dishwasher. Try to relegate all the reasons for not feeling to a file labelled "closed," even as bricks pile up and form a wall, even as the final brick, the basic foundation supporting all the rotting answers bubbling up from a fetid fen comes to the surface, and I relive the moment when—

Wren, age 65

"She's in the dayroom. We put her chair in the shade. She said the sun bothers her eyes. She was a little belligerent this morning," the nursing home attendant says.

"Mother, it's me," I say. I haven't seen her for a while, am not sure whether I need to introduce myself or whether she'll remember me—sometimes she does and sometimes she doesn't.

"I know damn well who you are. Why are you here? I told

you not to come," she snaps. It will do absolutely no good to remind her that the last time I came, she thanked me for coming. "I don't want to see you, Rivka." Rivka, the grandmother I was named after. The grandmother she often spoke of over the years as a person she disliked.

"I'm not your grandmother," I tell her. Maybe I shouldn't. At the Dementia conference I went to, they stressed getting into their world because they're incapable of getting into ours. "Therapeutic fibs," the experts say, but I have a feeling Mother knows exactly who I am and yes—I'm right.

"I know very well who you are. You're the one I never wanted. You should never have been born." There is nothing subdued or confidential about Mother's voice. It blares across the room. I can feel eyes turning toward us from all directions.

"Well, I apologize for that," I say, as if I had any choice about being born. I shouldn't ask, but curiosity overrides reason. "Why did you name me after Rivka?"

"Well that's easy." Broad smile smears Mother's face. "Surprised you couldn't figure it out for yourself. She was the most independent woman I knew. Went her own way. You were ruining my life by being born so I certainly couldn't like you. I knew I wasn't going to be there for you, that you'd have to be independent, so I named you after her."

"I need to leave. I've got to get back to Blossom Knolls," I tell her, and ask if she wants me to get her anything before I do.

"Ice cream," she croaks.

I get it for her, feed it to her while I digest the not-exactly surprising fact that I was never wanted.

And feel nothing.

The wall, built long ago, is reinforced by a truckload of bricks.

The last time I see her, she tells me a tale. It's disjointed, hard to follow, but I ask questions and somehow steer her into some semblance of a coherent story. It's as if she's trying to explain something about her life, and I'm deeply attentive. When she's reached what she seems to think of as the conclusion, she looks up and focuses, as if my face is zooming in to the point of familiarity. She looks me in the eye, and in a clearer voice than she's used in months, she says, "I never used to like you, but I see now that you're a nice lady."

"It's too late now," my mind-voice shouts, but aloud I softly say, "I forgive you."

Wren, age 72

I'm washing the dinner dishes hours later when it occurs to me that Mother enjoyed, was nurtured by, needed my failure. Needed proof that she was a far more competent, better person than I am. Snow White, I laugh to myself. "Mirror, Mirror on the wall…" The wall cutting me off from my feelings.

By the time I met Tim, the wall was so thick nothing could hurt me. But if pain can't pierce its way through, neither can ecstasy.

I attack a burnt-on section of the frying pan. Is it any wonder I mistook the simple pleasure I took in Tim's company for love?

Scene 48: <u>See Me, Feel Me</u>

Wren, age 72

I do my slow warmup, push the treadmill to three and a half miles an hour. Mere weeks to my granddaughter's wedding. I can't risk gaining back an ounce. One, and the zipper on my grandmother-of-the-bride dress will never close.

Damn! I should have turned my cell off. No reason to answer it. Let voicemail pick up. It does. I'll listen to it when I've completed my two miles.

Ringing again! Same number on caller I.D. No name. I slow the machine down to two miles an hour, answer the call.

"Wren, it's Grant—official Markettown police call."

Just the sound of his voice, before the name, before stinging words like official and police. My heart pounds, the room tilts, I hit the "stop" button. By the time he finishes identifying himself the treadmill is off. He must be up near Blossom Knolls. What has happened? Is it Janna? One of my grandchildren? A fire?

I'm racing toward the exit, phone glued to my ear. I'm at the door already when he says, "Are you at the COVE?"

Strange question. My heart beats faster. "Yes," I say, and before I can say I'm in the middle of treading and don't scare me, he's talking.

I grasp the handrail on the gym door for support.

"Tim's been in an accident up in Ira's Inlet. They're helicoptering him down to Markettown General. Ira's Inlet called my precinct to find you and get you there. You and Ethan are his medical proxies. I'm on my way—almost at the COVE."

"Yes, yes, on my way up to my room. I'll just change and get my things and—"

"No time, I'll be there in two minutes or less. Meet me by the front entrance."

I hear the blare of the siren as I race into the lobby. Time slow-motions, yet I seem to fly into the screaming car. Questions bounce around my mind like out of control bumper cars tuned up to race track speed. "What happened?" comes out first.

"Freak accident. He was up on a ladder, maybe fixing something up on the roof. The ladder slipped, or he lost his footing, or something. He hit his head on a rock when he fell. Hasn't gained consciousness. There was a hammer on the ground near him. He had a medical bracelet—EMTs called, got his records. They called Ethan—I guess they called him first because he's listed as a doctor. He said he'll get on the first plane out and be there as fast as possible but said you should make the decisions until he gets here. I was in the precinct when the call came in—said I knew you and would find you. I hoped you were somewhere at or near the COVE. If you were uplake, I'd have gotten someone from up there to drive you down."

I sit there, stunned. One question has to be asked. "Was he drunk?"

Grant turns his head slightly to look at me. "There was a half-empty bottle of wine on the ground."

I sit there, totally numb. Even my body has stopped feeling. My mind is an utter blank.

"Wren, maybe you should call your friends—have them meet you there with any paperwork you have—and some overnight stuff if you want to stay with him. I told the precinct to send someone up to Blossom Knolls and bring Janna down and have her call your other children."

I know Gracie is with her children, Maura is with one of her summer music groups, Shoshanna readying a show at an art gallery in Markettown. My mind is a blank. Thank goodness for the contact lists with phone numbers in my cell. Thank goodness I always keep my cell with me when I exercise. In case I hurt myself. The irony almost makes me laugh.

We drive in silence for a while. More crazy thoughts. He'd ticket me if I drove this fast.

Memories flash. Grant coming to assure me and the children that their drunk father had been found and was safe—and that the police would keep him away, keep us safe.

Memories of our decision to split—of years of Thursdays together in person or on the phone. Years of discussions and ideas flying between us and electricity sparked by ideas and the warmth and love—is it love?—that holds us together as long as we live apart.

We're getting closer and closer to Markettown. And I feel. Pain in every fiber of my body, ripping me apart with a silent roar of despair and torrents of held-back tears. I double over. Cold. So cold. I shiver so violently the whole seat shakes.

"Hey, Wren, are you OK?" Grant asks, and I morph most of the way back into the self that can't feel. I take a deep breath. I can still feel, but it's controlled. It's my mother standing over my three year old self saying "big girls don't cry." I sit as upright and still as I can, try to hold myself in, so my shivering doesn't make the whole seat vibrate. I'm terrified, and it's my feeling and not someone else's I'm picking up.

We get to the hospital. I walk, robotic step after robotic step behind the nurse, into the I.C.U. room with "Timothy Rose" in the slot on the door.

He's there, pale, blank, unmoving. Tubes. IVs. Surrounded by uniformed people busy, busy, busy. I push through them, cry out, "Tim, I'm here. I love you. I LOVE YOU." I'm weeping words I haven't ever felt before. Words I owed him from the day we met. Weeping words I'd closed off behind a wall of safety but love isn't safe. Weeping my love, as I've never in my life wept. Not when my children and grandchildren were born. Not when parents and friends and pets died. Not when my love could have given Tim something to hang onto so that he would have had me, not wine. I look at Tim, and along with my terror, I feel to the depths of my soul a love so strong it can't be contained. If only, Tim, I sob. "I LOVE YOU!" I scream as loudly as I can, loudly enough to break through the injury and brain swelling and drugs. Hear me, Tim! "I LOVE YOU!"

"Mrs. Rose," someone is saying. "Come over here. He seems to be trying to reach out. It's the first response we've had."

Someone in a uniform—a nurse or student or intern or resident—pushes me forward, helps me through and positions me next to Tim's hand. His eyes are closed. The blankness of his look! The aura of anxiety I've always felt coming from him is gone, replaced by a sense of calm acceptance.

"No, Tim, no. You have to fight. Come back, Tim," I plead. "I love you. I LOVE YOU!"

I take his hand, feel it tighten around mine, ever so slightly. Doctors behind me are murmuring about surgery to relieve the pressure, drugs to put him into an induced coma to let his brain heal.

"He's an alcoholic," I say to anyone listening. "Be careful about drugs," but I can see by the way they're responding that addiction isn't something to be concerned about.

They tell me my friends are here, but I won't leave Tim's

side, won't let go of the hand that is clearly holding mine. All I can do is hold his hand and tell him, as I haven't in forty years, how much I love him, over and over and over dripping in tears from the heart of my soul.

Just that. Just love, filling the spaces within cells, around cells, in the air and in every atom. Love.

Surgery. They reach Ethan when his plane lands. A new doctor comes in and introduces herself to me, says she's a surgeon, that she's spoken to "your doctor son, on the phone and he said you should sign the papers. We're just going to open a flap in his skull to relieve the pressure on his brain." Tim is wheeled away from me.

My cell vibrates. Mercifully, my children conference call, talk me through the wait while I'm not at Tim's side.

Janna arrives and sits with me. Gracie, Maura and Shoshanna are here.

"Surgery went well," the doctor says. "We're going to keep him sedated for a few days so his brain can heal, then we'll repair the flap we opened. It looks good. Go home and get some rest."

I stay. My friends keep bringing in food. I pick at it. Doctors and nurses come and go. Tim sleeps. I talk to him every moment I'm awake, broken only by visits from our children, Tim's uncle, our friends, family members. I repeat my declarations of love a hundred times over with apologies and remorse for the years when love was lost to me. I read him poetry, talk of the good times we had, the great discussions we had. The love that was there, underneath it all, whether I felt it or not. It came out in caring, but it was always love.

I'm in the midst of reading him a story. I feel—his eyes are open, looking at me, then turning, and taking in the star-studded sky beyond the window. "What are you doing here?" he asks. "It's not Thursday at four, is it?"

Hospitalization. Rehab. There's been significant brain

damage. Tim cannot live independently. The family convenes. "Blossom Knolls. With a caregiver," is agreed to by all— including Tim. He'll be surrounded by Janna, her husband, two of her children, grandchildren, by the Chew and Chat and Banquet staffs, by the home health aide who will be with him at all times. And I will be there, every Thursday at four, and as often as he wants me.

We sit under a tree, outside his cabin at Blossom Knolls. I tell him, as I have every time I've seen him, how at unexplained moments ever since his accident I'm overwhelmed by feelings of love. Not just for him, but for all people, for all that lives, for the universe beyond. As if my love for him has broken open the damn that's held back feelings all my life. "It's hard and beautiful beyond anything one small body can hold."

He takes my hand. We move on to discuss the book we read for today, Siddhartha, the book that brought us together in the park the day we met. We needed something familiar, something Tim will recall.

"To love is to risk losing, and suffering, so Buddhists preach detachment," I say, referencing ideas in the book. "I used to agree. I don't now. Suffering is part of being human. Part of being alive. A part I was missing."

I thank God for letting me risk love, even if it means risking suffering, and take the risk of repeating to Tim the depth of my love.

"Even if it's a Thursdays-together kind of love," Tim says, and starts to speak of the progress he's making toward walking.

It's so much more, I want to tell him, but he's taking the leap himself, saying, "I took three steps today, so Wren, will you do me the honor of walking down the aisle with me at our granddaughter's wedding?"

"If I have to drape you over my back and carry you, we'll get down that aisle together," I promise.

ACT XVII: <u>SOME ENCHANTED EVENING</u>

The Teacher

Streaming together in side by side boats, surrounded by family and friends, the four old souls come to a place of wonderment. For a moment, the turbulence of Time seems to slow, ever-changing Space to freeze. There's a sweetness to the air, colors intensify, insects, birds, and soft winds sing harmonies, emotions rest easily on surfaces that are at other times repellant. Kindness and respect hold All in their grasp, ruled by a Love every captive of Space-Time can feel. All is One. All is sacred in this stilled moment.

Scene 49: <u>Get Me To the Church On Time</u>

Maura, age 72

They don't get it, these children just don't get the music and there they are, all the grandchildren who are supposed to provide the music for the service and my goodness, they're so young so of course they never heard this music that Kayla and Luke want but it's from shows, and aren't old Broadway shows all that high schools can afford to put on without paying ridiculous royalties for new stuff—ridiculous for schools to pay, but right for copyright holders to charge because my goodness, people who write things we listen to forever should get paid forever but now —

"I don't know one of these songs," one of the younger ones squeals.

"Where did you dig these up?" Someone in the back demands.

"Hey, I didn't choose them, I mean it's Kayla and Luke's

wedding and you all know the story of how they met being counselors at an acting camp and fell in love so it's the music they fell in love to because camps just put on old shows so what could I do? It's the music they want and you're all going to learn these songs and you'll be glad you did because they're great songs." I throw up my hands.

"Maybe it will help us if we're ever on <u>Jeopardy,</u>" one of the middle-sized kids laughs.

"Old lady music," someone on the side mumbles.

"And this old lady says let's get going and learn it, all of it, because we have two days before it has to be perfect, and it's going to be!"

Gracie, age 72

Trees? Shoshanna wants me to hang tiny glass prisms from the reachable branches of the trees? And be done in time to shower and dress and get back down to the lake in time for the start of the ceremony?

I trust Shoshanna's vision. Everything she's ever orchestrated has been beautiful, but the trees are already gorgeous, their leaves just starting to turn. I can't envision what she has in mind. She's so busy getting the barn ready—has she been down here to see how the evergreens mix with the reds, yellows and oranges on the other trees? And the way the branches from separate trees entwine, as if their arms are wrapped around each other? Why do they need to be festooned with prisms? Didn't nature do a good enough job? I asked her why when she assigned me this task.

"The wedding canopy," she insisted, and taped X's on the trees I'm supposed to decorate.

It's ridiculous, I think. A wedding canopy? They're not having a Jewish ceremony. And if they were, the canopy would be cloth, not trees. But who am I to laugh? Didn't Ian and I wed beneath a rainbow of flowers?

A sudden wave of sadness. Tears glaze my eyes. No, I won't cry.

"Ian," I say, and I say it aloud because I want to be sure Ian hears me—and there's no one around to hear. "Ian, I want you to listen carefully. I know you're always with me, but I sense you with me sometimes more than others. Well, I need you to be here for me today—and tonight. For you, as well as for me. You've got to dress up for this—or think of dressing up because I suppose dressing isn't a thing you do in Heaven. You could wear a suit—I'm going to wear a lovely green dress that I'm sure you'll like. But in my heart, I'll be wearing my fairy dress, and I hope you'll choose to dress in the leprechaun suit you wore to our backyard wedding, after the suit and white-dress ceremony in the church. 'Twill be a joy of an evenin' Ian, and I'm lookin' forward to dancin' with y' later on."

I hear something coming—it could be a dog or a rabbit, but it could be a child, so I say a fast good-bye and busy myself hooking prisms onto tree twigs. Humoring Shoshanna, because for the life of me, I see no reason for it.

Wren, age 72

I walk—carefully. This damn dress wasn't shortened enough. "I thought you'd be wearing at least two inch heels," the seamstress whined when I complained. There was no time left for her to fix it. So here I am, in my dress, make-up and very flat flats, holding up the hem of my dress, mincing toward to the cabin Tim shares with Darlene, his home-health aide. I knock on the door, thinking how weird that is. If it was just Tim, I'd feel free to push the door open, or use my master key. But Darlene is here, and who knows if she's in the midst of dressing or—
She opens the door, fully dressed. "Wow, Darlene, you look lovely. What a gorgeous dress!" I'm delighted to see her attired for the occasion.
"Since you want me to help out at the banquet with Mr. Tim and with the darling baby during the ceremony, I decided I might as well fit in. I've been itching to wear my prom dress again. It's been sitting in the closet for two years waiting for a reason to be

worn," she laughs.

"It's perfect," I say, thankful again that we found an aide able to participate in all Tim's needs—and in this case—Shoshanna's great-grandson's as well.

Darlene looks at her watch. "He's going to be calling me in ten minutes, on the dot, to start helping him dress. Has he always been like this, Mrs. Wren?"

"Unfortunately, yes," I say. "So I guess I have nine minutes left to chat with him."

"Unless he has something scheduled I don't know about. He's just finishing his snack."

I go into the kitchen, join him at the table. "Can't believe our baby's baby is getting married," Tim says. "I missed so much, so many years when—I just couldn't do it. You and the kids needed spontaneity and I—I need structure. But I should have spent more time with them. I do regret it."

I feel his regret, feel my hands aching to touch him. He must sense some slight muscle movement—the barest lift of a finger. I feel his need to draw away. Speech. Just speech. The only form of human contact he can tolerate. I let words do the job of touch. "Tim, you can't berate yourself for what you didn't do in the past. You are who you are and you did what you could. You have today —that's all we ever have. Today. This moment."

I haven't lost him, so I continue. "The moment before you fell off the ladder, did you have any thought that in the next moment, your life was going to totally change?" I don't wait for an answer. "So grab today. And I do mean, *this* day. If dinner is served a half hour or even three hours later than your schedule, promise me— no—promise *yourself* that you'll stay, and enjoy the moments, and not make Darlene take you back to the cabin. You can enjoy today, Tim. I know you can."

"You don't, Wren. I love your faith in my abilities, but we're solipsists—both of us. We see the world through our own eyes. We might be able to walk in each other's shoes but we can't see through each other's eyes."

He looks at his watch. "And my eyes tell me it's time for me to start getting dressed. "Darlene!" he calls.

I turn from the room with the sad feeling that he's right, that most people can only guess at what others are experiencing, but I can't tell him—I'm not most people. I can do what other people don't seem able to do. I can feel others' feelings. For the first time, it's a thought filled with sorrow. My own.

"See you at the wedding, Tim. I love you," I call on my way
out.

"I love you, too," Tim calls back.

"But I can't live with you," we say in unison, and we laugh, laughter floating on a wave of sorrow, his, and mine.

I call Ethan, whose cabin is closer to mine than Zach's. "I'm sorry to bother you, but my dress is too long and I'll probably fall flat on my face walking through the woods down to the lake for the ceremony. Could you possibly walk with me and catch me if I trip?"

Is that a chuckle? I don't see the humor, but at least he's saying that it will be his honor to escort his shrinking mother, so I laugh, too.

"And I'll bring one of your granddaughters to help hold up the hem."

Shoshanna, age 72

I can hear Maura's chorus singing <u>Get Me to the Church on Time.</u> No one else is on the lake-trail. Everyone else is there already. I lift the hem on my dress and walk as fast as I can in these heels. Wren was right. I should have worn flats.

I get to the back of the "chapel" we set up this morning. Oh my! I had a vision, but this is—the white chairs, facing the sun setting over the lake. The prisms floating on the trees sparkling and reflecting the autumn-jeweled leaves. The children, all with clean faces and wrinkle-free party clothes, facing the audience. Ethan's son, standing to the side with his accordion, playing <u>Get Me to the Church on Time.</u>

Scene 50: <u>Marry Me A Little</u>

Wren, age 72

I hold my breath as Maura raises her baton and the children start to sing. She's always uptight about whether the kids will perform as well as they did in rehearsal, but today—"If they're as bad at the wedding as they've been at every rehearsal, all off-key, and half of them, more than half, not knowing the words to the songs and my goodness, they never heard these songs before and I YouTubed them and played them for the kids and you'd think the melodies would have gotten through to them but..."

But here they are, all on key, with the words clear and correct.

Emily, the friend of Kayla's who was ordained online so she could conduct the service, speaks. I look at Tim, sitting next to me in his wheelchair in the back row. We're up first. We'll walk down the aisle and sit in the first row on the left. During rehearsal, Darlene insisted on pushing his wheelchair and I walked alongside, holding his hand. The problem now is that Darlene is sitting across the aisle holding Shoshanna's great-grandson, ready to run back to the cabins with him if he starts to fuss. How am I going to push Tim's wheelchair and keep from tripping on my dress with only two hands available where four hands are needed?

Emily announces "Kayla's grandparents."

She should say "Kayla's grandmother, about to fall flat on her face."

I get up, turn toward the wheelchair beside me on the aisle. Tim is standing! Getting out of the chair! Zachary appears out of nowhere and hands his father a walker. Tim turns to me and says, "Surprise. Been practicing. Come on."

We didn't have music during the rehearsal. Maura insisted our song would be a surprise. What song could she possibly have found for a pair of can't-live-together-good-friends? She signals us—the chorus is ready. Are we?

We hesitate, inch forward. One careful step at a time. Tim

struggles with each step, struggles to trust the walker to hold him up. I clutch the hem of my dress, struggle to trust that I won't trip on it. They should be playing a "struggle" song.

Everyone else is laughing.

The chorus is singing. Tim and I look at each other. <u>Small Talk</u>. I giggle, Tim chuckles. The idea of no small talk between the two of us sums up our whole relationship. "We have something so much grander than small talk," I whisper to Tim. He can't turn his head. He has to focus on each step, but "yes," he says.

Janna's in-laws walk behind us, followed by Luke's maternal grandmothers and paternal grandfather. They come down the aisle together, three abreast, their steps in sync, both sides of his family blended into a loving unit.

When the grandparents are all seated, Emily invites the audience to stand.

Maura raises her baton, plays a chord on her keyboard and the chorus launches into <u>Marry Me A Little.</u> Luke fist-bumps in victory as he strolls down the aisle between his parents. He stands beside Emily and fidgets as his parents slip into their seats.

The chorus begins <u>Sunrise, Sunset</u>. Kayla, radiant in her frothy gown, floats toward him between Janna and Scott.

I look at Tim. Where did the years go? Our first baby. I look at Janna and relive my anxiety as I changed her diaper for the first time. I see her first skinned knee, her graduation from nursery school and then a heartbeat later her graduation from college. And now—she's the mother of the bride, freeing her baby bird to fly and build her own nest. I picture Janna handing me a tiny bundle swathed in pink. "Kayla wants to meet her grandma, Mom," Janna is saying.

And now she's swathed in white froth, gliding down the aisle. My little Kayla. Tim wipes his eyes. I hold out my hand. He takes it. Holds it. A moment to savor. A moment for memory.

Wedding vows. Poetry Kayla and Luke wrote for each other.

Emily declares that by the power vested in her by the state, they are now "man and wife." Still sexist language, I think and throw away the thought. Not for today. Today there are not one, but two glasses wrapped in towels, placed on the ground in front of Kayla and Luke. "To remember," Emily says, "not just the sorrows of the past, but to remind us as we feast today, others will go to bed tonight hungry. As we sleep in our cabins or the guest house tonight, others are homeless. As we turn on our faucets and get clean water, breaking the glasses reminds us that not all are fortunate enough to do that. As we rejoice in the multicultural, multiracial gathering that we are, let us remember that elsewhere, the walls separating us from others are still rampant, even in this country."

Emily nods. Kayla and Luke look at each other, hold hands, as each breaks a glass with a resounding stamp.

Emily turns to Luke. "You may now kiss the bride."

The mood is broken when one of the children pipes up "Don't they have to come up for air?"

It's a cue for Maura to sit down at her keyboard and lead the chorus into a jaunty version of From this Moment On, as Kayla and Luke join hands and skip-dance up the aisle, onto the path toward Banquet at the Barn, followed by the rest of the assemblage.

Scene 51: Always, Always You

Shoshanna, age 72

I have a strange feeling when Emily brings the ceremony to closure. I can't put a name on it. Anticipation? A combination of fear and desire? Something is going to happen. It's been there throughout the ceremony, simmering behind the rollercoasting of nostalgia and utter joy. A feeling of something unexpected, something that doesn't belong, but in a good way. Someone is watching me. Eyes that should be facing front have been glued to me throughout the ceremony. I can't turn around, that would be rude, and besides, I don't want to take my eyes off Kayla and Luke. There's a cloud of love—Wren talks about auras like clouds, and she's talking about individual people. The aura I'm sensing is pink and yellow and warmth and joy and love spreading over the crowd. Peace. A sense of Oneness. The sense of Love, and whoever is staring at me is a part of it.

I wait in my seat as Kayla and Luke prance up the aisle, guests streaming behind them starting from the first row. I'm three rows from the back. I wait. The eyes are still on me. I step into the aisle.

My heart stops.

There, coming toward me, is the man who hasn't taken his eyes off me, moving from the other side of the aisle. He stands beside me. In this single instant, fifty-four years dissolve. I want to shout his name, throw my arms around him, but I can't breathe. Can't move.

"Little Momma? My god! It *is* you! I had to get close enough to be sure. It's been so long."

"Leaf?" I manage to say. The man with short gray hair morphs in my mind into a young man, long black hair pulled into a loose pony tail, wearing a tie-died shirt over paint-splattered jeans. A face hidden behind a bushy beard. His eyes. His green eyes are enough. Leaf. My magic Leaf.

We stand there, looking at each other, blocking the aisle.

I sense the impatience behind me but am paralyzed, incapable of moving. Leaf takes my hand and pulls me back into the row of seats he just left, helps me into a seat.

We sit there, look into each other's eyes, say with eyes what words can't. Then the words start to flow—the mundane words of his marriage, his wife's last days in hospice care, his three children, five grandchildren, his job—retired now—as a shop teacher/carpenter. "It's Lee by the way. Lee Oakleaf, Luke's uncle. Please, keep calling me Leaf."

"I guess Little Momma won't do anymore. It's Shoshanna Free. I had another child, a boy, Pax. I'm not a seventeen year old Momma to be. Dandi Lion is a grandma now." I give Leaf a capsule version of my life thus far.

"My grandchildren used the cradle you made Dandi. Now my great-grandson is using it. Every time I see it, I think of you. That was my one regret when I left the commune. That I wouldn't see you again. I had to get away—the smoke in the house scared me. I didn't want my baby breathing it."

I take a long breath, bet everything I have, everything I am, on hope, and let my heart speak. "Who knows what might have been."

"Maybe what might have been can still be," Leaf says.

Silently, I reach for the hand of the gentlest man I've ever known. The one man I could talk to comfortably, armor-free. Something stirs in my body. A feeling once wrong, dangerous. Now, it feels right, and good, and welcome.

"But how can it be?" I muse, "with me on the east coast and you on the west?"

"As I said, I'm retired. No ties. I can move anywhere, any time. We'll work it out. Now, let's deal with the seating arrangements so we can spend the rest of today together."

I laugh. "As a matter of fact, it's already done. I wrote the table cards. My friends, Maura and Gracie, Maura's daughter, Gabrielle, and I will be seated with Laura and Mark Oakleaf, Jodie Creek, and Lee Oakleaf."

Scene 52: <u>To Life</u>

Wren, age 72

Who's that man Shoshanna is with? There's no one I can ask. Gracie and Maura won't know. When the reception on the terrace ends and we go into the barn for the banquet, I'll ask someone at my table. I know Luke's grandparents and two of his aunts and uncles will be seated with me, Tim and Darlene, my brother Geoff and his wife and—I swallow my disgust at the thought—

my cousin Deborah.

Someone blows a bugle—must be one of the teens. I laugh. Mess call. The doors of the barn swing open. There's a rise in the volume of talk, and then a hush, a sudden silence as people draw close to the wide entrance and see inside. A gasp, and then a quiet whispering, as if they're entering a sanctuary or a museum. The barn turned into the Haven in all its impossible beauty, impossibly captured by Shoshanna's paint. The Haven, but in keeping with Kayla's "spring into fall" theme. Trees shedding spring flowers, as if they were leaves.

I go to my table. Luke's relatives look befuddled. Why are they seated with us, why not with their family? They're too polite to ask, but the questions are there. As soon as we finish introducing ourselves, I explain.

"It's a family tradition. It started with Geoff, when he married Trisha, the girl next door."

"Plenty of room for a big backyard wedding, if we used both of our yards," Trisha interjects. "We agreed that everyone on the block would be invited."

She takes a sip of champagne. "Now, you have to understand that our street was half Jewish, which is what Geoff is, and half Catholic, which is what I am. When we started dividing the older guests for their tables based on who was friends with whom, we realized that one Acorn Oval table would be all Jewish, the other all Catholic."

"Because that's how our parents socialized," Geoff picks up the story, "and to their utter disgust we re-arranged the tables by having the odd numbered houses sit at one table, the even numbers sit at the other."

"It ended up," I say, "with people becoming friends who had lived next door to each other for years and never before socialized. When it came time for Janna and Scott to wed, they decided to mix their relatives, and it's been a family tradition ever since. So—welcome, we're all one big family now."

As dinner progresses, we start to meld. Different customs, different foods—we discuss them all. By the middle of the meal,

I feel as if I've been spending the evening with friends. I'm comfortable enough now to ask the question that's been a twitch in my thoughts all evening.

"Who is that gentleman—the one with the gray hair, dancing with the woman in the blue chiffon dress?"

Luke's grandmother smiles. "Why, that's my cousin Lee," she says. "Lost his wife two years ago." She sighs. "They do look lovely together. Dancing as if they've been practicing all their lives."

A chill runs through me. A chill that has no name. A thought too swift to catch. *Breaking up our group.*

Shoshanna, age 72

The dance music plays on in the distance. Together, Leaf and I walk through the gardens around the Barn. Stop. Watch. Over the mountains on the other side of the creek, a large orange moon rises. Smiling. I feel Leaf's arms around me. Together, our hearts beating as one. There's something sacred about this moment. Something about this night is pure love, pure peace. Togetherness with each other and with the universe. Holiness.

ACT XVIII: **HAPPY TALK**

The Teacher

Four streams meld in a placid pool. Sunlight floats down and warms the waters. Brooks and creeks feed into the lake and all is tranquil, all is quiet. Until the lightest of summer rains kisses the waters without clouding the sun, and a rainbow bursts forth across the sky.

Scene 53: **Feeling Good**

Wren, age 72

My caller ID is shouting Josie's name, but I'm on the other side of the room. I lunge for the phone, manage to hit the green button before she hangs up.

"Josie, I'm so glad to hear from you," I say.

"Then you'll be glad to hear I'm going to be visiting my daughter for the next week. Coming in for the Columbus Day weekend, and staying for a while because my grandchildren are going to be performing at The Lunch Club the following Friday."

I laugh. "The Lunch Club is really a soup kitchen," I start to explain, but she cuts me off. "My granddaughter explained—she said 'it's how they're helping people who can't afford food and iphones.' They're charging for the event—$5 a ticket plus $15 if the family guests want to buy lunch. I guess that's where the COVE comes in."

"Actually, it's my banquet chefs who are catering it, but yes, the COVE is providing volunteers to serve, help out in the kitchen, whatever. And Maura's Happy Tunes from the elementary schools are providing the entertainment." I push my unfolded laundry aside and plop down onto the couch.

"Great. We'll all get to see you, then," Josie says. "I was hoping, since I'll be around for a while, that we could get together for lunch, or dinner, or an afternoon hanging out—whatever. You, me, and any of the others who can join us.

For a nano-sec I'm dismayed, then I realize there's really no problem—just a fabulous solution. "Josie, I've got bad news and good news. Bad first—none of us is going to be around from Friday through Tuesday of Columbus Day week. We're leaving on Friday, the day after the Lunch Club event, for a weekend at Blossom Knolls. Everyone in our families who's off for the Columbus Day vacation who lives near enough to make three days together worth the travel. The good news is that more than half the family can't make it, so there are plenty of empty cabins—enough for you and however many family members you want to bring with you. Whatever your grandkids' ages are—they'll find friends."

Josie speaks to her daughter, calls me back. They'll all come up on Friday morning, have to leave after lunch on Monday. "So I'll see you then—with my daughter Carla, her husband Bob, and my precious grandkids."

The weather couldn't be more perfect. Everyone under seventy seems to be out and about enjoying fishing, boating, tennis, volleyball, kickball. Someone has organized races and games for the younger ones. We, those of us over seventy, are taking a walk. There are parts of the property Josie hasn't seen. We pass by Tim's cabin just as he's coming out. Cautiously stepping, leaning on his cane, Darlene close beside him.

"Morning ladies," he says. "I was just about to get some exercise. Care to join me?"

Our walk slows down to a leisurely stroll. I can see Tim getting tired, breathy, as we walk. "Want to stop for a while?" I ask.

Tim checks his watch. "I think I can make it down to the lakeside. I'll just rest for a few minutes there," he says.

Rest sounds good to my knees. We get to the lake. Darlene helps us pull the wooden chairs into a semi-circle. We continue the discussion of current events until we start repeating ourselves.

"So," Tim says, "I know how Wren, Shoshanna, Gracie and Maura got together, but where do you fit into the picture, Josie? Are you also one of those acorns?

Josie laughs. "No, I didn't grow up on Acorn Oval, but as a matter of fact, I did grow up down the street from the apartment building Wren and Shoshanna lived in when they were very young. I was even in their class in elementary school—one of four quote unquote Negro children allowed into the class for quote unquote bright children."

"Lovely system of de-facto segregation," I interject.

"I used to love watching Josie jump rope during lunch time," Shoshanna says.

"I was just plain jealous of everyone who could do Double-Dutch. Two ropes!" I say.

"No one would have stopped you if you'd come over to try it," Josie says.

My friends laugh. "My feet stopped me. I couldn't even jump in without getting caught in a single rope." I turn to Tim, Maura and Gracie—"You should have seen Josie. She was the champion. Feet faster than a cheetah's and height—sometimes I wondered if she had wings."

"Things of the past," Josie says. "I doubt if my knees could do it now. Anyway, to continue the story, they moved to Silver Birches and so did I, and we met again in junior high."

Shoshanna raises a fist in the air and shouts, "LOPs forever!"

Tim looks at her as if trying to determine where her mind has flown.

I pick up the story. "When teams were picked in gym class, Shoshanna and I were always the last ones picked. Never on the same team. Always the two leftovers the captains had to take. Well, there were some girls in our gym class who were just plain mean. So one day, after I'd accidentally tripped the most popular girl in the crew, they came to the lunchroom carrying loaded trays, and started bumping into girls at my table—who were all terrible athletes. Milk spilled on one of them, a few strands of spaghetti landed on my hair—and so on."

"But you got back at them," Josie says. "You should have seen them. The next day, they stood up at lunch, called for quiet. The tallest one climbed up onto a table and held up a sign— Shoshanna must have made it—a whole piece of oaktag with large letters covered in glitter—*The Last Ones Picked Club*, and in smaller letters, *L.O.P.s meeting here.* Everybody just stared. No one knew what to do. Wren and I were in a lot of advanced classes together—Shoshanna was in some, too. We did projects together. Wren would have been one of my best friends if our mothers hadn't made an outside-of-school friendship all but impossible. So I looked at the girls at my table—and yes, we were all African American. It's how things were back then. I said "Let's go." So we took our chairs and put them around the L.O.P.s table, and then brought our trays over to eat with them."

"And everyone else saw the best athlete in school and other great athletes coming to join us and some kind of miracle happened." Shoshanna says. "By the end of the lunch period the bullies were sitting by themselves, and everyone in the room was a L.O.P. I found a way to make L.O.P. pins, and almost the whole school started wearing them."

Tim looks at his watch. "Time to head back," he says. He and Darlene start walking. "We'll catch up," I say, because there's more to discuss about how the L.O.P.s incident broke the social/ racial barriers in Silver Birches Junior High, paving the way for our lasting friendship.

We're distracted by a shriek of pure joy coming from the other side of the wooded trail down to the lake. Two women are running toward us.

"Gabrielle!" Maura yells. "Are you OK?"

"Carla," Josie simultaneously calls out to her daughter, "What's up?"

Gabrielle and Carla plop down onto the grass in front of us, streams of speech pouring from both mouths.

"Carla," I start to say, but the joy I feel radiating from Gabrielle, as if the woman has turned into the sun itself, tells me this is her story. "Gabrielle, tell us what the commotion is about."

Gabrielle looks at Maura. "Mom, Mom, you know how you said you'd look into adopting me now—an adult adoption? Well, see, Carla recognized me from when I worked at Franny's Fine Foods, and I ended up telling her my story and oh, Mom! Carla is a judge, and she said all I have to do to get adopted is for you and me to fill out some forms and find a judge to make the whole thing official. And then, oh, Mom! she said she can do it and why not this weekend while we're all here?"

"Do you have the forms?" Josie asks.

"I don't. My laptop does." Carla turns toward me. "Do you have a printer?"

"Get your computer and meet me at the small cottage behind Chew and Chat. The office."

We get the document printed. Multiple copies in case anyone makes a mistake. Carla is ready to have Gabrielle and Maura sign on the spot, but I have another idea. "Can you wait until tomorrow? We're having a barbecue tonight, and if it's anything like barbecues of the past, everyone is going to get their food and scatter with their friends into little groups all over the place, but if we wait until tomorrow night, we can have a real celebration—a banquet that everyone can partake of together."

"I've waited my whole life. I can wait one more night," Gabrielle says.

I'm not sure if Maura can, but she goes along with the plan.

Scene 54: <u>Adoption Dance</u>

Wren, age 72

Somehow, Maura manages to stay calm until it's time for the event. The teens organized the younger children and together they filled the barn with flowers. Working without Maura, the chorus practices Ever After from Into the Woods to promise the "happy couple," as one child puts it, "a happy future."

"So why don't we make it a wedding ceremony?" one of the kids asks, and Carla thinks it's a great idea.

Gabrielle and Maura insist on writing their own vows.

Gabrielle goes first. "I promise to be a perfect daughter, to take care of you if you ever need care. I promise to be home by curfew, to clean my room, and to put the cap back on the toothpaste." She waits a moment for the laughter to end. "I promise to be a good mother to your grandchild, to let you spend as much time as you want with her, and not to stop you from spoiling her. Above all, I will love you no matter what—and I will not let a day—no, not an hour or a minute go by without being grateful to have you in my life. I love you, Mommy."

Maura starts to speak, her voice shaky, tears threatening to spill. "I promise to be the mother you've always wanted. Oh, Gabrielle," she says, and wraps her daughter and coming granddaughter, in a tight hug.

It's probably the shortest statement Maura ever made, and leaves everyone in happy tears.

Carla officiates, has Maura and Gabrielle sign the official document, and declares the two "Mother and Daughter."

Confetti fills the air, held aloft by jubilation.

Music, dancing, a sumptuous feast, champagne for the adults, bubbly grape juice for the youngsters.

Outside, a full moon shines down, and later, fireworks from across the lake light the sky. As if the whole world is celebrating what was always meant to be.

"What a coincidence," Josie says as a burst of glowing flowers fills the sky.

"My goodness, what about the coincidence of Carla being a judge, and having access to the paperwork, and what about just being here this weekend, and Carla recognizing Gabrielle just from working where she shops, I mean, it's as if everything that ever happened was coincidences and how—.

"Maura," Shoshanna interrupts. "I truly believe no coincidence is ever coincidental. Things happen as they are meant to. We just have to be open to them, ready to run with them."

Yes, I think. The coincidence of sitting on a park bench and meeting Tim. The coincidence of—something every day. I wonder how many coincidences we've all missed because they seemed inconsequential, or were never noticed. And how many coincidences we've caught and grabbed and made part of our lives, like the miracle of this weekend.

Shoshanna, age 72

I tie a ribbon around the box. I'll hold it until everyone is here. If I give it to Maura—it's safer if I hold onto it. The big thing will be to get Gabrielle to come up here to my apartment. It was Wren's idea. "We can tell her we're coming back to my apartment because Janna needs us to try out a new kind of cake her guests want for a wedding next weekend. So I guess we'll do it in my apartment. The gâtau château will be in my refrigerator."

"But you can move it to mine," I insist. "I have lots of space in my refrigerator and it will be easier for me to decorate my apartment, given that I live here." So here I am, tying ribbons around the box—and around my apartment.

Wren, age 72

"There's a perfectly good dessert here. Why do we need to go upstairs?" Gabrielle asks.

I explain about trying a new cake for Banquet at the Barn.

"But I have a thing for rice pudding. Can I grab a cup and bring it upstairs? I can try your cake tonight and leave the rice pudding in the refrigerator for later—or breakfast."

I assure Gabrielle she can have her rice pudding any time she wants—in fact, we'll all bring some up to store for her.

Shoshanna opens her door, invites us into a balloon, ribbon and flower filled partyland.

"What's going on?" Gabrielle asks.

Maura's babbling interrupts anything else Gabrielle might have wanted to say. "Wow! I like the oak tree in the middle of the room and all the acorns around it, and look, Gabrielle, each acorn has a name on it and here's one with your name," Maura says. She points to a large one under the tree.

Shoshanna slips the box she wrapped into Maura's hand.

"This is for you, Gabrielle, to welcome you into our family. Go ahead, open it already." Maura pushes the box into Gabrielle's hand, starts opening it herself mid-transfer.

Gabrielle gets it open. Gasps. There, on a gold chain, is a gold-plated acorn, almost identical to the ones Shoshanna, Maura, Gracie and I are wearing.

I see questions in Gabrielle's eyes as I help her clasp the chain around her neck. "We all grew up on Acorn Oval," I say. "When we were sixteen, we decided that instead of other gifts, this is what we'd give each other. Kind of a pledge we'd always be together, like a special kind of family. Acorns. We called ourselves Acorns. So we bought them at the same time, but no one was allowed to wear it until her birthday.

Maura picks up the story. "Then some of us started having children and my goodness, we couldn't do anything for the boys but when the girls had their Sweet Sixteens, we kind of initiated them into the club and gave them acorns to wear and then our daughters-in-law got them as engagement gifts and then granddaughters got them when they turned sixteen and my goodness, you're more than sixteen and it's your turn and you have to wear it and swear the Acorn Oath and—"

"Acorn Oath?" Shoshanna, Gracie and I chorus.

"There is no Acorn Oath," I laugh.

"I've noticed that sometimes Mom gets carried away," Gabrielle says.

"There's one more thing," Shoshanna says. She goes into her bedroom, comes back holding two tee shirts. She hands one to

Maura and one to Gabrielle. They hold them up for all to see. Gabrielle's has a picture of Maura on the front, with "My favorite Mom" inscribed on the back. Maura's has a picture of Gabrielle on the front, with the back proclaiming her "Number one daughter."

I go into the kitchen and bring out the cake. A fairyland castle, with a drawbridge and turrets and chocolate covered acorns all around the base.

Three take aways from tonight:

1. The cake will be placed on the Chew and Chat menu and be a Banquet at the Barn option.

2. Rice pudding is still Gabrielle's favorite dessert.

3. Gabrielle will never take off her acorn necklace.

ACT XIX: <u>AS LONG AS HE NEEDS ME</u>

The Teacher

A dream: A group of people, faces indistinct, identities unclear. Laughing and playing in a sand-covered park shaded by palms. One person suddenly seems shorter. "She's sinking," another calls. The others gather round as she sinks further and further under the sand. Carefully, they come closer, carefully, they reach for her, come close enough to grab an outstretched arm. But "No, no," she calls, almost gaily. "I can do it myself. I don't need your help." She scratches and claws and sinks, and sinks, and sinks, and...the others walk away. She has disappeared.

A moment later, the dream shows the moment she first begins to sink. Others gather round. Carefully come closer, reach for her. She stretches her arms back to them. Someone grabs one arm. Someone else grabs the other. People behind them form chains, pulling, pulling. Slowly the woman rises out of the sand, until she is out, safe, grateful, alive.

Scene 55: <u>I Cain't Say No</u>

Wren, age 72

My friends are flummoxed. Who was that about? What was that about? What is the quicksand a metaphor for?

"It didn't look like any of us," Gracie says.

"Maybe it's a metaphor for Markettown," Maura says. "My goodness, I mean what's happening to the schools there is a disaster and a half and the government could take over or something, there has to be a way people can band together to help the school or, well it's clear to me, things are so bad the whole district is sinking down to where no kids are getting any education and…"

"And you could be right," Shoshanna says, "maybe it was about the people in Markettown. How they have to band together to save their schools. Maybe the dream came to us to tell us to organize saving the system."

"I'm sure it was about people," I say. I don't add, I'm sure it was about us. One of us is drowning. Why else would we have had the dream? I just don't know who.

Gracie, Age 72

Elves have gotten into my sheets and totally tangled them. Serves me right for not making my bed this morning, but I was in such a rush. I straighten the sheets, get back into bed, turn toward Ian's picture on my night table.

"So Ian, here it is the end of October, when the school year has settled into a routine, and everything there is changing for me. They've asked me to do something new at the school, and it's for a horrible reason, but—Am I being selfish? Because it's bringing me great happiness. Great, great happiness.

"Let me tell you what happened: There was an accident—it was in all the newspapers. I didn't know the woman—Rebecca Dickenson. She was pregnant, walking with her wee lad, I think Charlie was his name and he was three. Ian, would you believe in this town there's a gang, call themselves the Red Stars, and another gang, the Yellow Champions and they were having a fight with Rebecca and Charlie right there in the middle of them. She tried to pull Charlie into a store but he wrapped himself around her leg so she couldn't move and—oh, Ian, she was shot and killed and Charlie was killed, but the happy part of the story is that the paramedics did a Caesarian right there in the ambulance and the wee babe survived.

"I read the paper and I grieved for the moment, but there's so much in the news. Something new breaking my heart every day. But today Gerard Pinkston, the high school principal, called me into his office while I was giving a heating pad to a twelfth grader who might have had menstrual cramps but I think just wanted to get out of math.

"'Grace,' he begins. 'Grace. That's what we need. Some grace in this situation.' Frankly I had no idea what situation he was talking about until he mentioned Rebecca Dickenson. Then he asked if I know Buddy, which of course I do, he's the custodian and the kids just love him. Always helpful with anything anyone needs, and a charm with the kids who teachers can't control. They call him the custodian but between you and me he's like a combination of a psychologist and chief discipline officer. Calms kids down with a look. Anyway, Gerard goes on telling me Buddy is Rebecca Dickenson's husband. I had no idea—we call him Buddy, don't use his last name at all. Then he keeps talking. It's hard to hear his words, my heart is breaking so. He tells me Buddy hasn't come to work since the accident, but he's ready to now, except he won't leave the babe. The teachers offered to pay for day care or a nanny, but Buddy won't hear of it. He'll come to school only if Becky—that's the baby's name—can come with him.

"Ian, I felt my heart lurch. I actually reached out as if I was reaching for someone to place a babe in my arms. And that's just what he did. Metaphorically. 'Someone in the elementaries mentioned how good you are with children and that you've had experience with babies,' he said. I'm ready to scream 'Yes!' but he keeps talking, saying how he knows I love the elementaries but they need to keep Buddy in the high school, given his rapport with the students, and—

"What it comes down to is some of the other women in the COVE who are nurses will be volunteering in the other schools, and I'll be at the high school five days a week, taking care of the poor wee babe. And the high school students. I can care for the child in the nurse's office and still give out heating pads and ice packs and call parents if there's something real, and give the kids who need a place to unwind a kind ear and a soft couch. And Buddy can come in as often as he likes to visit the babe and see that she's safe.

"Once it was all worked out Gerard asked if I could start tomorrow and I laughed and said 'right now.' I called Wren and she came over with my rocking chair in her truck, and Buddy came flying down to the school with the baby, her bottles, diapers, and a portable crib.

"Ian, I know this is a horrible situation, that it shouldn't be making me happy, but I am. Holding that baby, feeling so needed. It's my happiness. That's what I've always needed—being needed. That's been a part of me since I was a tot myself."

I turn out the light, think about being needed. How for the last twenty years, I've been so needed by Ian. From his heart attack to his bypass surgery, from his hernia to his detached retina, from his first bout of cancer to the cancer that finally did him in. One thing after another, I've been caring for him night and day. I turn back to his picture even though I can't see it in the dark. "You were my life, Ian. Caring for you was my life. When I lost you, I lost half of me."

I turn back to the side I like to sleep on, get comfortable. Of course, before care-giving for Ian, there were the children. And yes, I do have grandchildren now and certainly, I help out with them, but really, I'm just there for the fun of being with them. I'm helping my children with them, and I'm certainly not saying I'm not appreciated, but they could easily hire nannies and sitters. I'm useful, but being useful and being needed—it's not the same.

My mind drifts, comes to rest in my first memories:

Gracie-Faye, age 3

"You're gonna be a big sister-helper, my Gracie-Faye. Just like Patrick watches over y' and helps y' up if y' fall, y're gonna help y'r baby sister, Brigid. Y're gonna come get me if the babe is cryin'. Do y' think y' can do that?"

I feel so proud. "Yes, Mam," I say.

"And y' know how Brigid drools?"

"Yes, Mam," I say.

"Do y' think y' can take a tissue and wipe her face and her

clothes when she drools?"

"Yes, Mam," I say and go right to my Betsy Wetsy doll to practice.

Gracie-Faye, age 8

We're sitting at the lunch table. We've finished swapping sandwiches. I'm eating Carol Flynn's ham and cheese, Denise has my peanut butter and jelly and Carol has Denise's egg salad.

"So how was the circus, Gracie-Faye," Mary Ann-without-an-e asks. I start to tell them about the way it started with the clown trying to sweep up the spotlight. Someone—I think Mary Jo—tells her table, the one next to mine—to be quiet. She's going to the circus next weekend and wants to hear. I tell them about the bareback riders, the trapeze artists, the high wire act, the ring master. On and on—the elephants, the tigers, and the lions.

"I think I'll be a bareback rider," Carol says. She would. She loves horses.

"If I was in the circus, I'd lead the band and I'll have a beautiful red costume and maybe I'll be leading from a throne on top of an elephant," Maura says, until Mary Jo cuts her off with "I did a great job training Puss 'n' Boots to jump into my lap, so I think I'd make a great lion tamer," Mary Anne-with-an-e says.

They start going around the table next to ours and mine and then they get to me. How can I say I want to hold the nets under the tight rope walkers or the trapeze artists to catch them if they fall? Everyone would laugh at me. So I lie and say "tight rope walker." I'd rather have a sin on my soul and have to tell the priest when I go to confession, than have the whole third grade laughing at me. But it's what I really, really want to do. Like an ambition. I want to be a net-holder.

Gracie age 72

The last thing I can remember before falling asleep is the grateful face of Buddy as he walked in and saw his baby content and safe in my arms. The sweet feeling of having someone totally dependent on me.

Scene 56: <u>No One Knows Who I Am</u>

Wren, age 72

Shoshanna, Maura and I are sitting here at our table in the dining hall, waiting. We've been joined by Jane, Rayna, Claire and Nancy. I glance at Deborah, sitting alone at a table for eight, waiting for the last ones to straggle in, who have nowhere else to go but join her. I feel badly for her, but they're strict about keeping the tables to eight, and—And there's an empty chair at our table. Deborah keeps staring at it.

Lucy, our waitress is also staring. Glaring now. "If you don't want me coming back to you to let you know they've run out of half the things you've ordered, you need to order now. I'll get Gracie's order when she comes down. Maybe she's stuck in traffic or something. She knows what time dinner is."

Lucy's right. Gracie knows when dinner is, and she's never late. I'm getting a little concerned myself. I tried to call her a few minutes ago, and her phone was either turned off or out of power. Shoshanna quickly selects the vegan option, stands and lets us know she's going up to Gracie's room.

"Sleeping," Shoshanna says. "I woke her up, and she insists she's not hungry—just tired. She wants to take a nap before she meets with her dance club."

"She has to eat, my goodness, how can she do all that fancy stepping or whatever they do if she's half asleep and she hasn't eaten and–"

"Just what I asked her," Shoshanna says. "She said she'll heat a can of soup. I suggested that she skip the Steppers and we could bring a dinner plate up for her, but she was aghast. How could she possibly not lead the group? I told her that was ridiculous, that Colleen O'Rourke and Shannon Hennessey were both in Irish dance groups in high school and are perfectly capable of working on the Thanksgiving routine, which I think totally insulted her. She said she was going back to sleep and suggested that I go down and eat my dinner before it got cold."

"She's doing too much," Rayna says.

"The dance club after volunteering all day with that baby," Jane says. "I'm actually jealous of her for that. I'd love to spend time with a baby."

"Same here," Rayna says.

Shoshanna, age 72

I have to tell someone. I knock on Wren's door, and thank goodness, she's home. Wearing that schlep-around old shirt with the grease stains all over it. "Baking," she says. "It's the Chew and Chat baker's birthday tomorrow and Janna and I want to present her with a home-made cake."

I follow her into the kitchen. "Something's up with Gracie," I say.

She turns her flour-dusted face to me. "She was tired last night, so—we all have days when we just conk out," she says and dumps a handful of chocolate chips into the mixing bowl.

"No—something just now. I was driving past the front of the building, coming around to the garage. Sam's Car Service was parked in front of the main entrance, and I'm sure—I'm absolutely positive—Gracie got out and went inside. I thought maybe her car broke down or something, but when I got to the garage, her car was there in her spot. No damage, no flat tire that she didn't have time to take care of this morning—nothing."

"Are you certain it was her?" Wren asks.

"No one else here has a coat like hers, or walks like her, or —"

Wren, age 72

I open my door. Maura starts hummingbirding the moment she has one foot inside.

"We've got to do something and it's just not like her. I mean when I'm in the high school I try to stop in to the nurse's office around lunch time because she makes these fabulous salads and sandwiches and she knows I'm always there on Friday so maybe that's why she makes so much so there's always plenty for me to have some and maybe she makes extra every day because someone else has lunch with her on other days or she shares with the teachers but today all she had was an energy bar. She said she just didn't feel like cooking this morning and frankly, I don't like the way she's been looking."

"That's it," I say. "Tomorrow at breakfast—" I'm about to say we'll have to confront her, get through to her that we're concerned about her, that she's got to go to a doctor because she hasn't been herself, but—breakfast is at her apartment tomorrow. "Let's wait and see how she is at breakfast. Play it by ear," I tell Maura. I turn the discussion to the news, brew her a cup of coffee and make her a pb and j sandwich to replace the lunch she expected to get from Gracie.

It's worse than I expected. Let's face it, I'm not a housekeeper. I'm totally comfortable in a sea of mess. Clean mess. Unfolded clean laundry, clothes draped over chairs. Dishes on the drainboard, bed unmade. But my apartment looks like Mrs. Clean lives here compared to Gracie's. Claire comes in to clean every apartment in the building every other week. Except Gracie's. "I've always cleaned my own space and there's no reason in the world for me not to continue to," she always says.

But now there is. Her apartment smells. Garbage cans are overflowing. Dust is visible. Clothes worn days ago strewn everywhere. When I push the unlocked door open, Gracie is standing at her kitchen counter, staring at a bowl of eggs with a beater in her hand, as if unsure of what to do with it. She's still in her pajamas. No robe. Socks—the ones she wore yesterday—I remember the pumpkins on them. No slippers.

Shoshanna arrives, takes one look at the scene and ushers us to her apartment. "I have the frozen waffles I bought for tomorrow," she says.

Before Shoshanna starts to cook, we confront Gracie. "What's up?" followed by a litany of the things we've seen that concern us.

"The fairy folk have been enchanted by the spirit of the Forbidden Forest into thinking I'm the witch who has captured them. They're attacking from all sides, sapping my energy and enveloping me in a fog of fatigue and forgetting and confusion," Gracie says.

We look at one another. "Gracie," Shoshanna says so softly it's hard to hear. "You're sick. You've got to get to a doctor."

"It's time to let the fairies go and tell us what's going on. And let us get you to a doctor today," I say. And then realize no doctors work on Saturday.

"I guess I'll just go home," Gracie says, but she stays in the seat she's dropped into, as if it's holding her captive. As if she's incapable of standing up and leaving.

Maura sets the table, I put up the coffee and tea and bring out the can of whipped cream, the milk, sugar, lemon and tea bags. Shoshanna pops the waffles into the toaster, takes the defrosted strawberries out of the microwave. Their scent fills the air, but even that isn't enough to rouse Gracie to come to the table. Maura escorts her.

We pick at our food. Tell Gracie we're taking her to the doctor on Monday, because it just makes sense to take her to someone she knows rather than a storefront clinic with a stranger, which is our only option today.

Finally, she speaks. "It's back. My fibromyalgia. I mean, it's always here. I'm always managing it, but I'm having a fibro-flare. A bad one. I'm exhausted beyond exhaustion. That's why I'm having Sam's Service shuttle me around. I'm afraid I'll fall asleep driving."

"So let one of us drive you. My goodness, I go to Markettown to one of the schools every day and so does Shoshanna, and Wren goes a couple of times a week and we'd all be perfectly happy to drive and—"

"I'm helping Sam," Gracie says. "I'm not obligating any of you to go out of your way to drive me. Sam needs the money. And I can afford it."

"What do you mean by it's back?" I ask.

"Maybe you remember that I had mono when I was living in Oceanport. I was sick for a few weeks. Well, this is sort of like that in the way it feels. I started to feel that way again when the kids were young, but it never went away. Just calmed down to manageable. You hadn't moved up to Blossom Knolls yet when I had my first big attack. Ian and the kids and I were down in Harvey's Harbor so we didn't see you that often even after you moved up to the lake. No reason to tell you. I'd go to work each day, fall onto my bed with my clothes, sometimes even my boots still on, and sleep. I'd get up to put something together for dinner and then go back to bed. Ian and the kids cleaned up and took care of the house while I slept. And dreamed. Strange, weird dreams that went on and on through the night, leaving me as tired when I awoke as when I fell asleep. I was tired all the time. And everything hurt. Not all at once. One day my legs would hurt, another day, an arm. It was as if the discomfort of any minor, barely noticeable injury would be magnified and extended to the whole area. And I was confused. They call it fibro-fog. It feels like fog has rolled in and hidden short term memories, scrambled thoughts. It took a long time to get a diagnosis. Epstein-Barr, then Chronic Fatigue Syndrome, then Fibromyalgia. Take your pick. Most likely Fibromyalgia but it could be a combination. Nothing to do for it but pace myself. It's not like that always. Most of the time, if I pace myself, I'm barely aware of it. But I'm having what they call a flare now, and it's worse than usual, and I'll get over it, and there's nothing I can do about it.

"There. I've said it, so you can just get over it and let me be. Let's talk about something else."

Gracie, age 72

The folk of the Forbidden Forest have me tied to a tree. Fairies fly overhead, sprinkling the clouds with something until they rain down a fog that pushes in on my head from all sides. I'm free of the tree but I don't remember how I got here and where I'm supposed to go and there are paths and paths and I start down the one leading toward a baby that needs me but partway the path changes and suddenly I'm turned toward the man at the supermarket check-out and then I'm swimming in the ocean and it's cool and comforting but which way is the land? And how am I suddenly walking through a city I've never visited? I'm Dorothy in Oz and I need to get home but I don't know who I am or what direction I need to go to get there. Hands reach out to me, but I can't see whose they are and all I know is that no one but me can get me home.

And then I'm in my bed and the sun is peeping in around the curtains and my head is in a vise but at least I'm home and—Becky. I have to get dressed and get to school. Sam will be here to drive me, but—oh—today is Sunday. They're going to do something with me. Call my children. Make me see Dr. Joe when I know perfectly well what the problem is, and that there's nothing a doctor can do for it. I get out of bed. I get dressed. We ate at Shoshanna's yesterday. It was supposed to be my turn but I messed it up so we went to Shoshanna's because it was decided long ago that Maura would clean up for everyone and wouldn't take a turn cooking. So it's Wren's turn today.

She has bagels and lox and cream cheese and an egg scramble with onions and mushrooms. There's vegan cheese for Shoshanna. It's a nice breakfast and I'm so tired. I don't have the energy to chew a bagel. My hands feel as if they're made of lead when I lift a fork to my mouth but I make myself eat the eggs. They're good and I can chew them. I'm hoping we finish fast because maybe I'll be able to fall asleep, and sleep without dreaming, if I try to take a nap.

They want to talk. About me. Can't they see I'm too tired? Their words are like drum beats pounding against my head:

"Gracie you have to let people help you."

"Gracie, you have to let us drive you."

"Gracie, you have to let Claire clean your apartment, and come in at the end of each day to throw out your garbage."

"Gracie, you have to take time off from the dance club."

"Gracie, you have to stop volunteering at the school."

That's it. "Stop it, all of you!" I shout. "I'm not givin' up anything." I can hear my spunky child-voice coming back and I hang onto it, as if I'm standin' up to my brothers. "I have a happiness with that baby I'm not stoppin' and they need a nurse in that buildin' to give out sanitary napkins and let the girls lie down with heating pads and give the guys a place to get away from teacher-talk. And I'm not stoppin' the dancin'. "

We talk and we argue and it comes down to them callin' my children or me compromisin' which I'm good at. So I say, "OK, Claire can clean my apartment every other week like she does yours. And if I'm too tired Colleen and Shannon can lead the dancin'. And Sam can drive me. And I'll be fine."

I think they're fine with that. "Please, just ask us when you want us to do something for you," they say. I promise I will.

I know I won't.

"So Ian, I think I gave them what they want," I tell his picture. I try to sleep, but sleep doesn't come easy. Only when I'm driving. I could feel the waves of fog closing in on me a few days ago—I don't recall which one. So I stopped driving. I'm not going to do anything to endanger anyone. I won't fall asleep or forget what to do with the baby. I never had a problem when I was working as a nurse during other flares. It's like I get spurts of energy and focus where my head might hurt and a leg might ache but everything is light and clear and it's as if those times drain out every bit of energy I have, and the moment the reason for that burst of radiance is gone, the fog rolls in, the fairies start to dance, and I can't remember what I did two seconds ago, or keep weights from holding down my eyelids."

I turn from Ian's picture, but thoughts keep racing. "Ask," they keep saying. "I want to help," each of them says. "You don't have to go down to dinner. We could all eat at your apartment. Or eat downstairs and have your dinner sent up if you want to be alone." "We can drive you." "We can do your laundry." "We can…" "We can…" "We can…"

I know they can, but, I can't. I know how silly it seems. But I was brought up not to ask for help. To take care of myself. To take care of everyone else. I never learned how to ask.

I pray: "God, I don't know how to ask. Everyone tells me to ask for help, but I don't know how. It's not as if people were always asking me for help. Oh, sometimes someone asked me to help someone else, pointed out a need, the way Gerard asked me to take care of Becky. But Buddy didn't ask me. People don't ask. Women certainly don't. I did things for other people when I saw they needed doing, and my friends are doing that, but sometimes they don't know how, or don't know that I need help, and I don't know how to ask.

And I don't know who I am, because I was always the person who everyone else needed. How am I supposed to turn into the person who needs help? Who is she? She's not me. I don't want to be that kind of selfish person always asking for herself, as if I'm thinking I'm great or something and everyone should kowtow to me."

Wren, age 72

This has to work. We practically had to drag Gracie down, but here she is, sitting at our table. The alternative presented to her was calling her kids to tell them she was too exhausted to eat. We knew it would work. So she's sitting here, and we're all ready. We've scripted what we'll say, even rehearsed.

Claire starts. "I was thinking today, without joy, would life even be worth living?"

Everyone agrees. I almost laugh. Poor Deborah, who was invited to join us, is trying so hard. I can see her lips starting to mouth "hogwash," but she sees everyone's enthusiastic agreement with Claire, knows how important it is, and for once in her life, swallows her sarcasm.

We go around the table, call out words describing the feeling of joy. Get answers from "a peace so pervasive it's like floating in a sea of serenity," (Shoshanna.) To "So happy your whole body is singing and not letting you sit still because happiness is dancing you all over the place," (Maura.) To "something filling you up like a balloon and letting you soar above everything in your life that's not perfect," (Claire.) To "Having this flash of insight— hey, I'm happy!" (Rayna.) "Being around people you love," (Jane.) "It's being needed. Knowing that what you're doing for others is bringing them joy," (Gracie.) "And getting recognized for it. Joy is other people appreciating what you're doing," Deborah adds.

I don't say it. How can I say, "Joy would be being able to fully experience your own feelings? Even the painful ones." I say what I've rehearsed. It was inevitable that Gracie would say joy was serving others, or being helpful. "I agree with Gracie. Helping others is a sure path to happiness." I refrain from adding on "even if no one notices."

There's a break, while we order our dinners. Gracie just asks for a bowl of soup. "And she'll have the roast chicken," I add, and give Gracie the look that tells her she'd better eat at least half of it or that phone call would be made.

When the waitress leaves, I immediately turn to Gracie and ask her to talk about a joyful experience.

Of course, she begins with reminding us of her three weeks working with Becky, then adds, "I could fill a book with moments of joy, and every one of them would have been centered around helping someone else. I think the first must have been when I was about three or four, when my family was having a four-leaf clover hunt, and I slipped mine into Brigid's pile. It made me so much happier to let her win than I would have been if I'd won myself."

A micro-second of sound from Deborah's direction followed by her hand over her mouth amuses me. I'll compliment her later for sticking with the script.

I grab it and run with it. "So it made you joyous to give someone else happiness," I say, and throw in some words about putting a huge kettle over the fireplace where guests at Chew and Chat could drop in extra/overripe vegetables, to turn into "Stone Soup," free for all guests, for all passing travelers, for anyone needing free food, and how the extra, along with any other extra food we had, would be driven down to the Markettown Community Center and distributed to the hungry. "It makes me happy to think of it."

Shoshanna speaks next. "Yeah, I like that. Making other people happy. OK, an incident—a specific—not something big like being a parent. This is such a little thing, but it really made an impression on me. I was having an art club meeting in the high school, and I saw this girl peeking in. Shy, almost creepy looking. I went to the door, invited her to join us. "But I'm not an artist," she said. "I told her it wasn't necessary to be perfect, that art could be fun for anyone, and I kind of escorted her into the room. I gave her paint, and she started slashing on colors—darker and darker but different tones, balanced beautifully, and "Wow!" I said as I walked past, "You really do have talent. I hope you'll come to the club, and that you'll try an art elective next semester. You know, your work is really making me feel something deeply emotional. You're capturing the essence of sorrow." Which, I must say, scared me—I hoped I wasn't saying too much. But the smile on her face! I'll never forget that. And then she asked if she could start another painting, and of course I gave her a fresh piece of paper and she painted the same thing on one half of the page, but on the other half, it was all light and yellows and pinks with lines that looked like they were dancing, and it was so beautiful and so joyful, my eyes filled with tears."

Maura says, "I I overheard a student saying her father is very sick in the hospital and the only food her mother can afford is spaghetti and cereal so that's all they get to eat, so I took up a collection from the teachers and dropped off bags of food and my goodness, they were so happy it made me sing all the way home."

"I used to work in a corporate office," Claire says, "making a lot of money, but it gave me no satisfaction. Now, when I come into your apartments, or clean this room tonight after you leave—it just gives me a sense of doing something worthwhile, something you might not even notice—but you'd notice if I didn't do it. It makes me happy."

"Deborah," I say, holding my breath, but she comes through, giving the specific about how happy it makes her to do the taxes for all the residents who can't do their own.

"Helping others," Gracie says. "There's no joy greater than giving joy to others. Like helping Buddy with the baby."

This is the cue Rayna and Jane have awaited. It was almost inevitable that it would come. Almost in unison, they jump in with "You're so lucky to have that opportunity," and "I'm so jealous. I'd love to spend time taking care of that baby."

"Do you think you could share some of your happiness?" Rayna says.

"Do you think we could possibly come and spend some time with you—like, share taking care of Becky?" Jane asks.

The beautifully rehearsed tag team, I think. Perfect. If Gracie doesn't fall for this…

"You really could be helping Rayna and Jane if you let them," I say.

Not to be outdone, Deborah pipes up, "I don't like babies," she says, to no one's surprise. But I also like to do things for others, so I'll be dropping off lunch for Gracie each day."

"And don't forget us," I say, indicating Maura and Shoshanna with my hand. "We also get joy from being needed. So you're going to give it to us by letting us do your laundry, get dinner for you if you don't feel like coming down to the dining room, and get everything you need on the weekends. But you'd better ask, because if you don't, you may find yourself getting more of us than you want," I add, and am happy to see a glimmer of a smile.

Scene 57: <u>My Favorite Things</u>

Gracie, age 72

Everything changes. Everything becomes joyful. Being able to hand off Becky, to just sit and watch her playing with one of my friends. The thought of Deborah lunching with me was frightful, but she never stays. She takes one look at Becky, practically throws the food at me, and disappears.

Walking outside, breathing the fresh air, seeing the leaves greening the trees, the ripples on the lake, with someone I've asked to accompany me in case I lose my balance, because there are moments of dizziness, moments of confusion, is a joy.

Being with my grandchildren—and letting them bring me things, asking them to do things I really don't need help with just to let them feel as if they're doing something important—wow!

I've learned a new skill, and I love it. Asking for help. Helping others by giving them the joy of feeling needed.

PART FIVE: <u>SEASONS OF LOVE</u>

SECTION C: <u>LIFE GOES ON</u>

ACT XX: <u>WHAT YOU MEAN TO ME</u>

The Teacher

The force of the stream carrying three pulls strongly, yet the fourth stream sidles off on its own path. The soul riding the errant stream has no fear, this is just a detour, a slight turning toward sunlight sparking rainbows in water, toward mountains clothed in pine boughs and fields strewn with sunflowers. She feels the magnetism of the welded waters her friends travel and is confident of her stream's return to them. But the attraction of the ocean is strong.

I send a dream to all: A stream drifting off from a river floating boats with each of the women. The boat floating Shoshanna drifts into a side stream. Just that. I end the dream.

Scene 58: <u>And This is My Beloved</u>

Shoshanna, age 72

Shoshanna's Journal

My friends were all bonkers when we met for breakfast. What did the dream mean? Was I about to pack up and leave the COVE and move in with Leaf? I had to admit it was a possibility—way in the future. But the reality—more chance of Leaf moving in with me here than of me leaving my friends and moving to the west coast. You'd think I was committing to the crime of the century when I said the dream made perfect sense. Leaf has invited me to spend Thanksgiving vacation at this resort in the mountains. "Not for the skiing—that's for the youngsters," he said. "For you—for the scenery. It's the most beautiful winter spot I've ever seen. I really want you to see it," he said. As I said, my friends reacted as if I were plotting a murder or something. Not to come to Blossom Knolls for the traditional Thanksgiving weekend! When my children and grandchildren plan to be there?

I reminded them that we'd all just been together at Kayla's wedding. I assured them that those of my family who weren't doing their alternate year with their in-laws would still be there. I promised that Leaf and I—or I alone—would be at their Christmas/Chanukah gathering "Which," I reminded them, "is only a month away."

"Which," they reminded me, "might not be happening this year since Gabrielle's due date is right in the middle of the week, and we need to stay down-lake at the COVE to get her to the hospital. Our families will probably get together, though."

I promised I'd be with them for Christmas, Easter, and New Year's wherever they are. "You can live without me for one Thanksgiving," I said.

End of discussion.

This, they don't understand. Or maybe they do— maybe it terrifies them. The thought has entered my mind that Leaf may propose during this trip, and I'm sure it's entered their minds. I'll never leave them, never move far from where they are. Leaf could move to the COVE! But —

Throughout my life, the emotional scars of my childhood scream in pain when anyone touches me. Even a hand on my arm makes me want to pull away. Throughout my life, I've needed to see a clear path to the exit wherever I am: to take the aisle seat, to take the restaurant seat facing the door. Except:

Once upon a time, as Gracie would say, I met the kindest, gentlest man in the world. I was seventeen, scared and lost, and he, it turns out, was 23. I thought he was older. He became like a father, or big brother, who got me through the roughest time in my life. But that's all been written in journals of the past. What hasn't been written is the effect he's having on my body. No man has ever made me feel physical pleasure. No man, until now, with Leaf. I never understood what the talk, the songs, the poems, even the jokes, were all about. Now I do. Now, being with Leaf.

Once, I was a scared, pregnant teen and Leaf was like a big brother. Now, we're close to the same age. I look at him, and see love. He is still the kindest, gentlest man in the world. When I am with him, I feel safe. When I am with him, it's as if I'm wrapped in peace. It's a soft thing, as gentle as he is. It's almost as if he's turned the whole world into love.

Since I met him again at Kayla's wedding, I walk down the crowded streets of Markettown and want to go up to every person and hug them, tell them I love them. I've always thought—or thought since I was fourteen and started reading about other religions—that God is everywhere, in everything. I think people and animals have free will—that God throws us into situations and we react. And I believe that our choices are guided by how in touch we are with God within us. People like Mother Theresa, Pope Francis, the Dalai Lama—when I see them in videos or on TV—I get the feeling that they're touching God, guided by God. As if there's an aura of Love around them, glowing from within. Maybe it's sacrilegious to say this, but being with Leaf is like being in the presence of God. I feel safe with him. His touch is soothing. Something my friends just don't understand.

And this, too, no one understands. My voice is getting stronger. It turned from a whisper into sounded speech when I forgave Ima, but it was still soft. Now—it's filled with feeling, filled with music. I catch myself singing. As if loving Leaf, trusting Leaf, is a balm, sealing over the wounds of the past.

Scene 59: <u>Finishing the Hat</u> (Reprise)

Shoshanna, age 72

"Oh, Leaf! I forgive you for waking me up so early. I. Oh!" I squeeze Leaf's hand, but can't take my eyes off the perfect ball of orange rising out of the lake, gliding into the sky. Mountains on the far shores seem to be bowing down to it. I've seen plenty of gorgeous sunrises in my life, but never one like this. Never. "Oh, Leaf!"

We stand here for a while, watching, aware only of the sunrise and of each other. When the sun finally settles in the sky, Leaf gently tugs me back to the lodge.

"Must we?" I ask.

"If we don't want to miss breakfast, yes. And check out is in an hour," Leaf says.

"I wish we could stay forever. This is the most glorious vacation I've ever had. I wish it could go on and on into eternity." A thought—Leaf, I wish you would say something about forever.

There's something sad about his eyes, as if he's in pain. "Everything ends, Shoshanna," Leaf says softly.

It's a chilling thought. My bones shiver as he continues, "Nothing goes on forever. But I promise you this. The trip isn't over. After we leave, there is one more thing, not far. Something so beautiful it will make this pale in comparison."

"We'll see about that," I laugh, and feel warmed by possibility.

The sign says "Private Property. No Trespassers." A road has been cleared—it looks as if it stretches to the top of the mountain.

"No problem," Leaf says. He drives up to the gate a few yards past the sign, gets out of the car, and takes a key from his pocket that unlocks the gate. "I know the owner," he says.

We drive through stands of snow covered pine, to the top of the mountain. There's a small clearing. We get out, crunch over the snow to a lookout with a fence protecting viewers from falls.

It's like looking out over the Haven. Different, but with the same unearthly beauty. Trees, fields, houses whitewashed by snow. A universe made of marshmallows, cotton balls and sparkling sugar crystals. More shades of white than I ever thought possible. The frozen lake, shimmering in the sunlight, breaking up into colors as if the lake were made of a gazillion prisms. The wind now, whispering music. And love coming from Leaf, with his arms around me. Love so strong it hurts.

Gently as the first dawn light-brushed the planet, Leaf feather-touches my eyelids. It's as if the scene changes, morphs into the Haven, as if I'm looking at it for the first time.

"Oh Leaf, what happened?" I hear the wonder in my voice. To my own ears, it sounds as if it's coming from far, far away.

Shoshanna

"I love you," Leaf whispers, kisses me, and draws out my last breath.

I am in his arms now, floating through time, floating through space, floating through colors and light and a confluence of space and time and energy and matter where everything is one thing.

I look at Leaf and see, not Leaf, but my Grandma, Leah Greenbaum, who loved me and nurtured me and protected me until her passing, when I was sixteen. It's the face of Leaf when we were in the commune when I was seventeen, and it's the face of Leaf, as he is today. It's the face of my protector, of all the protectors who were there to catch me whenever I fell.

I'm in the Teacher's arms, placed here so gently, so gently I didn't know Leaf was handing me to her. She releases me, and I understand that I must gather all I've learned through all my lifetimes on earth into one word. A memory of a dream the Teacher sent—a password given to Shoshanna, a different one to each of my friends. My word, for me, alone. Leaf. "Leaves," the factories from which animal sustenance springs. I whisper the word with the reverence it deserves.

It's as if a veil is lifted, a door opened. All the beauty of the Haven explodes into a marvel beyond anything imaginable. Colors never dreamed of, but they are not colors to look at. They are colors around me, within me. The colors of Eternity. And music. How Maura would love the music! Notes no human ever heard. The song of Angels.

I feel a wholeness, as if something was missing all my life, and sense around me all the selves I've been forever and beyond. As they press against me, I meld with them. My Shoshanna persona drops from me as easily as taking off my clothes at the end of a day, and I become one with the essence and learnings of all the persona's we've entered in the past.

And now! All around us are the souls, the eternal wholes of people who have loved us and been with us throughout time.

And Leaf, or the essence that once also was my grandmother —"You were always here," I whisper wordlessly.

"And always will be," I hear in my soul.

"Welcome to Om-eh", the Universe sings.

Scene 60: <u>Something's Missing</u>

Wren, age 72

"It's open. Just come in."

"Is it here yet?" Gracie asks. "There's no way I could have eaten leftover turkey in the dining room."

"I'll be right in," I say. "I'm just finishing dividing the leftovers Janna threw in the car. Packing them for freezing. Some single packs for each of your freezers if there's ever a night or lunchtime you want to eat it alone, and several large packs for all of us. I have room in my

freezer."

There's a knock on the door. Maura walks in, followed by the pizza girl.

"Would you believe it? I was just getting to your door and

here's Benita, one of my high school sopranos, all loaded down with—what did you order besides pizza?"

"Salad," I call from the kitchen. "Maura—my bag is on the table out there. Can you get a tip out of it?"

We're just sitting down to eat. "I thought Shoshanna was coming back tonight," Gracie says.

"So did I," I say. "She still could be. They might have stopped for dinner somewhere. Pass the dressing, please."

"If you pass me the garlic bread, my goodness, it's so—aren't you going to answer your phone, I mean—"

"Quiet, Maura, so I can hear if the caller leaves a message. Probably a telemarketer," I say.

"Wren," we all hear. The voice sounds funny, as if the speaker is choking. Or crying. We get very quiet. I walk in from the kitchen, move toward the answering machine. "This is Karen Free. Please call me back as soon as—"

I lunge across the room and grab the phone. "Karen! What's —"

"Are you alone?" Shoshanna's daughter-in-law asks.

"No, Maura and Gracie are here, why—"

"Please, put me on speaker. Everyone, please sit down." I can hear her voice cracking, hear her deep breath, her struggle for control.

Maura, already seated, wraps her arms around her stomach and presses against it.

Gracie, on the couch beside her, turns pale.

I stand, frozen beside the phone.

"I'm sorry," Karen says. "I have some very bad news." Her voice breaks. I hear a sob. "My mother-in-law passed away."

"What?" I scream. An unearthly animal howl. I can hardly believe it's coming from me. I fall into a chair.

"NO!" Maura shrieks. "NO, NO, NO!" She picks up a pillow and slams it across the room, dissolves back onto the couch in tears.

Gracie melts into sobs. She mutters something like, "May she find comfort in the arms of God." I think she's praying.

I manage to control my weeping enough to ask what happened.

"They—she and Leaf, were at a mountain look-out on the way home. Leaf said she was overwhelmed by the beauty and then just collapsed into his arms. By law they have to do an autopsy when a seemingly healthy person suddenly dies. We'd want one anyway—in case she had a genetic condition the family needs to be on top of. They think it was a heart attack or a stroke. Whatever it was, it was instantaneous. Oh, God!" Karen cries.

We pick at the pizza. Most of the food ends up in my refrigerator for another night. "We can have it for dinner tomorrow."

"For sure," Gracie says. "For sure we're not going to want to eat in the dining room with every person in the building coming over to our table to offer their condolences."

The Teacher

I send a dream, bring them to the Haven, to a scent of pine, the silence of sound, muffled by the muted white of deep fallen snow. Shoshanna and I walk atop the snow, leave no footprints. Together, we kneel, dig a hole in the fluffy whiteness. I unclasp the necklace Shoshanna is wearing, hand her the acorn that was around her neck. She places it in the hole. We cover it with snow.

As we stand and watch, a tree sprouts from the ground.

As we stand and watch, leaves cover the branches, and the whole Haven greens.

As we stand and watch, summer turns to autumn, leaves fall. Three flame-bright leaves lie on the ground, resplendent as jewels.

I let the women awaken. Each walks, in her own time, to her window to open the shades. Each sees, on the ledge outside, a brightly colored fallen leaf. Each looks, and is surprised to see no tree shedding leaves nearby.

And knows.

Wren, age 72

I look at myself in the mirror, could swear that my brown and gray hair has turned totally gray in the last two days. Gracie looks like she's shrunk, and Maura's been almost silent. On the ride up to Blossom Knolls for the green funeral Shoshanna outlined in her "Bucket's been Kicked—What Now" document, no one says a word. What is left to say? For the last two days, we've shared every Shoshanna memory we have.

A multitude of people gather to bid our farewells, grouped together along the roadway edging Blossom Knolls. Everyone's here, from all of our families. The COVE bus just arrived, bringing our friends for the funeral, and a Markettown school bus bringing students and faculty members will be here any minute.

We prepare to say goodbye to what feels like a part of our very souls.

Shoshanna

What a crowd there is! Even my cousin's family from the west coast. It seems like everyone I've ever met! All there, all standing at the site I selected, now a hollow grave.

A horse drawn wagon comes toward them and they step back to create a path down the center of the gathering. My son, Pax, his wife, Karen, my daughter, Dandi Lion, her husband, Dustin, and my grandchildren come forward to lift the basket woven of bamboo and flowers off the wagon and place it in the prepared grave. My Shoshanna body lies within, as if asleep. Leaf stands beside me in Om-eh, yet Leaf stands beside my friends, close to my family.

Dandi, my first born, comes forward to speak: "My mother named me Dandi Lion. Dandelion. The name of a weed. A weed that grows everywhere, anywhere a seed falls. A name that tells me I will survive, wherever I find myself. A name that tells me I wasn't planned, but a seed fell to fertile soil, and I sprang forth. And I was loved. By God! I was so loved by the woman I called

Mom…"

Oh, Dandi, you and Pax have no idea. I feel the weight and pain, the jubilation and the grief of that love and I can't listen. I can't say goodbye. I love you, Dandi.

And Pax. Now Pax is speaking. "My name is Pax. Peace. Everything my mother did was about Peace. She dedicated her life to bringing people together, to creating peace…"

I see us now as we were, see myself carting babies off to marches and teens marching alongside me as Pax speaks. Why did I let my children speak? I cannot bear this pain. And now! He's almost finished. Just a half page of the words he's reading are left:

"She honored the differences between people, our varying beliefs, and she believed to the depths of her soul that we are One. One human race, one family. She quoted the Dalai Lama, saying 'My religion is kindness.' She tried to make it hers."

I watch him turn toward the casket, hear him say "Mom, you're a hard act to follow," and know I'll never hear his voice again.

And now my friends. We called ourselves forever *but my forever with them is ending, and it's more—it's*

They're singing the final medley. No! It can't be over. Not this fast.

My grandchildren come forward, lift shovels, are the first to pitch the freshly dug soil over my casket before handing the shovels to their parents, and then on to my friends and other family members.

With each shovelful, I feel myself drifting away, leaving the mourners, leaving my mourning. With each shovelful, I feel myself fading into the Oneness of my former selves, becoming fully a part of a single soul, a Me made up of all the me's that ever cloaked it.

ACT XXI: <u>SOMETHING HAS HAPPENED</u>

Shoshanna

Om-eh: Everything made up of all the time and space that ever was, the Eternal Now, the Eternal Is, the Omnipresent Everywhere.

The Teacher comes to me, soundlessly speaks: "I need you. You have earned an eternity in Om-eh, but I need you. The peoples of the world never understood Kindness, and things are going to get a lot worse, so much worse. An old soul, one that has learned all lessons and completed its journey is needed to be reborn. Someone who will remember not her personas, but the learnings of her past selves. Someone who will lead the peoples of the world from Me to We. I need you, who was once Shoshanna."

My soul, which has touched eternity, understands: "Yes. I will go."

Scene 61: <u>Everything Changes</u>

Wren, age 72

It's an ache, a stab in the brain every time I prepare breakfast. Stray thoughts. "I can't use milk—Shoshanna's lactose intolerant." The automatic grasping of four sets of cutlery to bring to the table. The empty chair. A glimpse of a woman across the street, the sudden thought, that's Shoshanna," the realization that it's not.

An ache. A hole. A reminder. The conversational stutters. "What would Shoshanna say? Or "remind me to tell Shoshanna," or "Let's buy that for Shoshanna."

Shoshanna's absence when we all go down to Gabrielle's new

apartment in nearby Ira's Inlet. Decorating the nursery. Choosing drapes for the living room. This should have been Shoshanna's job. She should be telling us where to hang the pictures, what angle the couch should be positioned at.

And yet, being here is a balm. Planning for the new baby. Helping Gabrielle settle into a life of security, of knowing she'll always have food, always have a roof over her head and a soft pillow beneath it, knowing she's a part of a family and will always be loved.

I'm in a deep sleep and someone is playing the drums. No. Someone is banging on the wall. Maura. The emergency knock. I jump out of bed and race next door. Maura is half dressed, trying to pull on a tee shirt upside down.

"Gabrielle's in labor! I'm so nervous I can't drive to get her and I can't even get this shirt on and—"

I grab the shirt from Maura, turn it right side down. "Get a hold of yourself. I'll slip into some clothes and drive you there." I call Gracie and tell her to meet us at my car or the hospital—she says she'll be down at my car before I am.

I drive as rapidly as is safe, while Gracie calms Maura. There is no way they're going to let her be the birth coach if she's this unstrung.

We get to the apartment. Fly in through the unlocked door, expecting heaven knows what, but Gabrielle is sitting calmly in the living room, her suitcase by the door.

"I told you, Mom, no rush. The contractions are ten minutes apart. Dr. Brooks said I could come in but not to race until they're five." She stops to breathe. I can sense her pain, but she's in control.

"We're going now, not a second to lose. My goodness, let's get going!" Maura practically pulls Gabrielle off her chair the moment the contraction ends. I pick up the suitcase, but I'm thinking it's Maura I should be carrying. Gabrielle is supporting Maura, not the other way around.

I know Gabrielle feels as if every contraction lasts an hour and that they're coming at ten second intervals, but time means something different for each of us. For me, this labor is taking forever. One hour, two, three, four, five—and then—"It's crowning," the nurse says. She's familiar with Gracie, knows she's not Gabrielle's mother, so she looks at me and tells me to come with her to scrub in. She directs Maura to the waiting area, but Maura corrects her.

"My goodness, I'm her mother and I'm her coach and we practiced and I'm going to be a grandmother and I'm going to be in the delivery room and you can't say—"

"Come with me, then," the nurse chirps. "You can sit with Gracie in the waiting area," she tells me.

We sit, and wait. Gracie struggles with knitting needles, determined to finish the blanket we found started in Shoshanna's apartment. Yellow and white. "I told her what colors I wanted," Gabrielle said. I pick up a magazine, but the words are dancing around the page. I sit there and relive sitting in this same room, awaiting the birth of my grandchildren. They all came out fine, I remind myself. This little girl will be just fine. Gabrielle will be just fine. But I worry.

Scene 62: <u>When I'm Being Born Again</u>

Shoshanna

We understood, the entirety of our soul agreed. "Yes, we will go."

Now it is time for leaving. We take a last glimpse of Om-eh and turn toward our future.

For an instant we know where we're going. For an instant, we feel a gladness, knowing we will be with those who loved us over lifetimes, for an instant knowing we will be nurtured and aided in our mission knowing the She, we will become.

She, the babe, feels the heaviness of a human body. She feels hands and arms. She looks into the eyes speaking love to me and sees the face of Gabrielle. She smiles.

She takes her first breath as we, her soul, becomes earthbound and forgets past lives, forgets Om-eh. Becomes She, whose name will be—

Wren, age 72

Maura comes out, tears streaming down her face.

I feel my heart drop to the floor. No! "What?" I manage to ask.

"Her name, the baby's name! Gabrielle was going to call her Maura but my goodness, that wouldn't work, I told her because what if I'm in the same room as the child when she's a little older and someone calls 'Maura'—we won't know who she's talking to, so I told Gabrielle to come up with another name and she said she had this dream that told her a name and what a wonderful idea it was and it wasn't too long, which the whole name would have been because how awful it was to have a long name, Gabrielle told us the trouble she had and so did Shoshanna and Gracie-Faye writing all those letters in first grade when everyone learned to write their names, so everyone told Gabrielle to choose a short name so she did and it's a shorter name and I can hardly say it," she stops to wipe her eyes.

"The baby's name is Shanna," she finally says. "Shanna Maura Rossi. And this is so strange, but a song was going through my head the whole time she was in labor, that Laura Nyro thing about how when she dies and a how a child will be born to carry on, and—"

I don't think any of us hears what she says after that. The other people in the room stare at us sitting there crying. Gabrielle is fine, the baby is healthy, and one child was born to carry on. A little girl, named Shanna.

PART SIX: <u>TOMORROW</u>

The Teacher

Quietly, tranquilly, streams slip through space-time, joined now and then by a brook making its way downhill into the path of the united streams. Now a new creek, bubbling joy, wends its way downstream to join the ever flowing waters. A stream that will merge with the others, and change the nature of the waters for all time to come.

ACT XXII: I AM WHAT I AM

The Teacher

One child watches, senses the joy foaming into her life. One child sees, and makes a pronouncement.

Scene 63: Marrying for Love

Gabrielle, age 37

I'm a blithering mass of walking anxiety, waiting for my date from Perfectpairs.com to arrive. He sounded nice over the phone. Conversing was easy, but I've learned not to expect too much. Wasn't the last man who sounded nice over the phone almost twice my age?

He walks in. The form says his name is Emmanuel Leavey, but he introduces himself as Manny. I look at him and something happens. I don't know what it is. As if I recognize him, and know I can trust him. But more—there's something so loving, so safe so—. He has the most beautiful green eyes. Can eyes be peaceful? As if he's projecting rays of peace and love and—

"The baby sitter seems to be late," I say and offer him some wine. We sit and—talking to him is like talking to an old friend. We're in the middle of a conversation. I can hear Shanna walking toward the living room where we're sitting and I wish there was some way to signal her to leave us alone. No such luck. She pirouettes into the room in her princess costume. I introduce her to—I start to say "Manny," change to "Mr. Leavey."

"Well, what do we have here? A fairy princess? What a cute little girl you are," Manny says. He gets up and actually bows. "Pleased to make your acquaintance, little princess."

Instead of thanking him or saying any of the things I've

trained her to say, Shanna turns to me with this "I want ice cream NOW! look on her face and blurts out, "Marry him, Momma. Marry Mr. Leavey."

I'm ready to die of embarrassment. Manny actually starts to say something like, "You never know, maybe some—" and then the doorbell rings. Shanna races to her room to get something she wants to show the sitter, and I lurch toward the door faster than I've ever moved before, to let the sitter in.

Why would Manny want to celebrate the four month anniversary of our first date? Sixth—half a year maybe—but four months? And insist that Shanna be with us, and why at the Ice Palace, which is Shanna's favorite restaurant—a family type place? He's been taking me to fine restaurants—without Shanna.

We laugh and talk our way through a veggie burger (Shanna,) a stuffed portabello mushroom (me,) and a ridiculously huge eggplant parm sandwich (Manny.) I'd suggest asking for the check—I'm stuffed, but you don't bring Shanna here without ending her meal with a hot fudge sundae. Manny orders one for her and one for us to share. "I'll take one bite," I promise. "You get the rest." How can he eat a sundae after that sandwich?

We're awaiting our desserts, watching Shanna color her placemat, when Manny turns to Shanna and asks "Do you remember what you told your mother to do the night we all met for the first time?"

How is a three year old going to remember, even one as smart as Shanna?

But she pipes right up: "I told Momma to marry you."

And then he's down on one knee, asking me to be his wife, telling Shanna to tell me the answer.

"Marry him!" she shouts.

I can barely get the word out. "Yes!"

Still on his knees, Manny turns toward Shanna. "And will you do me the honor of becoming my daughter?"

"You don't think I'd tell Momma to marry you if I didn't want you to be my daddy," she says.

By then the whole restaurant is clapping and cheering and the waitress is bringing hot fudge sundaes with candles flaming and I don't know whether to laugh or cry so I do both. Somebody from another table orders champagne for us and—there's no room for me to drink it or eat the ice cream—I'm too filled up with happiness.

Wren, age 75

Maura is so hyped up I'm thinking of sitting on her. Three-year old Shanna is marching around the Bridal Shoppe at Sophisticated Styles "practicing to flower-girl."

"What's taking Gabrielle so long?" Maura asks.

"Buttons," I say. "Those buttons all the way down the back. If she chooses this gown, we're going to have to leave lots of time to get her into it."

Maura takes out her wallet out while we're still waiting for Gabrielle to come out of the dressing room, and pulls out a stack of pictures she took of Gabrielle, Manny and Shanna. Something is familiar about Manny. I turn to the next picture. His face. His name. It hits me then—who Manny reminds me of. "Leaf?" I whisper to Gracie. She pales, mouths "Yes." A shudder goes through me just as the fitting room door opens and Gabrielle walks out, looking like an angel.

"Seems like we're going to be spending a lot of time buttoning her up before the ceremony," Gracie says, eyeing the back of the dress.

Maura opens her wallet, waves her credit card toward the salesgirl. Gabrielle studies herself in the mirror. "No," she says.

We assure her that she looks gorgeous, that the dress looks as if it was made for her.

"No, that's not it. It's a magnificent dress, but not the kind of dress and not the kind of wedding I want. For most of my life I was unwanted. I'm shy, too—I just don't think I can handle being the center of attention at the kind of wedding Kayla had. I'd be embarrassed to death, and I don't think it would be good for

Shanna. I want something very small—just the three of you, and those in your families who I've come to know well. A few of the grandkids who are Shanna's friends. Manny's family and friends —he said there are very few who'd be able to come. Just people who love us. Not everyone who knows us or even likes us. We're not getting married to become a couple. We're getting married to become a family, and Manny and Shanna and I just want people there who really, really care," she says.

With great reluctance, Maura says she'll go along with Gabrielle's wishes.

Sometimes something simple is best. Sometimes you have to trust. Nothing could be more perfect for Gabrielle, Manny and Shanna than the wedding we hold at Blossom Knolls on a warm spring day, beside the flower garden. We were going to have the luncheon at Chew and Chat, but the weather is so glorious that we move the tables and chairs outdoors, and sit at our tables for the ceremony.

Josie's daughter, Carla, who has become a good friend of Gabrielle's, performs the ritual, declares Gabrielle and Manny husband and wife, tells Gabrielle she can kiss the groom.

Voices start to rise, and someone flings a handful of confetti toward the kissing couple. Carla holds up her hand for quiet. "We have another surprise ceremony," she says, and calls up Shanna. Some legal paragraphs are read, vows are taken, documents signed, and then Carla bends down to Shanna, asks her if she wants to take Emanuel Leavey as her father.

"Of course! Why else would I have said Momma should marry him?" Shanna declares, as she does whenever she has the chance, and Carla proclaims them a family.

The Teacher

Nothing is inevitable. The stream carrying the angel now called Manny flows into Gabrielle and Shanna's lives. The angel who guarded the soul once known as Shoshanna in her incarnations through time, the angel who guarded Shoshanna as her grandmother, the angel who was Leaf, whenever she needed him in her life, will be here to shelter Shanna and help her guide her skiff as it sails her life stream.

It is all I can do. It is for her to float her vessels beside his, or for her to steer her vessel to the far side of her streams, to keep separate from him. Her stream will go on, as it must, but now, to the extent that I can be joyful, I feel joy. And contentment. All is as it should be.

Scene 64: <u>Another Opening, Another Show</u>

Wren, age 76

It happens. Any day but the Fourth of July, which is Barbecue Day at Blossom Knolls and Fireworks For All at the Lake Kinde Residents' Beach. We sit through it every year on the Fourth of July weekend. The Talent Show at Blossom Knolls. Every child gets a chance to perform, even the abysmally untalented. Maura tries to organize it so there's at least one good act following each dreadful one, but it's not always possible. This year, so far, hasn't been bad. Which really doesn't matter—the only ones in the audience are people who adore these performing children, to whom even the worst act is nothing short of marvelous.

It's a shock when Maura opens the show to announce the year's M.C. There's a stirring in the crowd. Which recent high school graduate will it be? Maura's voice rings out over the whispers of the crowd. "...and after the auditions, the announcer elected by the graduating seniors is none other—" a slight pause, as parental breaths are held. The winning student knows, but no one else does—"elected in a unanimous landslide—Miss Shanna Maura Leavey!"

Shock waves! Cheers from the teens congregated at the rear. Confusion on the faces of those who didn't witness the auditions.

Four year old Shanna? Is this some kind of a joke?"

From the moment she steps onto the stage, it is understood why she was chosen. She is poised, articulate, keeps the show flowing, and interjects appropriate humor at adroitly chosen intervals. "They wanted to keep the program short this year, so they chose the shortest M.C. who tried out," she says to the befuddled crowd, and then immediately introduces the first act.

The youngest ones open the show. My two year old grandson, Liam, with his three and a half year old sister, Olivia, are the essence of adorable. So what if she shows signs of inheriting my clutziness and utter lack of rhythm? A child dancing is a child dancing is adorable. Especially if they're your grandchildren. Shoshanna would have loved seeing her four year old great grandson.

Act after act goes on. Encore after encore. Shanna keeps things moving along.

They're up to "the final act," Shanna announces, and introduces herself. "I wrote this story myself," she says. "The world is having a lot of problems with people getting along with each other, so I wrote a story about how some animals got together to bring peace and kindness to their realm."

I turn toward Gracie, see her turning toward me. See eyes all around questioning each other, and "who really put this child up to this?" written on faces.

Expressions which turn to wonderment as Shanna opens a folder, and begins to read.

Roaring applause, stamping, whistling and shouts of "encore," follow the moment of stunned silence at the story's end. Shanna follows this with an original poem. Again, an encore is demanded, but Shanna holds the mic in front of her, waits for quiet, and says, "Sorry, but it's past my bedtime," and skips off the stage.

"She has a publisher," Gabrielle tells us later. "The book will be out in three months. She's illustrating it herself."

"She's supposed to start kindergarten. The principal wants her to start in second grade. We forbid it. She's a four year old child, who happens to be gifted in reading, writing, and artwork. But socially, she's like any other child and she needs to socialize with children her age. If she's bored with reading lessons, she can sit next to a child having difficulty and be a helper," Manny says.

I watch Shanna the next day, playing duck-duck-goose and making sand castles beside the other youngsters. There is no way a stranger would pick her out as having unusual talents. She's enjoying her life as a child. What could be better?

PART ZERO!

INTERRUPTION!!!
(The music stops)

The Teacher

Three united streams bubble along over small rocks, flow around corners. Small tributaries join, as if the waters themselves were having a party. Nothing is inevitable, but the stream of contentment flows on, seemingly headed for uninterrupted jubilation.

And then! Had I a heart to stop, it would. As if a curtain has come down in the middle of one of those human shows. As if the sun itself has turned off and turned the world to blackness. There is a bend in the river path, and I can see nothing beyond it. Only blackness. I send a dream, but can show no more than I know. I let Gracie, Wren and Maura stand beside me in the Haven, as darkness falls as far as the edge of earth's atmosphere and fast as the flick of a light-switch.

Scene 65: (soundtrack: silence)

Wren, age 77

It's my turn to make breakfast. Omelets. I'm just cracking the eggs when Maura and Grace show up. The dream. They're going to start gushing about the dream. My thoughts are still tied to the original story Shanna read us last night. As if she knew something bad was coming and wanted to remind us to find the joy hidden in the worst of moments. And I know, because I heard the news, and most likely, the child did, too. I know what is coming, because it's here already, in parts of our globe that seem distant, but nothing is distant in the world of jet travel.

"It was the craziest dream. I mean, the whole world went dark. My goodness, we've never had a dream like that and—"

"I think it was a warning of some kind," Gracie cuts off Maura and says. "Someone's going to die, or something really bad is going to happen. Maybe 9/11 over again, or something like that. Or—any hurricanes predicted? Or earthquakes?"

"A virus," I say. "It's all over China and moving into Europe. Yesterday there was a case in Washington—the state. They're calling it a pandemic. People are dying. A lot of them. And it's going to come here."

"My goodness, what are we going to do? What's going to happen? What's—"

"Breathe, Maura," Gracie says, and starts to hum <u>When You Walk Through a Storm.</u>

What happens is a shut down. What happens is stopping the world as we know it. Closed businesses, schools, theaters… everything that differentiates humans from other species. What happens is that overnight, herd animals must turn into animals that roam the world as solitary beings. Smiles hidden behind masks. Hugs and handshakes turned into "distancing."

A new world order, a new vocabulary: Lockdown. Isolation. Distancing. Handwashing. Zoom weddings, birthdays, religious ceremonies, meet-ups with friends. Zoom funerals. Zoom. Who knew anything about Zoom and FaceTime before? Now they're the fragile threads holding together the privileged who have devices and understand how to use them. As for the others, I weep.

But before we understand that, on the day COVID arrives in our part of the state, but before it gets to the COVE, they tell us to stay in our apartments. Those who want food from the dining room will have it left on trays outside their rooms. More new vocabulary: Rely on delivery services to order food and other necessities. Contact-free delivery. Curbside pickup. Remote learning. Twenty second hand washing—sing <u>Happy Birthday</u> twice. Quarantine. Distancing. Masks. Masks. Masks.

No contact.

NO HUMAN CONTACT.

At the COVE, dinners will be ordered a day in advance and left on trays outside doors.

With numbed minds, Gracie, Maura and I make a fast decision. Toss clothes, toiletries, medications, whatever food we have in our pantries into our cars, break the speed limit, race up to Blossom Knolls.

Janna, two of her children and a slew of grandchildren are already living at Blossom Knolls. So are Gabrielle, Manny, and Shanna. Tim and his aide. One of the cooks, Beulah, decides to stay. We meet Claire as we're running to our cars and she accepts our offer of a cabin, insists that she'll help with the cooking, and do our cleaning for us. "It's what makes me happy," she says, and we're glad to know we'll have her company for the duration.

Chew and Chat and Banquet at the Barn are, of course, closed. We set up roadblocks. No one can enter the Blossom Knolls property without our consent—and a quarantine in an isolated cabin before joining the rest of us.

For the first two weeks, everyone stays in her own cabin area for the fourteen day incubation period. Beulah has offered to cook and leave dinners at our doorsteps. Bless you, Beulah!

Actually, those first two weeks aren't bad. We're apart, but if we sit in front of our houses, we can see each other. I can hear most of them. For those whose cabins are a little further away or hearing impaired, we use cell phones as we sit in front of our homes and chat. It's kind of fun.

"We need school," Shanna insists. The only child who does. Between my training in teaching reading and interest in science, Maura's music education, Gracie's health expertise, Janna's husband's proficiency in history and Manny's willingness to try to teach math, we put together a school. If this keeps up, others in our family will join us here, bringing families who will quarantine for their two week stint, when their children will join the school-in-progress. Life during COVID won't be so bad, we tell each other.

And then the deaths start to add up. We sit, numbed, in front of TVs, watching scenes of trucks outside hospitals. Refrigerated trucks, to hold bodies cemeteries and crematoria can't keep up with. Pictures of people on ventilators. Stories of hospitals running out of equipment, patients sharing ventilators. Not good for either patient but better than choosing one to help fight for life and one to die.

Instant hospitals are set up in tents in parks to serve the hospital overflow. Medical staff abandon families to work never-ending shifts.

Funerals we can't go to. Friends. Cousins. Phone calls with friends whose husbands died in nursing homes and hospitals, who were not allowed to visit them for the last days, sometimes weeks, of their lives.

Weeks turn to months. Over a year goes by.

Rayna's sister dies, and she can't go to the funeral. No one can. No one can sit shiva.

No human contact.

Alone.

Friends leave the COVE to live with their children. Isolated together, they get on each other's nerves. But they're the lucky ones.

My cousin Sue lives plane rides away from Blossom Knolls. Impossible for her to get here. Impossible for her to get to her children, who also live afar. Days, weeks, months—over a year goes by when her only human contact is on the other side of a phone or screen. Isolation. Loneliness. "But ALONE is different," she says. "If I'm lonely, I can call you. But I'm still alone." I listen as she sobs. The same thing Gracie said after Ian died. But Gracie had us. Sue has no one.

Our roadblocks stand firm, but Lake Kinde is a community and Blossom Knolls is a part of it. Janna's son, Jordan, garbed in mask, gloves, full protective gear, drives around the lake each day delivering food from Blossom Knolls to our neighbors, dropping the packed meals they order in front of their gates and doors. They do the same—dropping off our order of eggs, dairy products, organic produce, chicken, and fish right outside our gate. Stores send their trucks and drop off other necessities.

No human contact.

We become FaceTime and Zoom experts. Gracie watches a granddaughter's wedding: The bride and bridegroom, wedding officiant and photographer—and faces on a computer screen. I wonder if Ethan's toddler knows I'm a real person, not just another face on a screen. I wonder if I'll ever hug him again.

At Blossom Knolls, we find a way to go on. Shoshanna's daughter, Dandi, her children and grandchildren join us. After they finish isolating, her children join Shanna, and Janna's grandchildren for "school." Zoom classes now, from their home schools, supplemented by Maura's music lessons and games. I help with the academics. Musical programs, arranged by Maura.

When Dandi's quarantine ends, she sits with us around a campfire—after sticky marshmallows and melted chocolate has been washed off the children and they've all been safely tucked in for the night. She's still teaching her second grade students online. "It's a joke. My school is mixed—middle class kids with educated, computer literate parents. They're doing fine. But half of my class is impoverished. Welfare kids. Uneducated parents.

Half of them—or more—are functionally illiterate. The other half don't speak English well enough to help their kids. Yes, they were all given computers, but if the parents have to rely on the kids to even know how to turn it on, how are they supposed to help?"

There was always a divide, we agree. The virus is shining a spotlight on it. This will only serve to widen it, broaden it.

One more thing to mourn.

In front of the others, I smile, talk, interact as I always did. Alone at night, I weep. I think the others do, too.

We each deal with it in our own way. Maura gathers the children and willing adults and puts on shows. Claire becomes Mrs. Fix-It, our on-the-spot plumber, electrician, carpenter…

And Gracie. Gracie leaves the grounds, goes to Markettown General, dons as much protective gear as an astronaut on a spacewalk, and treats hospitalized COVID patients. Falls into a bed for a few hours each night at the Markettown Manor, now a refuge for hospital workers.

We sit around in the evening, luxuriating in our togetherness. Openly acknowledging the guilt we feel at the relative normalcy of our lives, at our protected health, at our freedom to feel air on our faces, to see each other's smiles, to live isolated from the world in a place where we can be together, mask free. A place where thanks to Shanna's idea, and the internet, we have a school, routines, some strange sense of routine and normalcy.

Scene 66: I Don't Know How to Love Him
(A scream in the silence)

Wren, age 77

"One more lap?" Maura says, and I can tell she's out of breath because that's all she says.

"How about up to Chew and Chat and then turn around and do a cool-down back to our cabins," I suggest. We've already done almost twice our usual cardio walk.

We step out of the path to let a child on a tricycle pass us. Hear a scream from the direction of Tim's cabin.

I race, breathe a prayer.

Hear myself scream "Tim!" before I have time to process what I'm seeing, knowing only that he's lying on the floor. At least a second passes while my scream goes on before I'm aware that he's having a stroke. He's struggling to talk, to move, but he can't seem to manage his right arm and leg and the words —just sounds come from his grimaced mouth.

"I called 911," Darlene, his aide, says. She lifts his head and puts a pillow under it. "He likes pillows, she apologizes.

I start to say it's OK, that I don't expect her to know what else to do that she's—

A thought. The gate! No one is around to open it to let the ambulance in. "Open the gate," I hear myself scream, and two of the teens—I'm too upset to register which ones—start running screaming "Emergency—open the gate for an ambulance," passing the cry along to others who are closer to the periphery.

"Masks!" Everyone put on your mask!" someone in the crowd gathering outside Tim's cabin shouts, and that, too, is passed along while parents frantically run to find their young children, cover their faces and shepherd them indoors.

The crowd disperses, runs for the safety of their homes. We have practiced this drill. We carry masks in our pockets. We thought we'd need them whenever a new family joined us, for the brief moments they moved into their cabin for their fourteen days of total isolation. We didn't think of emergencies.

I haven't been seeing Tim as often as I should. I was annoyed. He took the isolation thing way beyond anything rational. We're isolated, all of us. Until this moment, with the ambulance entering our grounds, there's no way anyone here could be contagious. It occurs to me that we'll all have to isolate for two weeks again. Tim never left isolation. With therapy, his speech returned, never as before, but enough to communicate, enough to discuss. But he wouldn't leave his cabin, not even for our Thursday discussions. Not even for dinners. "I don't want to die," he said, and really, I should have—I was his wife—I still love the man—I should have stood outside his window and talked to him, let him know I care about him and his ideas, and.

And I ignored him. He was safe there with his live-in-aide, who he allowed to eat with the rest of us at Chew and Chat— and then at Banquet at the Barn when Chew and Chat became crowded. He mandated that she eat at a separate table at least six feet from everyone else. Let's just say what he didn't know couldn't hurt him.

He has Darlene. Honestly, the way he treats her aggravates me, and it shouldn't. I know what makes him tick. It was wrong, totally wrong for me to be annoyed with his ridiculous isolation. I knew it wasn't ridiculous to him, and now "Tim," I cry. I move toward him, see the terror in his eyes. "I love you, Tim," I say. Knowing this might be the last chance I'll ever have to see him, I say it again. And yet again.

Visitors aren't allowed in hospitals, and who knows what kind of care he'll get. Gracie has told us how woefully understaffed Markettown General is.

But, it turns out, she never told us that Markettown General now has only one floor available for non-COVID patients. Never told us that the rest of the hospital is now treating the virus.

Tim catches it.

The hospital calls. They put him on FaceTime, let me say what could be my last words to him before they sedate him to put him on a ventilator. I tell him how sorry I am that I didn't spend more time with him. Between gasps for air, he whispers something that sounds like "I knew you were there."

We both say "I love you" at the same moment.
They are his last words.

Scene 67: <u>A Whole New World</u>
(woven in and out of silence)

Wren, age 78

The children are the first to notice it. They're screaming and running out of their cabins to see it: Fireworks, being shot off across the lake. We turn on our TVs. A vaccine has been approved. <u>A Whole New World </u>I hope, when I first hear the news. As if a switch will be flicked and life will open up as quickly as it shut down.

A mandate: Vaccinate the elderly first. Somehow, it seems backwards. Shouldn't the children be protected first? But they haven't tested it on children yet. So what about their parents? Teachers? Young adults? What sense does it make for me to be in the top priority group? The first to receive it? And the grim answer: because we're the ones most likely to die if we become ill.

Another thought. The vaccine is a new technology. We're all guinea pigs. If there are dire effects, we're the most expendable.

We don't hesitate. It takes hours on the computer—our teens are the ones who finally secure appointments for those of us over seventy to get our shots. We wear double masks, leave Blossom Knolls for the first time in over a year, drive to the pharmacy in Harvey's Harbor, and drive back, vaccinated. Quarantine, because we've been off-grounds.

Time goes by. All Blossom Knolls adults are vaccinated. Enough in the outer world, for precautions to be lifted. We come to a decision. Tables and chairs are moved from Chew and Chat to the lawn outside it. Tables are spaced wide apart. The gate to the public space of our property is lifted. Chew and Chat opens.

Teens are vaccinated. Then children.

Masked, although masks are no longer required, we make cautious forays off the property. To the small towns first. Then Markettown. The day comes when we go to Oceanport. Theaters reopen. It's a whole new world—until a new variant comes. Until they realize immunity wears off. New rounds of vaccines. New variants. New…again, and again, and again.

Will we always wear masks when we're near anyone we don't live with? There are anti-vaccers around who won't get the vaccine. Years from now, I'm hopeful never to see masks again—except in the winter. How wonderful they are at keeping faces warm! For now, I'll keep mine on even outdoors in the summer if I'm around strangers who may not be vaccinated.

I'm not the same person I was before COVID. I don't think anyone is. We've learned to value life, learned to value human contact. Even confirmed loners have learned to value being with others.

At the COVE, about a year into the virus, major changes occurred. Behind the scenes, with no one aware until the deed was done—clandestine meetings, secret signings—property ownership transferred. The COVE now belongs to the Righteous Flock. We can keep our apartments and adhere to their religious rules, or be reimbursed for the price we paid, minus a "refurbishing charge." We invite those friends who are left at the COVE to move to Blossom Knolls—we'll build more cabins if necessary—or maybe a small apartment building. But our friends yearn for families they haven't seen for over a year, and are all eager to move near their children. Gracie, Maura, and I are staying here. Claire is buying a camper, and planning on travelling "to every state and Canadian province. But Blossom Knolls will be home base," she promises.

In the outer world, there are big changes in the way people work, shop, participate in politics. Awareness of social/racial disparity loomed and won't go away. We join groups, support and attend marches and rallies.

In the outer world, as waves of variants bring fresh bouts of illness, waves of Me-ness loom above We-ness. Waves of disdain and maltreatment of people, races, and cultures falling under the heading of "Different from Dominant Here," turn the ground beneath our societal feet to thin ice.

Shanna's "Stories and Poems for A Peaceful Planet" is wildly successful—even the children are pitching in. All of us, doing whatever we can to bring justice, equality, and true democracy to a nation that has forgotten who it is.

In her videos, Shanna implores, "They say universal vaccination could get rid of this virus, so wouldn't universal kindness and respect solve our societal problems? I'm just a kid, but I really don't understand why the grown-ups, especially our leaders, don't get this."

Oh, Shanna! The bottom line is that adults *don't get it.* I love your dream of fixing the world, but I'm getting old, and the best I can do is help you spread your message, and see that at Blossom Knolls, on a day to day basis, life goes on, with an awareness that makes every moment a celebration.

And as life goes on, so, too, does COVID. A step forward to communal life opening up. A step backward with each new variant, to life behind a masked, distanced from other humans.

But we're alive, and together, and life goes on...

PART SEVEN: <u>LIFE IS</u>

The Teacher

Time passes. Dimmed light brightens. Blossom Knolls has become home, where streams of time float gently, softly.

But time is relentless. The pull of the ocean is strong. Someday, streams will part. One stream at a time will reach the sea. Water will be received by water, and all will be One.

ACT XXIII: <u>WHEN I LOOK UP</u>

The Teacher

For one stream, the tidal pull of the moon, the pull of the waters toward the sea, is overwhelming.

Scene 68: <u>Something's Coming</u>

Wren, age 81

I flit out of the house, walk next door as fast as my arthritic legs will allow me and yell through Maura's screen door. "Ready yet?"

"I'm not deaf and no, I'm not ready and you said—oh, it is eight o'clock—well, packing takes time and I still need a few more minutes and—"

"Twenty, I say. "You have twenty minutes."

I call and report to Gracie. "On schedule. She should be ready in about an hour. I told her twenty minutes."

What with the bathroom stops, the food stops, the "gotta stretch my legs" stops, the four hour ride takes seven hours. Just as I planned. I honk the horn in my son, Ethan's, driveway. My grandchildren bound out of the house, nearly knock us over with their exuberant hugs.

Dinner is—torture. For me—and I feel it from Gracie and Maura. Kate is a lovely woman, the perfect daughter-in-law. But the most imperfect cook on the planet. And Ethan! How can Tim's son eat this food? It's hard to swallow, but rules of politeness coupled with hunger and no-way-to-slip-out-and-go-to-a-burger-chain make us eat every drop of leather-dry chicken, half-baked potatoes, and over-cooked, watery broccoli on our plates. It's nutrition, I tell myself.

I put on my pj's, slather moisturizer on my face, wonder how my son and his children survive. On love, I think. On laughter. Food was a disaster, but dinner was a blessing. The stories, the respect each family member has for each other and their guests. The excitement building up for tomorrow's eclipse: "Yes, we have glasses for everyone." "Yes, we brought the big TV out to the porch and we'll be able to watch right where we'll need to be to see it live when it happens here." "Yes, we have enough chairs." "Yes, they're predicting good weather."

No, I'm not going to get a moment's sleep. I love Maura. I love Gracie. But we're all together now on pull-out beds and a cot, down in Ethan and Kate's family room. And Gracie is snoring. Loudly. When she stops for a minute, Maura takes up the chorus.

I can wake them up and tell them to stop, and they will. Until they fall back asleep and the concerto starts again. I might as well let them get some sleep.

Murder. Holding pillows over their heads might work. I search through my bag. Surely I must have a pair of earplugs in here somewhere. I know I packed them, in case the kids insisted on playing what they call music at ear-splitting volume. I find them, put them in my ears and a pillow over my head. And sleep. Sporadically. Between the verses and the chorus of snores.

Maura, age 81

This is it! I'm overwhelmed by my wake-up thought. My goodness, it's been on my bucket list since the last eclipse seven years ago and we were at the COVE so we only got seventy percent and even that—the sky darkening, the big black ball, the small chunk of bright orange around it and then the ball shrinking, the orange growing until the black was just a sliver, a crescent, the orange sun reborn. Why, my goodness, it was like getting a glimpse of the invisible God, so there was no way I was going to live seven years waiting and not get to see a total eclipse and when I heard where and how soon the total eclipse was going to be, well, I begged and pleaded and Wren called Ethan who lives right where it's going to be total and here I am, the day I've lived for and I'm here and just knowing today is the day is more happiness than I can hold.

Gracie, age 81

Happiness is seeing how happy Maura is. I almost didn't come. My hip's becoming a bit of a problem, and sitting in a car that long wasn't exactly pleasant, but I'm so glad I came.

"Could we have gotten better weather?" I ask, and everyone agrees the sky without a cloud, the temperature just right for sitting outside is as perfect as perfect can be.

We gather hours early, sitting on the porch, snacking, thank goodness, from a tray prepared in a deli, able to make our own sandwiches and all. We don't talk much or look at each other, which is a shame, because looking at their faces and the happiness there, especially Maura's, is a happiness in itself. Mostly, though, I'm like the others, with my eyes glued to the TV, rejoicing in seeing the eclipse glide through the sky across the country. Every once in a while someone puts on the glasses we all have ready and reports, "Nothing yet."

And then. "A black spot. Lower left on the sun."

We turn the TV off, put our glasses on. Take them off again. On again. Off. And then. ON!

Silence. Darkness blackens the air around us. Breath held. As if the air itself has stopped moving. As if the earth itself has stopped spinning. As if all there is, is the black ball covering, and covering.

Until a crescendo of bright light rims the moon.

Scene 69: <u>Stranger in Paradise</u>

Maura, age 81

Music. Does anyone else hear it? The heavens are singing—
I've never heard anything like it in my life, as if the angels are
singing. I want, I need to get closer, to hear the music, to sing
with the music, to be part of the music. My goodness! the orange
sun is bursting forth around the black sphere, slowly, inch by inch
overwhelming the darkness. Oh, my goodness! I need to get into
the music and I am—I feel myself wafting toward it, toward—

*I'm in the Haven now. Oh, my good—The Haven is music!
I'm inside the music and the Teacher is here, and Chris, Chris
who I haven't seen for years upon years is standing before me,
singing to me, holding me now, and "Forever," I hear in the
music. "You can stay here forever."*

*I open my mouth and "Yes," I sing back. "Forever." Forever
in bliss beyond the imagination of mortals. Forever in the music.
Forever, together with Chris.*

Wren, age 81

I take off my glasses, blink my eyes. How can it be over so
fast? But Maura was right. It was worth schlepping here. It was
worth listening to Maura and Gracie snore all night. I turn to look
at them. The look of bliss, of exquisite peace on Maura's face. A
calm she's never shown before. But.

"Maura, are you awake? Maura? MAURA! SOMEONE
CALL 911! ETHAN! GRACIE!"

I reach for her pulse. Gracie pushes me aside and begins
CPR.

Maura

*I see myself sitting in my chair, people gathered around me,
Wren being pulled away by Ethan, Gracie pushing on my chest.*

Ethan telling her to stop. Gracie weeping. Sadness washes over me and yet, sadness is swept away by knowing, yes, knowing—

"It's part of life," the Teacher says, though without a voice, the words resonating within my soul and the shades of people and people and people who have housed this soul as it journeyed through time learning lesson after lesson. All this, I know, and it comforts me. Comforts US, for I am now part of a single soul with many pasts.

I feel the souls around me who were my parents, siblings, cousins, friends. Shoshanna? She's shadowy, half here. I sense her eternal soul, but a part is—"Where?" I ask.

"Her persona is here," the Teacher says, "merged with all the personas of her soul's past, but a part of her soul, the lessons she has learned through eons of personhoods, has chosen to incarnate again, to teach what her eternal soul has learned."

I hear the music, the incredible music that bore me here. It's still off in the distance, still drawing me toward it. I need to get to the source, to join with it. I need—

"You yearn for what some call Heaven, some call Nirvana— every culture has its own name for Om-eh, the place beyond. You have earned the right to enter," the Teacher tells us.

"Where?" we ask.

"In the reaches beyond. In Om-eh, where all music is born. The soul you knew as Chris lives there, and you will, too—just tell me the key," the Teacher says.

It was given to Maura in a long ago dream. I remember following music, being stopped by a hedge, given a key and told to remember it, because the time would come to use it. The time is now. But what was it! What was the key? To Maura, the word "key" wasn't just something for opening doors. For her, the key was the setting for the song. One note, one chord controlling the notes around it. The key? I listen to the music. Not A, B, C, D, E, F, or G. Not a sharp or flat, not a major or minor. "All keys," I wordlessly say. "Each voice a different key and all blending together perfectly."

"And now add yours," the teacher says. As I do, hedges off to

the side part. We glide through the opening into a wonderment of living music, peace, love.

Wren, age 81

I'm in a place beyond grief. Numb. Past the point of feeling. Gracie calls Manny's cell. It will be better for him to tell Gabrielle, to wrap himself around her and help her bear the unbearable. I call Kevin and Bobby, Maura's brothers, and yes, I promise. We'll wait the extra day for their families to get to Blossom Knolls for the funeral.

We drive back in silence, Gracie as numb and distant as I am. We find Maura's "Bucket's Been Kicked" instructions and it surprises us. It wasn't something Gracie or I expected of Maura. A wake, a funeral mass. Gracie makes the arrangements. I deal with the other logistics, organize the green burial in a plot beside Shoshanna's. Plan a post-funeral repast with the staff at Chew and Chat.

In private moments, every cell of my body sobs for the loss of my friend.

It is a blessing to see Maura lying in her open casket at the wake, cradling the urn containing Chris's ashes, her face softened by bliss.

I see the crowded room, the lines of people waiting to pay their respects to Gabrielle, Manny, Shanna, Kevin and Bob, and their families, who stoically stand, accept hugs and words, but there's a curtain between me and the room. I don't really hear a thing.

I find Janna on the other side of the gathering. "I know," she says. "I see the crowd. I already called the staff to switch tomorrow's repast to the Barn, with the tent up for extra seating outside."

I look around the church. It's as if every adult who was ever a child Maura taught travelled to be here. Everyone who knew

Maura—"Would you believe? People we went to high school with!" Gracie whispers to me. Everyone from our Silver Birches neighborhood, to work associates, friends from Oceanport and Markettown, and it seems like everyone who ever knew Maura on the Lake or at the COVE. The priest does a beautiful job, with prayers, hymns, and a thumbnail summary of the good deeds Maura gifted us with.

"No eulogies," Maura noted in her list of instructions. "My goodness, I annoyed people with all my run-on talk. No need for more!"

It helps to know the esteem my friend, my sister-in-spirit, was held in. But it's only when Maura's distinctive voice rises joyfully above the singing of the throng, it's only when Maura's voice drowns out all the other voices as her favorite hymn, Hail Mary, Gentle Woman, is sung, that I understand. Maura will always be here, filling the empty space her death left behind.

The crowd at the burial spills past the cemetery onto the road and the neighboring farms. It's OK, the neighbors are here and welcome all to their property. As per her instructions, the high school students sing a song from a show they're rehearsing. How could she have known they would be working on Cotton Patch Gospel days before her death? How could she have known they'd select When I Look Up, the perfect song about nature and love surrounding us, bringing peace to all? How, Maura? I look up and ask the Teacher, "How?"

As Maura's casket is lowered, we all join in singing Amazing Grace. Once again, Maura's voice stands out. I wipe my eyes.

You will always be with me, my friend.

ACT XXIV: <u>HAPPINESS</u>

The Teacher

Carrying memories of the past, streams run on, drawn by the ever-strengthening pull of the sea. Yet one fledgling stream forges a new path as it grows from creek to stream to river.

Scene 70: <u>Days Gone By</u>

Shanna, age 9

I want something of Grandma's to hold onto. I have all the gifts she gave me, but I want something of hers. Not her clothing. Not her jewelry. "You wear the pearls," I tell Mom. Grandma wrote a note in her will that I should get them, but what kid my age needs pearls? "I'll borrow them when I'm older if I need them." I can't explain it. What I want is memories. I want to know what Grandma was like before I was born and started remembering. I want to know what she was like way before. I'm nine now. What was she like when she was nine?

Mom and Dad tell me all kinds of stories about things they remember, but they don't go back far enough. "Go ask your aunts," they say. I kind of balk at the thought—they're both so sad. But maybe talking about good memories will help them.

Aunt Wren starts to tell a story about helping Grandma learn to read. It doesn't surprise me that she had problems. Gracie goes out while she's talking, and comes back in with a stack of notebooks with fancy covers. "Here's what you're looking for, I think," she says. "Shoshanna made us journals every year. The covers all show something that happened during the year. They were her New Year's Day gifts from the time we were around your age until she died. Your grandmother didn't do any writing, but she kept a scrap book filled with theater programs and photos and souvenirs. Shoshanna did some writing, but mostly she drew pictures. Wren and I used the journals essentially as diaries. All our secret thoughts. You're welcome to mine."

"And mine," Wren says. "There's loads of stuff about Maura in all of ours. The four of us were always together."

I'm thinking and thinking where in my room I can find the space for them, and for a table to put them on when I'm going through them, when they tell me the most amazing, spectacular thing there is: In Cabin 14—the one on the end that never gets used, there are all the rest—books from every one of the four friends for every year since they got to know each other! Shoshanna's and Wren's from when they were six, and then Maura's and Gracie's from when Shoshanna moved to Silver Birches. They made a kind of library for their families, and usually they just give the key to the cabin to older "responsible" teens, but they'll make an exception and—

Holy Acorns! Gracie pulls a key out of her pocket, hands it to me, and says "It's yours. Just be sure to wash and thoroughly dry your hands before you handle the books."

Wren adds, "The journals from the last ten years are always kept private. Gracie and I have the keys to the room they're in. The other rooms are open. When the last of us dies, the room can be permanently opened."

I race to Cabin 14. I'm shelving the books Gracie gave when one falls onto the table, lands open to a page with a picture on it. So it's Shoshanna's journal. I look at the picture and—how can it be? It's a picture of the place I dream about. The place I call Peaceland. Every detail is the same. I tell Mom, and she says "Shoshanna drew pictures like that all the time. You must have seen them and dreamed about them."

But when I tell Dad, he says "Mom is right," but he has a kind of look, like, maybe he dreams about it, too.

Shanna, age 13

Oh my! It's the easiest assignment in the world, but it's too easy. "Interview an older person, or a few older people, and write about what their life was like when they were thirteen." So here I am, in cabin fourteen, with the volumes from the time Shoshanna, Grandma, and my aunts were thirteen, and holy acorns! I could write a whole book! Mrs. Rhodes wants two to four pages!

I manage to keep it to four: How the four of them took the train from Silver Birches to Oceanport and went to the road-show of a Broadway play—all for $8.53 a person, with the prices for the train tickets, the restaurant lunch, and the theater ticket included. Grandma going to a drugstore soda fountain and sharing a malted float on her first date. Shoshanna's family getting a two tone Chevy Bel Aire, and the girls all wishing it was the new Chevy Corvette model. I Love Lucy. I don't say anything about Grandma's struggles in school, Gracie's boyfriend, Wren being bullied for being inept in gym, Shoshanna having trouble accepting her family's strict religious rules.

But the things I don't include keep swimming around my mind. Maybe I will write a book, I think. Not yet. But someday.

The thought simmers for a few days, and here I am, with a blank notebook in front of me, starting the book when they are seven, and have their first dream.

I tell Wren and Gracie, and they make me promise not to ever show the book I'm going to write to anyone, until the last of them dies. And then, "Make it a biography of our friendship," Gracie says, and Wren agrees. So that's what I'll do. Whenever I have some time, I'll add to it, and—someday. Who knows? Someday maybe, when the last of them dies, I'll have a book. But that had better be many, many years from now.

Scene 71: <u>Bring On Tomorrow</u>

Wren, age 93

"You go, Wren," Gracie begs me, but I can't leave her here alone.

"They'll zoom it and we'll watch it together. End of discussion," I say.

She starts apologizing, as if having fragile bones were something she has control over. As if a ball whizzing past us, inches from her head was something she could have ignored. As if taking her eyes off the ground and not seeing the tree root popping up in front of her was done on purpose. As if falling and breaking her leg, and her hip, were something she chose to do.

As if having her leg shatter, as if its being held together now by pins and plates is something she can ignore...

"No," Dr. Johnson said, "I don't care what the event is. She's not sitting in a car going over potholes and bumps for four hours."

So, "You go, Wren. I'll be fine here. I'll hire an aide. I'll be OK. I'll watch on the big screen. I'm not going to miss Shanna's graduation, and I'm certainly not going to mess it by falling again."

I won't leave. For one thing, Gracie is my forever friend, and you don't leave a friend when she's in need. Besides that, we're a team. This is the kind of experience we've always shared, and I'm not going to break that tradition now. For another thing, if we learned nothing else during the COVID episode, it was how to Zoom. Now we have a choice. Zoom or half a dozen other carriers.

The kids set it all up for us. All I have to do is wait for one o'clock, tap the screen and—

Gracie is settled on the couch. I'm in the seat at the table beside us, where I can reach the controls. I put my hand out, touch the screen, and there they are. The whole family, sitting in three rows of chairs near the outdoor stage decorated with the huge Ivy University banner. I press another button and they pick up their devices, smile and wave at them. Gracie and I wave back.

"It will start in ten minutes," Gabrielle tells me. "You can talk." She reminds me that she, Manny, Maura's family, Shoshanna's family, Gracie's children and mine will all be wearing earpieces so they can hear anything Gracie and I say. "Just be careful not to say anything you don't want us to hear."

She holds up a program, shows us the section headed "Future Plans," moves through pages until we can see Shanna's name: Gabrielle turns it around and reads it to us: "For the past four years, Shanna has been spending summers working at Clear Ideas, the internationally acclaimed think tank. She'll be moving on to an internship in the office of U. S. Representative Zoey Xavier. In addition, she plans to continue the weekly podcast she's had since she was fourteen, and she's thinking of writing another novel. 'But probably not next year,' " she adds.

I have to laugh. Where does the girl find the time? I know she sleeps!

Gracie and I chat with our gathered family and friends, watch the procession until "Gracie do you see her! There, on the lower left!"

The president of Ivy University makes his speech. Other dignitaries speak. I keep glancing at Gracie, ready to wake her up if she falls asleep, but she's bright eyed and alert, even through speeches so soporific I have to stop myself from nodding off.

Awards are given. Gracie pulls herself to standing and applauds along with the crowd on our screen every time Shanna is called up for one.

The president finally says, "Now for the speech you've been waiting to hear. It is with overwhelming pride that I introduce the moderator of the podcast, *Pathway to Peace*, the author of this year's bestseller, *It Starts With You*, which is slated to come out as a film next year," he stops and waits for the murmurs in the audience to quiet, "innumerable poetry books, and children's

books which she began publishing at the age of four, and—
without further ado, I give you this year's valedictorian, Shanna
Maura Leavey."

Gracie raises her arms, I stand, and together with the crowd
we cheer.

Shanna, serene in front of the microphone, in her white cap
and gown, fills the screen. Whichever teen is the videographer
zooms the camera in on her face.

"I don't want to disappoint you," she wipes sweat off her
brow, "but you're all feeling the same heat I am, so I'll keep this
short. Many of you have heard my podcasts or read my books, so
you have a good idea of what I'm about to say. For those who
haven't, if you want to hear more, the podcasts are always
available. For today, I want to thank Ivy U. for allowing me to
follow my dreams and take the courses I wanted without
fulfilling major requirements. I think I've sampled every
department, and I think it's important for me to have gotten that
kind of broad background for me to use my talents most
effectively. I did actually, unintentionally, complete a philosophy/
religion major. It was just so interesting I couldn't stop taking
courses! And that's what I want to say about my hopes for all of
you. I hope you all felt that way about your majors. I hope you all
felt about your professors the way I felt about mine. I can't single
one out. Each one was brilliant, entertaining, mind-blowingly
informative—and a nice person. Thank you, thank you, thank
you.

"Thank you to my parents, and the huge extended family that
has nurtured me and sustained me and put up with me for the past
twenty-one years. I love you all.

"Now, you're expecting some kind of speech spewing
wisdom that will send you off into the world ready make of your
life something grand and wonderful, but you don't need those
words. You know them, you've lived them. You are, after all,
graduating from Ivy U. You are gifted, you are special, and you
are now educated by the finest faculty any school ever had, so—
go for it! But please, go for it in a profession that brings you the

joy and excitement you felt in your best courses, with your favorite professors. Go for it in a way that is meaningful, and worthwhile. Go for it in a way that lets you look in the mirror each day and say 'I'm living the best life I can.' Best for you, best for All." She reaches for her water bottle, takes a sip.

"In the end, I have just two words to say: If you live by two words, make the first *We,* and make *We* include our planet, and all that lives upon it. *We* means kindness to all. *We* means acceptance of all. *We* means tolerance of all. *We* means respect for all. And the second word? *Kindness.* Let every thought and every act be guided by kindness, for you, for All.

"I'd like to end with the Pledge for a Peaceful Planet. For those who know it, please say it with me:

"I pledge allegiance to the Planet Earth and all that lives upon it. One planet, indivisible, where every human strives for liberty, justice, and equality for all. One planet, where kindness and respect rule, and peace is shared by all."

I listen to the thundering chorus of the voices joining hers, and hear hope for our world.

We chat for a few moments with Gabrielle and Manny, and then I excuse us. I want to heat up the dinner our chef left in our freezer before she went to the graduation. It's been defrosting in the refrigerator long enough. It should be ready by how. The other guests are going out to celebrate—why shouldn't we? Seafood paella, along with a side order of happiness and contentment, at having been able to share this experience.

Scene 72: I'm Flying

Wren, age 97

"No," I tell Gabrielle for the hundredth time. "I'm OK. Perfectly comfortable, and I still have a half a cup of tea. I don't need more, and if you offer me another cookie I'm going to eat it and I'll split out of my dress!"

Gracie's already sprawled on the couch in Gabrielle and Manny's cabin, crowded around the TV. Waiting. Waiting. The results are starting to come in, now.

"Quiet!" Manny yells. A picture of Shanna and the man she's running against flashes onto the screen. The announcer starts to say something, stops for a moment as if he's listening to something. The camera zooms in on his face as he announces:

"…We have a projected House of Representatives winner in the Lake Kinde region of the state. With fifty eight percent of the vote in, it appears that Shanna Leavey will win in a landslide. At twenty-five, the minimum age for a representative, Ms. Leavey will be the youngest member of the house.

Down in the Oceanport area, the incumbent…"

Manny helps Gracie into her wheelchair and starts running with it. I hoist myself onto my scooter, join the throng racing toward the Barn where our gathered friends and relatives, the TV crews and Blossom Knolls staff have been watching and waiting for this moment. Shanna, her staff, and her life-long friends, are alone in Shanna's cabin, awaiting her opponent's conciliatory speech. Or she should be, because there they are, scurrying toward the Barn like the rest of us, Shanna fist-bumping the air as she dances down the path. I think about what she said when she told us she was running.

"Sometimes, it's just easier to make big changes from the inside. Like the changes Wren made in her sorority."

Yes, I think, remembering how for the three years I was a member, not one woman who wanted to join was turned away.

I sit in the barn, surrounded by my grandchildren, by my friends' families. Sadness wafts over me like a sudden draft. What Maura would have given to see this moment. Her jubilant granddaughter standing beside her friends, fulfilling her dream. Walking along her path to peace, and taking the world with her.

ACT XXV: <u>SO LONG, FAREWELL</u>

The Teacher

The ocean, the wellspring of all life, flows on. Sunlight warms the seas. Droplets drift skyward. Rains fall on mountainsides, in valleys, on plains. Water finds water and creeks coalesce, streams form and run together into rivers. Water is never still. Water moves onward, relentlessly, to the sea. Where sunlight will warm it, so that rains will fall, and new streams flow.

Scene 73: <u>Over The Rainbow</u> (Reprise)

Gracie, age 97

Look at this day! My great granddaughter is just learning to walk. What memories that brings. She's so cute. And Shanna! Little Shanna, elected to be a Representative to the U.S. Congress!

Under the eaves, near the door to my cabin, two robins are working together to build a nest. White fluffy clouds, like angels in the snow, are floating lazily through the sky. A memory: The first day it snowed after Shoshanna moved to Acorn Oval, Maura and I took her outside and started making angels in the snow. She was appalled, and so scared! Was this something Jewish girls were allowed to do? One thing she was sure of—her mother would never approve of her lying down in the snow and getting all wet. We tried to explain that she wouldn't really get wet— maybe a little damp. "The snow has to melt for it to get you wet," I told her and suggested that we go to my backyard, where her mother couldn't see her every time she looked out the window. Years later, when I brought up the incident—or maybe Maura did —Shoshanna said it was more important to her to make new friends than to obey every religious rule. If there even was a rule.

People walking toward my cabin draw me from my reverie. Wren and—Josie?

"Josie, when did you get here?" I ask.

"Just stopped by to say hello," Josie says. "I'm playing hooky from a conference at the college, but I couldn't bear to be this close and not see you."

I want to say "It's OK if you came to say good-bye. I know I don't have much time left. You have to understand, I've had ten wonderful, glorious years since the gremlins got into my hip and made the ride home from seeing the eclipse where Maura died such torture that I went to the doctor. Ten years with this stage four breast cancer. Now it's all over and the side effects are diminishing the quality of my life, so, no more chemo. Time to move on." I can't say it. I have to let others take the lead, and if all Josie is saying is that she wants to see me, what can I say but "Well, hello, then."

We chat for a while—what a lovely day it is, what our kids and grandkids are up to, the conference Josie is at—As they said on that Seinfeld show—"yada yada yada."

Josie looks at her watch. "I really have to get back to that conference."

We say our good-byes. Maybe Josie doesn't want to say it, but I thank her for "being a truly good friend. My life is richer for having known you."

She thanks me—I don't know whether for the compliment or for giving her permission to let her say good-bye. "The honor is all mine. You're a beautiful person, Gracie. The world has been graced by your presence in it."

She's gone, in the blink of an eye, before I can jump on her overdone pun.

It's certainly been a glorious day, but I've been feeling unusually tired since dinner. I'm alone in the cabin. No one will mind if I go to bed a little early. I do, sometimes. I'm in the cabin next door to Wren's. She watches my lights and my shades. If the lights are off and the shades are drawn, she knows I'm resting. In the morning, our raised shades tell each other that we're alive and awake.

I'm so tired. So, so tired. I pull down the shades, turn out the light and lie down on top of the quilt. It's a warm night. I say the prayer I've been reciting since I learned to speak. "If I should die before I wake, I pray the Lord my soul to take."

I close my eyes, awaken to softness and peace. A sense that all is right and all is good. A sense of someone in bed beside me. Ian. Of course, Ian!

"So where did you tell me you wanted to go for our honeymoon, my Gracie-Faye?" he says.

"Over the Rainbow. Oh, Ian, I wanted to spend my life over the rainbow with you. And we did, didn't we?" I ask.

"It was lovely, Gracie, but look, I brought you a real rainbow. Would you like to fly over it? For I love you more than the rest of the world put together. I've been waiting for you to be ready to go over the rainbow with me.

I reach out to touch him, to hold his hand, but his arms are around me, embracing me. I try to speak, to tell him I love him, but he puts a finger on my lips and lifts me. So gently. So tenderly.

I'm flying now, in his arms. Flying through my childhood— and there are Mam and Da and those of my brothers and sisters who are departed, all in their front yard on Acorn Oval, searching for shamrocks and four leaf clovers. Flying through my teen years with Ian, while he's standing beside me, walking me home from school, reciting poetry he wrote for me. He's flying with me through the Acorn years, flying through the day he walked into the coffee shop with his pot of gold. On and on through the child-rearing years, the years and years and years of friendships and love. Holding me and flying me, and the feeling of safety, the feeling of softness and peace. A sense that all is good, and right.

Now a sense of something holy. Something so grand and perfect that I would weep were I not made of air.

For I look down. My body is lying on my bed and I'm flying in Ian's arms, far above. Slowing now, landing. In the Haven! Winter. White snow. The Teacher is here. The Teacher is saying, "Welcome to Om-eh." But she isn't the Teacher! Not the Teacher of my dreams. She is the Blessed Mother exactly as she looked in the picture across the room from Brigid's bed. The picture I looked at when I knelt to pray each night.

The Blessed Mother is holding me now, as if I were a precious child. "Welcome to Om-eh," she says again. "Welcome home."

Jesus stands beside us, strokes my face, wordlessly welcomes me.

There's a gathering of spirits around me now. Shades and shades and shades of people and people and people I once was. They come together. I feel myself united with them.

Home. I am home. I am One, one spirit, with all the learnings and growings of lives lived in the past. Around Us now are all the lives Ian has lived, loving me in every lifetime. And there—Mam and Da, my sisters and brothers, cousins, teachers, and all who have been my friends. All, all here.

Two spirits approach from the side. As Gracie, I never met them, yet the part of me that still sings the song that is Gracie knows them immediately. With all the spirits around me, I am drawn to them as if by a magnet reaching deep within me to a place of unquenchable longing.

"Our daughters?"

"Yes," Ian lets me know. Their souls moved on to other personages, but yes, they are the daughters who died before they could be born." I would fall to my knees if such were possible. I would take their hands, throw my arms around them, breathe life into them. Their spirits touch mine and longing turns to bliss.

I'm made to understand there is a place beyond the Haven, Om-eh, where flowers sing and shamrocks dance. I'm made to understand that I have the key. I think back and back to my life as Gracie, to a dream, to—"A rainbow, God's promise to Humankind," I silently say. "And a stone," I add. "The substance of the planet itself. The reality and the promise. Matter and Faith." Hedges split apart and there—yes, the flowers are dancing. I spring up and join them, dancing with all the joy and dreams I danced with when I was young. Dance free, without the encumbrance of a human body.

I hear music, and know—Maura's soul is here, in the choir of angels. Yes. Yes. That's her voice, soaring over the flowers dancing at my feet.

Wordlessly, I ask if this is my eternity, if I can stay here forever with Ian, with my daughters, with my siblings and parents and—

Wordlessly, I'm told that I can, but if such is my wish, with Ian by my side, I'll occasionally be sent to earth, allowed to embody as a human when people need two angels to guide them.

The blessing of being needed! With gratitude, I consent.

"Like Josie," Ian lets me know. "Josie is an angel who comes to earth when humans are in need. So we'll be here most of the time, and go where we're needed, clothed in flesh when necessary, as Josie is.

I look at the spirits nearby, and know—when part of a fully evolved soul materializes on earth, a part of it remains ever in Om-eh. I see Shoshanna, and know part of her has been reborn as Shanna, know that part of her Leaf is living within Manny, for the work Shanna has to do on earth is great enough for her to need the guidance of a bodhisattva—a soul reborn, and an angel, incarnated. An angel who once stepped in and guided a man named Leaf.

The Teacher looks at me and Ian. "As time goes by, Shanna will need two more angels by her side."

She doesn't have to ask. "It would be an honor," I silently say.

Scene 74: <u>Prayer</u>

The Teacher

I send Wren a dream: She is in the Haven, in its winter whiteness, winter silence, winter stillness. Two people walk across the snow. Lightly, lightly. The snow is deep and soft. A rabbit hops across and leaves footprints, but the two people seem to float along the surface, leaving no impression at all.

They come closer, close enough for Wren, standing knee-deep in the drifts at the entranceway, to see it clearly. Ian and Gracie. Gracie and Ian. Light as air, and glowing, beaming. To Wren, it is as if joy and love, peace and something holy are radiating from them. The sense grows stronger the closer the two come.

Ian is leading Gracie toward someone. Someone who belongs in the Haven. The Teacher? But it is not me, as Wren has ever seen me. Wren recognizes me as I appear to Gracie—the Blessed Mother, as she appeared in the picture in Gracie-Faye's childhood room. Mary, reaching her hands toward Gracie and Ian, as if welcoming them to her home.

Wren, age 97

I awake from the dream, drag myself out of bed. Gracie. It's four A.M. The middle of the night. You don't go barging into someone's cabin because you had a dream.

But.

But.

I throw on a robe and slippers, take a flashlight and walk next door. Gracie, asleep atop her bed, still wearing the jeans and shirt she wore to dinner. Gracie, with a look of peace, of a happiness that is—ecstasy—beatitude, I think.

I find a blanket and cover her, call Arwen and Oberon. Call her hospice volunteer. Call her priest.

The wake is—it's as if I'm half in a daze. I know I'm here. I see the room filled with flowers, Gracie in her coffin looking so lovely in the green dress Arwen selected. I see all the chairs facing her. I see groups of people gathered around the room. Groups from our years at the COVE, people I recognize from the Markettown schools. Becky, who she's cared for, as if she were her grandmother. The room is packed. Arwen and Oberon and their families. Gracie's living sisters and brothers and their families standing in the longest reception line I've ever seen. Throngs of people patiently lined up outside the funeral home, waiting to pay their respects. I know I'm here, but I'm not here. It's as if none of this is real, as if Gracie is going to pop up any moment and say, "Surprise! The gremlins knocked me out for a moment, but I'm back!"

Friends come up to me and offer their condolences. "We know she was like a sister to you. We're so sorry for your loss," kind of thing, and it's almost as if they're speaking a language I don't understand. My loss? Is Gracie really gone? Am I the only original Acorn left? I stand here like an unfeeling statue, but everything inside me has turned to tears.

Gracie's children speak first at the funeral. Obie speaks of growing up in a house where faith and magic were a way of life, but "Kindness ruled, above all."

"She was always there, whether I needed advice about boyfriends, or a last minute baby sitter. Always ready to give up whatever plans she had to come over and help," Arwen says. "But what I'll remember most is magic. Magic. She let me in on a little secret. 'Magic,' she said, 'lets you imagine. And maybe if you imagine hard enough, it will be so. But rainbows? Rainbows are from God.'"

There's a hum from the audience like a communal smile, and "yeah," as if everyone who knew Gracie can hear her declaring, as if she's here, "Sure, rain will dampen your life. But even surer, there'll be a rainbow at the end."

Her grandchildren and great grandchildren speak. "The funnest great granny." "She always made me laugh, and she had the best stories ever." "I'll never forget how she taught me to make Irish soda bread and claimed it was the Leprechauns who made it explode over the sides of the pan." "She came to every little league game I ever played and cheered so loud I could hear her on the field." "You always made me feel how much you loved me, even when I misbehaved." "Granny, your hugs were everything." "I miss you, Granny." "I miss you, Granny," "I miss you, Granny."

I talk about the times the group of us got in trouble with our parents, and how Gracie would explain to them in the most serious voice that it wasn't our fault, that we couldn't help it if the elves ate the whole cake my mother made for her ladies' organization or that the fairies made the ball go through the Gallagher's window. "She always got whoever was angry at us to laugh, and kept us from being punished." I go on to speak of her years upon years of service after service—how she lived to "do" for others.

One speaker after another makes note of particular volunteer activities, of her quiet acceptance of all the illnesses and strife she endured. How she never lost her faith, or the joy of a magical world.

My eyes are drawn to her coffin, and glory be! Gracie is floating above it, sitting with her legs crossed the way she used to when she was young. We make eye contact, and she smiles.

The mass continues. Gracie remains, seems to enjoy it. When it's finally over, the coffin is wheeled out to the waiting horse-drawn wagon, with Gracie still hovering above it.

The Catholic cemetery is a short ride away. Rain starts to pour down as we leave the church, is still raining when we reach the gravesite, beside Ian's. Umbrellas open. A fleeting thought—like the day they first met under Gracie's umbrella.

Prayers are said. As flowers rain down on the casket, a rainbow fills the sky like a canopy guarding the grave.

Scene 75: <u>**Sunrise, Sunset**</u>

Wren, age 97

Six months after Gracie's funeral, Shanna weds. It's almost as if one of my own grandchildren is getting married. No. Screw the almost, I think. My great grandchildren can't hear my thoughts, can't be shocked by the refined old lady they think I am, using words like screw.

But screw it. Shanna is my grandchild. In spirit, if not in genetics or legality. Wasn't Maura my sister in spirit? And when Maura, as a single mother, fostered Gabrielle as an infant, didn't Gracie, Shoshanna and I fill in as a substitute second parent? When Gabrielle returned weren't we with her almost as much as Maura? Didn't we all kind of fall into place as grandparents when Shanna was born? And after Maura died—weren't Gracie and I there to parent Gabrielle, and grandparent Shanna? So yes, I answer myself. My granddaughter is getting married and—even Shanna says I'm walking down the aisle, "Like a grandma." Walking alone. I still can't accept that I'm the only one left.

I think back to all the weddings we've had at Blossom Knolls and my eyes fill with tears. All the children, now parents and grandparents. All of my generation—gone. Two of the young women are pregnant. Eva and Carlotta. I can't keep track of whose children they are. And now a new person is marrying Shanna and becoming part of the family! A man named Craige Angelli. And his sister, Ina, Shanna's friend, who introduced them. Marry one of us and your whole family becomes part of ours. I make a note to check on the work being done on the new cabins being built. One for Shanna and Craige, and one for Ina, a sister-of-the-soul friend of Shanna's, I think, the way Gracie, Shoshanna, Maura and I were friends.

ACT XXVI: <u>NEVER, NEVER LAND</u>

The Teacher

It began with a dream, with a glimpse of serenity, and eternal peace. And so it will end.

Scene 76: <u>Memory</u>

Wren, age 100

I sit on my porch. Just sit and think. I do a lot of that these days. The night is clear, the air crisp. No light is needed. The full moon, the sky speckled with stars so thick and close they almost touch, provide all the light I need. I sit and rock, think about the wonder of reaching a hundred. I think about the changes in the world over the last century, and it saddens me. Those terrible years in the late twenty teens up through much of the twenty-twenties. The hatred and meanness, the intolerance of difference. Seeing it tore me apart. And the plague, the virus. Sometimes I think God sent it to make people stop and realize what really matters. Examine their values. Too many people died, but it did have an effect. In many ways, it brought out the best in people.

And the worst in some. I can't deny it. The meanness—the ME-ness that came out was a disease in itself. Thank God and Goodness, and yes, thanks to Shanna, we're past that now.

Shanna—the way that young woman graduated from college and went into politics. My goodness, as Maura would have said, what a difference she's making.

I stop thinking about the world and start reflecting on myself, where I am now. They humor me. Invite me to the kitchen to be the "ultimate taster" at Chew and Chat and Banquet at the Barn. Whenever children are around they come asking, always asking, about the "old days."

It's a good life. A day doesn't go by without joy, and peace, and so much love. And laughter—especially when they walk away whispering, "Poor Wren must be losing her hearing. Her voice just keeps getting louder and louder." Balderdash! I hear their whispers, don't I?

Whispers—about loneliness, "Now that all her friends are gone." Of course I miss them! Gracie, Maura, Shoshanna. I miss Tim. I miss my brother. But look who I have here! How could I be lonely? How is that possible, when I'm surrounded by my children and grandchildren and great-grandchildren—and everyone else's? One big family, with so many new faces I can't keep the names straight. But I remember their personalities, their interests, their likes and dislikes. There's always love, always caring. You don't need to remember names to share the feelings.

I pull my sweater around me, pull up the lap blanket someone knitted for me, watch the changing expressions on the face of the moon, think about the first time I visited the Haven and met the Teacher and wonder. Just wonder.

Scene 77: <u>Circle of Life</u>

The Teacher

I watch as the last of the four streams flows serenely onward, drifting through Space along Time-worn paths. Pulled ever onward, relentlessly, toward the sea.

Wren, age 101

Thank goodness, they listened. "No party," I insisted. "Yes, the family can come together for a dinner at the Barn—the way we do for every holiday. That's it. Nothing special. Nothing crazy like last year.

Last year. OK, one hundred is a big deal. But a whole weekend of non-stop revelry? Don't they realize that a person who's reached a hundred needs some downtime? That just breathing takes energy and being bubbly is exhausting?

At least this year, they listened, and as soon as dinner was over, I popped onto my scooter. Sort of. One of the teens hoisted me onto it. He wanted to escort me back to my cabin but as soon as his hands were off me I hit the gas and took off. They think I'm sleeping now. Who goes to sleep when there's a party going on and cake hidden in my pocket?

I'm here on the back porch, where they can't see me. No lights. I like sitting in the dark. Besides, the air is so pure that starlight makes artificial light unnecessary. I sit in the dark, breathe the green scent of the land, watch the start-dusted sky and drink in the wonder of the news about the planets being discovered on distant stars—planets designated as most like ours. Planets our unmanned spaceships are aimed for now. What if they find life there?

What if? The question my friends and I always asked. A question with no wrong answer.

I think of the century I've lived through. Spaceships. Imaginings in comic books when I was growing up. Pure fiction. Even planes were a novelty. People did travel and go to Europe—on big ocean liners. I remember going to see my friend Lisa's parents off when they set sail on the Queen Mary. Now folks get on planes and are there in a few hours. Just enough time for one of those dreadful plastic-coated cardboard meals.

Yesterday, on my actual birthday, they sat me down in front of a screen on some kind of new device whose name I can't recall. Turned it on and up popped my grandson sitting at a desk in Scotland. It was so nice chatting with him. But then, they hit a few buttons and there was my great granddaughter, in Japan. It all makes me remember travelling to London—I think it was in the 1960's. They didn't have jets yet, just planes with propellers, and barf-bags ready at every seat. I'd been mandated to call home and let my folks know I arrived safely. Big mistake. With static and connections and heaven knows what, it took around an hour—or it felt like an hour—to make a three minute call. Telephones. When someone told me they'd have phones you could carry around with you, as small as credit cards—I thought it was a fantasy. Credit cards? I wonder what happened to them. The memory of huddling around the radio to listen to a comedian named Jack Benny. The shock of seeing him for the first time when we got our TV when I was eight.

How the world has changed. I take a sip of the water I carry with me. They—my children—insist. I have to carry water around. Like I'm an old dried up prune that will shrivel away if I don't keep "hydrating."

Hydrating. The world is moving too fast. When I was growing up, we didn't hydrate. If we passed a drinking fountain, we took a few sips. Do drinking fountains still exist anywhere on this planet or did they disappear into the same landfills as phone booths?

Changes. The world has moved on and I haven't. That's OK. There's a lot of good in the world moving on. If Shanna gets her way—follows her dream and is elected Senator, then goes on to be President and who knows from there—that's not the dream— it's the vehicle for it. Her dream is to bring peace on earth. Real peace, encompassing the entire planet. Isn't that worth the other changes—worth the price of all the new technology I can't keep up with?"

Ah, enough musing. I go inside, brew a cup of tea. I'm supposed to watch my sugar, but it's my birthday! I brought a piece of chocolate cheesecake back from the Barn. Not easy. Took careful planning. I had a plastic bag in my pocket ready to slip the cake into with no one seeing. I'm proud of how well I did it—didn't get a drop of frosting on my jacket. I take a bite, chew it mindfully. I can taste the chocolate, the cheese mixture. Just the right touch of vanilla. Not too much sugar. The love.

The thought makes me laugh. There was once a court ruling that a bakery couldn't list love as one of the ingredients. Love. When something is baked with love, you taste it. Ridiculous ruling.

I wipe the crumbs off the counter, top off my half-drunk tea and head back outside with it.

The full moon is right overhead now. A gently gliding soft white cloud interrupts the pattern of scintillating stars. I'm back on another night, when I was a teen. Another night, another full moon. A crying moon. I was with Shoshanna. We both saw it. The teardrop slipping from the moon's eye. A cloud, shaped like a hand, cradling the moon. Now, just as then, the cloud stops moving, huddles beneath the moon, as if Love itself is holding the moon in its palm. The hand of God, I think, just as I did as a teen.

The cloud moves now. Not across the sky, but beneath it. Slowly, serenely, its softness sinks downward until I feel myself wrapped in it—the softest, warmest, most loving blanket I've ever been swaddled in.

Ah so. So now.

The Teacher

I watch the stream flow downward to wed with the sea. Cloudlike, I lift Wren, ferry her to the Haven. Watch, as new waters are welcomed and made one with the ocean. Watch in the distance, as warm air lifts droplets skyward, melds them together to form clouds. In the far distance, new streams will form, flow, find their way to the sea...

Wren

I'm in the Haven, the Teacher beside me. She lifts me lightly from the cloud. I feel myself merge with all the personas my soul has ever worn, feel my Wren personage drop from me like a robe as I melt into my soul. All around me are the souls of all I have ever loved throughout the eternity of Time. All the personas each soul encompasses.

I know, for the Teacher is within me, speaking to me, that I must produce the key to the realm beyond. To Om-eh, where all love is born. Had I hands, I would reach for the chain around my neck. "Acorn," I silently say. "An acorn, a vessel of possibility, holding within it keys to life. Holding within it an oak tree, which will bear more acorns, sprouting more oak trees, and more life, ever onward."

"Yes," I hear the Teacher say, and the Haven opens to Love itself.

In silence, the Teacher speaks to me. I understand. I have a choice to make. It has taken eons, but my soul has learned the lessons humans are put on earth to learn. I can stay here, luxuriate in all the beauty and peace. Or I can stay here, but with a job—one more difficult than anything my earthly mind could imagine.

"It is time for me to move on to joy everlasting," the Teacher says. "If you will have it, my job will be yours. You call me a teacher. Humans will call you something else. Their guardian angel, their guru, their guide. Every so often, you will be granted new souls to mentor, as old ones move on to Om-eh. For generations to come, these new souls will look to you in times of need until they have learned all the lessons Earth has to offer, and come to live in eternal perfection. Would you like to watch over them, guide them, and—"

"Yes," my soul sings. "Yes."

I understand that I won't be Wren. I will be a part of the Soul holding all the personas I've had through all time, all the lessons and learnings my soul has gleaned. The teacher tells me of Gabrielle, wedded to an angel Wren originally knew as Leaf, living as Manny. I will be responsible for guiding Gabrielle, and the soul of my Tim, whose soul is now within a little boy, with an angel for a little league coach, an angel Wren knew as Claire. I'll guide the young soul Wren once knew as Deborah, reincarnated as a little girl, and assist her mother, the angel Wren knew as Josie.

I'll also support Shanna, housing the soul Wren knew as Shoshanna. I understand that she finished her earthly travels, and chose to incarnate to teach the world. "Helped," the Teacher says, "by two angels, her husband Craige, once living as a your friend Gracie, and his sister, Ina, also an angel, Gracie's beloved Ian. Two souls, bound forever."

I ask about Tim and Deborah. "They arrived at the Haven," the Teacher leads me to understand. "Neither could find a door. It wasn't a matter of no key—It was a matter of learning, and learning takes many turns on earth. They're young souls. You will guide them in many personas. You haven't asked about Maura," the teacher notes.

"I didn't have to! I can hear her, leading Om-eh in song."

"As Gracie understood."

The Guide, once the soul of Wren

I, who will ever after be known as the Guide, watch in awe as the Teacher seems to thin, to spread and spread and spread so that she is no longer a discrete soul. Spread so thin that she joins and melds and merges into the omnipresent, infinite Sea of Bliss: The Holy Oneness, Love, God, the Fountainhead, The God Particle, the Eternal Goodness that is a part of all things material, all energy, all things spiritual throughout the vastness of the universe.

The Teacher

I feel myself merging with the Eternal Oneness, beyond the bounds of earth-bound Om-eh. The Guide will take my place. New babes will be placed in her care. Clouds, heavy with water, will release rain to mountain streams, waters will flow to the seas, droplets will rise to clouds. The never-ending cycle, will repeat again, and yet again, in the circle of love.

From the depths of the Holy Oneness, I sing my final words: Hush, listen. My name is Love.
Hush, Listen, I am within you, all around you, before you,

after you. Hear me. Feel me. Be me.

Frantically I whisper in the fading that is the ending of all I ever knew myself to be, which is the beginning of all I ever was and am and will be.

Hush, listen. Listen to the silence within the sounds, to the space between atoms, the empty spaces within atoms, the soft sound of a breath, the sob beneath the smile, the smile beyond the sob, the broken heart of an orphaned animal, the kiss of the wind, the song of the acorn.

Hear me, as I enter into the Oneness that is All, that is God, that is Love, that is You—

You who read these words or dream these words or think these words or hear them in the silence beyond all words, know them, and be them. Listen to the goodness glowing in your heart, let it flow toward the goodness in the Other. Always.

Hush. Listen.

APPENDICES

On The Road to <u>As Miraculous And Ordinary As Acorns:</u>
Acknowledgements, Plus

Questions For Discussion Or Thought

Also Written By Author Ellen Belitsky

Everything You Need To Know About The Song Titles

On the Road to <u>As Miraculous and Ordinary as Acorns</u>

Acknowledgements Plus

In order to understand the enormous gratitude I owe to my "writers' salon": Kathleen Kubik, Lynn Lehrfeld, Ann Letzter and Jackie White, you need to understand the process by which this book came to be.

It was not an easy birth. It was certainly the longest labor of any book I've created—and my attendants were with me every step of the way, reading draft, after draft, after draft, after… Change after change after change after…

Many of the major changes were based on feedback from my salon. Others were brought about by changes in life: In my personal life, in the politics of the time, and finally, by COVID. With each external change, I changed, and as I changed, my characters did, their stories did, even the landscape did.

Originally, there were five women, all living at the COVE, all gathering in one apartment for breakfast and dinner, on a daily basis. And that's where the action took place—in their meal-time conversations, punctuated by flashbacks. Deborah, originally the fifth friend, became a secondary character, dining with the group as infrequently as they could manage. Beverly, one of the originals, became a minor character, and Wren took her place. While their backstories had similarities, they reacted differently to events, and became polar opposite personalities. Josie and Marfa had large backstories and larger parts, but with growing awareness, I dropped them because—how could a middle-class white woman understand what life was like for a black cleaning woman and her daughter well enough to make them real? Deborah had a daughter—one version after another, but as the book evolved, they didn't belong. Wren had a succession of husbands until Tim introduced himself, and I knew he was "the one."

As time went on and drafts went by, the action moved out of an apartment dining room and into the outer world. Blossom Knolls grew, the COVE opened its doors to action in Markettown and Oceanport, and the lake. As my life changed, the characters grew and changed. When I transitioned from being a caregiver to a widow, my understanding of Gracie grew, and her portrayal changed. With COVID came an understanding of how interdependent the people living on the shores of the lake adjacent to Blossom Knolls had to be. The lake became Lake Kinde, and the idea of a fine for unkindness took root.

Toward the end of the writing process—Shanna grew up, went through several changes, and became the character you met. The narrator changed from the Teacher to Wren, and finally to Shanna.

There were other editorial changes: The original manuscript took place in the women's seventy-second year, revolved around months, and presented most of the past in flashbacks. Several sections were omitted. Each month culminated in a discussion club meeting. Too didactic and preachy. Too boring. They were omitted. Thank the Salon!

Writers have large vocabularies but I can't come up with a word large enough, grand enough, heart-felt enough to thank the four women who have been my writing mainstay through the years of changes outlined above. Each one deserves an award for brilliance in editing, and superhuman patience. Thank you a gazillion times over to these talented women: **Lynn Lehrfeld** and **Jackie White**—talented writers whose works deserve to be published soon. **Ann Letzter**, author of <u>The Vanishings </u>and <u>Miriam, Ever Watchful.</u> **Kathleen Kubik**, author of <u>Neither Sand Nor Sea,</u> and the prize-winning <u>The Autumn Of Her Years.</u>

Without their help, this book never could have come to be what it is today.

Toward the end of the writing process, we decided that the book needed "fresh eyes." Were some of the things I deleted necessary to keep in? Were there unnecessary repetitions? Were parts boring, unneeded, contradictory? For that feedback, I thank a long-term friend, Helene Leibowitz, and some new friends: In the midst of the early stages of COVID (back when we thought it would be over soon,) I moved from a house to a newly-built apartment complex. Fiction is often based on life, but in moving to my new home, life seemed to be based on fiction. While my new residence is not an 'over-fifty-five', the older women in our buildings have found each other, and formed a close group, making it feel like the COVE. Two of my new friends stepped forward, slogged through reading the entire book online, and provided valuable feedback. Huge thanks to Dana Asher, and to Paula Heitzner, author of <u>Yoga and You For A Year</u>.

My thanks to Erica Virvo Hackman for assisting me in the technical process of self-publishing and cover design.

And now, thank <u>you</u>, for reading my book and staying with me long enough to read this passage! Be well, stay safe, keep trying out books by authors you're not familiar with, whether traditionally published or self-published. You just may find the book you've waited for all your life!

Questions for Discussion or Thought

1. The Teacher points out to each main character that she has a flaw she needs to overcome in this lifetime. She refers to them as lessons. What did each have to learn? Were all of them successful? What about Deborah and Tim—what lessons did they have to learn? Were they successful? What do they have left to learn? What about you….?

2. Each of the characters has a different view of life, and its purpose. What is the opinion of each of the characters? What is yours?

3. Several of the characters went through major changes in their views of God and religion. What, if any, were the changes in each character's opinions? What were the experiential influences that precipitated whether or not her view changed? How did each think of the relationship between God and religion? Did, and if so, how, did each character's opinions change, and why?

4. What were some of the differing views of love?

5. Deborah and Wren had very similar mothers, yet they ended up with extremely different personalities and outlooks on life. To what do you attribute this? To what extent did the mothers of the other children influence who they became?

6. Discuss or think about the COVID section of the book. Terrible things happened to the characters at Blossom Knolls, but so did wonderful things. What were some of the good, and the bad? What impact did COVID have on your personal life?

7. The last section of the book deals with the years after death. What happened to each of the characters. Why?

8. Some of the characters fully overcame their flaws. Some still had a bit more to learn, yet the four friends were all welcomed into Om-eh. Without giving anything away to anyone reading these questions before finishing the book—One of the characters is given the task of becoming the next Teacher. She learned most of her life-lesson, but not to perfection. Why do you think she was given the Teacher role, when another character(s?) may have seemed more suitable?

9. Did you identify with any of the characters? Who? Why?

Also by Ellen Belitsky

Books

PRISONERS OF PURPLE: You know from the outset that three doctors are engaged in clandestine research. You know that a writer is hospitalized, a prisoner of locked-in syndrome. But how did five other women start the day in different parts of the United States, and all end up imprisoned in the same purple house? And what will happen next?

IMAGINE IF... A Love Story: The events of 1968 are in the background, folk music the sound tract when a shy teacher and a charismatic draft dodger fall in love, only to be driven apart by the actions of their nemeses. Forty years later, they meet again, and the pattern repeats. Will the ending be different this time?

THE LONGITUDE AND LATITUDE OF LIFE, A Collection of Stories: Fifty stories, some long, most short, add up to the longitude and latitude of life. Stories about people and stories about ideas. Realistic stories and fantastical ones. Stories that will make you laugh, cry, shiver and smile. Stories filled with characters as strange as the snake in the Garden of Eden and as familiar as your best friends.

SOARING WITH BROKEN WINGS, Collections: Poetry and Other Pieces: Eight collections dealing with illness, aging and hope; friendship and romance; light, amusing poems; poems about education and writing; pieces dealing with war, hunger, inequality, and the environment; and above all, poems of hope.

Publications in National Magazines

Stephanie Alone, in the Stories for Free Children published in **MS.**, July, 1984: A story about a miscarriage, written for children.

I'm Just a Girl Who Can't Say No, an essay written in response to a questionnaire about addiction, about addiction to volunteering. Published in **MS.** February 1987

A Breathtaking Lunch. A story about a child who saves another by using the Heimlich technique. Published in **CHILD LIFE.**

Various essays published in the **Writer's Write** section of **The SUN,** most recently, September 2020

Everything You Need to Know About the Song Titles

Key*:*
Song Titles Used as Part/Section/Act/Scene Titles,
Title of Show the song is from,
C, composer_
L, lyricist
Composer/lyricist, or unknown which credited person performed which function—no indication, just the name. Last name only after first mention.

Once Upon A Time and Long Ago, **Peter Pan,** C: Julie Styne &/ or Mark Charlap, L: Betty Comden & Adolph Green &/or Carolyn Leigh

A Dream Is A Wish Your Heart Makes, **Cinderella**, Mack David, Al Hoffman, Jerry Livingston

Somewhere, **West Side Story,** C: Leonard Bernstein, L: Stephen Sondheim

Don't Rain On My Parade, **Hello Dolly,** Jerry Herman

Mr. Cellophane **Chicago**, C: John Kander, L: Fred Ebb

The Impossible Dream, **Man of La Mancha**, Mitch Leigh, John Darion

No One is Alone, **Into the Woods**, Stephen Sondheim

What Have I Done, **Les Miserables,** C: Claude-Michel Shonberg, L: Alain Boubil, Michel Shonberg, Jean-Mark Natel

Who Can I Turn To? **The Roar of the Greasepaint, The Smell of the Crowd,** Anthony Newley

Happy Talk, **South Pacific,** C: Richard Rogers, L: Oscar Hammerstein

Bali Hai, **South Pacific,** C:Rogers, L:Hammerstein

Getting to Know You, **The King and I,** C: Rogers, L: Hammerstein

I Won't Grow Up, **Peter Pan,** see above

Neverland, **Finding Neverland,** Gary Barlow, Elliot Kennedy

Oh, What a Beautiful Mornin', **Oklahoma!,** C: Rogers, L: Hammerstein

Friendship, **Anything Goes,** Cole Porter

We Go Together, **Grease,** Warren Casey, Jim Jacobs

Something Sort of Grandish, **Finian's Rainbow,** C: Burton Lane, L: Y.A. Harburg

I'm All Alone, **Spamalot,** Michael McGrath and Tim Curry

Bosom Buddies, **Mame,** Jerry Herman

As We Stumble Along, **Drowsy Chaperone,** C: Bob Martin, Don McKeller, L: Lisa Lambert, Greg Morrison

Falling Slowly, **Once,** Glen Hansarb, Marketa Irglova

If This Isn't Love, **Finian's Rainbow,** C: Lane, L:Harburg

Hurry Back, **Applause,** C: Charles Strause, L: Lee Adams,

I Got Lost In His Arms, **Annie Get Your Gun,** Irving Berlin

No Other Love, **Me And Juliet,** C: Rogers, L: Hammerstein

Soon It's Gonna Rain, **The Fantasticks,** Tom Jones

On My Own, **Les Miserables,** C: Claude-Michel Shonberg, L: Alain Boubil, Claude-Michel Shonberg, Jean-Mark Natel

Movin' Out, **Movin' Out,** Billy Joel

Move On, **Sunday In the Park With George,** Sondheim

What I Did For Love, **A Chorus Line,** C: Marvin Hamlish, L: Edward Kleban

A New Life, **On A Clear Day You Can See Forever,** C: Lane, L: Alan J. Lerner

I'll Know, **Guys and Dolls,** Frank Loesser

A Wonderful Guy, **South Pacific,** C: Rogers, L: Hammerstein

The Best Night Of My Life, **Applause,** C: Strause, L: Adams

Something Bad, **Wicked,** Stephen Schwartz

I'm Not At All In Love, **Pajama Game,** Richard Adler and Jerry Ross

It's Too Damn Hot, **Pajama Game,** Adler and Ross

No More, **Into the Woods,** Sondheim

Maybe This Time, **Cabaret,** C: Kander, L: Ebb

Life's A Funny Proposition After All, **Little Johnny Jones,** George M. Cohan

The Way Back, **Jekyll and Hyde,** C: Frank Wildham, L: Wildham, Leslie Bricusse, Steve Cuden

Change, Change, Change, **Menopause, the Musical,** Norman Whitfield, Barrett Strong

The Telephone Hour, **Bye Bye Birdie,** C: Strause, L, Adams

I Belong Here, **The Grand Tour,** Jerry Herman

Good Friends, **Applause,** C: Strause, L: Adams

Consider Yourself, **Oliver**, Lionel Bart

Finishing the Hat, **Sunday In The Park With George,** Sondheim

Open A New Window, **Mame,** Herman

Who Am I? **Les Miserables,** C: Shonberg, L:Shonberg, Boubill, Natel

Seasons of Love, **Rent,** Jonathan David Larsen

The Little Things We Do Together, **Company,** Sondheim

Here We are Again, **Do I Hear a Waltz?** C: Rogers, L: Sondheim

Willkommen, **Cabaret,** C: Kander, L: Ebb

Doin' What Comes Natur'lly, **Annie Get Your Gun,** Irving Berlin

Love Makes the World Go Round **Carnivale!** Bob Merrill

My Funny Valentine, **Babes In Arms,** C: Rogers, L: Lorenz Hart

This Time of the Year, **Finian's Rainbow,** C: Burton Lane, L: Y.A. Harburg

Jubilation, **Cotton Patch Gospel,** C: Tom Key, Russell Trayz, L: Harry Chapin

Nobody Told Me, **No Strings,** Rogers (C & L)

Seasons of Love, **Rent,** Larson

Being Alive, **Company,** Sondheim

My Child Will Forgive Me, **Parade,** Jason Robert Brown

All That Matters, **Finding Neverland,** C: Scott Frankel, Gary Barlow, Elliot Kennedy, L: Michael Koric, Barlow and Kennedy.

Let The Sun Shine In, **Hair,** C: Galt MacDermott, L: Gerome Ragni, James Rado

Miracle of Miracles: **Fiddler On The Roof,** C: Jerry Bock, L: Sheldon Harnick

Where Do I Go? **Hair,** C: MacDermott, L: Ragni, Rado

Luck Be A Lady, **Guys and Dolls,** Frank Loesser

The Best Night of My Life, **Applause,** C: Strauss, L: Adams

This Is The Moment, **Jekyll and Hyde,** Frank Wildhorn, Leslie Briscusse

If I Only Had A Heart, **The Wizard Of Oz,** C: Harold Arlen, L: Harburg

It's a Hard Knock Life, **Annie,** C: Strauss, L: Martin Charnin

See Me, Feel Me, **The Who's Tommy,** Pete Townshend

Some Enchanted Evening, **South Pacific,** C: Rogers, L: Hammerstein

Get Me To The Church On Time, **My Fair Lady,** C: Frederick Lowe, L: Alan S. Lerner

Marry Me a Little, **Company,** Sondheim

Always, Always You, **Carnivale!** Bob Merrill

To Life, **Fiddler On The Roof,** C: Bock, L: Harnick

Feeling Good, **The Roar Of The Greasepaint, The Smell Of The Crowd,** C: Anthony Newley, L: Leslie Bricusse

Adoption Dance, **Annie Get Your Gun,** Berlin

As Long As He Needs Me, **Oliver,** Bart

I Cain't Say No, **Oklahoma,** C: Rogers and L: Hammerstein

No One Knows Who I Am, **Jekyll and Hyde,** C: Frank Wildhorn, L: Bricusse, Wildhorn

My Favorite Things, **The Sound of Music,** C: Rogers and L: Hammerstein

Comes Once In a Lifetime, **Subways Are For Sleeping,** C: Julie Styne, L: Betty Comden, Adolph Greene

What You Mean To Me, **Finding Neverland,** Gary Barlow, Elliot Kennedy

And This Is My Beloved, **Kismet,** C: George Forrest, Robert Wright, L: Luther Davis, Charles Lederer

Something's Missing, **Come From Away,** Irene Sankoff, David Heim

Something Has Happened, **I Do! I Do!** C: Harvey Schmidt, L: Tom Jones

Everything Changes, **Waitress,** Sara Bareilles

When I'm Being Born Again, **On A Clear Day, You Can See Forever,** C: Lane, L: Lerner

Tomorrow, **Annie,** C: Strausse, L: Charnin

I Am What I Am, **La Cage Aux Folles,** Herman

Marrying For Love, **Call Me Madam,** Berlin

Another Opening, Another Show, **Kiss Me Kate,** Cole Porter

I Don't Know How to Love Him, **Jesus Christ, Superstar,** C: Andrew Lloyd Webber, L: Tim Rice

A Whole New World, **Aladdin,** C: Alan Menken, L: Howard Ashman, Tim Rice, Chad Beguelin

Life Is, **Zorba, The Greek,** C: Kander and L: Ebb

When I Look Up, **Cotton Patch Gospel,** C: Key, Trayz, L: Chapin

Something's Coming, **West Side Story,** C: Leonard Bernstein, L: Sondheim

Stranger in Paradise, **Kismet,** Forrest, Wright, Borodin

Happiness, **You're a Good Man, Charlie Brown.** Clark Gesner

Days Gone By, **She Loves Me,** Bock, Harnick

Bring On Tomorrow, **Fame,** C: Steve Margoshes, L: Jacques Levy

I'm Flying, **Peter Pan,** C: Julie Styne, Mark Charlap, L: Comden& Greene &/or Carolyn Leigh

So Long, Farewell, **The Sound of Music,** C: Rogers and L: Hammerstein

Prayer, **Come From Away,** Sankoff, Heim

Sunrise, Sunset, **Fiddler on the Roof,** C: Bock, L: Harnick

Never Never Land, **Peter Pan,** C: Styne, Charlap, L: Comden & Greene, &/or Leigh

Memory, **Cats,** C: Andrew Lloyd Webber, L: T.S. Elliot, Trevor Nun, Richard Stilgoe

The Circle of Life, **The Lion King,** C: Elton John, L: Tim Rice

Other Song Titles Mentioned Within the Narrative

Rock Around the Clock, Max C. Freedman and James E. Myers

Singin' In The Rain, C: Nacio Herb Brown, L: Arthur Freed

Look To the Rainbow, **Finian's Rainbow,** C: Lane, L: Harburg

A Cock-Eyed Optimist, **South Pacific,** C: Rogers and L: Hammerstein

I'm Not Down Yet , **The Unsinkable Molly Brown,** Meredith Wilson

Be Not Afraid (Hymn), Bob Dufford

The Hearse Song, Harley Poe

Another Opening, Another Show, **Kiss Me Kate,** Porter

I Think I'm Gonna Like It Here, **Annie,** C: Strauss, L: Charnin

At The Hop, Artie Singer, John Medora, David White

Peggy Sue, Jerry Allison, Norman Petty

Bye, Bye Love, Felice and Boudleaux Bryant

Lollipop, Julius Dixon and Beverly Ross

Let There Be Peace On Earth, Sy Miller

Small Talk, **Pajama Game,** Adler and Ross

From This Moment On, **Kiss Me Kate,** Porter

Ever After, **Into The Woods,** Sondheim

Hail Mary, Gentle Woman (Hymn), Cary Landry

Amazing Grace (Hymn), John Newman

And When I Die, Laura Nyro

Happy Birthday. (disputed) Patty Hill and Mildred J. Hill, or Preston Ware Orem

www.ingramcontent.com/pod-product-compliance
Lightning Source LLC
Chambersburg PA
CBHW030403180626
46812CB00005B/1914